THE DYING MINUTES

Martin O'Brien was educated at the Oratory School and Hertford College, Oxford. He was travel editor of British *Vogue* in the 1970s and has written for a number of international publications. After more than thirty years on the road Marseilles remains one of his favourite destinations.

MARTIN O'BRIEN
THE DYING MINUTES

A Daniel Jacquot Mystery

arrow books

This paperback edition published by Arrow Books 2013

10 9 8 7 6 5 4 3 2 1

Copyright © Martin O'Brien 2012, 2013

Martin O'Brien has asserted his right to be identified as the author of this work under the Copyright, Designs and Patents Act 1988

First published in Great Britain in 2012 by Preface Publishing

Arrow Books
Random House, 20 Vauxhall Bridge Road
London, SW1V 2SA

An imprint of The Random House Group Limited

www.randomhouse.co.uk
www.prefacepublishing.co.uk

Addresses for companies within The Random House Group Limited
can befound at www.randomhouse.co.uk

The Random House Group Limited Reg. No. 954009

A CIP catalogue record for this book is available from the British Library

ISBN 978 1 84809 0 620

The Random House Group Limited supports The Forest Stewardship Council
(FSC®), the leading international forest certification organisation. Our books
carrying the FSC label are printed on FSC® certified paper. FSC is the only
forest certification scheme endorsed by the leading environmental organisations,
including Greenpeace. Our paper procurement policy can be found at:
www.randomhouse.co.uk/environment

Typeset in Times by Palimpsest Book Production Limited,
Falkirk, Stirlingshire
Printed and bound in Great Britain by Clays Ltd, St Ives plc

For Olly and Chris,
Jaimie and Jacqueline,
and for all the fine times
around *la table noire*

November, 1972
Madrague de Montredon

She was strong and she was fit and she was young.

And very determined.

Matched the two men she worked with, the older and the younger, load for load, back and forth, from truck to vessel.

The night was black as pitch. Somewhere in that dead, silent space between three and four in the morning. There was no moon, so no real form or shape to the blackness, just a few distant lights across the harbour, glimmering over the water. Even the stars had gone, put out by a band of low storm clouds that had moved in the evening before, filling the air with a salty crackle of electricity. She may have been sweating but she could feel the hairs on the back of her neck prickle with fear and excitement.

None of them checked the time but it had to be three hours since the take. And they were nearly done. Better than expected. Ahead of schedule. Maybe thirty bars still stacked on that pallet. Three bars at a time. Ten more trips between the three of them. They'd brought the truck as close to the boat as they could but it was still thirty metres between pallet and mooring.

Slotting the bars into the sailcloth waistcoats she'd made for them, panting past each other, back and forth, coming and going.

No shadows, just that inky blackness, the repeated shuffle of their feet, and the hungry suck and slap of water on stone. All that,

1

and the heavy clunk and clink of the bars as they set them down in a double line from for'ard cabin to aft deck, spreading the weight.

A ton of gold.

A little over nine hundred kilos.

Seventy-five bars.

If their arms and shoulders didn't cramp from the loads, or their legs buckle as they scuttled back and forth across the quay, they'd be away. Another thirty minutes and they'd be free and clear.

And very, very rich.

Everything had gone so well, so smoothly. Just as they'd planned. Up in that chill midnight air on the Col de la Gineste, and down here in the port of Madrague. While she and her older companion had prepped the boat, their man on the inside had hidden out with the others, up among the rocks on the high pass road between Marseilles and Cassis, city lights spread out beneath them like gems twinkling on a cloth of black velvet.

They'd crouched there from ten until midnight, twenty in the gang, either side of the road, waiting for the convoy in that whispering darkness, finally spotting the headlights winding up towards them, hearing the engines rumble and strain on that last juddering bend before they brought the makeshift barriers crashing down. Ahead of the convoy and behind it. No way on and no way back, the three trucks brought to a standstill, brakes wheezing on the slope.

In short order they'd dealt with the four outriders, then cracked the three trucks. A cake of C4 taped to each windscreen, primers set, had seen to that. Security crews scrambling out, their own crews clambering in. The C4 bars removed.

Six minutes after springing the trap, the higher barrier was pushed aside and they were out of there, one after the other, a seamless operation, up over the ridge and down into the city. Three security trucks, in a tidy line, nose to tail along the tree-lined straight of boulevard Michelet, only splitting up when they reached the higher Prado roundabout: the first truck straight on, through the green lights, direct to the city centre; the second truck taking the first exit off the roundabout, up along boulevard Rabatau to the A50 cross-town; and their man, driving the third truck, taking the last exit, south, as planned, towards the beach. Three different routes through the city to minimise any hold-ups, to lessen the odds, each truck heading for the same rendezvous in the unlit railyards behind the docks of La Joliette.

Except their man had taken a left, not a right, at the statue of David on Prado Beach, had somehow got rid of his four companions – neither she nor the older man had asked how he planned to do it, just knew that he would – and made it alone to Madrague, switching off his headlights as he coasted down rue Tibido, turned in to the quay, reversed and braked. Engine killed, doors swung open.

And now it was nearly done, just the last bars to shift, the older man staying on the boat, just her and the young one jogging back to the truck, breathing hard from the effort, waistcoat pockets empty, arms loose and aching at their sides, legs almost weightless from the work-out.

It was then that a single gunshot rang out across the quay, the sharp cracking sound of it clattering and battering its way around the houses on the far side of the harbour, followed by a second and a third shot, brief muzzle flashes from the corner of rue des Arapèdes.

And her companion, running beside her, suddenly grunted and pitched sideways, the breath punched from his body when he hit the stone quay.

She knew when she touched him that he was dead. One of those three shots a lucky one to the side of the head that left the back of his skull mushy, warm and splintered.

She couldn't believe it. Wouldn't believe it.

Not now. Not him.

Behind her, from the boat, she heard the older man call out. A desperate, whispered scream, 'Vite, vite,' not knowing what had happened to them, out there in the darkness, with guns firing.

Then she heard the engines turn, chortle, splutter and catch, and she knew she had to run, knew she had to leave him, and prayed she'd make the twenty metres of open ground without another lucky shot taking her down.

She pressed the young man's shoulder, slick with blood, whispered her farewell and, stripping off her cumbersome waistcoat, she turned for the quay.

This time the gunshots were closer, the bullets too, zinging past her like hot, angry hornets as she made her crouching, zig-zag dash for life and freedom.

But now the twenty metres were thirty, and lengthening.

While she'd delayed, the older man had cut the boat loose from its mooring, backed it out from the slip and turned it, low in the water now, heading for the harbour entrance, pushing the throttles forward.

'Jump!' she heard him call from the wheelhouse, his voice louder now, over the engines. 'You'll have to jump.'

And as the bullets whined past her, she ran with what little strength she had left in her legs, reached the end of the quay and flung herself from it, flew through the air, arms and legs wheeling, into the darkness.

Part One

1

August, 1999
Madrague de Montredon

SOMETIMES IT BEGINS WITH A death.

Not a murder, just a natural passing.

This one had been long and slow and painless, ending in an old man's single bed. At night. In a shadowy, shifting darkness, with the distant shuffling sound of the ocean drifting through slanted wooden shutters and the sharp scent of sea salt and dried netting dampening the air he breathed. Long, slow, painless breaths, drawn in over toothless gums, sleeping breaths that softened, shortened and, in the dark hour before dawn, ceased with a final, wet, fluttering cough that might have woken a younger man.

But not this one.

Not Philo.

Philo was a fisherman, born in the spring of 1922 in a *cabanon* on a calanque slope past Sormiou. Of course, Philo was not his real name, and nor was he French despite his place of birth. His father was Greek and his mother Italian, and it was her surname that she'd given him since she couldn't remember the father's.

Whatever his real or adopted name, this old fisherman was known among friends and acquaintances as Philo, *Le Philosophe*, the scholar. Not that he was particularly clever or wise, not that he even thought he was, but because for as long as anyone could remember Philo had always had a book in his hand, something to read. He might just have been a fisherman, supplying local restaurants with the daily makings of a *bouillabaisse*, but he was a reader too. And in the port of Madrague de Montredon where Philo moored his six-metre skiff, there weren't too many fishermen who lay back on their drying nets to read a book.

If it was the sea that had given Philo his living, it was to the sea that he was returned, like a debt repaid, nine days after his thin, cold body was found in his bed.

An hour before dawn, with stars still glittering in the night sky, at the very time he had taken that last rattling breath, a twenty-metre sloop set out from Madrague a few kilometres along the coast from Marseilles. The air was still and cold, no breeze to fill the sails, just the oily scent of diesel and the rumbling chug of the sloop's motor, a verdigrised prop churning up a steady phosphorescent wake, a lengthening lifeline leading back to land.

There were five men aboard: one at the wheel, three in the cockpit, with Philo's body stitched into a stiff sailcloth wrap, secured to the deck railing beside them, and weighted with a length of anchor chain. Four kilometres past the breakwater, heading south-west, a sharp slap of spray came off the bows, out of the darkness, stinging their faces, and the skipper ordered the jib and mainsail up. Cutting the engine, he spun the wheel to port, set a course south-east and felt the sloop heel and pull as the sails caught the breeze and they surged forward, four knots, then five, faster than the engine had driven them. But now there was no engine sound, just the splash and lash of the water, the straining tug of taut, stretched canvas and the creak of varnished timbers. Sounds each one of them knew well, fishermen all, coming to them as the steep slopes and crags of the Îles de Maire and Riou and Pénitents loomed ahead, jagged, crouching shadows set against a lightening dawn sky.

'Old Philo would have liked this,' said the man at the wheel, breathing in the sharp sea air.

8

'Coming home, he wouldn't,' replied the netmaker from Madrague, wiping the salt spray from his cheeks.

'He'd have stayed over at Sormiou,' said the oldest man in the party, now that Philo was gone. 'Or maybe chanced it closer to shore, other side of Jarre and Calseraigne.'

'Anyone for more coffee?' said the fourth man, making for the hatch.

'Calva, too,' the skipper called out, bracing his thighs against the wheel, legs apart, bare feet in tattered espadrilles. 'Bring the Calva this time. In the cupboard under the charts. That's what Philo would want.'

An hour after they'd set out from Madrague, warmed by the coffee and apple brandy, the skipper had the sails trimmed and brought the sloop round into a stretch of dead black water down-wind of Île des Pénitents, the furthest of the islands. Up in the bow a trailing anchor was thrown out and the sloop began to turn and drift astern, the distant mainland lights of Sormiou twinkling into sight as they passed the headland seven kilometres offshore.

'He always did well here,' said the netmaker from Madrague, as they unclipped the tags that secured their old friend and shifted him closer to the railing. 'Just smelled them down there, he did.'

'Anyone want to say anything?' asked the skipper, heaving up the length of chain and cradling it in his arms.

'À Dieu should do it,' said the oldest man among them. 'That's all he needs now.'

'And fat nets, wherever he's going,' said the man who'd brewed the coffee and found the Calva.

'And pretty girls, too. Don't forget the pretty girls,' added the netmaker, as the three men got a grip on the sail-cloth shroud and hoisted it up to the railing.

'Philo first,' said the skipper, and he watched as his three companions heaved their friend overboard, the canvas cocoon smacking on to the water, bobbing on the surface and starting to twist like the points of a compass, as though trying to decide which direction to take.

9

There was only one direction.

Leaning over the rail, the skipper let the length of chain unravel through his arms and splash down into the dark, lapping sea.

For a moment more Philo bobbed there in his sailcloth coat, and then he was gone, as though snatched by an unseen hand, taken down into the depths.

2

Three weeks later

THE LAWYER, CLAUDE DUPONT, DID not hear the phone ringing. The call came through as he breakfasted on the terrace of his home off the Niolon road. He'd smeared the last of his *petit pain* with the remains of the plum jam, popped it into his mouth and was reaching for his newspaper when his wife, Francine, came out with the phone in her hand, a long lead snaking out behind her.

'*C'est pour toi*,' she said, offering the receiver with one hand, the other holding closed the front of her dressing gown. There was a tight, disapproving expression on her face. Francine Dupont did not like business calls coming through to the house, particularly at the weekend. She had made it clear often enough. Business was office, home was home – *n'importe quoi*. No matter what.

Dupont swallowed his bread and jam, wiped his fingers on his napkin and took the phone with a nod of thanks and a weak smile.

'*Oui*? *Allo*?' he said, curtly, so his wife would register his annoyance as she left the sunlit terrace for the villa's cooler, shadowed interior, a shared irritation at this unwanted, unexpected intrusion.

It was Jules Ranque, assistant warden at Les Baumettes prison on the other side of Marseilles. After the formalities, Ranque came straight to the point.

'He wants to see you. Today.'

11

There was no need for Ranque to give a name. Claude Dupont might have had more than a dozen clients currently confined in Les Baumettes but he knew exactly who wanted to see him.

Prisoner LB67-426.

Also known as *L'Hippocampe*. The Seahorse.

Real name Pierre-Louis Lombard.

Five years into a twenty-year stretch for the murder of a Marseilles hoodlum who'd had it coming. Lombard had done the State a service, but he'd still got the maximum. Sticking to his 'not guilty' plea hadn't helped either. After two failed appeals, and no parole, he'd be in his eighties by the time he got out.

Ten minutes later – apologies rendered to his wife; he'd likely be late for their lunch with the Rosseaux – Claude Dupont passed between the villa's high wooden gates, drove up the winding lane towards La Rove and turned right onto the road leading down to L'Estaque. He would follow the coast, he decided, around Marseilles' Vieux Port, along the swooping curves of the Corniche Président John F. Kennedy, and up Avenue du Prado. It would take him longer than driving cross-town, following *Toutes Directions*, but the sight of the sea on his right-hand side would calm him, distract him, give him time to prepare.

In his professional capacity as a defending advocate in the Marseilles *Judiciaire*, Dupont had spent a considerable amount of his working life in prisons. But that didn't mean he had ever grown used to them. At sixty-two years of age, after a lifetime of prison visits and as senior partner in his own law firm, Maître Dupont would normally have instructed one of his colleagues to make the trip he was making now. Pascal, the most junior, or Fabien who was eager for advancement in the firm. But Dupont knew that the summons he had received that bright and sunny Sunday morning demanded his presence, and his presence alone.

As he turned off Boulevard Michelet, passing the Mazargues war cemetery en route for Morgiou, Dupont felt a deep weariness slide over him. It was always the same. In just a few moments he would exchange the sunlight and verve and vibrancy of this ancient sea port for the daunting, deadening compound of Les Baumettes – its brooding windowless walls, its tightly coiled wreaths of razor wire, and its grim watchtowers. He'd exchange, too, the sound of birdsong and rolling surf and traffic and distant ships' horns for the jangle of keys, the echoing slam of steel doors and the dread finality of a turning lock. Even worse, the piney, salty scent of fresh air slicing through his open window would be replaced by the confined, foetid reek of sweat and food and fear that seemed to pulse through a prison like the flow of blood through veins, clinging to his clothes for hours after every visit. And if all that were not enough to ruin his day, there was that sudden, crowding proximity of evil, of lost hope, of brutal desperation, diluted out in the real world, but here distilled into a shoulder-hugging closeness.

Up ahead, through the BMW's windscreen, Claude Dupont saw the walls of Les Baumettes rise up on his left-hand side, shaded by a line of plane trees, walls and trees stretching the length of a broad dusty boulevard. There was word that renovations were due, that the sixteen hundred or more inmates might soon enjoy less cramped and savage surroundings. Dupont had heard the rumours, but he knew that any improvement in the prisoners' living conditions was still a long way off. He parked the BMW in a patch of shifting leaf shadow, listened to the tick of the engine die, then got out, locked the car and walked to the gate.

The assistant warden, Ranque, in a crumpled linen suit and tasselled loafers, was waiting for him at the entrance to the hospital wing. He was taller than Dupont, but where the lawyer was healthily tanned and scrupulously clean-shaven, Ranque was as pale as paper, his cheeks pock-marked, and his greying moustache in need of a trim.

'He's HIV-positive,' Ranque told Dupont as they climbed the polished concrete stairs to the top-floor isolation ward. 'Rape . . . Needles . . . Who knows? *Enfin*, he may have had it before he came to us. Whichever, it's full-blown now. We've done as much as we can, but the doctor says he's close. Not much longer.' The assistant warden shrugged as they reached the landing, with a what-else-can-I-say wave of a hand. He pushed open the door and stood aside for Dupont to pass.

The news of Lombard's illness stunned the lawyer. When he'd been directed to the hospital wing, he'd imagined an injury – a fall, a fight, an operation maybe. Not this. He felt a chill sweep of apprehension as he stepped into the ward and Ranque let the door close behind him.

It was eighteen months since Claude Dupont had last seen Lombard, in Marseilles' Palais de Justice at the hearing for his second and final appeal. He'd been inside for three years by then and had held up well. A lifetime along the Marseilles docks would have given him all the skills he needed to survive in Les Baumettes. But now, not two years later, the man Dupont had known, the man Dupont had defended, and the man whose testimony he had believed in and whose freedom he had fought for, was dying.

There were eight beds in the room – four a side, each set between barred and pebble-glassed windows – but only one of them was occupied. It was breathtakingly hot, stifling, in that high, narrow room, and as Dupont walked towards his client in the far corner the heat closed in on him, wrapped around him. Pulling up a chair, he felt the sweat slide down his back, sucking his silk shirt against his skin. He didn't look at the man in the bed until he'd settled, but when finally he did, his breath caught and he reeled back. It was just as well his client's eyes were closed, but the sudden scuff and creak of the chair brought them open.

There were three reasons why Pierre-Louis Lombard was called The Seahorse.

First, his place of work, his *milieu*. The city's quays – every ship, every official, every *permis*, every bundle of contraband – all in his control; nothing happened along the Marseilles waterfront, from L'Estaque to Madrague, without The Seahorse having a hand in it.

Second, there was his style of operation. He was quiet, discreet, blending into the background, hard to find, tricky to pin down. He worked alone, lived alone. No wife, no children. But when he lifted

14

the phone, made a call, people scrambled to do his bidding – or faced the consequences.

Finally, his eyes. The third and major reason for his nickname. In his late twenties a thyroid condition had resulted in exopthalmia – and once gentle, mischievous grey eyes now bulged wildly from their sockets, seeming to swivel in opposite directions as though run by two separate motors.

Just like a seahorse – eyes everywhere.

These same eyes – or, rather, one of them – settled now on Dupont.

The lawyer managed a smile, nodded.

'Pierre-Louis. A long time.'

'It is good of you to come, Maître,' whispered Lombard, working his lips painfully, scraping a dry tongue across them. The man's skin was jaundiced, the colour of old ivory, dappled with raised black lesions that seemed to throb with malice, and his bare arms lay on the sheet like thin kindling.

Dupont's first reaction to these words was one of relief. Relief that he was able to hear them. If the voice had been any softer he would have had to draw closer to the bed. And he certainly didn't want to do that. Instead he started to say something, he didn't really know what, just something appropriate, suitably cheering.

But Lombard slowly shook his head, as though he knew what was coming and had no time for idle talk.

'I want you to know I was guilty,' he began, without preamble. 'I want you to know that I lied to you. It *was* me who sliced up that arab *con*.' A small smile stitched itself across those peeling bluish lips.

Dupont was taken aback, shocked out of any discomfort. Despite his client's reputation he had believed every word the man had told him. Every detail, every nuance of his alibi, from the very start, in that holding cell at police headquarters on rue de l'Évêché.

Now he felt a shiver of irritation at the deceit, at being taken in and played. It wasn't the first time it had happened, and it wouldn't be the last, but given a choice he'd have preferred not to know.

15

There was something damning in such a casual revelation, something that made him feel complicit in some way. And irritation swiftly sharpened into an unsettling anger, even if the man in front of him was dying.

But Lombard wasn't finished.

With some considerable effort, enough for Dupont to wonder if he should help, Lombard pushed himself over on to his side, brought up his knees and squared his shoulders. A warm waft of stale bed breath fanned up from beneath the sheet and Dupont was hard pressed not to cover his nose or sit back. With eyes swivelling wildly, Lombard reached one arm slowly behind him, and seemed to rummage for something. He closed his eyes, pursed his lips and his brow creased with the strain. A moment later he rolled back, wiping his fingers on the sheet. He was holding something. Before Dupont could do anything about it, Lombard reached out and caught hold of the lawyer's wrist.

'My pension,' he said, pressing a warm, rubbery package into Dupont's unwilling hand and closing his fist around it. 'I won't be needing it now. But I'm sure you can have some fun and games with it. For me, you understand. Debts to settle. There's people out there who owe me, and I want you to see they pay. It's all there.'

He squeezed Dupont's hand then released him, sinking back on the bed, breath short and fast now.

'As for the rest, Maître, consider it thanks for your professional services. Past and future.'

And with that, Lombard closed his eyes and waved the lawyer away.

Ranque was waiting for him on the landing.

'A last request?' he asked, pulling a handkerchief from his pocket, blowing his nose, wiping it vigorously. 'Was that what it was?' He bundled up the handkerchief and pushed it away.

'You could say,' replied Dupont, feeling the small weight of the wrapped package in his trouser pocket, desperate to find somewhere to wash his hands.

3

'YOU CALL ME AS SOON as you get there, okay? Paris, and the island.'

It was midday, a Sunday, in the Departures Hall at Marignane Airport outside Marseilles, and Claudine, Midou and Jacquot were heading towards passport control. Mother and daughter had checked in their cases, stopped for a final coffee with Jacquot, but now their flight had been called. It was time to part.

'As soon as we arrive, I promise,' said Claudine, turning to take his face in her hands, kissing him lightly on the mouth, the cheeks, then hugging him tight. She wore cream slacks, brown mocassins and a blue denim shirt that showed her tan, her long black hair caught in a mother-of-pearl clasp. When she was done with him, she stepped back, tears brimming, lips tight, and her daughter took her place.

'I'll take good care of her, just you see,' said Midou, and slid her good right arm up round his neck, her left arm still in its plaster cast.

If Jacquot had straightened his back, if he'd been able to straighten it without feeling wincing shafts of pain lance through his left hip, he could have lifted her off the floor.

'I know you will,' he said. 'You have fun, you hear?'

With sad smiles and nods and waves the two women turned

away from him, and Jacquot marvelled at the passing of time, and regretted it. Just last week it had been days before their departure. Then a day. Then hours. And now . . . within a minute they would be gone from sight, and he would be alone. He watched them approach the passport desk, Midou first, then Claudine, nearly five months pregnant yet not a sign showing beyond a rounding swell to her belly, and just the faintest limp as she stepped forward, not as marked as Midou's, all that was left from their ordeal in that basement in Pélissanne. Passports were handed over, examined with a brisk formality, returned with a nod, and then, with a final turn and wave and a blown kiss, the doors slid together and shut behind them.

Now they really were gone.

Turning on his stick Jacquot wheeled round and stumped off across the concourse, pausing one last time at the Departures board. Air France Flight 360, Marseilles to Paris Charles de Gaulle, departing 13:25. By the time he got home they would be flying somewhere above him. And this time tomorrow, when he woke in a lonely bed, they'd be landing at Pointe-à-Pitre on the island of Guadeloupe in the French West Indies.

And it had all been his idea.

They had come out of hospital within a week of each other, just a month earlier, Claudine first, with gauze bandaging taped over the entry and exit gunshot wound in her left thigh. They had given her a crutch, but by the time Midou was released a few days later, her shattered arm pinned in two places and coated in a plaster cast, the crutch had been discarded in favour of that light, tip-toe limp, as though she were about to start dancing.

Jacquot had been the last of them to leave hospital, the 9x19mm bullet that he'd taken in his hip chipping away a splinter of pelvis, and tearing its way out of the back of his thigh. In addition to these not insignificant wounds were the raised pink scars from the two operations carried out to repair the damaged bone and to secure the shredded muscles.

Age played its part too, Jacquot was sure. The two women were

18

younger, fitter than he, and possibly their wounds were not as serious, or rather not as restricting as his. When Claudine came to collect him from the hospital, pushing his wheelchair to the waiting car, helping him into it, making him comfortable, no one would have believed that she had been shot as well. But for all the show, Jacquot could see the wounds still there, hidden behind her smile, the memory of those terrible moments when a killer's gun had been levelled on her and her daughter, and a trigger pulled.

And so he had suggested, without really thinking, after dinner one evening, that when Midou returned to Guadeloupe, maybe Claudine should accompany her, to assist on the journey and settle her daughter back into her island home.

Claudine had been the first to object, but just as he saw the wounds behind her smile so, too, he could see the flash of excitement at such a proposal – spending more time with her daughter, visiting the island for the first time. Beaches, sunshine, the warm Caribbean . . .

'But . . . but what about you?' she'd asked. 'How will you manage?' Before adding, 'And I'm pregnant. I can't fly when I'm pregnant.'

All of which he'd waved away, assuring her he'd be just fine, and that a five-month pregnancy shouldn't hold her back; she should go.

At which point Midou, equally delighted by the sudden prospect of having her mother come to stay, declared that she knew of women nearing full-term pregnancy taking flights. And the sun would do her good, a break . . . And the baby too.

And so it had been settled.

And now they were gone.

At his own insistence.

And he was on his own.

Just as he'd known it would be, the millhouse outside Cavaillon was empty without them, silent, just the sense of them there, their softening fragance, a dim memory of their voices, soft echoes reaching down the hallways, on the stairs, in their rooms, as Jacquot made a slow and painful journey round the house.

19

Alone.

Tut-tutting at his melancholy, he went to the salon, poured himself a shot of Calva and retired to the kitchen, losing himself in the preparation of a late lunch. The last of a duck rillettes, some slices of country sausage, a bowl of olives, a length of warm baguette. A bottle of Fleurie. Some cheese.

An hour later he was loading the dishwasher, stooping over the racks like an old man, when the phone rang.

He checked the time. They'd be there by now. Paris.

He picked up the wall-mounted kitchen extension.

'So you got there?'

'I got where?' The voice was not Claudine's nor Midou's. It was Jean-Pierre Salette on the end of the line, the old harbour master in Marseilles, just as gruff and throaty as ever.

'I thought you were Claudine. I was expecting a call from her.'

'*Alors*, you'll have to make do with me. Why? Where is she?'

Jacquot told him about the trip to Guadeloupe.

'Good idea,' said Salette. 'Just what was needed. Because there's a lady I'd like you to meet.'

4

IT WAS LATE THAT SAME Sunday when Francine Dupont finally switched off the television and prepared for bed. She came out on to the terrace, kissed the top of her husband's head and told him not to stay up too late. He'd been out there an hour now, taken a thin cheroot and glass of cognac with him, waiting impatiently for just this moment. He gave a little shiver, starting to feel the chill out there on the terrace, and assured her he would be up presently, listening to her slippers slap across the tiles and up the stairs. He waited ten more minutes, watching the bats flicker past the stars, listening to a distant surf crash against the rocks below the villa, the night air heavy with the damp salt scent of the sea, as strong as the smoke from his cigar. Then he went to the garage and opened the boot of the BMW.

The hold-all Dupont had picked up from a long-term left-luggage locker off the main concourse of the Gare Saint-Charles was just as weighty as he remembered. At the station he'd found a trolley to get it to his car, but now there was no such convenience. Grunting with the effort, he hauled the bag from his car and dragged it through the house, two-handed, stooped over, kicking aside any rug to move it more easily over the tiles. At the railway station, anxious not to be too late for their lunch with the Rosseaux, he'd resisted the temptation to examine the contents. Now, after locking

21

the study door and pulling the case to his desk, Dupont slipped the catches, worked the zipper and looked inside.

The first thing he saw was the gold. A dull yellow glimmer at the bottom of the case. Two long bars. They were loosely wrapped in sheets of waxed paper and looked like rolled slabs of Isigny butter. Reaching in with both hands, he lifted one out, set it heavily on his desk, let his fingertips trail over it. He was surprised how warm it felt, as though it were a living thing, its thick skin dented and scuffed and scarred. There were also various markings stamped on to its surface. An assay mark – 999.9/1000; a 24-carat brand; and the legend *Banque Nationale d'Algérie*.

Turning back to the case he pulled out the other bar, similarly weighty, similarly scuffed and stamped, and laid it beside the first with a hefty clunk. A dozen kilos each bar, he estimated. At what? Say, sixteen hundred francs an ounce? He reached for his calculator, tapped out the figures. Tapped them out again, just to be sure, then sat back in his chair with a dazed look on his face, wide eyes fixed on the two gold bars, sitting there on his desk, seeming to suck in the light from his desk lamp.

With a long disbelieving sigh, he pushed them aside and reached back into the case. One by one he lifted out half a dozen linen drawstring bags and lined them up on the desk. He untied the first and dumped out its contents. Wads of banknotes bound in paper collars and rubber bands, each wad as thick as a paperback. He did the same with the next five bags, also filled with bound bundles of banknotes, each bag a different currency: francs, dollars, Swiss francs, sterling, lire, deutschmarks. Each bundle a high denomination. The francs were green, Marie Curies, 500 a note. The US dollars bore the image of Ben Franklin – 100 dollars apiece. Some of the denominations – the dollars and Swiss francs – were brand new, hardly used, tight and tidily rectangular, like a sealed pack of playing cards. The others were older, dirtier, fanning out at either end like a bow-tie. Once again he sat back and looked at the haul – a walled stack of currency twenty centimetres high that occupied pretty much the length of his desk.

But there was more. In a zip-up pocket set in the case's lining, a pocket that had crunched against his knuckles as he lifted out the gold bars and the bags of currency, he found three black velvet pouches, the nap worn away in patches, their long necks loosely knotted. With shaking fingers he undid the knots and spilled out the contents of the first pouch into the palm of his hand. Diamonds, maybe thirty or forty stones, cut and rough, sparkling and winking, dull and dirty, ranging in size from an olive pip to a sugar cube, all of them sticking to his hot clammy skin. In the second pouch were emeralds, green as wet moss, and in the third pouch a spill of deep blue sapphires, their polished sides glancing with the light from his desk lamp.

Just as he'd done with the currency and the gold bars, Dupont set the three pouches on his desk where they settled with an oily scrunch. Millions of francs. Millions and millions. A treasure trove covering his desk, its value impossible to calculate. Dupont's heart hammered. So much money. He couldn't believe it. And Lombard had told him that all this was payment for services rendered. Past and future. It was clearly stolen, but still . . .

Tearing his eyes away from the haul on his desk, Dupont reached back into the case and pulled out two cellophane wraps secured with strips of duct tape. They looked like bags of flour, packed so tightly that the powder within hardly registered the press of his fingers. Heroin or cocaine, he guessed, laying them carefully beside the money. Three or four kilos of a grade-A narcotic was not the kind of thing a practising advocate should have in his possession, and, wondering what he ought to do with them, he reached into the case again for the last item in it – an office folder that so far he'd ignored. Stiff cardboard covers, secured with a faded red cord.

He slipped the knot and the folder sprang open. It was an expanding wallet, like an accordion, maybe a dozen compartments filled with scraps of paper, notebooks, Zip-lok plastic baggies, cassette tapes, photos, videos. He slipped out one of the baggies – containing some shell-casings – then dealt his way through a wallet of photos, flicked through some of the hand-written notes and let the breath whistle through his lips.

Finally he put everything back in the folder, retied the red cord and set it down beside his slippered feet.

Fun and games, Lombard had told him.

Fun and games indeed, thought Maître Dupont.

5

IT WAS FIVE DAYS BEFORE Jacquot made it down to Marseilles – five days since he'd driven Claudine and Midou to Marignane – stopping twice at service stations to ease a cramp in the back of his thigh and stretch away a pulsing ache in his left side. A month after that 9mm slug had slammed through his hip, Jacquot had learned that any movement that entailed bending his left knee or leaning forwards from the waist, was going to hurt. Driving a car involved both, with the added discomfort of having to twist round for a seat belt or to check his blind side, the kind of movements one never really thought about in real, uninjured, life.

And getting out of a car, he had also discovered, was a great deal more painful than getting in. Which was what he had to do after finding a space in the underground car park below Cours d'Estienne d'Orves a couple of blocks back from Marseilles' Vieux Port. Reaching for the door handle, he took a deep breath, and managed the entire movement – open door, bad leg out, swivel, good leg out, and push up from the seat, and stand, and turn, and close door – with a whispered and extended 'ay-ay-ay-ay-oh-shit-that-hurts'.

Jacquot had called Salette that morning, told him he'd be down for lunch.

'A week. You left the good lady to wait a week?' Salette had complained.

25

'It's Friday, J-P. Five days. And I've had physio every one of them.'

'When I was your age . . .'

'. . . you were sitting on your arse in the *Capitainerie*, telling people what to do. Nothing's changed.'

'So your tongue still works, *salaud*.'

'What time and where?'

'The usual. Not before eleven-thirty because I won't be there.'

'And you're bringing your lady friend with you?'

Salette had grunted. 'You'll love her.'

Taking the car-park lift, not the stairs, Jacquot limped out into the blustery, mistral sunshine on Place aux Huiles and took in a lungful of salt air off the old port – all sea and blue sky, bobbing masts and balconied facades. It always gave him an appetite, that smell. Just as well, given that he was lunching with Salette.

His friend was alone, at the back table, Bar de la Marine, in the shadow under the stairs. He was old enough to know better than to wear a blue Levi jacket with a singlet beneath, but somehow the old boy managed to carry it off, the jacket tattered at the elbows and faded to a milky blue, the cream cotton trousers he wore rough and coarse but stiffly clean, his espadrilles worn down at the heel. And for a man in his seventies the chest and shoulders were still broad and strong enough to fill the jacket and tighten the singlet, the skin round his neck brown and tightly corded. With a baleful eye he watched Jacquot ease himself down on to his chair and slide the stick under the table, without any offer to help. But that, as Jacquot knew, was Jean-Pierre Salette through and through.

'A walking stick? You need a walking stick?' the old harbour master began.

By the time Jacquot had got himself settled, his left leg stretched out beside the table, one of the older girls who worked the Marine bar had arrived with a pitcher of water and two pastis, one for Jacquot and a second for Salette, a dish of olives, and a short, warm *flute* roughly broken. Her hair was long and black, her T-shirt cut low, and the skirt, Jacquot decided, altogether too short to mention.

'Shot in the arse, Josette. Shot in the arse, he was,' said Salette, nodding at Jacquot.

He rolled his eyes, reached for his cigarettes.

'*Pauvre*,' said Josette, smoothing her knuckles over Jacquot's cheek.

'Finished as a man, of course,' Salette continued. He shook his head, turned down his mouth.

'Why, all he needs is the right woman,' purred Josette, slipping the tray under her arm and pressing it to her, a manoeuvre that gave a generous roll and swell to her breasts, a movement that was hard for Jacquot to miss. She felt warm so close to him, close enough for him to smell the shower gel. With a '*plus tard*' – later – she ruffled his hair and swung back to the bar.

'So where's your lady friend?' asked Jacquot, lighting his cigarette, dashing some water into his pastis.

'Patience, patience, *mon brave*. All in good time. First we eat.'

And eat they did, none of the food that appeared at their table ordered by either of them, and none of it on the Marine's laminated menu or on the list of *plats du jour* chalked on a blackboard behind the bar. Before one dish had been seen off another arrived: flash-fried fillets of red mullet; a grilled pepper and anchovy *salade des Pecheurs*; a couple of *pavé* steaks; a platter of cheese; and, finally, baked apples in Calva.

And all the while, working at the food, the two men talked. The Cabrille affair, Jacquot's most recent case, and the shoot-out in Pélisanne, the reason Jacquot was hobbling around on a stick.

'The old man was a psycho,' said Salette, of the gangster Arsène Cabrille who'd milked Marseilles like a cash cow for more than fifty years – prostitution, drugs, racketeering, protection. 'And his daughter, Virginie, no different,' sniffed Salette, of the woman who'd come so close to ending Jacquot's life, and Claudine's and Midou's, in that basement in Pélissanne – before eventually questioning him about the gunshot wound he'd received, and how bad it actually was. 'But that's nothing,' he'd declared when Jacquot described the bullet's progress through his left hip. 'A pin-prick.

A flesh wound. Jesus Christ, you kids . . .' Only softening when their talk turned to Claudine and her daughter.

'Claudine . . . what a woman! You don't deserve her.'

'You're right, I don't.'

'The good Lord works in mysterious ways.'

Jacquot nodded. 'So what about your date?' he said, finishing his coffee. 'Looks like she's stood you up, old man. Constance, you said?'

'That's right. Constance.' Salette glanced at his watch. 'And time for introductions. Think you can make it, Peg-leg?' he asked, throwing down his napkin and pushing away from the table, leaving Jacquot to look after himself. As he passed the till, Salette tapped a finger on the bar and thumbed behind him. 'My friend in the wheelchair's paying,' he told Josette, and stepped out into the late-summer sunshine.

By the time Jacquot had settled their bill and been offered Josette's telephone number, Salette was across the road and unlocking one of the security gates in the white wire-mesh fence that protected berths on the old port. Leaving it open for Jacquot, he headed off along the quay, mistral flapping around his Levi jacket, tugging at his white curls and cotton trousers. Fifty metres on, he stepped to the right and down on to one of the many pontoons laid out like ribs into the harbour, four back from the entrance to the Carénage, the pointed bows and cropped sterns of yachts and cabin cruisers tied up to its sides, fenders squeaking, halyards snapping against masts. At the end of the pontoon, Salette came to a halt, turned, waited for his companion.

'Constance lives on a boat?' asked Jacquot when he caught up, feeling the lap and suck of the sea beneath his feet.

Salette grunted, as though surely Jacquot would have worked it out by now.

'*Constance* is the boat,' he replied, and turned to clamber aboard what looked like a motor cruiser under its stretched tarp cover.

'Won't take more than a moment,' he called out, edging his way around the craft, releasing the ties. In just a couple of moments, it seemed, Salette was back where he'd started, gathering in the now loosened covering into his arms. And as it lifted away, sliding over

28

the superstructure with a salt-stiff shushing sound, snatched by the breeze, snagging here and there but shaken free with an encouraging flap and tug, *Constance* revealed herself. Maybe twelve metres, Jacquot guessed, a curving black hull, an open wheelhouse, the varnish on her woodwork a little grey and flakey here and there, the brass portholes he could see greened, dull and blistered.

'It's been a while,' said Salette, dumping the cover on the aft deck and kicking it into a corner, out of the wind. 'But she's in good order. Nothing a little tender loving care won't correct.'

'You've bought another boat? Wasn't the sloop enough?'

Salette smiled ruefully, shook his head.

'I haven't bought anything, thicko. I'm just taking care of her. Until the new owner arrives.' He leaned down and hauled up a gangplank, swung it down on to the pontoon. 'Come aboard. Take a look.'

Wincing, Jacquot manoeuvred himself up the plank, over the stern, and felt the gentlest tip and sway as he let his weight on to the deck.

'Of course, it's not a real boat,' continued Salette, by which Jacquot knew he meant that it didn't have a sail. 'But I suppose it's . . . *utilisable*, serviceable.' He looked around, shrugged. 'Built 1954. A pilot boat, turned Customs cutter. Used to work out of Toulon. And a good berth to go with her,' he continued. 'End of the rack. Properly out in the harbour, and clear of the traffic.'

Jacquot looked back towards the quay, a hundred or more metres away. It was true. Out here, thought Jacquot, you were just at the point between city and open sea. It was beguiling. And bothersome, too. What was Salette up to? he wondered.

'So who's the new owner?' Jacquot asked.

Salette gave him a look. He reached into his pocket and pulled out a knotted piece of rope with two keys attached. He tossed it over.

'Why don't you open her up? Invite me in?'

Jacquot looked at the keys, the boat, and then at Salette.

'For a Marseilles boy,' said the old harbour master, 'and a *flic* to boot, you can be pretty dim sometimes.'

6

WHILE JACQUOT WAS BEING INTRODUCED to *Constance* in Marseilles' Vieux Port, Olivier Roquefort put down the phone in his office overlooking the loading wharves of La Joliette and felt a red tide of anger sweep over him.

The voice had been calm and precise.

Was he Olivier Roquefort?

Oui – *who was this calling?*

Was he shipping regulator at the Joliette Docks?

Yes, and what of it?

Was his wife called Christine?

Now look here . . .

That's when the caller explained the purpose of his call, his delivery of the facts – the who, the when, the where – smooth and certain. And with every word, the anger slid deeper into Roquefort's heart.

Who is this, who is this? Roquefort kept asking. But no name was provided and the call ended as abruptly as it had begun.

It was a short walk along the docks from Roquefort's office to the Customs Hall where the duty sergeant told him that the boss, Jean Grandet, had left for a late lunch.

Where? asked Roquefort.

Maison Blanche, replied the duty sergeant.

It was a stiff ten-minute walk from the docks to Maison Blanche and Roquefort could easily have returned to his own office, taken his car and made the journey in half the time. But he didn't think of it. He simply left the Customs Hall and set out on foot, each step increasing the swell and pulse of his fury. By the time he reached Maison Blanche, a small neighbourhood brasserie on rue Guillot, he could have punched a hole in a brick wall and felt no pain.

Roquefort had known Grandet since the late eighties, when Grandet had moved in from Toulon down the coast and taken over the top spot at Customs. He was tall and slim and younger than Roquefort, with cropped black hair and matching cold black eyes. He was single, looked good in a uniform, and took suspicious care of his appearance: the razored sideburns, the polished nails; regulation black tie always tight to the collar; uniform jacket tailored, waisted; shoes laced and shiny. It didn't take long for word to spread along the quays that Jean Grandet was not gay as previously thought but a serious and serial philanderer and that there were few women who could resist his attentions.

Now, in a single phone call, Roquefort had learned that his own wife was one of the younger man's conquests. According to the anonymous caller, the affair had started only a year after Roquefort and Christine had married and had lasted nearly six months. It might have been years before, but for Roquefort it might just as well have been yesterday. He loved his wife, had imagined that she loved him, and he found it hard to believe that such a thing had happened. And so soon after they'd married.

And yet . . . and yet . . . Somehow, deep down, Roquefort knew that the man at the other end of the phone line was right.

Striding along, he tried to recall that time: his wife's moods, her occasional inconsistencies, those sly smiles, those unexplained absences, an often flustered look, and how, sometimes, inexplicably, she had denied him. Not tonight, I'm so tired, it's the wrong time, *chéri* . . . Just how often – and astonishingly for those early days of a marriage – had she refused him? Certainly enough times for him to remember them now.

He also wondered how Grandet and his wife could possibly have met. The where and the when. As shipping regulator, it was a requirement of Roquefort's job to inform Grandet's office of incoming traffic – ship, skipper and shipper, crew, load and berthing quay – so that Grandet, as Head of Customs, could decide on the appropriate action. A cursory examination of the captain's papers, or maybe a thorough search of the holds. It all depended . . . But although that work brought the two men into frequent contact they had never, so far as Roquefort could recall, met out of hours – either at parties, or by chance in bars or restaurants.

That wasn't all. According to the caller, it was Jean Grandet who had ended the affair, not Roquefort's wife. Which somehow made it worse. As though Christine was not good enough for Grandet. A passing indulgence, someone with whom to wile away the odd afternoon. Nothing more than that. A whim. A fancy.

Increasing his pace, stepping out onto rue Tamberle without looking and earning himself a glaring klaxon blast from an approaching truck (which served only to increase his fury), Roquefort suddenly recalled those months of quietness, reserve, almost sadness in his wife. It had worried him, so soon into a marriage, and he had done all he could to lighten her mood – gifts, outings, extravagances he could barely afford on his supervisor's wage – to bring her out of her *ennui*. Eventually their life together had settled back into its old routine, but it had been hard, and Roquefort remembered the way it had been, remembered his disquiet.

And then, more galling still, he wondered how many other people knew about it? Did his staff know? His friends? Did they laugh behind his back? Was he the only one not in on the joke? He felt a boiling mix of anger and shame, and a sudden, aching need for revenge: to take that primped-up, smug, little Toulonnais *con* and teach him a real lesson, a Marseilles' lesson he would never forget.

At the corner of Tamberle and rue Guillot, Roquefort slackened his pace and paused by the stone bollards that closed Guillot to traffic. Catching his breath, heart pounding, he looked across the road at the front of Maison Blanche, its pavement parasols packed away and its striped awning wound in. If the mistral hadn't started up, Roquefort knew that Jean Grandet would have taken his usual table outside, making sure he could lean back in his chair to catch some sun and work on his tan. He'd seen him do it enough times. But this afternoon, with the wind whipping along the street, he'd be inside.

Maison Blanche was a favourite lunch spot for the higher ranks of dock worker. If you wore boots and *bleus* and worked the quays you brought your own packed lunch, or snuck across to Ali's where a bowl of couscous and tub of salad gave you change from a twenty. But if you had a desk and an office, you'd come to Maison Blanche. The food was good, came in large portions, and didn't stretch the budget too far. Roquefort usually managed a couple of times a month; Grandet, a single man, a great deal more often.

Pushing open the door, Roquefort smelled the hot *daubes* and *rôtis* from the kitchen, but felt no answering call from his belly. Instead he cast round the room, a line of tables down each side, and a shorter line down the middle, each covered with a red gingham cloth, every seat taken. He spotted Grandet straight away, sitting in the far corner, uniform jacket hung off the back of his chair, shirtsleeves up. He was one of four at the table, none of whom Roquefort recognised. Making his way across the room, he reached the table and caught Grandet's eye.

'Join us?' asked Grandet, casting round to see if there was a spare chair. He probably knew there wasn't, not that it would have worried him.

'A word, Jean. That's all,' replied Roquefort, somehow managing to keep a hold on his anger, even managing a brief, apologetic smile.

Grandet sat back, spread his hands. He didn't need to say anything. *Sure, go ahead, we're all friends here*, was what he meant.

Roquefort shook his head. 'There's a problem with one of the new arrivals, docked this morning. I'd rather we went outside, if

33

it's okay? Shouldn't take a moment, but you need to know.' He hadn't planned the exchange; the words just came to him.

Pulling the napkin from his collar, Grandet made his excuses, eased away from the table and followed Roquefort out of the restaurant. By the time he stepped onto Guillot, Roquefort was a dozen metres away, waiting for him by one of the bollards, the wind blustering through his hair and ballooning his shirt.

What followed was swift and vicious, Marseilles-style.

Grandet had just reached Roquefort and was pulling a pack of cigarettes from his pocket when Roquefort reached up his hands around Grandet's head as though to embrace him, then jerked it down, smashing the man's face into the top of the bollard that stood beside them. Grandet had no time to react, to defend himself. There was a crunching, splintering sound of bone and teeth and a whiplash of Grandet's blood splashed across Roquefort's shirt. Without waiting a moment, Roquefort hauled Grandet off the blood-crowned bollard by the shirt collar and waistband, and heaved the limp, stunned and wheezing body across the back of his neck. Then, getting a grip on a leg and arm, he hoisted Grandet above his head like a weight-lifter, paused for a moment, took a breath, then slammed him down onto the pavement. The head hit the kerbstone with a juicy slap, the body crumpled into the gutter and more blood spilled out on to the road.

If that had been all, Grandet might have survived the attack. But Roquefort wasn't finished. His blood was up, his heart pumping, muscles singing. This was his moment. This was where he settled the score. Once and for all.

His breath short and sharp, Roquefort took a couple of steps back and then lunged forward, aiming a running kick at the side of Grandet's head.

The right leg swinging through an arc from the hip, toe pointed, arms spread out for balance, like a striker in the penalty box, shooting for the net.

A working shoe. A steel cap.

*   *   *

34

Christine Roquefort was in the garden, pegging up washing, when her husband returned home an hour later, pulling up his car in a cloud of dust. She turned in time to see him striding across the lawn, but she was not in time to protect herself from the fist which landed fair and square in the centre of her face, breaking her nose, splitting her top lip and snapping three teeth from her upper jaw. The force of the blow sent her staggering backwards through the line of washing before she dropped to the parched grass like a sack of rice.

Knuckles burning, panting with the effort, every ounce of energy and hatred suddenly spent, Roquefort dropped his chin to his chest as the sound of sirens approached, turned into his street.

7

'TELL ME THIS IS A joke,' said Jacquot, as he followed Salette
through the wheelhouse hatch and down into the main cabin, feeling
a wince of pain on every one of the five steps. There was a warm,
stale smell below deck but the varnished wood and brass fittings
gleamed. 'I hardly knew the man.'

Salette waved the objection aside. '*Ça n'importe*,' he replied,
reaching up to open the skylight. A draft of fresh salty air spun
through the opening and stirred the small curtains on the three
portholes either side of the cabin. 'Philo knew your father, fished
with him. You didn't have to know him. And it's what he wanted.
For the boat to be with someone who would take care of her.
Someone who would cherish her. Love her. As he did. And he
appointed me, as executor, to make sure it happened.'

'And he specified me? Daniel Jacquot, the cop, the son of
Vincent? Something written in a will.'

'Not in his will, no,' admitted Salette, working now at the screws
that latched down the portholes. 'But he mentioned your name.
Many times, always asking after you. Vinnie's boy. The *flic*. And
since Niko had no family, never married, kept to himself . . . He
just gave me the papers. With instructions to hand them on. To
whomever I thought should have them.'

'Niko?'

36

'His real name. Niko Emanetti. His mother was Sardinian, I think, and his father Greek.'

'Emanetti doesn't sound too Greek.'

Salette latched the last porthole open and threw Jacquot a look. There was no need to say anything. Jacquot knew what the look meant. When a child took a mother's name it was usually because the father was not known. Maybe the 'Niko' was a nod to the man who had sired him, but that was all.

'*Écoute. Écoute-moi*,' Salette began again. 'Listen to me. It's not a joke, and there's no mystery here. It is straightforward. Niko . . . Philo . . . He just wanted *Constance* to go to a good home, and told me to make it happen. That's what I'm doing.'

Jacquot started to chuckle, started to shake his head. 'You make me drive all the way down here to give me a boat?'

'I have the papers. A *notaire* waiting. You just have to sign. Three copies only. *C'est tout*. It's yours.'

'It can't be for nothing, J-P. There must be money involved. A boat like this? Too much for me, *c'est certain*.'

'The berthing, servicing, a few bits and bobs. That's it. And it'll do you good. Get you out of the office.'

'It can't be.'

'It's me he asked to sort it. And I'm sorting it,' replied Salette, a little testily now, as though he couldn't understand Jacquot's reticence. Why there should be any objection? All these questions. He pushed aside a cushion and settled himself at the table, started tapping a finger against its edge.

Jacquot remained standing – unwilling to risk the discomfort that sitting might entail – and looked around the cabin. For the first time he took in the books, every spare centimetre shelved and laden with books, down in the for'ard berth, too. Books everywhere.

'It's like a library,' he said.

'That's Philo for you. You remember him?'

'Late-seventies? Brown as a nut. Not many teeth . . .'

'None.'

37

'A gentle, quiet man as I recall.'

Salette nodded. 'But tough too. Old-school tough. No whining, no excuses. So, what do you think?'

'What I think is . . .' Jacquot couldn't help himself. 'What I think is, how did he get his hands on a boat like this? Even with no wife, and no kids to support, a fisherman's nets wouldn't have brought in enough for something like this.'

'Hard work and luck,' replied Salette. 'Old Philo was always lucky. Cards and women, both.'

'He won the money, or some admirer bought this for him?'

Salette spread his hands. 'Who knows? Like I told you, he kept himself to himself. None of us ever really knew. He never said. And we didn't ask. It was just . . . his. That's all he'd say. And now . . . it's yours.'

Jacquot started to shake his head, tried to order his thoughts, was about to turn it down, get off that boat and drive home, leaving Salette with an earful for wasting his time. It was all just too . . . ridiculous. Impossible. He lived in Cavaillon now, not the city. And a boat? In the Vieux Port?

But then he paused, let his eyes take it all in, felt another gentle sway and tip as a cruiser passed down the channel and out to sea. And he smelled the salt air, stronger out here at the end of the pontoon.

'Be good for the boy,' said Salette, with a sly glance.

'Boy?'

'Or girl. Whichever.'

There was a moment's silence, filled by the distant, rising wail of a siren. Mention of 'the boy', his son, 'or girl', his daughter, had caught Jacquot unawares. As Salette had meant it to.

'So tell me about *Constance*,' Jacquot asked, still playing for time, still undecided, but knowing that soon he'd have to make up his mind.

Salette smiled. 'Mahogany hull, new epoxy sheath. Teak decking. Twin Volvo diesels that'll give you close to twenty knots. Turns in her own length, cheap to run. You want, you can take off the wheelhouse roof, too – go topless . . .' Salette chuckled. 'Sleeps six if you're friendly. And all the gadgets.' He nodded to the chart desk that Jacquot was leaning against. 'Radio. Radar. Depth finder. Solid stuff.'

Then he smacked the palms of his hands on the table, got to his feet. He had said enough. No more.

'So. Are we going to that *notaire* or what?'

8

JACQUOT DID NOT RETURN TO Cavaillon that afternoon, nor the afternoon that followed. After parting company with Salette, who refused an invitation to stay for supper on board *Constance* – 'the two of you need to be together,' he'd told Jacquot. 'Get to know each other.' – Jacquot had gone to a quayside chandlery and bought himself a sleeping bag, and to a small corner store on Sainte-Catherine for a toothbrush, toothpaste and other basic supplies. Back on *Constance*, he fired up the galley stove to heat some water, found a mug, made coffee, added a dash of Calva and took the brew up on deck. The sun was low, sliding towards the battlements of Fort Saint-Jean and the wind had dropped to a flighty, gusting breeze. Finding cushions in one of the seat lockers on the aft deck, Jacquot laid one out – sun-faded blue canvas stiff with salt – made himself comfortable and tried to take it all in.

As Salette had promised, it had taken just twenty minutes at the *notaire*'s office: the scrawl of his signature, the official's secretary as witness, and the duly notarised exchange of papers confirmed with a triple stamp-stamp-stamp with ink from a pad that had almost run dry. And *Constance* was his. All he had to do now, Salette informed him as they left the *notaire*'s office, was to signal the change of ownership with the *Capitainerie* in the morning, deposit a quarterly berth fee, and he was done, formalities dealt with.

Jacquot sipped his coffee and reached for his cigarettes. Twelve hours earlier, he'd been stumping around an empty house in the Lubéron, missing Claudine more than he could have imagined, and now he was here, berthed in the old port, on a boat that had come into his life without warning and was very quickly capturing his heart – as Salette had surely known it would.

There was just something about *Constance*. The shape of her, the curving lines, her age and elegance, thought Jacquot. The sun-whitened teak decking, smooth and sturdy underfoot, with its finely tined caulking; the brass-framed dials on the instrument panel with their salt-speckled glass and black needle-thin arrows; the occasional gentle creak from the timber planking in the wheelhouse when she rode a swell; and below deck the pair of warm, snug cabins, wood-panelled, lit by gimballed oil lamps, with portholes for windows and blue gingham curtains the size of napkins. And being out here in the middle of Marseilles' Vieux Port, watching a sun set through a metal fencing of swaying masts, the lights round the harbour and stars above twinkling now into strength, traffic circling the quays just a distant hum, was a simple yet invigorating delight. The blackening sea all around him, deep and dark and shifting, the warm breeze over its light-shimmering surface, the slap and snap of halyards and the hollow suck of the water beneath the pontoon. All utterly seductive.

But maybe the attraction was not so surprising, he thought. It was in his blood, after all. His father had been a fisherman, lived in Le Panier and worked right here in the Vieux Port, and Jacquot recalled the times as a boy when Papa had brought him aboard whatever fishing boat he'd been working – the smell of the catch, of drying nets and seaweed, of oil and petrol and rusting chains. There'd been something magical about it all back then, Jacquot decided, and there was something just as magical about it now. But whether it was *Constance*, or where she was, or the fact that this lovely old boat now belonged to him – no matter how unlikely or impractical – he had to admit that the spell she had cast had caught him as surely as a tightly knotted net. Just a few hours afloat and he was lost.

After finishing his café-Calva and two more cigarettes, Jacquot set about exploring his new home, his first real inspection, starting with the seat lockers on either side of the aft deck. Secured with simple brass clasps, he opened them up and sorted through their contents. In the one he'd been sitting on, there was another seat cushion, a folded rug, some smaller cushions, and a pair of rusting hurricane lamps, fuel still sloshing about in their tanks. Turning to the other seat, he lifted the lid and found a set of wet-weather gear: a yellow, waxed jacket that was far too small for him, a sou'wester, and a pair of old rubber boots, also a couple of sizes too small. Beneath them was a heavy-duty waterproof torch (batteries dead), a set of fins, mask and snorkel – useful, he supposed, if something snagged round the rudder or propellers, a fishing rod broken into sections and wrapped in a green plastic sleeve, and some hand-held wooden lines with the hooks neatly bedded into the twine. Right at the bottom, tucked away in a corner, were old cans of varnish, a glass jar filled with a collection of screws and nails and tacks, an opened packet of sandpaper, and half a dozen paint brushes held in a thick rubber band, their soft bristle tips cleaned and ready for use.

Satisfied there was nothing else of any interest, Jacquot closed and secured the seat lids and made his way down into the cabin where, gimbal lights lit, gingham curtains drawn but portholes left open, he continued his search, as detailed and thorough as any scene-of-crime investigation. Taking it all in: the smell of her, the feel of her, judging heights, testing his weight before leaning against anything.

The main cabin was five paces long from wheelhouse steps to the sliding door leading to the for'ard berth, and Jacquot was a big man; high enough, too, to allow him a reasonable clearance in the centre of the cabin; and a good few centimetres wider than a full stretch of his arms. These proportions might not have been overly generous on land, but here they had been cleverly organised to provide enough space for a small galley on one side of the wheel-house companionway, a chart table on the other, and a booth-style dining area that would comfortably seat six, which, as Salette had demonstrated, could be turned into a second double berth by dropping the table to seat level and using the cushions for a mattress. Between the outside banquette and bulkhead a worn strip of deck led forward to a Formica-skinned shower stall, a marine head, and the for'ard cabin where Jacquot had dumped his sleeping bag.

There was also plenty of storage space, all of it ingeniously accommodated: a number of drawers, cabinets and stow-spaces containing a basic range of cooking implements, cutlery and crockery (mismatched, two of each), a school-kid's geometry set, a see-through plastic ruler, a GPS handset on a worn rope collar, a white tin box with a red cross on it, and a fairly comprehensive collection of hammers, pliers, spanners and screwdrivers all neatly secured in metal clips. As Salette had said, a tidy, well-kept, and well-found vessel.

And books, of course. Books everywhere. Two shelves running the length of the main cabin, both sides, squared off to keep the portholes clear, with another shelf along the top of the bulkhead and three narrower ones the other side in the for'ard berth. There could be few small boats, Jacquot reckoned, with such a large and extensive collection, paperback and cloth-covered, dog-eared and fat with use.

Slowly, Jacquot worked his way along the shelves, tipping his head to read the spines. Everything from Rabelais' *Gargantua* to Camus' *La Peste*, not to mention other Nobel laureates like Sartre, Gide and Mauriac, old masters like Balzac, Dumas and Zola, as well as collections of short stories, poetry and philosophy. And text books, too, but text books of a high order, with titles in French, German, English, Italian and Spanish on subjects ranging from celestial navigation to marine engineering, their pages filled with finely detailed drawings and lengthy footnotes. It wasn't just the languages that impressed – Jacquot's own father had spoken Italian and Spanish as well as French, Salette was equally fluent, as were many other French trawlermen who worked in mixed-race crews – it was the wide scope of the subject matter: classic fiction from the sixteenth to the twentieth century, and non-fiction works that would have demanded a certain level of academic and intellectual aptitude, clearly showing that Philo was altogether more than just a fisherman. Only in the for'ard cabin were the books any lighter. Thrillers this time, and crime fiction, from Marseilles' very own Jean-Claude Izzo to John Grisham, from Clive Cussler to Jack Drummond.

Jacquot reached forward and pulled a book from the rack. One of the cloth-covered titles. De Maupassant. Short stories. He turned to the contents page – *Moonlight*, *The Practical Joker*, and *Forgiveness* – and flicked the dry pages through his fingers, a stale smell of dust and age coming off them. No damp here then, thought Jacquot. Books would have been the first to give the game away. He was about to put the Maupassant back when he noticed an ex-libris sticker on the inside cover. Librairie Santal. Jacquot knew the shop, a second-hand *bouquiniste* just a few hundred metres along the quay, two blocks back from the Opéra, with open, trestled stalls set out on the pavement. He replaced the Maupassant and pulled out another book, Gide's *Trois Contes*, and checked the inside cover. Not the Santal sticker this time but a stamp from the Lycée Simon on Cours de Valerie. A school-book. Of the ten books he checked, five had come from second-hand bookshops, two from the Lycée Simon, with three belonging to someone called Edina, the signature in pencil. An old lady's signature, Jacquot decided, or a young girl experimenting: the careful, studied curls to the letters, the tidy little underline brought back off the tail of the final 'a' and prettily looped beneath the 'E'.

And in most of the books he examined there was a bookmark. The same bookmark. A thin laminated strip with Philo's initials. A neatly worked 'N' in red ink at the top left of the strip, and the 'E' in green in the bottom right, the two capital letters separated by a column of numbers . . . the same numbers, Jacquot noticed, on every bookmark: 4305, 1022, 4023, 2836. Page references? Favourite verses from the Bible? Phone numbers? 43-05-10-22; 40-23-28-36 reading across; or reading down 43-10-40-28;

44

05-22-23-36? Alternatively they could have been the combinations to a set of locks? Or a bank account number, perhaps? Or maybe credit-card pin numbers. Even fishermen had credit cards. And an old boy like Philo, getting forgetful, what better place to note them down? On a bookmark, rather than scribbled on a slip of paper in his wallet. Clever boy, thought Jacquot, slipping the marker between the pages, closing the book and putting it back on the shelf.

Somewhere beyond the pontoon another cruiser motored past, coming in too fast, its wake slapping against *Constance*'s hull and gently tipping the deck, enough for Jacquot to reach out a hand to steady himself against the tilt and rock, shallow as it was. Being out at the end of the jetty might have distanced him from the sounds of the city, but it put him closest to passing traffic in the harbour's main channel, and at the mercy of inconsiderate sailors. In time, he was sure he'd get used to it, just like all the other things he'd have to get used to: trying not to bang his head on the ceiling when he reached up to close the wheelhouse hatch, or when he leaned forward to blow out the main cabin lights, and having to turn sideways to reach the for'ard cabin, spreading out his new sleeping bag over the foam rubber mattress wedged into *Constance*'s curving bows, a bed so short that he could only stretch his legs out straight if he kept the cabin door open.

And in the darkness of that for'ard cabin, slanted with moving lights from the distant quays, Jacquot settled himself down that first night aboard *Constance*, trying to accommodate the ache and spikes of pain in the top of his leg, the distant hum of traffic broken every now and then by a distant siren wailing through the city, or the high-pitched revving scream of a Friday-night trail-bike accelerating along the quay. And in the deepening silences between them, he listened to the whispering gusts of breeze around the open cabin portholes, felt the gentle, lulling rock of the ocean, and with a sigh of puzzled contentment, he fell asleep.

9

THEY WERE ALL DYING NOW, mused Patric Polineaux, putting down his cognac and taking a deep pull on his Cohiba Robusto. The lucky ones that is, the ones who had made it through to the end without collecting a bullet in the head, or a wire round the neck, or a knife in the guts. Difficult to say which was worse: the gun, the wire, the blade or, years later, the stroke, the cancer, the sudden, searing heart attack. All of them just as deadly, of course, the only consolation a long life to look back on, but lives now rapidly unravelling. Hugo, down in Antibes, dribbling into his nappy until that last final bursting in the brain just a week before; that bastard Colonese in Menton, with his twenty-seven-year-old widow left everything; and old Bouri, the Algerian, who'd filled the Nice–Cannes section of the A7 flyover with more calcium than concrete, the decaying bones of anyone who'd crossed his path and thought the Arab's gentle stammer and exquisite manners were genuine. A big, big mistake.

Each of them – Hugo, Colonese, Bouri and a dozen more – killers all. Utterly ruthless. Had to be, of course, to make it through.

But not one of them as bad as that old coot Cabrille, who'd passed away just a few months earlier, whose funeral Polineaux himself had attended. A foggy Sunday in Marseilles. No more than a small handful of the old guard there to pay their respects: René

Duclos, from Toulon; Jean-Claude Rachette, also known as The Hatchet, after his weapon of choice; and Guy Ballantine, stooped and greying, in his fancy London suits. Now it was the youngsters taking control, and only a few of those prepared to turn up for a gangland *adieu*. Too busy with their casinos and their hookers and their fancy cars to honour the passing of an old-schooler, even if Cabrille had been a certifiable psychopath.

And his own turn soon, thought Polineaux with an icy stab of dread.

With a rug tucked round the stumps of his long-lost, bullet-shattered legs, he sat in his wheelchair on the terrace of his home, high on the western slopes of Cap Ferrat, watching the lights twinkle around the bay of Villefranche. So much prettier, he thought, than the buzzing orange glow of Nice, and Cannes, and Antibes. Taking another long draw on his Robusto, he remembered how the same stretch of coast had looked some fifty years earlier, when his father had bought this house. No golden glow then, no smudged orange shimmer reaching to the stars and running from Mont Boron to the shadowy pleats and folds of the Esterel Hills. Nowadays you needed sunglasses at night. If you'd lived long enough to see it. But Villefranche, seen from out here on the Cap, from the terraces of Hauts des Pins, was little changed, just as it always had been.

Polineaux knew that he had been one of the lucky ones. An invalid for the last fifteen years, tucked up in his wheelchair, with a hoist in his bedroom and bathroom, a live-in nurse to wipe his arse, and an oxygen tent on hand for one of his 'episodes' – that terrible breathlessness, the blood pumping up his neck and into his head, until his face felt as tight and red as a ripe tomato. But at least he was still around. He might know what the cold blade of a knife felt like, and the terrible slicing and shredding of a fusillade of lead, and by all accounts he should be dead. But he wasn't. He was still at the top of his game, keeping the youngsters in line. Legless he may be, but there was life in the rest of him.

Polineaux gave a little shiver, tapped the ash from his cigar and held the red tip to his cheek. It was starting to turn chill and he felt the Robusto's heat, knew they'd be out for him soon – the new nurse, Delon, with those long, slim fingers and that ridiculous waxed moustache, and his old butler, Jarrive, in his striped green waistcoat. But with just one Cohiba a day permitted to him, he wasn't going to let them spoil his treat because it was getting a little cold. He'd stay till the damned thing was ash between his fingers, and they could choke on it.

He was closing his lips around the fat cigar when he heard the door slide open behind him. He could tell from the soft footfall that it was Jarrive, and prepared to send him packing. But Jarrive beat him to it, starting to speak while still some distance from the chair.

'Monsieur Didier has arrived. Shall I ask him to step out?'

Polineaux frowned for a moment. Didier? Didier? And then he remembered. Of course, of course. He had sent for him an hour earlier, asked him to drop by. He raised the cigar and waved it over his shoulder. 'Show him out. Show him out.'

A reprieve. Now he could finish his cigar in peace.

'And bring me another cognac,' he called after Jarrive. A second cognac would certainly help warm him up.

A few moments later Didier Lacombe stepped out on to the terrace. He was formally dressed for the casino in Beaulieu, from whose *salle privée* he had just excused himself following Polineaux's late-night summons, and he tugged at his cufflinks and straightened his bow tie as he came closer.

Polineaux glanced up at him. Mid-thirties, curly black hair that would likely fall out by the time he was fifty, a long nose, black eyes and thin lips . . . thin as a blade of grass. Tall and slim and deadly. And loyal – loyal to a fault. A winning streak at the races, or a good hand at the tables, or a tasty lady – Didier would dump them all when he got the call from Hauts des Pins. Not many around like that any more.

'You wanted to see me?'

Polineaux waved him to a chair, then pointed at the cream-coloured envelope on the table. Didier picked it up, peered inside, pulled out the contents. He looked at the photos then read the covering note. It was short, precise, and written in neatly sloping capitals.

FOR YOUR INFORMATION . . .

'The cars look old,' said Didier, putting down the letter and shuffling through the images again. Three of the photos showed two men talking to one another. Grainy long shots, black-and-white. In a shopping street somewhere, in a car park, outside a bar.

'They are,' replied the old man. 'Twenty-seven years old, to be precise.'

'You recognise the men?'

'The shorter of the two was one of ours.'

'One of ours?'

'Back then, yes. Monsieur Bernard Suchet of Transports Suchet International. Gone straight now, so they say.'

'And the other guy?'

Polineaux studied the picture. 'The other one's a cop. Can't be sure, but he's got that look about him. Probably working both sides. Out to bulk up his pension, you know?'

Didier nodded, came to the last two photos. Polaroids.

'And these?'

Polineaux didn't need to look. The flash of colour. Almost blinding. Nothing black or white or grainy. In one, a single bar of gold sitting on the front page of Thursday's *Le Figaro*. The other, a close-up of the same bar. The assay marks and stamps easily made out.

'Before your time, but no need to tell you, I expect.'

Didier nodded. 'You know who sent this?' he asked, sliding the note and photos back into the envelope.

Polineaux turned down his mouth, pushed out his bottom lip – a long red shiny slug – and spread his hands.

'It can only be that shit Lombard. Going that far back.'

'Can't be Lombard,' replied Didier. 'He's in Baumettes, remember? A long stretch.'

'Then someone who knows that swivel-eyed freak. Someone he's brought in. Someone who knows which bells to ring.'

49

Polineaux pulled in a mouthful of cigar smoke, let it lick the inside of his cheeks, slide over his tongue, then blew it out in a thin whisper that made his lips tingle. For the first time that day, since the envelope had arrived, he had his wits about him. That's what Cohiba Robustos and a good cognac did, the second of which Jarrive was even now setting down on the table. No better medicine known to man.

'A cop. Or a lawyer,' said Didier.

'That's my guess,' said Polineaux, reaching for the cognac, nodding to the butler; the nurse, Delon, would never have allowed it. 'Someone he's got his hooks into, someone on the outside. That's who sent it. And that's . . .' Polineaux waved his glass at the envelope '. . . that's who's got my gold.'

Somewhere below the terrace, in the gardens of Hauts des Pins, the sprinklers started up and a frog began to croak.

'You want me to make some . . . enquiries?'

'Enquiries? Oh, yes. And just as soon as you can, please.'

10

'YOU HAVE UNTIL MONDAY, SISTER. On Monday you will all be gone.'

The voice was low and steady. No emphasis, no sense of threat, just a message delivered with unwavering certainty. A dozen words that rang in Sister Mercy's head as she watched the man turn on his heel and cross the open yard. His jacket had been tightly buttoned but the breeze still caught at it, similarly the grey trousers, and he lifted a hand to push back a lock of hair. Although Sister Mercy didn't take it in, he wore trainers too. It was a strange look, given the suit and the briefcase. At the gate her visitor passed the postman coming in, pushing his trolley. As she took the letters and package he had brought her, wishing him a '*bonne journée*', her heart tightened and her voice caught as the message finally registered.

She had known it would happen, sooner or later, but she hadn't been prepared, hadn't been ready for it so early in the morning. She had buzzed open the outside gate, thinking it was the postman, then gone to the front door. And there he stood, shoulders as wide as the doorway, as clean-shaven as he was ever going to get, jacket buttoned, tie a grease-darkened red, a double chin bellying over his collar. Even before he said a word, she knew who he was. From the landlord's office, as a result of a month's unpaid rent on the small factory space that she and Sister Odette occupied. Eight years

51

they'd been there, and every month the rent had been paid on time. But one slip and they were on to her. Letters first, then the visits. This was the third man to knock on her door in as many weeks.

She knew why, of course, this speed and enthusiasm to observe every last tiny phrase of their lease, to follow minutely every sub-clause and condition of tenancy: to have them out, as swiftly as possible, because the landlord wanted to develop the space, an old soap-making factory that had closed down twenty years earlier and lain damp and deserted until Sister Mercy from the Convent of the Immaculate Conception had taken a short renewable lease on it, the rent paid through donations and sales from the print-works they'd established. But times were hard. The summer had been long and hot, outgoings had increased but income had fallen. And so, the shortfall. Which was why they'd missed that month.

Money. Money had always been tight, but they'd always managed to make ends meet. This time things looked bad. Because of that misunderstanding with the bank and a bounced cheque from one of their retailers, they had to leave on Monday. Three days. No, not even that.

Either take up the ten year lease remaining, payable in full – a little over a million francs – or leave by Monday. Either / or. That simple.

Clutching the mail, Sister Mercy closed the door and turned down the passageway towards her small office. There were three polychrome prints of the Virgin Mary on the wall between the front door and her office – the Madonna's skirts as blue as the sky above Marseilles that morning – and at each one Sister Mercy made a hurried sign of the cross, kissing her thumbnail on the last, before bustling into the box room she called an office and dumping the mail on her desk. Above her, on the first floor, doors opened and closed. There was the sound of footsteps on the lino-covered passageway, a burst of children's laughter, an accompanying scream to counter it, and voices – women's voices. In an hour, the children would be breakfasting in the refectory before crossing the yard to nursery and classes, their mothers to work on the presses or in the office or around the house. Working for their room and board. And safety. Just like any other day. The chanting from the classroom, the rackety-rack of the printing machines, the smell of cooking from the kitchen wing . . . just as it always was.

Until Monday, he had said. And Sister Mercy had known he meant it.

Then it would be over. They would be out of there. All of them, women and children, out on the street. For Sisters Mercy and Odette there was always the convent in Aubagne, but for the thirty-two women and eleven children who lived at the refuge there would be no such fall-back position. A hostel, a friend's apartment, maybe a parent's house. Or, more likely, out on the street or back home for more of the same abuse from the drunken husbands or unforgiving pimps who had driven these poor women out in the first place, taking their children with them. For years now the two Sisters had provided shelter, work and food for hundreds of such women, each given six months to find her feet and move on. The Sisters were as strict about that as the men who wanted to evict them on Monday. A deadline was a deadline. A deal was a deal. There were other women waiting for a place of safety. Six months was enough to sort something out and move on to make room.

But Monday . . . It was just hours away, thought Sister Mercy, and her chest tightened with another drum roll of fear and anxiety. What on earth could they do? Where would they all go? How in the good Lord's name would they manage?

And then Sister Mercy did the only thing that she knew would make her feel strong enough to face the challenge ahead. She got down on her knees, rearranged the folds of her habit, then rested her elbows on the desktop and lowered her forehead to her clasped hands.

And as she prayed she felt the tightness in her chest ease, her heartbeat settle and the weight on her shoulders fall away, drawing in her breath at the end of every line of her prayer to begin the next, a whispered litany of thanks and blessings and faith.

It was after breakfast when Sister Mercy got round to the morning's mail. She'd told Sister Odette of the deadline, but no one else, and as the two women sat together trying to come up with some kind of plan, Sister Mercy started on the mail, slicing each envelope open with the penknife at her belt, unfolding the letter within, reading it with a sigh – always official, always a request for money – before adding it to the pile.

The package was the last item she opened. A bulky brown envelope, crumpled from the sorting office and the postman's trolley, postmarked Avignon and addressed to her.

She sliced it open, put away her penknife and peered inside.

For a moment or two, she didn't say a thing. Wasn't able to say anything. Couldn't believe her eyes, which started to prick with tears.

'*Le Bon Dieu*,' she whispered at last, and her hand trembled.

Across the desk, Sister Odette's kindly old face, pinched tight by her wimple, creased with concern.

'What is it?' she asked. 'You're white as a ghost. Are you all right?'

Sister Mercy swallowed. 'I don't know . . . I don't understand . . .'

And she turned the package in her hand and tipped out its contents on to the desk.

Tightly wadded rolls of green, each the size of a man's fist, each secured with a rubber band, a tumble of paper tubes that rolled across the desk and spilled on to the floor. Sister Odette reached down and picked one up, turned it in front of her disbelieving eyes, her mouth opening in a silent 'Oh' as she registered the thickness of the wad, its particular shade of green and the engraved face of Marie Curie.

Five-hundred-franc notes, rolled into a tube.

Many thousands of francs, certainly.

Thirty thousand? Forty thousand? Just the one roll was heavy enough.

And so many rolls. Forty? Fifty? Maybe more.

For a moment the two women looked at the surface of the desk, at the pile of money between them.

A million? Two million? More?

And then, together, they began to laugh and cry, and they stood, and they hugged, and they patted their chests to ease their pounding hearts, and took handkerchiefs from their sleeves and wiped away the tears.

Laughing and crying at the same time.

The good Lord had provided.

The lease was theirs.

There'd be no leaving on Monday.

11

JACQUOT KNEW WHERE HE WAS before he opened his eyes. On a boat. His boat. Berthed in Marseilles' Vieux Port. In the heart of the city.

At the millhouse in the Lubéron, he woke to the summoning buzz of the bedside phone, or the low peep-peep-peep from his alarm clock, or the smell of baking bread or perking coffee on those occasions when Claudine got up before him. Here, it was the cackling screech and stuttering caw-caw-caw of seagulls, and the distant mournful hoot of a cargo ship leaving the docks of La Joliette, that had broken into his dreams. And when he finally opened his eyes, rubbing the sleep from them, he saw not the beamed ceiling of their millhouse bedroom and the cypress trees outside their windows, but the planked roof of the for'ard cabin and a square of deep blue sky through an open skylight. And somewhere, hardly registering, there was a sense of motion, a lulling, barely discernible pitch and tilt.

And as he lay there, loosely covered by the unzipped sleeping bag, listening to the sounds of the harbour and the city, Jacquot thought of Claudine, on the other side of the world, beyond the curve of the globe, on an island in the Caribbean. With their baby inside her. Very soon he was going to be a father, and he thrilled at the thought. Boy or girl, they had no idea, had agreed not to ask, though there'd been a moment's hesitation when Claudine's doctor asked if they wanted him to tell them. But it was just a moment, and afterwards they'd smiled – 'For a moment there . . .' 'Me too . . .' – and then laughed, happy and relieved that they'd resisted.

The prospect of fatherhood filled Jacquot with a warmth and a wonderment he had never known. Claudine had been pregnant before with Midou, knew what it meant, this new life growing inside her. But for Jacquot the feelings were new and urgent and exciting.

But what, he wondered, would Claudine make of this? The boat? *Constance*? She'd love it, he knew that, and he could see her – and their child – sitting in the shade of the wheelhouse as he motored them along the coast, to the islands, to the calanques, to Cassis. To small coves and deserted beaches, and to three-table shack restaurants where they grilled the morning catch under slatted split-cane roofs.

But knowing Claudine she'd be sensible, too. The practicalities. And all the impracticalities that he had not thought – or chosen – to consider. At least there was no large financial burden for her to settle on, to take into consideration. A few thousand francs a year, that was all. They could manage that, even with the new addition on his or her way.

And soon, in another couple of weeks, Jacquot would make the introduction and Claudine would see *Constance*. He'd lead her down the pontoon, telling her nothing, doing what Salette had done to him. And let *Constance* work her magic.

But first things first, thought Jacquot, throwing off the sleeping bag, and crawling from the bed, feeling that tight morning ache in the back of his thigh and hip. What he needed, he decided, was a good breakfast, and a little light exercise. Struggling into his clothes, he knew exactly how to get both.

12

THE PHOTOS WERE DAMNING, SHOCKINGLY explicit. Seven of them. Black and white. A little creased and faded. Interior shots. Église Saint Ignace off Marseilles' rue Kléber, the stone panels of its altar clearly visible. And equally visible, the action being played out on the altar's runnered steps that long-ago night.

As far as Curé Pascal Dominici could tell, the photos had been taken from one of the side chapels, without a flash. Someone hidden. Someone they hadn't known about. And in each of the photos there was Curé Pascal himself, younger, fitter, and with more hair, a white, lacy shift-like *rochet* riding up over his thighs as he clutched hungrily at his young companions. Three of them. Choirboys. Thin and lithe, naked as the day they were born.

Eighteen years ago. A parish priest just a few years out of the Seminary of Saint-Joseph in Équirre. Now assistant secretary-general to the office of the Archdiocese of Avignon. Forty-seven years old, nearly thirty in the service of the Church, with elevation to a full position on the Curia only a matter of weeks away.

The photographs had arrived that morning, mercifully not opened by his secretary thanks to the *Private and Confidential* instruction on the front of the envelope. Not that it mattered now. Standing at his office window, with its angled views of the Place des Papes and the misted countryside north of Avignon, Curé Pascal felt his stomach twist and clamp and turn chill as he shuffled, disbelieving, through the photos, hands shaking, reading and re-reading the brief note that accompanied them. It was written on a plain sheet of cream paper, heavily milled, silky to the touch, the words in the very centre of the page, just above the fold, in short, business-like capitals, so there could be no mistake with the message, the meaning:

AH, THOSE WERE THE DAYS . . .

Just that one line.

And beneath it, also in neat capitals:

COPIES TO THE RESIDENCE OF THE ARCHBISHOP.

With the full and correct address written below. The small second floor apartment below the Petit Palais overlooking the Bénézet Gardens where His Grace was even now considering applications for the post of Secretary General to the Office of the Archdiocese, a post which he, Curé Pascal, had recently applied for, a post he had every hope of securing.

But no longer.

Turning back to his desk, a wide oak table drawn up beside a brick-floored hearth, a Cardinal's tasselled *galero* carved into the high stone mantle, Curé Pascal placed the photos and the note on his blotter and felt another icy shudder spread through his belly. With the strength draining from his legs he slumped into his chair, put his elbows on the desk and laid his head in his hands. He stayed like that for more than a minute, trying to steady his breathing, trying to calm his nerves.

Somewhere beyond his window, the bells for morning Mass started up. Their clear ringing peals seemed to revive him and with the shaking now under some kind of control Curé Pascal got to his feet, pushed away from the desk and like a man on a tightrope steered himself across the room to a high, glass-fronted cabinet. Opening one of its doors he reached in and pulled out a packet of cigarettes, a lighter, and a small silver disc, like a woman's compact, that served as a portable ashtray. He slipped them into his cassock, and from a cupboard beneath the shelves he drew out a bottle of Glenfarclas 30 year old and a thick glass tumbler. Back at his desk, he poured a large measure and left the bottle uncorked. There'd be a second and a third, he reckoned, lighting up a cigarette, before he was done.

And as he smoked and drank, he tried to work out who had sent those photos.

The person who had taken them in the first place? All those years ago.

Or someone else?

Someone from his past?

Or from his present?

One name sprang to mind. Massanet, the Curé from Saint-Sulpice, who had also applied for the Curia post. Pascal Dominici wouldn't have put it past him. A weasely individual with small greedy eyes and a tight thin mouth. The man didn't drink, didn't smoke. The two of them had never got on . . .

But how had he got hold of those photos? And after all this time.

Not that it mattered any more. It was all over. Massanet was a certainty now. Nothing he could do to change that. Except pour another shot of Glenfarclas, light another cigarette and weigh up his options.

It didn't take Curé Pascal Dominici long to realise that he didn't have any.

Or rather, just the one.

An hour later, at ten thirty that morning, the Curé's secretary knocked at the door and waited for a response. He was carrying a hand-delivered letter from the Bénézet Palace, a summons from the Archbishop's office, his seal stamped into a puddle of blue wax on the back of the envelope. When no answer was forthcoming, the secretary knocked again and reached for the doorhandle.

He had closed the door behind him and was three steps into the room before he smelled the cigarette smoke and saw the whisky bottle on the desk. The next thing he registered was an overturned chair and Curé Pascal Dominici dangling above it, a pair of pointed black shoes peeping from beneath his cassock.

13

IT HAD TAKEN JACQUOT NEARLY thirty minutes to hobble round the quay, increasing the weight and pressure on his left leg and hip, just as the physio had instructed, and using his walking stick for just the last twenty metres, when he was brought up short by a green light on Quai des Belges and had to wait at the kerb for passing traffic.

Despite the time it had taken him to make the journey, Jacquot managed to arrive early enough at Café Samaritaine on the corner of rue République to find his favourite table unoccupied. With a grateful gasp, he pulled out a chair and settled himself carefully on it, pleased to note that the pulsing ache in his hip and the back of his thigh – a few centimetres below the crease where buttock properly becomes leg – had started to ease by the time the waiter returned with his *petit pain*, conserves and café-Calva.

Jacquot loved the Café Samaritaine. There were plenty of cheaper places in Marseilles to order up a café-Calva breakfast but none that offered such a sunny, bustling view: the quays, the traffic, the apartment blocks on the far side of the harbour, still in shadow, rising up like a stone pedestal beneath Marseilles' hilltop Madonna, the golden Dame de la Garde. Four years back, when he'd been working homicide on rue de l'Évêché, the Sam had been a regular stop. He'd sit here at this same table working through a case, a list

61

of suspects, or simply observing the other customers, watching the little dramas that played out at surrounding tables: shop girls whispering about their previous night's activities; single ladies of a certain age feeding their poodles pampering titbits under the table; tourists with suitcases and backpacks sorting through their small change or tickets or hotel reservations; and always lovers, or soon to be lovers, or lovers who'd moved on but were still friends, leaning over their tables, fingers touching, oblivious to everything around them. All life was here, he thought. You just had to look around and take it in: the whispered bustle of the café and, out on the pavement, the daily ebb and flow of people passing by, with their briefcases and shopping bags and prams and dogs, brisk or dawdling, old and young, all of them heading somewhere – things to do, people to meet.

Jacquot liked bars, too. Much the same kind of shifting dynamic and lay-out as a café – all the comings and goings. Yet somehow darker, more conspiratorial: the whispering barman, the dodgy businessman with his tie pulled loose, the local soak with his *demi* of beer or *petit jaune*, and after dark the working girls and the pimps and the thugs, night-time people with an altogether different agenda.

And whether it was here in Marseilles or up-country in Cavaillon, Jacquot always had his *tables préférées*. At Samaritaine it was out on the terrace, where he now sat, in the left-hand corner, under the awning, with his back to the wall. At Café de la Paix on Sadi-Carnot, the table was inside, in the small corner alcove, two steps from the front door where you could keep an eye on the street and every table in the room without moving your head. At La Tasse, it was the rickety tin table on the pavement unless it was raining when he took the table inside by the newspaper rack, or at Aux Coqs the table furthest away from the hiss and rattle of the ancient Gaggia.

As for bars, it was usually a favourite stool, elbows on the *zinc*, always on the corner where it turned towards the cigarette machine or coat-rack, never with his back to the door, unless there was a mirror he could keep an eye on. Théo's on rue Delion in Le Panier if he wanted a quiet word with someone, or Chinou in the fifth *arrondissement* where the lawyers gathered, or Mer Rouge if he wanted to know what the hacks from *La Provence* were talking about, or, back in Cavaillon, at Fin de Siècle, first booth on the right, behind the front door.

But this morning Jacquot wasn't thinking about any ongoing investigation, or what the journalists or lawyers or informants were talking about. He was on sick leave, recovering from wounds received in the line of duty. Four months off. Another three to run. Instead he was thinking about the previous day. His lunch with Salette, his meeting with *Constance*, and the impossibility, the sheer implausibility, of his suddenly owning a boat, with a berth on the Vieux Port. And for nothing.

As he sat there, watching the sun glance through his glass of Calva, he wondered whether Philo would have been pleased with Salette's choice of owner for the boat. Jacquot certainly hoped so. Because he knew without a shadow of a doubt that he was going to keep *Constance*, and love her, just as Philo would have wanted. And when the time came to pass her on, he'd do just the same. Give her to someone who'd love her too. His son? His daughter?

But for now, there was work to be done. Some catching up to do. Supplies for life afloat. Some fresh paint and varnish, some oil for the lamps, batteries for the torch, washing-up liquid, brass polish . . . he'd need to write a list, call in at the chandlers again, at the *supermarché* on Sainte-Catherine.

He finished off his Calva and checked the bill, smiling to himself as he slid a couple of notes under the empty glass. Twenty-four hours earlier, back in the Lubéron, he'd spent a lonely breakfast thinking of Claudine. Now there was another woman in his life, and he had time on his hands to knock her into shape. He couldn't think of a better way to spend it.

14

FIFTY KILOMETRES ALONG THE COAST, in Toulon's Mourillon Gardens, René Duclos, head of the Famille Duclos, let out the extendable dog lead and continued on his slow, shuffling way. A dozen steps behind him his poodle bitch, Salome, settled her haunches on the sidewalk and hunched her back. She lifted her snout, flared her split black nostrils, and her thin white woolly body seemed to stiffen and shiver.

When he got to the full extent of the lead, Duclos turned and flipped it, sending an irritable snap rippling down its length.

'*Alors. C'est tout. Viens*,' said the old man.

With a delicate shake and bound, the little poodle hurried up to him. Ten metres behind them, Duclos' minder, Beni, bent down with a carrier-bag glove and scooped up what the poodle had left him.

Duclos was not a man who lost his temper easily, but this morning he was angry. Very, very angry indeed. The envelope had arrived in the morning's mail, clearly sent by some smart-arse shit-stirrer, and the photo and photocopied document it contained spoke for themselves. Most eloquently.

A long shot of Jean Garnolle, hailing a taxi. Fanning his hat in the air like he always did, to attract the driver's attention. The bald head, the big ears. Unmistakable. His friend, his advisor, the only man Duclos had ever really trusted. Nothing out of the ordinary, nothing remarkable.

What was remarkable was the photocopied document that came with the photograph. A trading receipt made out in Garnolle's name dated 13 February 1973. The letterhead on the receipt a finely scripted copperplate, elegantly and expensively printed by the look of it. The address, Bahnhoffstrasse, Zurich, Switzerland. Telephone numbers, fax numbers, and the name *Jéromes Frères, Négotiants Suisses*. With the single word 'Gold' in brackets beside it.

The receipt had been delivered to Garnolle's old address in Toulon, before he moved to Marseilles, confirming the sale of 12.267 kilogrammes of 24-carat fine gold. A single bar. Delivery Standard. Assayed at 999.9/1000. Bearing the legend *Banque Nationale d'Algérie*. The agreed price of three hundred and fifty French francs per troy ounce less non-resident tax, handling fees and commissions. Just that one bar and his old friend Garnolle was a little over a hundred thousand francs richer.

A lot of money back then.

Just the one bar.

But how many more might have been traded, in the days and weeks and years that followed? Duclos wondered. How many more bars for which there were no receipts? From Jéromes Frères or some other unscrupulous *négotiant* in gold bullion. The transactions spread around over time, between dealers. Garnolle had always been a cautious man.

And thanks to that stamp – *Banque Nationale d'Algérie* – René Duclos knew exactly where that gold bar had come from. How many bars there had been.

And he now knew that Garnolle must have been involved.

Somehow. Somewhere along the line.

But his friend had never said a word about it. Not a fucking word. Kept the Famille Duclos right out of the loop. The first he, Duclos, had heard about it was on the news the morning after the heist. Three security trucks, seventy-five bars in each. Two picked up fully loaded, the third . . . empty. A ton of gold missing. The newspaper, *Le Figaro*, had even printed a picture of what a ton looked like. The bars were stacked high in a metal cage. On a pallet. That much fucking gold.

And Garnolle had known about it.

And said nothing.

'The fucking two-faced, cheating, bastard traitor,' whispered Duclos through gritted teeth. A *con-salaud* of all *cons-salauds*.

As he passed beneath the slanting shade of the Mourillon Gardens' palms that Saturday morning, with Salome skipping about his heels, it was that sense of betrayal, even more than the gold, which really bothered René Duclos, the fact that his old friend had fucked his arse.

And he, René Duclos, hadn't known.

René Duclos had been taken for a fool, and had played the part to perfection.

Duclos felt another tug as Salome paused to sniff at the base of a prettily-trimmed palmetto. Without turning he pulled at the lead, hard enough to elicit a yelp in return and hear the skitter of the dog's claws on the polished stones.

15

BERNARD SUCHET, OWNER, CHAIRMAN AND chief executive of Transports Suchet International, put down the newspaper and sighed. *Plus ça change, plus c'est la même chose*. Murder in the street. In broad daylight. A savage, fatal beating, Marseilles-style, and hang the consequences. Arab or Jew, Muslim or Christian, communist or conservative, black, white or yellow, Marseilles never changed. Always ready with its fists and its guns and its knives to settle a score whenever a score needed settling. Which was what had happened on rue Guillot just the day before, according to a stop-press paragraph, bottom-right on the front page of *La Provence*. A fatal assault. One man dead, another man arrested.

Normally Suchet would have turned to the business pages but this particular stop-press item had caught his eye. A familiar name, the man who had died. Jean Grandet, head of Customs at La Joliette. There was a photo accompanying the piece, but Suchet didn't recognise the face. Just knew the name from somewhere. For a minute or two he racked his brains – Grandet, Customs. Grandet, Customs. And then he had it. Of course . . . Grandet! That thieving bastard down in Toulon a few years back. Twice this Grandet character had delayed quayside loading and unloading for TSI rigs. No reason; he'd just pulled them over. Spot searches. Documents check. Other firms had been brought in too, but most of the rigs were TSI rigs. That's what Suchet's chief of operations had reported, adding that said bastard Grandet would be happy to ease the inconvenience on receipt of fifty thousand francs. And on two separate occasions Suchet had nodded it through and TSI had paid the bribe. They'd been hit again when Grandet moved to Marseilles, more rigs pulled over, further 'considerations' put his way. But now, it appeared, the man was dead. *Tant pis*. Tough shit. What goes round comes round, mused Suchet.

Of course, Grandet was not alone in his grafting. Everyone did it, one way or another. It was the way business worked; the way Marseilles worked. And in his time he had done his fair share, thought Suchet, getting up from his desk and going to a window. He was in his private office, a newly refurbished suite of rooms on the sixth floor of an eighteenth-century townhouse on rue Grignan in Marseilles' prestigious seventh *arrondissement*, so high that his view of the street was seriously diminished. All he could really see were the top floors of the buildings opposite and a tiled and leaded roofscape that stretched as far as the rising slopes of Le Panier. He wasn't high enough to see the sea, but he knew that if he opened a window he'd be able to smell it.

Now, looking towards those distant slopes and the unseen quays beyond them, Suchet remembered the days when he had crossed the line. A little more stylishly, a little more professionally than Grandet, he hoped, but still a crossing of the line. Three or four years of it, back end of the sixties and early seventies when he was starting out, with a young family to support. It was scary and tough, but exciting too. That pump in the balls you'd get when a game was going down. The thrill of it. And when it was over, watch out whatever girl happened along! Stiff as a flagpole, he'd be; bursting for it. But he had changed. He might have been down there once, with blood on his hands, but not now. Now he was legit, more than twenty years on the straight and narrow, just that horseshoe-shaped scar across the top of his broken nose to remind him of those distant times, and a fading memory of the bent cop who'd given it to him.

There was a tap at the door and Monique, his senior assistant, came in. She was in her fifties, elegantly turned out, and a formidable barrier between him and the outside world. She carried a cream-coloured envelope in her hand.

'This just arrived,' she told him, placing the envelope on his desk. 'The courier said it was urgent. And for your eyes only.'

'*Merci*, Monique,' he said, coming back to the desk, dropping into his chair.

'And Bruno is waiting downstairs. Your flight to Paris . . . ?'

The flight to Paris. A weekend of meetings. Another big step for TSI. This time next week, all being well . . .

Suchet reached for the envelope, his name and address handwritten in slanting capital letters. But not a familiar hand.

'Tell Bruno I'll be down in a moment,' he said, and as Monique turned for the door Suchet slit open the top of the envelope and tipped out its contents.

16

AFTER THE LATE-NIGHT MEETING WITH Polineaux, Didier Lacombe had returned to the casino in Beaulieu in an attempt to recoup his earlier losses. Didier was not a man who liked to lose – money, games, women, anything – and the hundred thousand francs he'd wagered between a 'split' pair of nineteen and twenty at the baccarat table had seemed a certainty . . . until the croupier slid a two and a five of hearts from the shoe to add to his three of clubs, six of spades and five of diamonds. *Vingt-et-un. Merde.* A hundred thousand he could ill afford to lose.

By the time Didier made it back to the casino's *salle privée*, however, the croupier with the magic numbers had been replaced by a woman. And Didier didn't like playing against women. You might take them to bed with you, you might use and abuse them, but you never played games of chance with them. Even if they looked like the replacement croupier, tall and lean and stripper pretty, with a large swell of something luscious hidden away beneath her tightly buttoned white shirt and accentuated by the equally tight lines of her black waistcoat. Nothing more than a clever ruse to divert attention from the cards, to distract the players. Didier was no fool, and distractions were for another place and time.

Since there was only the one baccarat table in the room, he settled at the *petite roule* with its mahogany wheel, cherrywood track and numbered ivory slots, splitting his remaining chips between the seven and eight, and the *Rouge* and *Impair*. When the tiny ivory ball accommodated these various wagers, he placed fifty thousand each on *Impair* and *Noir* and left his chips – and subsequent winnings – in the same positions for two further spins. When he left the casino an hour later, he was three hundred thousand up on the night, fifty thousand of which he had paid in to the casino account of a certain Madame de Ternay. Thirty minutes after returning to his apartment in Nice's old town, one of de Ternay's girls was fitting a shiny, high-heeled red Louboutin between Didier's naked thighs and asking him to take off her stocking.

The girl had stayed two hours and left with another ten thousand francs for her time and her . . . engaging expertise. Now Didier lay in his bed, watching the TV morning news and wondering how best to initiate the enquiries required of him by his boss the night before.

The first place to start – the only place to start, he decided – was Baumettes. A prison visit with Pisco, one of Polineaux's boys serving a three-year stint for receiving. Pisco would find out all there was to know about Lombard, if he didn't know it already, which would leave Didier free to work out how best to deal with Monsieur Bernard Suchet.

If the gold was out there somewhere, Didier was going to find it.

And if he did, and if there was any of it left after all this time, who was to say the old man need ever know about it?

17

THE FOLLOWING MONDAY, ISABELLE CASSIER peeled off the A7 autoroute, rattled across the reedy bed of the Durance river and drove into Cavaillon. It was four years since she'd last made the journey here from Marseilles and when she reached the centre of town, she turned to the left, down Cours Bournissac. The street hadn't changed: the Vietnamese restaurant with its pink paper lanterns strung up in the window; the *pâtisserie*, Auzet's, with its mouthwatering confections; and the pavement fruit stall under its striped awning, always ripe with the sweet smell of melons. Slowing down she leaned over the wheel and looked up at the rooftops, between the branches of the plane trees, until she spotted the three mansard windows set in a tilting row, and, behind them, the one-bedroomed loft apartment she had found for Daniel Jacquot and where she had spent every weekend with him for three long months.

But she didn't stop. She carried on through place Tourel and up Sadi-Carnot, turning into police headquarters a hundred metres short of the traffic lights and parking in the shade.

'Isabelle Cassier, for Daniel Jacquot,' she told the desk sergeant, flipping open her wallet to show her badge.

'*Alors*, he isn't here, Chief Inspector. On sick leave, he is.'

'I know that,' replied Isabelle. 'What I want to know is where can I find him? His home?'

'Ah . . . that would be the millhouse. Out on the Apt road. A left past the turning for Goult and Saint-Pantaléon. But I don't think he's there.'

'Any idea where he might be?'

The desk sergeant spread his hands. 'Would you like to leave a message?' he offered. 'I'll see he gets it.'

'No. No message. I'll leave a note at the millhouse instead. Thank you.' And with that, Isabelle Cassier returned to her car and followed the sergeant's directions, out of town, taking the road for Apt. Twenty minutes later, at the top of a steep country lane that petered out into a stony farm track, she pulled in through the gates of the millhouse and drew to a halt under the shade of a drooping willow. She switched off the engine, pushed open the door and stepped from the car's air-conditioned interior into a blaze of late-summer, mid-morning heat, the still, breathless air filled with the battering static of insects.

Leaving her bag and badge in the car she went to the front door, a hefty piece of timber blanched to a grainy grey, studded with blackened nail heads and hung on four banded iron hinges. She rang the bell but knew the sergeant was right; the ground floor shutters were open but all the windows she could see, on both floors, were closed, no sound from within – no radios, no voices, no creak of floorboards or approaching footsteps in answer to the bell.

She rang again, waited a few moments then stepped away from the door and set off around the side of the house. Maybe there was someone in the back, someone who hadn't heard the car or the doorbell; she knew it was unlikely, but it gave her an excuse to poke around, take a look, see where Daniel had ended up.

It didn't take her long to discover that her old lover had done well for himself. Set on a stretch of level ground half-way up a steep slope of land and canopied by a belt of holm oak, willow and cypress, the millhouse was everything that a Provençal dwelling should be: centuries old with a low pantiled roof, stone-collared windows, and planked shutters painted the palest blue. At a set of

French doors she stepped close to the glass, held up her hand to cut the reflection and peered inside. Fat, plump sofas, bookshelves, paintings, an enormous stone hearth leading up to a vaulted ceiling, and in a shadowy corner what looked like the original wheels and gearing for the millhouse. Lived in certainly, a little worn maybe, but beautifully and stylishly renovated – the kind of house that, if it came up for sale, would take its own page in the property magazines. And the asking price? Isabelle wondered. Eight million francs? Ten? Maybe more.

And flowers everywhere, the garden and pathway bordered with terracotta pots and tubs and stone urns and chiselled troughs draped with blossoms – scarlet, pink, blue and white. Not the kind of display she'd expect to find after such a long, hot summer. But then this was a millhouse, probably built near some ancient spring – a likelihood confirmed when Isabelle came round the back of the house: a lawn as green as new moss, banks of flowering shrubs along the borders and a vegetable patch thick with growth sloping up to the trees that edged the property.

And a familiar smell. Sweet, sun-warmed and heady. Isabelle walked along the side of the vegetable patch, until she found what she was looking for. Three thickly stemmed plants more than two metres high, the weight of their swollen heads bending the branches. She reached out a hand, fingered the tight, sticky buds. Ready for harvest. Same old Daniel, she thought with a fond smile. So some things hadn't changed.

From the vegetable patch Isabelle strolled back to the house, noted the swimming pool off to her left, two hammocks strung out in a copse of trees, and stepped up on to the terrace. It was enclosed on three wisteria–clad sides by the house, with a firepit and spit grill in its centre, a pair of wickerwork recliners and an outside *cuisine d'été* furnished with a long oak table and a dozen canvas-backed chairs. She pulled one out and sat herself down, looking across the terrace to the garden. She could see him there, cooking at the firepit or smoking one of his spliffs in the hammock, dressed in his signature shorts, T-shirt and battered espadrilles – big and strong and lumbering, yet always calm and gentle – and she wondered about the woman he lived with. A painter or sculptor, early forties according to the boys in the squad. A divorcée who'd lived there alone until Daniel turned up. As far as Isabelle had been able to establish they'd been together a few years but had yet to marry, their affair probably starting soon after she and Daniel had split up.

Isabelle sighed, took one last look around the terrace then pushed away from the table, walked back to her car, trailing her fingers along the stonework.

Sooner or later she'd find him.

Sooner or later she'd see him again.

Because she had to.

There were questions that needed to be asked.

And Daniel Jacquot was the man who might know the answers.

18

IT HAD BEEN A HELLISH few days. When Suchet landed at Marignane airport on Tuesday evening he should have been thrilled at the way everything had worked out during his meetings with the bankers and the brokers and the lawyers in his suite at the Plaza Athenée: a new share issue, more funds, and a long anticipated, meticulously-planned expansion into eastern Europe. With its workforce in excess of four thousand in France alone, a growing fleet of articulated Scania and Route-King lorries, twenty-six garages and workshops around the country to service that fleet, and nearly a million square metres of temperature-controlled warehousing shared between twelve regional depots, TSI was one of the biggest names in Europe's road haulage market. And now it was set to be bigger still. The biggest.

Yet through it all – the dealing and negotiation and fine-tuning that had led to the final, satisfying thumbs-up – all he'd been able to think of was the cream-coloured envelope that had landed on his desk the previous week.

Bernard Suchet had come a long way from his 1966 two-seater Peugeot transporter running small loads – no questions asked – at competitive prices between La Pomme and the quays of La Joliette. Hard work, good luck and a little bending of the rules early on had seen him become a very rich man, with a seventeenth-century bastide in the countryside outside Aix, a six-bedroom chalet on the Salvette ridge in Hauts des Aigles, and a thirty-metre Pegasus cruiser berthed in Saint-Tropez, which his wife and daughter were currently using as a base for expensive shopping jaunts. In six weeks his daughter was marrying the son of a Minister in the Chirac government, and life, and business, looked set to become a whole lot more interesting.

But now, suddenly, all of it was in jeopardy following the arrival of that envelope marked *Private and Confidential*, underlined twice, an envelope that contained nothing more than a parking ticket and a shell casing in a Zip-lok baggy. At first the two items had made no sense. But Suchet's puzzlement had lasted no more than seconds.

After all this time, his past had come back to haunt him.

When everything in his life was about to come together.

Just that one slip. That one mistake.

Taking the wrong job, and paying for it big time when that fucking cop came after him.

And a single shell casing and grubby ticket stub were enough to bring it all back.

No note. Nothing.

Didn't really need anything else.

Sooner or later he'd get a phone call, or another *Private and Confidential* envelope, outlining what would happen if the shell casing's three missing companions were to fall into the wrong hands, and what it would cost to stop that happening.

And the call would come from Pierre-Louis Lombard. That slimy, two-faced, double-dealing little *con* with his duck-arse hair and swivelling eyes.

Even behind bars the bastard was still a threat.

What Suchet couldn't fathom out was why now?

What was the point?

And how much would he have to pay to make this go away?

He'd find out soon enough, he thought.

19

IN THE HOMICIDE SQUAD ROOM three floors above rue de l'Évêché, sitting at her corner desk, Isabelle Cassier played the tape for the third time that morning, the volume low, just a murmur. Voices on a phone, back and forth. Two separate calls.

The tape and two accompanying Zip-lok baggies had arrived in a large cream-coloured envelope the previous week, addressed to Yves Guimpier, her boss, who had promptly handed the investigation over to her, her first solo job since rejoining the team. Nearly four years away, working with the Paris *Judiciaire* and watching her mother die. Waiting for her mother to die. There had never been any love lost between them, but Isabelle was an only child, no one else to keep the old lady company, caring for her until she was moved to a small hospice in Neuilly, then visiting every week. Three years watching her die, a year spent tidying up, cutting the links, and then walking away.

Across the room, Isabelle saw Laganne cruise between the desks, heading in her direction. She switched off the recorder and took her feet off her desk. She shouldn't have worn a skirt. She could see Laganne's eyes sharpen as she tucked her legs down under her desk. Laganne . . . sweet, lovely Laganne; he'd tried so hard. A good-looking guy, no question, with the smile and the toothpick and those smoke-squinched grey eyes. But the bitten fingernails cut him out of any running. The thought of those fingers on her, sweet as he was . . . no way.

'Any luck?' he asked, sidling up to her desk.

'I've been up there twice. The house is empty. Locked up, but not shuttered. According to the local boys the woman's on holiday. With her daughter. No one knows when they're due back, but Jacquot didn't go with them.'

'And no sign of him?'

Isabelle Cassier shook her head, wondering what was coming. She knew Laganne well enough to realise that he knew something she didn't. That slight, hovering smile, the way the toothpick moved as he chewed.

'Out with it,' she said, bending sideways to pull on her shoes, regretting it immediately as she saw Laganne's eyes latch onto the gap at the top of her blouse.

Jesus. Men! Didn't they ever stop . . . ?

As if the roving eyes and chewed nails weren't enough, Laganne now perched on the edge of her desk. Something else that she didn't much like. Some man's arse parked on her desk without so much as a by-your-leave. Did she do it to them? Perch herself on their desks? No, she did not. Even if they might have liked it.

The toothpick swivelled to the other corner of Laganne's mouth.

'He's here. In Marseilles. Charlie bumped into him the other night at Gallante. Seems he's got himself a boat. Moored off Rive Neuve. Couple of the lads have been over, dropped by for a drink, and it's like Danny's turned sailor boy.'

'And no one thought to mention it to me? That he's here, in Marseilles. That I didn't have to haul myself all the way to Cavaillon and waste a couple of days . . .'

Laganne tipped back, not expecting the broadside.

'Me. I'm here, aren't I? I'm telling you.'

Isabelle drew a breath, calmed herself. She'd overreacted. She knew why. Finding the house in the Lubéron all closed up had been a relief, truth be told. Not having to face him again. Postponing it. Even after four years. But now there was no avoiding it. The time had come. He was here, in Marseilles. In the Vieux Port. Just minutes away from rue de l'Évêché.

'Address? I mean, a mooring? A name?'

'Tasty little cabin cruiser, Charlie said. Old, but nice lines. Very snug . . .'

'Name?'

'Ah,' said Laganne.

Isabelle didn't need to ask. Charlie, and whoever else had called in on Jacquot, had probably drunk too much, couldn't recall what or where. She reached for her phone, nodded a curt thanks to Laganne and dialled the switchboard.

'Can you get me the *Capitainerie*? That's right. Le Vieux Port.'

20

IT WAS STRANGE TO BE back in the city and not working, Jacquot decided. For nearly twenty years he'd been with the *Judiciaire* on rue de l'Évêché, just the other side of the harbour, working with the homicide squad and rising to Chief Inspector before a forced reassignment to run a serious-crime unit in Cavaillon. He'd recognised a dead-end posting when he saw one, but so far Cavaillon had kept him surprisingly busy. It wasn't Marseilles, but six months into the new posting he'd met Claudine again, and his life had changed, and he was happy with it and settled.

Yet now, without planning it, he was back in the city, right in the heart of it, the city where he'd been born as well as worked. A true *Marseillais*. And apart from an overnight stay at the mill-house on Sunday, to check the place was still in one piece, to pick up supplies and some suitable clothes, and for his final session with the physio Monday morning, he'd been here for six days now. Six days afloat, and loving every minute of it, each day simply divided into mornings and afternoons and evenings, with nothing more serious than lunch and supper to consider, and nothing beyond a few simple jobs to see to on *Constance*.

As Salette had said, there wasn't much that needed doing beyond a little care and attention here and there. The interior was immaculate, the panelling, shelves, drawers, table and decking smartly varnished and in good order, and thanks to the tarp cover the exterior had been spared the worst of the damage sun and salt could wreak. Apart from a few scuff marks from the fenders on the curved black-painted hull, there were just a few patches of woodwork that needed sanding and varnishing, and some blistered paint on the cabin roofs to deal with – all of them small jobs that took little time to complete, paint and varnish drying quickly in the sun.

He'd also set up a sound system, with a simple tape deck that didn't drain too much of *Constance*'s batteries, and had brought in a selection of tapes from his car. Maybe down the road, he thought, he'd fix some speakers on deck, but for now just the background hum of some old favourites coming up from below was just fine. And as he worked – sanding the woodwork on the mahogany transom, laying the varnish over the smoothed timbers – he listened to those old favourites, a pleasing, gentle soundtrack to his new life afloat: Stan Getz, some Nina Simone, J. J. Cale, Ella and Clapton; blues and Latin and samba and rock. Never too loud, just there, at the level of the breeze, enough to cover the murmur of traffic.

As for the accommodation on board *Constance*, it may have been cramped quarters after the millhouse, and the bed in her for'ard cabin neither as wide nor as long nor as soft as his bed back home, but what *Constance* lacked in space, she made up for in one particular and important regard. With Claudine away, the millhouse had been cold and lonely, but on *Constance* there was nothing of her to pick at his guts or trouble his mind. And while he still missed Claudine, and longed for her return, he had to admit that his time with *Constance* had not only eased the loneliness, it had been an unexpected delight. Indeed, he wondered how he would have coped without her.

He'd also got to know his neighbours. Not that there were many to know. From Friday evening until he left for Cavaillon on Sunday afternoon, the pontoon had swayed and squeaked with weekend sailors, at least twenty of the sixty or so craft moored along his pontoon visited by their owners: tinkering around, taking them out, even just coming for a lunch or a dinner on deck in the late-summer sunshine. But since he'd got back on Monday afternoon, there'd been hardly a movement, just a sense of the two other resident boat owners living on their vessels between him and the quay.

When you live on a boat, on a hundred-metre length of pontoon, it's not easy avoiding your neighbours, that slatted pathway between sea and dry land taking you close enough to them to exchange some form of greeting, introduction, explanation, an instant closeness and comforting camaraderie not often evident on land. Contact was made on Jacquot's first morning back after the weekend sailors had departed, on his way to the *boulangerie*.

'If you're passing Chamère's, be a darling and bring me back a couple of almond croissants.'

The voice, rich and gravelly from too many Gitanes, belonged to a woman in her early-sixties, rising out of the hatchway on a beaten-up old ketch called *Joya*. She had ashy grey hair that was more straggly than straight, and was dressed in a dirty cream shift that looked like one of Claudine's studio smocks. Her name, as he discovered when he duly returned with her almond croissants and was invited aboard, was Gala Desfornado – her maiden name, she informed him after the introductions had been made. Jacquot liked her immediately. A big, bold woman who didn't look like she took too many prisoners.

She asked if he had met their other neighbour – a wiry, tanned fifty year old who lived close to the quay on a twelve-metre Jeanneau named *Les Vents* – and when Jacquot told her that he had not, she told him all he needed to know.

'Michel's his name. Michel Charbon. The pair of us are divorced. Not from each other, you understand. It's just the way we ended up. His ex took the house and left him the boat. Me, I took the boat and left that *salaud* I married with the house he'd grown up in. A mausoleum, it was. No loss. As for Michel, he's a nice enough fellow. Keeps to himself, he does, and a real sailor. Always off on jaunts. Me, I stay put. Last time this old bird was out – the boat, not me – Giscard was running the country.'

Michel Charbon might have kept himself to himself, but later that afternoon he'd called by asking for a ball-peen hammer he'd lent Niko a few months earlier. Jacquot had invited him on board, found the hammer and returned it, and offered a glass of wine, which Michel had accepted. Twenty minutes later, after explaining how he'd inherited *Constance*, just as he'd told Gala, he learned that Michel was off the following day for a one-hander to Corsica.

'A lovely island,' Michel had told him. 'Have you been?'

When Jacquot informed him that his father was Corsican, and that he had been there many times, Michel beamed.

'Then I'll bring back some *prizutto* to make you feel homesick. Best ham in the world. I'll be gone a month, but when I return you must come on over and have some.' And with that, Michel had taken his hammer, bade Jacquot *adieu* and *bonne chance*, and scurried back along the pontoon to complete his preparations for a dawn departure.

By the end of that first week, Jacquot felt as though he'd spent a lifetime aboard *Constance*. He'd met his neighbours, bumped into some old friends on his trips into town, gone to some of his favourite haunts, and in just a few days *Constance* had a shine to her, if not as good as new then certainly close to it, as though Jacquot's gentle pampering and attention and simple occupation had brought something to her, like a woman flattered, spoiled and loved. The painted cabin roof shone, the varnished woodwork gleamed, the wheelhouse windshield and the glass faces of the instrument panel had been polished free of salty deposits and the brass framings of the portholes buffed to a rich golden glow. As for the engine, a pair of Volvo turbo diesels recently serviced, Salette's assurances were borne out when he took Jacquot out on his maiden voyage.

'She's a tough old girl,' Salette told him as they left the main harbour and met heavier water beyond the bar. 'But not wide enough to take a big wave from the beam, or head on. Whenever you can, take them on the shoulder, so she'll rise to them.'

It was evening and the sun was setting behind them, a shimmering gold disc that sank into the shouldering bulk of the Sausset headlands. As they passed Cap Croisette, riding between Île Maire and Les Goudes, they followed the bare white limestone slopes until Salette told Jacquot to bring her round to port, pointing out where he wanted to drop anchor in the narrow calanque he'd selected.

'If you take her out on your own, you're going to have to be able to do all this without my help. So, *fais attention, s'il te plaît.*' And he'd guided Jacquot through the approach and the manoeuvring until the anchor was over and Jacquot left panting up in the bow, just a warm ache in his buttock and thigh reminding him of his injury. '*Voilà*, we'll make a sailor of you yet.'

They'd stayed overnight, moored in the calanque, warming up a thick, meaty broth that Salette had brought with him, spooning it up under a narrow canopy of stars, talking about *Constance* and Philo and the old days when Salette had crewed with his father, Vincent. They'd stayed up too late, talked too much, and drunk too much – the sea seemed to do that, Jacquot decided – and by the time he'd successfully reversed into his Vieux Port berth the following morning, Jacquot was relieved to find that the heavy head had lightened. Something else the sea seemed to do.

An hour later, Salette long gone, Jacquot was back at work, down on his knees and greasing the brass runners on the cabin hatchway, when a shadow fell across the deck.

'Permission to come aboard, skipper?'

21

IT WAS A WOMAN'S VOICE. A voice Jacquot knew. That familiar lilt, the softness bordered by a rougher edge. He looked up, wiped a forearm across his eyes, and squinted into the sun.

'They said I'd find you here,' the voice continued.

And then he saw her.

'*C'est pas possible* . . . I don't believe it.'

He jumped to his feet without thinking and a sharp pain started up in his thigh, as though the muscles were a beat or two behind any sudden movement.

'Old age?' she asked, as he came down the gangplank and stepped carefully on to the pontoon.

'A nine-millimetre slug that passed perilously close to all I hold dear.'

He brushed off his hands against his shorts and reached for her, brought her into his embrace. 'I don't believe it,' he said again, stepping back and holding her at arm's length, the better to take her in. She looked just the same. The slim wiry figure, the lightly tanned skin not quite dark enough to cover the scatter of freckles across the bridge of her nose, the straight black hair cut to the shoulder, long enough to pin up at the back, or to swing to and fro when she laughed, when she made love . . . 'Isabelle Cassier, as I live and breathe.'

'The same. Also living and breathing,' she replied, eyes twinkling with delight, her smile bright, dimpling her cheeks.

'I bumped into some of the boys the other night,' said Jacquot. 'They told me you were back.'

'So I heard,' she replied. 'Quite a reunion, I believe.'

Jacquot grinned. 'You know how it is. But I'm forgetting my manners. Please, won't you come aboard? Here . . .' And he held out a hand, helped her along the gangplank and down on to the rear deck, taking in the laced black bootees with a small heel, the tailored black blouse, a black skirt that looked tight on her but which he knew would be loose enough to run in if she had to, with a matching three-button black jacket that was roomy enough to take her badge and conceal the bulge of the Beretta service pistol she'd be carrying. Right side for a left-hander, and at the hip not under the arm like most of the boys working homicide on rue de l'Évêché.

'You're looking good,' he said. And then, softly, 'I heard about your mother. I'm sorry.'

Isabelle shrugged it away. 'It was time. For her, and for me. So here I am, back in Marseilles.' She gave him a sly look as she dropped into the canvas chair he opened up for her, set in the shade of the wheelhouse. 'And I missed the sun. You know it's raining up there this morning, in Paris? Who'd want that?'

A silence settled between them, and as Jacquot brought out another chair, set it up and sat himself down, Isabelle Cassier took the opportunity to look him over. The same large hands, the same deep scar-like laughter lines set around those green eyes, the same low, smoky voice. And in his shorts and T-shirt it was clear his body was just as she remembered. He may have lost some weight but he still looked hard and muscly. There was only one thing missing.

'I see the ponytail's gone.'

'Line of duty,' he replied, making himself comfortable. 'Maybe I'll grow it back.' Then he nodded at the briefcase at her feet. 'But I'm guessing this is not just a social call.'

'You're right, it's not,' she said, and for the first time Isabelle looked uncomfortable. 'I'm afraid I have some questions you need to answer.'

Jacquot gave a little grunt of surprise. 'That sounds a little formal.'

'And that's exactly what it is.'

22

'TELL ME ABOUT GILLES BARSIN.'

Jacquot's head snapped back as if he'd been slapped. This was something he hadn't been expecting. Barsin. Just like that. Out of the blue. After all this time. Twenty-five years – maybe more?

Jacquot could see him now. In the blink of an eye. Tall, with stooped shoulders. The close-cropped grey hair, the drooping, tired eyes, the big tombstone front teeth over a rat's chin. And those silvery sharkskin suits he wore with the narrow lapels, the elastic-sided boots with the tabs to pull them on, and usually a blue and cream tie, Marseilles' Olympique club colours, loosely knotted in a grimy unbuttoned collar.

'You know the name, of course.'

'Oh, yes. I know the name.'

'You worked together.'

'A long time ago.'

'And?'

'What's this about, Isabelle?'

'Just tell me what you know. That's all you have to do.'

'Tell you what exactly?'

'About Barsin and you. Whatever you can remember.'

'Should I call a lawyer?'

'Do you want to?'

'Do I need to?'

Isabelle shrugged, tried on a smile for size. It didn't quite work.

Jacquot saw it, and smiled back. She might have caught him on the hop, but sensing her discomfort made him feel just a little more in control. *Et alors*, there was nothing to lose, nothing that he *did* need to worry about . . . as far as he could remember. But internal investigations, as he well knew, had a dynamic all of their own, and this looked like the start of one. Forget direct complicity or implication, sometimes simple association was enough to end a career. The wrong place, at the wrong time.

'Barsin was bent,' he said at last, keeping it brief.

Isabelle gave him a patient look. She tipped her head to one side, held out a hand, as if to say, *Tell me something I don't know*. Then she gestured with her fingers, like a gambler asking for another card. She wanted more.

'We worked together . . . years ago, back in the early seventies. A year at the most. If that.' He stopped, remembered something and chuckled. '"American Pie". That's when it was. When that song came out. He was always singing that line about the Chevy and the levee and those good old boys . . .'

'I know how it goes.'

'Well, that's when it was.'

'And?'

Jacquot gave the question some thought before he answered, gathering his memories.

'He always liked to be first at a crime scene, I remember that. See a body, the first thing he did was check the wallet. And not just for identification. Any cash . . . it was gone, into his pocket. And if there was no wallet, he'd go through the pockets – loose change, didn't matter.' Jacquot smiled at the memory, shook his head.

'You ever say anything?'

Jacquot continued shaking his head. 'I was a rookie, new on the squad; he was a twenty-year man. Chief Inspector. I was with him to assist – from fetching him coffee to putting on cuffs – learning the ropes.'

'He ever offer to share what he took, bring you in on it?'

Jacquot didn't have to think. 'Once, yes. Early on. He emptied a hooker's purse and offered me a couple of fifties. She wasn't even dead. Standing there against a wall, she was, watching the whole thing. Just a shake-down. He did it all the time. Some hooker, some pimp. Cash. When he needed it. Even if he didn't. He must have put away a fortune.'

'And you took them? The fifties.'

'*Non, non.* I said I didn't want them. So he tucked them into my jacket pocket, like a handkerchief. When he was finished with her, and I thought his back was turned, I made to hand her the money back. Barsin saw me. Snatched it off me, and punched the hooker in the face. "You don't want it, I'll have it," he told me. He was not a nice man.'

'And after that, did he ever offer you anything again?'

'Nothing. I was off his radar. I'd played my hand, shown him my cards, and that was that. He never bothered after that.'

'And he knew you'd never say anything.'

'If I'd said anything, I wouldn't be here now. Simple as that. Barsin was . . . an operator. Worked both sides. You didn't mix it with Barsin.'

A breeze caught the hem of her skirt, lifted it from her knees, but, unlike Laganne, Jacquot's eyes remained fixed on hers. She couldn't decide if she was pleased or not. 'Anything else?'

'He wasn't what you'd call a team player. Preferred to be on his own, work things his way. If he decided someone needed a hiding, that's what they got. Dispensing his own kind of justice. He'd hand it out himself, like he did with the hooker. But what he really liked was putting out a whisper, getting someone else to do the dirty work. So-and-so's got a big mouth, something like that. A week later, a month later, that same so-and-so would end up in hospital with a broken jaw or his tongue stapled to his lip. When he heard about things like that – someone else doing the dirty work – he'd . . . you know, he'd be walking along and kick out his legs to the side and click his heels. Like he was some kind of dancer. Quite extraordinary.'

'So what happened to him?'

'You mean, you don't know?'

'Tell me.'

'He was shot dead, here in Marseilles. In an underground car park. Around Christmas.'

'Where were you?'

'Training. An evening session in Aix. I was playing rugby back then, for a club and the Police. And rugby, at a certain level, always came first. Which suited me just fine. Working with Barsin was not your usual buddy-buddy experience.'

'What cases were the two of you working on around that time?'

'Nothing particularly big. Some starting out, others getting to the end. *Non*, *non*. *Attends*. I'm wrong. It was the Gineste heist. Everyone was working that one. He was shot soon after.'

'Did he ever confide in you?'

Jacquot shook his head. 'I was the rookie, remember? And I hadn't taken the money. My card was marked.'

'So what do you think happened? That night in the car park?'

'I think he played the wrong hand, in the wrong game. Like everyone else on the squad said, the ones who knew him, knew the way he operated. That night he took a step too far and someone just got . . . tired of it. Suddenly he was getting to be a nuisance, getting in someone's way. Or getting greedy. Bang-bang and that was it. So tell me, why the interest in Monsieur Barsin? After all this time.'

Isabelle reached down for her briefcase, pulled out a sealed black plastic evidence bag and handed it to him.

'I'm assuming you've got a sound system on board.'

23

AFTER THE SHADED, BREEZY COOL of the wheelhouse, the main cabin felt suddenly close and hot. While Isabelle settled herself at the table, Jacquot reached up and pushed open the two aft-portholes, latching them into place. He held up a hand and felt a soft current of air shift through his fingers. If he'd opened them a little further, he'd have got a stronger draft but this was enough to freshen the air.

Dropping on to the banquette opposite, Jacquot realised suddenly that Isabelle wasn't wearing a bra. There was a looseness inside the black blouse, a tight swing as she made herself comfortable, something he was aware of, peripherally, without actually looking. As he settled himself at the table, the thought of her breasts stirred him. He had seen them, caressed them, licked and bitten them. And now there they were, just a hand's reach across the table. He shook away the memory.

'There's a cooler under the corner seat,' he said, 'if you want a drink. Water, beer, mixers?'

'I'm fine,' she replied, and nodded at the plastic bag she had given him. Jacquot held it up, shook it, put on a clown's exaggerated frown, then opened it and tipped out the contents. A cassette tape came first, followed by an A4-sized envelope, two Zip-lok plastic bags and a folded sheet of paper.

He picked up the two bags, one by one and examined their contents: the first with what looked like a blue ticket stub inside it, the second with three .45 calibre brass shell casings. Jacquot put down the bags and turned his attention to the envelope, the name 'Yves Guimpier' and the address for police headquarters on rue de l'Évêché written in small slanting capital letters. There were no stamps; the envelope had clearly been delivered by hand, dropped off at the reception desk. The paper was stiff but silky, high-quality stationery.

'I remembered you liked to see the real thing, not photo-copies or photos.'

'And you were right. I do.'

Putting down the envelope Jacquot picked up the folded writing paper. Like the envelope, it felt stiff and expensive. He checked the watermark – Tyvek: Luxembourg – then raised the paper to his nose and sniffed. No perfume. So not from a woman. Then he sniffed again, frowned, tried to place the scent. Woody, but sweet, with maybe a hint of . . . coconut? Talcum powder? He tipped the page towards the light from the portholes. No sign of talcum smudges, no shiny powdered marks. Soap, he decided, it had to be soap, the distant scent too dry for eau de cologne or after-shave, but no less expensive.

So a man, then. The writer was a man. Jacquot was certain of it. A man with money enough to afford fancy soaps and fine imported stationery.

Carefully unfolding the paper, he read the single line in the middle of the page, written in the same small slanting capitals as the name and address on the envelope:

SOMETHING I TRUST YOU WILL FIND OF INTEREST.

Jacquot read the line a few times, thought about it.

An educated man, too.

Something I *trust* you will find *of interest*.

That *trust*. What was wrong with 'hope'? And *of interest*. Why not just 'interesting'? So, a professional man. There was something corporate about the tone. A memo, with edge. And something of the pedant, as well. A doctor? A lawyer?

He looked up, held Isabelle's eye. 'And?'

'The envelope arrived at headquarters last week. The note, the two bags, and two tapes – the small ones. From an Ansaphone. We had them copied on to the one cassette.' She nodded at the tape on the table. 'Guimpier gave it to me to handle, see what I could turn up.'

'How is he? Guimpier.' Despite their occasional differences, Jacquot had a soft spot for the Boss. Guimpier was a man you could trust, somehow keeping the politics at bay, allowing you room to move.

'He's fine. Trying to hold everything together, and everyone apart, as usual. It was Guimpier who mentioned that you had been Barsin's partner at the time of his death . . .'

'But knowing you, you'd probably already found that out.' Jacquot reached for the bag containing the ticket stub and held it up to her.

Isabelle smiled. 'Parking La Caboucelle, seventeenth of December 1972. 11:57 p.m. Where Barsin's body was found. Since he'd been alone, after hours, I wanted to know who he'd been working with. His partner.'

'Me.'

'You.'

'Any prints?'

'Nothing on the letter or envelope. Nothing on the Ansaphone tapes. But a partial on the ticket stub thanks to a smudge of dirt – oil maybe – on a thumb.'

'And the casings?' asked Jacquot, pushing at the bag with a finger.

'Just smears. Nothing more. Probably a thumb and forefinger on each of them, but too deteriorated to be of any use. Time. The explosive heat of the gunshot. You know how it goes . . . But they'd still match to a gun, if we could find one.'

'If I recall Barsin was shot four times,' said Jacquot. 'Twice in the head, twice in the chest.'

Isabelle smiled. 'Correct. As if the killer wanted to make sure.

Which suggests it wasn't a professional job. Workman-like, but not polished.'

'Yet here we have only three casings.'

Laying down the bag, Jacquot picked up the tape, slid out of the booth and went to the chart table where he'd rigged up the cassette player. He slotted in the tape and pressed 'Play', and as he sat back down he pulled a pack of cigarettes from his pocket. He knew Isabelle didn't smoke, but offered her one anyway.

She shook her head and smiled.

'I don't, remember?' It came with a whimsical smile, as at a shared memory.

Jacquot nodded, as though he'd forgotten, and lit up. As he put down the lighter and reached for the ashtray, there was a crackle from the speaker above the chart table and the sound of a phone being picked up.

24

'*OUI. J'ÉCOUTE.* I'M LISTENING.'

A man's voice, gruff and business-like. Not so much a question, more a confirmation, as though the call had been expected.

There were no greetings. Whoever was calling came straight to the point.

'*So where are they? The boss wants to know. You said you were going to deliver them.*'

'*No, I said I was going to get rid of them.* C'est pas la même chose. *It's not the same thing.*'

'*Well, Monsieur S wants 'em. No argument.* Et vite.'

'*Well, he can't have them. Like I said, they're gone. Down a drain in Arenc, if he wants to go looking.*'

'*Monsieur S will not be pleased.*'

'*As if I could give a shit! If he wants to play with guns, tell him he'd better learn to do it properly. If I hadn't been there to tidy up after him, he'd be sweating it in Baumettes right now. Cop killer. Tell him that. And tell him he owes me big-time.*'

The connection was broken. The tape hissed.

Jacquot was about to speak when the tape came alive again.

A phone being lifted. A connection made.

'*Oui?*'

'*I am not happy, Pierre-Louis.*'

97

Once more there was no greeting. It was clear that this 'Pierre-Louis' would have known who was speaking, recognised the sharp, flinty voice.

There was a pause before 'Pierre-Louis', whoever he was, replied, '*Your concern, not mine.*'

'*Is that the way to speak to an old friend?*'

There was another pause. Jacquot could almost see the answering shrug.

'*I'm told the casings are lost,*' continued the caller, presumably the Monsieur S mentioned in the previous call. '*Or do you still have them?*'

'*Got rid of. So how can I have them?*'

This time the silence came from Monsieur S's end of the line. And then, '*You're certain of that?*'

'*Like I said to your man, go look if you don't believe me.*'

'*So I'm going to have to take your word, am I?*'

'Ça me fait rien. *I couldn't care less whether you do or you don't.*'

'*I'm a bad man to fool with, Pierre-Louis.*'

'Moi, aussi. *Now fuck off.*'

Once more the connection was broken, the tape hissed.

'That's it,' said Isabelle.

'Anything on the other side?'

'Nothing. Just those two phone messages.'

Resting his cigarette in the ashtray, Jacquot retrieved the tape and dropped it back into the envelope.

'Strange there are no other messages,' he said, sliding back on to the banquette. 'Just two Ansaphone tapes, and those two conversations. Must have been expecting the calls and had the machine primed. Wanted to tape whatever was said.'

'Any idea who they are? This Pierre-Louis and Monsieur S? They're clearly tied in with Barsin.'

Jacquot reached for his cigarette, took a last drag and stubbed it out. He had started to shake his head when the name just came to him, as though someone had whispered it into his ear. *L'Hippocampe . . . L'Hippocampe.*

'I remember . . . He was called *L'Hippocampe*. The Seahorse,' Jacquot began. 'Had some problem with his eyes, and kept a very low profile. I never met him, never knew him back then but I remember hearing Barsin mention his name one time when he thought I wasn't listening. I got the impression he was one of Barsin's insiders. Someone pretty big.'

'You have a real name . . . something I can look up? An address?'

'Oh, yes,' replied Jacquot. 'Lombard. Pierre-Louis Lombard. As for an address, you could try Les Baumettes. He was sent down a few years back for knifing a local scumbag called Antère who ran a posse of girls around Joliette. Last I heard he was in Les Baumettes. A long stretch.'

'He was one of the men we matched to the Christian name, but we couldn't be sure.'

'Nor am I,' corrected Jacquot. 'It's just a guess.'

'It's good enough for me,' said Isabelle. 'I'm glad I called by. What about this Monsieur S?'

Jacquot gave it some thought, trying to drag something back out of that time, all those years ago. He remembered he'd been seeing a girl called Agnès around then. She'd worked in the ferry office, and for some reason he couldn't shift the image of her out of his head. Tight jeans, fluffy Angora jumpers. A small black mole just beneath the lobe of her ear. A petite brunette a few years younger than him. She smoked Boyards . . . Jacquot shook the memory away, and concentrated.

'Two possibilities,' he said slowly, reaching for another cigarette. 'And both of them are guesses. I mean, real guesses. The first name that comes to mind is Stokowski. Armenian. He's a big *gorille*, used to have one of those droopy black moustaches and long sideburns. He ran a couple of gambling joints, high-bet tables, without a licence. If Barsin had found out about it, and was putting the screws on him, Stokowski wouldn't have hesitated pulling a gun. A nasty piece of work.'

'Does he have a record?'

'Oh, yes, and you'll find prints on file.'

'Is he still around?'

'Still around the last I heard, and probably still dealing the cards, spinning the wheel and loading the dice. He had a place out at Samena.'

'And the other guess?'

'This is a long shot . . . Suchet. Monsieur Bernard Suchet.'

'Sounds familiar.'

'You've been away too long, Isabelle. Bernard Suchet . . . head of Transports Suchet International. One of the country's biggest road freight transport companies, with its operations centre and headquarters right here in Marseilles – on the quay at La Joliette and an office in town. You see his lorries all over. Even in Paris.'

'Sounds just a little too respectable to be involved . . .'

'Isabelle, he's *Marseillais*, born and bred. And this is years ago. Back around the time Barsin was shot, Suchet would have been starting out, and like any ambitious *Marseillais* from some slum in the suburbs he was likely prepared to do whatever to get on. Now, of course, he's whiter than white. Got what he needed and went straight. Or rather, he never got caught; he's never been tied in with anything as far as I know.'

'And Barsin knew him?'

'Oh yes. Barsin knew him. Two or three times while we were working together, they met up in some bar while I kept the motor running. Back then he was a real tough – rolled-up sleeves on his T-shirts, a swagger, a belt and buckle he used for more than holding up his trousers. A real piece of work, believe me.'

Jacquot remembered the last time he'd seen Suchet, just a few years back. He was having lunch at Mirador, a big Mercedes parked at the kerb. He was wearing a blue silk suit, the kind that catches the light, and had a big bald head that did the same. He might have been a chief executive by then, but he'd still looked like a truck driver.

'So you think one of them, Stokowski or this Suchet, might possibly be in line for a cop killing? Even a cop like Barsin?'

'Possibly, possibly. But like I said, I'm giving you guesses here. You'd have to find the gun first. Or a witness. Or get Pierre-Louis

Lombard to tell you his side of the story. But what all this looks like . . .' Jacquot waved to the envelope on the table, '. . . is someone out for a reckoning, a settling of accounts. Or maybe just mischief, who knows? And after all this time, it's all long shots now.'

'There's a link already. We're not the only ones who got a letter like that.'

'And the link is?'

'There was a suicide in Avignon. Some priest – quite high up. When the police arrived they found an envelope, just like that one. With a selection of photos . . . The action was here, in Marseilles, about eighteen years ago. Which is how I got to hear about it.'

'Post or courier?'

'A Marseilles postmark.'

'And you're checking it out?'

Isabelle nodded.

'So what's your feeling? About whoever sent these letters.'

'Well, it's reasonable to assume that Lombard – if that's who it turns out to be – made the tapes in the first place.'

'Possibly. But he didn't send them. He's in prison, remember. And he doesn't have access to fancy stationery and couriers. And none of them – Lombard, Suchet or Stokowski – wrote that accompanying note.'

'What makes you so certain?' she asked.

'Because they've all got too much to lose by sending material like that to the police. And because the note was written by an educated man. A professional. If I had to guess . . .' He glanced at Isabelle.

'Go on. Guess.'

'If I had to guess, I'd say someone in competition with Suchet or Stokowski – if that's who this Monsieur S is. Someone in the same line of business, out to bring one of them down. But what I don't understand is how that ties in with your Avignon priest . . .' Jacquot spread his hands, a *there-you-have-it* gesture. 'Whatever happens, I think you have yourself an interesting case, Isabelle.'

'It'll be my first down here. On my own.'

'You'll do it well, I have no doubt. And any help I can give you, just ask.'

Isabelle gave him a long, appraising look – the grubby T-shirt, the paint-stained shorts, sawdust in his hair.

'You have any decent clothes, sailor?'

Jacquot frowned.

'I thought I'd take you to lunch,' she said. 'To say thank you. You do still like lunches, don't you?'

25

JACQUOT LIT A CIGARETTE AND watched Isabelle Cassier at the bar, talking on the phone. A few calls. That was all. A couple of minutes, she'd said, wiping her lips and throwing down her napkin. They had feasted on new-season *oursins*, the sea-urchins' purply-black spines scissored away and the mouthparts opened up to reveal the puffy orange gland sacs. A wad of lightly toasted bread between thumb, middle and forefinger was all that was needed to dab into each shell, buttering fingers and bread with the golden spread offered up. They had followed these with a shared sea bass from Chez Ma Mère's brick oven, and worked their way through a bottle of Sainte-Trophyme rosé. Coffee had come and gone, but Isabelle had drawn the line at a Calva. Through a wreath of cigarette smoke he saw her push a hand through her hair, loop it over an ear, and noted that her blouse had come untucked from the waistband of her skirt. Whoever she was talking to, she looked at ease, in charge, and getting what she wanted.

No surprise there, Jacquot decided. From the moment she'd joined the squad, back in the days when he was still working Marseilles, before the Cavaillon posting, there had always been something steely and confident about Isabelle Cassier. If she wanted something, she usually got it. And that included him. Within weeks of being on the squad she had just homed in on him, like a bee to blossom. Asking him out for a drink, her boss. And not taking no for an answer. *You can fight it all you want, but I'm going to have you, Mister.* That was the message that came over loud and clear. And have him, she did. That's how it had been.

She was just as pragmatic when things didn't go her way. It was Isabelle, after all, who'd given him his marching orders, not prepared to take what little he was offering when she finally lured him to bed. She'd read the writing on the wall, decided it wasn't what she wanted, and did something about it. Rang him up from Marseilles, to say she wouldn't be coming up to Cavaillon that weekend. His heart wasn't in it, she'd told him, and that just wasn't good enough. Not for Isabelle Cassier.

As he watched her at the bar, Jacquot wondered why, exactly, his heart hadn't been in it. Perhaps it was all down to timing. Bad timing. Back then, he'd been living with an Air France stewardess called Boni who'd seduced him on a night flight from Paris and moved into his Le Panier apartment soon after. They'd been together some time, and then, one day, he'd come back home and she was gone. No message, no nothing. And Isabelle, standing there at the bar, had helped him get over it, Boni and the subsequent transfer to Cavaillon, and as he watched her tapping her fingers on the *zinc* he felt a wince of remorse at the way he had treated her.

But that was then, and this was now, and she was putting down the phone, thanking the barman and heading back to the table wearing a pleased expression.

'One of your guesses is out of the frame,' she said, taking the jacket from the back of her chair and pulling it on. Lunch was clearly over. 'Stokowski,' she continued, tucking some notes under her coffee cup. 'Killed in a car crash three years ago. He was sober, the other driver was drunk.'

'He wouldn't have put odds on that,' said Jacquot, pushing away from the table and pocketing his cigarettes and lighter. 'Or maybe he would.'

'Which leaves Monsieur Bernard Suchet.'

'These were just guesses, Isabelle. That's all.'

'I know, I know. But still . . .'

'*But still* what?'

'According to Laganne, Suchet's office is just three blocks away. I thought we might drop by.'

'Isabelle, this Suchet is big time. You don't just barge in and expect . . .'

'*Exactement*. Which is why I called ahead,' she said, taking Jacquot's arm as they left the restaurant, clamping herself to him. 'And made an appointment. Two-thirty. Which gives us exactly eleven minutes.'

'I don't have my badge,' said Jacquot.

'Don't worry. I'll do the talking.'

26

MUCH TO HIS AMAZEMENT, SUCHET had heard nothing more from Pierre-Louis Lombard, or whoever else had sent him that envelope. He'd been expecting some follow up, but so far there'd been nothing. It was because of this that he felt a nervous fluttering in his stomach as the door to his penthouse office opened and Monique ushered in two police officers.

Had the cops also received something?

Had they been on the mailing list?

Was Lombard, or whoever it was, really trying to stir up trouble? It certainly seemed possible, with the *flics* suddenly calling on him.

Of course, it would have been easy enough to postpone the meeting. He was a busy man, with a tight schedule. But he needed to know the reason for their visit. Whether all this was somehow linked in. Even if it was more than twenty years ago now. Water under the bridge. Any river there, long dried up.

Fixing on a welcoming smile, Suchet pushed himself away from his desk and came around to greet them. A young woman – surely too young to be a Chief Inspector? – stepped forward to shake his hand and offer her identity card for examination, followed by an older, but apparently junior, colleague dressed in a creased linen jacket, an open-necked shirt and jeans. Suchet gave the man a nod and gestured to the chairs drawn up at his desk.

'You have a beautiful office, Monsieur Suchet,' said the young woman, taking in the panelled room, the four balcony windows and the extensive rooftop views.

Suchet made himself comfortable, spread his hands.

'Thank you. Yes, it is delightful. We have been here three years now, since we decided to separate day-to-day operations from planning and strategy. A central address is also more convenient for meetings – banks, investors, the computer people. IT – that's the way forward in our business. Nowadays, it's logistics and programming . . .' Suchet was about to settle into his favourite subject, his eyes drifting to the front of her blouse, when the Chief Inspector cut him short.

'But we musn't waste your time, Monsieur. So if you wouldn't mind? There are just a couple of questions I would like to ask.'

'Go ahead, please,' he replied, indicating that the floor was hers. He realised, too, to his dismay, that he had been blabbering. He would have to watch himself. Time to play the Chief Executive Officer of Transports Suchet International.

'Have you ever heard of a man named Gilles Barsin?'

If the envelope he had received and this visit from the police were linked, Suchet had known that the name would come up at some point in the conversation and he was prepared. As he always had been.

'Barsin . . . Barsin . . . No, it is not a name I know.'

Yet all he could see, as he spoke the words, was the snarling, spitting face of Gilles Barsin in La Caboucelle car park, up close to his, and the snatched image of that bastard cop's pistol smashing into his nose, the cartilage grinding and snapping, blood spilling out of his nostrils. That was the moment, sprawled on the ground, with Lombard standing in the shadows, that he'd reached for his own gun, a small stubby Colt .45, firing with concentrated energy as Barsin leaned over him and smiled his ratty little lick-spittle smile. At such close range it would have been difficult to miss – two bullets in the chest, one in the left eye and the last in the right cheek. Barsin had dropped his gun, lumbered backwards on to the

107

bonnet of his squad car and dropped to the oil-stained cement floor, the sounds of the gunshots echoing, multiplying, around the various levels of the car park. How no one had heard the shots, or come running, had astonished Suchet. But they hadn't. And with Lombard's encouragement he'd stumbled to his car and managed to drive away, leaving Lombard to clear up.

Suchet laced his fingers and smiled, as though inviting another question. Anything he could do to help.

Across the desk, the Chief Inspector nodded as though she had expected this answer. It was clear to Suchet that she believed him, and he was pleased with his performance.

But she wasn't giving up. She caught and held his eye in a most disconcerting manner. This young woman was not one to underestimate.

'Gilles Barsin was a policeman. A Chief Inspector, here in Marseilles. He was killed in the line of duty.'

Killed in the line of duty. Suchet liked that one. In normal circumstances, he'd have chuckled at such a description. But he sensed a trap, delicately laid, and put on a suitably concerned expression.

'I am so sorry to hear that. I truly am. Was he married? Are there children?'

The police officer shook her head.

Suchet sighed, spread his hands. 'But Marseilles is a tough town, as we all know.' Then he paused, frowned, preparing to lay down his ace. 'But there's been nothing in the papers. I would have read about it. Surely such a thing would have been reported . . .'

'It was, Monsieur. Twenty-seven years ago.'

Suchet managed a little gasp of surprise. 'Twenty-seven years? But that's . . .'

'But that's just a day when someone murders a police officer, *n'est-ce pas*? That kind of thing is never forgotten.'

Suchet gathered himself. '*Mais, bien sûr*. Of course, of course. And it shouldn't be forgotten . . . something like that.' He started to shake his head. 'Such things, such horrible crimes, should not be allowed to go unpunished. But I can't see how I can possibly . . .'

108

'What about Lombard?' she asked. 'Pierre-Louis Lombard. Also known as *L'Hippocampe*.'

He'd been cut short again. It was something Suchet wasn't used to, something he didn't much like. He felt his face start to harden, took a breath to settle himself, to loosen the tightness in his cheeks and chin, to ease the gentle clenching of his teeth. He must not let this policewoman, or her doltish-looking colleague, think that he was discomfited by their probing.

Everything under control.

Wits about him.

Chief Executive Officer.

But there was still a tightness in his belly, below the level of the desk, a chill crawling in his guts. They knew something. That *con* Lombard . . .

Suchet tried a smile; easy, complicit. '*Ah, mais oui*. Now that is a name I do remember.' He tipped back in his seat, looked up at the ceiling, as though better to remember, and then settled his eyes back on Chief Inspector Cassier, with a glance at her colleague, out of politeness. 'Now I never met the man, you understand, but I have certainly heard of him. Years ago now, when I was starting out. Back then, believe me, if you had any business on the water-front, Lombard was going to cross your path sooner or later.'

'But you say you never met him?'

'Not Lombard, not personally, but a couple of his thugs on a few occasions . . . In those days you had to . . . pay your way, if you understand me. I didn't like it then and I don't much like it now, but there you are. Call it insurance. Protection money.' Suchet spread his hands. A small confession. Nothing for him to worry about. So long ago now. 'Back then a few hundred francs every month,' he continued, 'and no one fired my trucks, or sugared my tanks, or shot out my tyres. I'm a bad man to fool with, Mademoiselle,' he replied, deliberately discarding the use of her title, 'but I know when I have to play the game. Businesses like mine, along the waterfront, have gone down for less. Always have and always will.'

'Quite so, Monsieur. Just one last question. When did your relationship with Lombard cease?'

'I would hardly call it a *relationship*, Chief Inspector.' This time he did allow himself a little chuckle.

'The paying off, then.'

'With Lombard, about six or seven years ago. I believe he was sent to prison.'

'There've been others?'

'That's two questions, Chief Inspector . . .'

A little joke, a little lightness, didn't seem such a bad idea at this particular point.

But she didn't bite. She waited for his answer.

Suchet shrugged. 'Now and again, of course. Something *sous table*, some extra protection. That's the kind of world it is, Mademoiselle. *Ça, c'est Marseilles, non?*'

And that's how it ended.

The Chief Inspector thanked him for his time. He demurred. Hands were shaken. Suchet saw them to the door, watched them cross Monique's office, waved briefly, then closed the door behind him, rested his back against it.

He was in the clear.

They had nothing on him.

Whatever Lombard, or whoever else, had sent to them, he was not in any kind of trouble. Serious trouble. If he had been, he'd have known it. The interview might have been testing but he'd performed immaculately, kept everything under control, and the way it had ended left no room for doubt.

He would not be hearing from Chief Inspector Cassier again.

27

'WELL, IT'S THE SAME VOICE,' said Jacquot, as he and Isabelle stepped out on to rue Grignan, the last of the mistral snapping at shop awnings.

'The same voice?'

'You didn't hear it: *"I'm a bad man to fool with"*? Just like he said it on the tape.'

'I missed that.'

'But you did get his fingerprints.'

She shot Jacquot a look.

'Making him take your card, like he needs to examine it? Usually I drop mine, wait for them to pick it up for me. But neatly done, all the same.'

'Thank you. I thought so too.' She looked around, saw a café-bar a few metres down the road. She looked back at him, tipped her head. 'Coffee? You got time? Tell me what you think?'

'Only if I get the Calva to go with it.'

And that's how they spent the next hour, going over the interview with Suchet. Neither of them was in any doubt that the man they had just met in his sixth-floor penthouse office in the building across the road was the Monsieur S of the tapes, and that for the last twenty minutes he'd been lying through his teeth. He had known Barsin, and had probably killed him, too, in that underground car park. Any print match would confirm it – on the car-park ticket or possibly the casings. And if it was his voice on the phone, it was also clear that he'd known Lombard too, though he'd made a good fist, with both names, of pretending otherwise. In short, Monsieur Bernard Suchet was in a very great deal of trouble.

They were discussing how Isabelle should proceed – bring Suchet in or keep a watch on him – when Jacquot tapped her knee and pointed through the bar's window. She gave a start, then looked where he was pointing.

Across the road, Bernard Suchet stepped out on to the pavement. Winding a white silk evening scarf round his neck and tucking it into the lapels of his jacket, he set off at brisk pace along rue Grignan.

Jacquot and Isabelle moved fast. Calva tossed back, a scatter of francs to cover the bill, and they were out of the bar in seconds. They spotted Suchet half a block ahead now, crossing rue Lulli and heading for rue Paradis. Shoulders hunched, head down, hands plunged in his trouser pockets, he had a clipped kind of swagger to his walk and was easy to mark. As he closed on the corner of Grignan and the busier Paradis they lost sight of him for a moment when a large black van drove past, slowing for the intersection. By the time the van had moved on, turning left into Paradis and accelerating away, Monsieur Suchet had disappeared from view.

'I wonder where he was off to,' said Isabelle Cassier.

'You'll never know now,' replied Jacquot.

28

BERNARD SUCHET COULD STILL SMELL the Chief Inspector's perfume. Faintly. But it was there. Musky. Oriental. It reminded him of Pamlin, the last girl he had called up from Madame Jacqueline. A Malay. Quite exquisite. He wondered how Madame found them. And thinking of Pamlin and Madame and the quite delightful entertainments he'd enjoyed with her firm over the years, and with his wife in Saint-Tropez, what better opportunity?

Still a little unsettled following his interview with the police, Suchet picked up his phone and called the number he knew by heart. He left a message. In the next fifteen minutes – no more – she would be back to him. He waited twelve minutes, enough time to pour himself a drink.

'De Ternay Investments on the line for you, Monsieur,' came Monique's voice.

'Put them through, please.' He waited a beat. 'Ah, Jacqueline, so good of you to call . . .'

Twenty minutes later, Suchet passed through his assistant's outer office.

'I'm going out for a while,' he said without pausing.

'I'll have Bruno bring the car round,' said Monique, reaching for the phone.

'No need,' Suchet called back. 'But have him meet me outside the Mercure at eight forty-five.'

And then he was swooping down in the old Edoux caged lift and stepping out into the street, his mind fixed on the young lady he was about to meet in a serviced apartment owned by de Ternay Investments on rue Balon, the relevant information passed to him in the usual financial shorthand. A new stock, Madame had informed him. A Japanese fund with interesting yields. The usual commissions, of course, but well worth the investment. The call had ended with a formal confirmation from him that he would buy in at the rate she was quoting. If anyone had been listening in, it would have sounded as though broker and client were agreeing the details of a sale – in which assumption they would not have been mistaken.

From the moment Suchet had put down the phone, the phrase 'interesting yields' had lodged in his brain and his imagination had gone into pleasurable overdrive. And Japanese, too. So she would be small and delicate, with long black hair and slanting almond eyes. She would whisper to him in a language he would not understand, and her hands and fingers would work him in ways that would be interesting and arousing. There was, he knew, a wet room in the apartment where they would meet, and he had a certain idea that some kind of Japanese water therapy would be involved in the coming attraction.

So bound up was Suchet in his imaginings, as he set off up rue Grignan, wondering what the new girl would be like, what little tricks she would have up her sleeve – and wherever else she might keep them – that he quickly forgot his visit from the police, and who had sent that damned envelope, and was in no way aware of the black van that slid past him and slowed as he approached the corner of rue Paradis. The driver's window was down and the driver leaned out and called to him, slowing the van to a walking pace, as though seeking directions. There was no one else close by to whom he could have been appealing, so Suchet turned, drew closer the better to hear, to help.

And in that instant, the side door slid open and strong arms simply lifted him off the pavement and bundled him on to a stinking mattress in the back of the van.

So swift and sure was the manoeuvre, his arms clasped tight to his sides, his hands still in his pockets, that there was no time to struggle, no opportunity to react. All he was aware of was the van's side door sliding shut, darkness filling its interior and a sudden swinging turn to the left that would have rolled him off the mattress had he not been held steady by strong hands. As the van straightened up and the driver put his foot down, working his way through the gears, Suchet felt the sleeve of his jacket being pushed back up and the sharp slide of a needle on the inside of his forearm.

29

DRIVING BACK TO THE MILLHOUSE that evening, Jacquot decided that Isabelle Cassier hadn't changed a jot. Four years on, not so much the new girl now, she seemed even ballsier than she'd been when they'd worked together on rue de l'Évêché, and when she'd helped him make the move from Marseilles to Cavaillon, sharing his bed, and filling his empty weekends in a strange town. The last time he'd seen her, she was getting dressed on a Monday morning in that loft apartment she'd found for him on Cours Bournissac in Cavaillon, after he'd been thrown off the squad in Marseilles and been posted to the Lubéron. Four days later she had phoned from Marseilles, told him that she would not be coming up that weekend.

And that had been that. He hadn't seen her, and they hadn't spoken, not since that last Monday and that final Friday phone call. That weekend, alone in Cavaillon, had not been fun. And the days that had followed had been equally dull and restless, week after joyless week spent at his provincial cop's desk, new colleagues to meet and work with, new routines to get used to, and just the three options for his time off: stay at his desk and work late, drop in somewhere for a drink, or go home and watch television. And a hundred times he'd thought about picking up the phone, calling her, to see if he couldn't retrieve the situation. But a hundred times

116

he'd held back. Because she'd been right. His heart hadn't been in it.

Later he heard that she'd left Marseilles and transferred to Paris; her mother was ill. And that had been the end of it. She really had made a break, gone to another city, taken on another life, and that sudden distance between them, a real, geographical distance, had made a phone call redundant.

What was the point?

Did he want to sleep with her? Yes, of course he did.

Did he love her? No, he did not.

That's all there was to it. Time to move on. Just as she had done.

And Isabelle, he knew, would have been feeling a great deal worse than him, because she plainly had loved him, or had been in danger of doing so. Whereas he . . . well, he'd just felt lost and lonely and needed the companionship, her warm body beside him in that lumpy, squeaking bed, under the eaves on Cours Bournissac, her breathless whispers and gentle caresses . . .

Soon after that final phone call, he'd pulled himself together. He'd taken a spring ski break, on his own, stayed longer in the mountains than he'd intended, and by the time he returned to Cavaillon he'd banished the blues and started to settle into life in the Lubéron. Not long after that, covering a case in Luissac, he'd met Claudine.

And now Isabelle was back.

As the sky started to darken in his rear-view mirror, and up ahead the day slid away in layered bands of red and gold and scarlet, Jacquot wondered what he thought about it, meeting her again.

Well, she was still goddamn sexy, and no mistake. Walk into a crowded room and look around and hers was a face and a body that would catch your eye, that you'd linger on. And, if you had the nerve, you'd do something about it. Four years earlier, at her invitation, he had done just that. They'd been lovers once, but now they weren't. Not that he didn't enjoy thinking about it. Remembering.

He wondered, too, about her. How had she felt about meeting up with him again? He'd have been surprised if the encounter hadn't come freighted with a certain . . . tension, after all this time. But she'd handled herself well. Cool and professional when she came aboard *Constance* to quiz him about Barsin, and just friendly and enthusiastic when she'd caught hold of his arm outside Chez Ma Mère. Apart from that little start she'd given when Suchet came out of his building and he'd tapped her on the leg, as though the touch was somehow electric, there had been no indication that she still had any feelings for him beyond the kind he had for her. There had been no mention of their time together, their abrupt parting, and no sense for Jacquot that they were now anything other than friends. Friends and colleagues, playing on the same team. The rest was history. She'd moved on, and so had he. All in all, he was happy with the way things had turned out.

Up ahead, he saw the slip road sign for Cavaillon and swung up through the toll, crossed the Durance river and skirted the town heading for the Apt road, and the millhouse. Claudine was due back and the old place was in need of a wash and brush up.

Or she'd want to know the reason why.

30

'WHERE'S MY GOLD, YOU SON-OF-A-BITCH?'

Bernard Suchet blinked in the darkness.

As the words settled into his consciousness – the sharp sound of them, if not yet their exact meaning – Suchet became successively aware of a number of sensations. His shoes and socks had been removed and the stone floor was cold. He was in shirt sleeves, shivering in fits and starts, and his wrists and ankles had been bound with wire to the chair he sat on. A hard wooden chair with a flat seat and a straight back that reached as high as his neck. And the darkness wasn't real; he could see a band of light across his chest where the black hood over his head ended, and peering through its folds and weave he was aware of four dim shapes.

'I said, where's my gold, *salaud*?'

It was a man's voice, an old man's voice, low and level, and without thinking Suchet turned to his right, to the shortest of the four shapes. That was where the sound had come from, maybe three or four metres away. Someone sitting in a chair. But not tied, not like him. Not restrained, or that was the impression he got.

And gradually the words began to take on some form and order and sense.

A question had been asked.

Something to do with gold.

119

'Is he conscious yet?' asked the old man in the chair.

'Oh yes,' came another voice, from his left. A younger man this time, with a stronger, deeper voice. 'Just look at the feet.'

Suchet realised that they were talking about his own feet. And realised, too, that he was wiggling them up and down, the bony balls drumming on the stone floor, the binding wire cutting into the skin. He hadn't even known he was doing it. He stopped moving them.

There was a grunt from the shape in the chair, and the old man's voice started up again.

Same tempo. Same level. Just as chilling.

'1972, scumbag. Not so long ago. Not long enough to forget. Or forgive.'

And with every new word, Suchet began to put it all together.

Where he was. What was happening. What this was all about.

My gold, the man had said. *My gold*.

And suddenly Suchet wanted to pee very badly – which was maybe why he'd been drumming his feet. Because now he knew who the old man in the chair was, who that chilling voice belonged to.

He'd never met him, but he knew who this was.

Patric Polineaux.

And Suchet knew, too, what gold Monsieur Polineaux was talking about.

Seventy-five bars, twelve kilos a bar. A ton of gold. And it had gone missing. More than twenty years ago. All that was left just an empty truck on the quay at Madrague. Four bodies on a side-street in Pointe Rouge, and a fifth body, the driver's, left by the truck.

'So where is it? What did you do with it?'

Suchet opened his mouth to reply but discovered that his tongue was as dry as bone, almost glued to the roof of his mouth. He gagged rather than spoke.

'Give him a drink,' said Polineaux, and for a moment Suchet expected the hood to be raised and a glass put to his lips. He was wrong. The shape on his far left seemed to step forward and swing something in his direction. The next instant he felt a massive smack of icy water dashed over him, flattening the shirt against his chest, the black hood against his face, making him gag even more, gasping for a breath through the cloth, trying to suck in some of the water, trying to sluice it around his mouth to unglue his tongue, then swallowing, then reaching for another breath, for more water. Icy. Icy.

'I don't know . . .' he began.

'Oh yes, you do, you piece of shit! Yes, you most certainly do. And you're going to tell me.'

'Lombard. He's the one you should talk to.'

'Yeah, yeah, Lombard. I know all about Lombard. Did me a favour, he did. Sent me some pretty pictures. Photos. Of guess who? Just the head man at TSI, that's who. But playing pally with the *flics* way back when.'

Suchet's heart nearly stopped, his guts twisting and cramping.

So he hadn't been the only one to get an envelope. Lombard must have sent one to Polineaux, too. That was why he was here. After all this time, for whatever reason, Lombard had decided to drop him in it. But what photos? What had Lombard sent? What had Polineaux seen?

'Barsin,' Suchet whispered. And then, clearing his throat, a little louder, 'Barsin.'

'The cop? That's his name?'

'That's his name.'

'So you know who I'm talking about here? Your friend. The other one in the photos.'

'I know who you're talking about,' said Suchet. 'But he's no friend. He came after me. After the heist.' The words felt sticky, unnatural in his mouth. As if his tongue was somehow too large, still too swollen, to operate, despite the water he'd managed to suck in through the hood. That's what it felt like. The drugs, he decided. Whatever they'd given him in that van.

'After, not before?'

121

'Afterwards. Two, three days later. Wanted to know about the gold. Where it was. Who'd taken it.'

'And why would this cop, Barsin, think you'd know something like that?'

'*Merde alors*, I don't know. Because I got out? Because I didn't get taken at Le Canet? Who knows? Maybe because a couple of my boys were in that third truck? But look what happened to them. Shot. Left on the side of the road, they were.'

Silence settled as Polineaux considered this.

'So why don't you tell me about that third truck?' he began again. 'Tell me how come it ended up in Madrague?'

'That's what Barsin wanted to know. Like he had a personal interest, nothing to do with the cops. Said it was me who had set it up. Had my boys go off plan, take a different route. But I hadn't. I didn't know anything about it, I swear. All I knew was we did what we'd been told to do.'

'Which was?'

'Everything by the book. That's how it went down. Just as planned. The information was good . . .'

'Of course it was good. It was me who got it.'

'. . . The convoy came along right when it was supposed to. Up that hill. The right number of trucks. The right number of outriders. We had the road blocks ready, and we got the gold. Three security trucks. I was the lead driver. Drove them on into town, taking separate routes at Prado like we were supposed to. But only two of us made it to the rail-yards. And then the cops were everywhere. We were set up. Had to be. Someone knew, someone talked.'

The more Suchet spoke, the easier it became, just a roughness now at the back of the throat.

'And that someone wasn't you? Telling this Barsin all about it, so the cops would be at Le Canet and you'd be able to pull a fast one over in Madrague?'

'That's crazy. If it was me, then why wasn't I driving the third truck? Why would I drive to Le Canet if I knew the cops were going to be there? Me and a couple of the boys, we only just made it out.'

'Tell me about the driver, the one in the third truck. Was he one of yours?'

'I didn't know the other drivers. They were brought in from Nice. I got the job as lead wheels because I knew Marseilles, and I had some lads on my crew who were up for the game; fit boys, knew the city, too, and how to handle themselves. But Barsin didn't believe me. Kept on at me. Where was the gold? Who'd taken it? That's all he wanted to know. Took out a gun, threatened to use it. It was him or me. He was crazy. He was going to finish me.'

'*You* shot him? That cop in the parking garage? That was you?'

'I told you, I had no choice. He had his gun stuck in my face. Lombard was there. He'll tell you.'

'And I'm sure he will. But in the meantime it's you in the box. It's you telling me what happened. And it better be what I want to hear.'

'I swear to you, I'm telling the truth,' Suchet began. 'Whatever happened that night, I didn't know about it . . .'

'Oh, I don't think so. I think you know a lot more than you're letting on.'

There was a chuckle from the outline on the left, and the unmistakable snick-snick of an automatic pistol being primed.

Jesus, there are guns, thought Suchet.

And then he thought, Of course there are guns. This is Polineaux. They were going to shoot him. He was a dead man.

'*Écoute* . . . Listen . . .' he began.

The sound of the gunshot was little more than a whisper, a kind of compressed, pneumatic *phut*.

But the pain exploding in his left ankle was nothing short of gigantic, and he gasped then screamed at the size and pitch of it.

'So where did it go, Ber–nard?' asked Polineaux, drawing out his name. 'What did you and your cop friend set up?'

'*Rien*. Nothing . . .'

There was another *phut* and his right knee shattered in a blast of splintering white heat.

'One more time. Where is the gold? What did you do with it?'

'I don't know . . . I don't know . . .' a weeping Suchet managed to splutter, somewhere between a scream and a whisper. 'If I did, Christ JESUS, don't you think I'd tell you? I just . . . I just don't know . . .'

'Not good enough.'

'No, no, wait. Listen . . .'

'Listen? Listen to what? All I want to hear about is the gold. And all you do is tell me you don't know, or you tell me to listen. And then, when I'm listening, you tell me absolutely nothing.'

'That's because there's nothing to tell. I don't know about the gold. Where it went. Who got it. I don't know about Madrague. All I know is that Barsin was involved – and not as a cop, like I said. Lombard too. He was always around.'

It was as if Polineaux hadn't heard a word.

'The trouble is,' the old man continued, 'you think it's all too far back to matter, don't you?' Polineaux's voice was level, unhurried, thoughtful. 'And you think that now you're too big to be involved. To explain. To take responsibility. But when it comes to the family, this family, no one's too big, Monsieur Ber-nard Su-chet, of Transports Suchet International. No one. Not you. No one.'

As Polineaux spoke, Suchet became aware of the shadow on his left moving closer and then passing out of sight, somewhere behind him. There was the whining sound of an electric wheelchair and he could see Polineaux reversing away from him, and the two other shapes on his left stepping back.

That's when he felt something hard press against the side of his head, through the hood.

He knew what it was.

There was no time for fear.

He took a sharp, deep breath.

It was his last.

Part Two

31

CLAUDINE ARRIVED AT MARSEILLES' MARIGNANE
airport on a Wednesday, shortly before lunch. She had arrived in
Paris earlier that morning after a three-day delay in Guadeloupe;
the tail end of a hurricane whipping past the island had grounded
all flights. Making much of her condition at Charles de Gaulle
airport, she had managed to get on the first connecting flight south
to Marseilles. Waiting for her bags at the carousel, still a little
ashamed of her small deceit – a six-month pregnancy that still
hardly showed was poor grounds for preferential treatment – she
suddenly felt tired and heavy and creased, and longed for a shower,
for her own soft, warm bed. And for Daniel, of course. What was
it about pregnancy? she wondered. One minute she felt fat and
unattractive, the next all she wanted to do was . . .

After a long wait, long enough for her to look around for somewhere to sit, the carousel started up and the cases began to appear,
sliding down the chute. All, it seemed, except hers; the penalty,
she decided, for jumping a flight at the last moment. But then, she
reasoned, if her case had been the last to be loaded at Paris Charles
de Gaulle then surely it ought to have been the first to appear in
Marseilles. But of course it wasn't, and she watched as other
passengers stepped forward to claim their bags and leave for the
Arrivals Hall. And each time the sliding doors opened for those

passengers whose cases had appeared on the carousel before hers, Claudine peeped through to see if she could spot him. But the doors never seemed to stay open long enough, and the angle was too tight to see anything more than the scrum of waiting friends and family gathered excitedly at the barrier, and the wall of stone-faced drivers in suits holding name boards.

When she finally came through the doors with her case and her carrier bags of duty-free, a quick look round established that Daniel wasn't there. No sign of him. She felt a twist of irritation – another unfamiliar response she put down to pregnancy. They had spoken the previous day, before she'd finally boarded her flight in Pointe-à-Pitre, and he'd promised – he'd *promised* – he'd be there.

And then she saw him – or rather someone who looked like him but clearly wasn't. Younger, slimmer than she remembered. Leaning against a pillar, hands in pockets, one foot crossed over the other. A deep tan against a white T-shirt, an old cream jacket, faded blue jeans and espadrilles. And then, of all things, she recognised the jacket. His jacket. Daniel's. The very same.

And then the man's eyes latched on to hers and he was raising an arm, waving, pushing away from the pillar and coming towards her. In that single moment, she felt an exquisite curl of delight and excitement. It was him. Daniel. Looking better than she could believe. A big warm smile as he drew closer, the gleam of his teeth making the tan even deeper. And no walking stick, just the slightest stiffness and a roll to his walk, favouring his stronger leg. He really did look very good indeed.

For the last week in Midou's cottage in the hills above Pointe-à-Pitre, mother and daughter had joked about her homecoming, how Daniel would look after being left alone, without her supervision. How much weight he'd have put on. All those lunches and dinners pressing against his belt, and no real exercise beyond a little light gardening and housework. Clothes a little rumpled, a little unshaven. In short, they'd agreed, he'd have let himself go.

On the phone, of course, he'd sounded fine, still the same old Daniel – telling her about the house, how things were his side, asking about the baby, how she was, then letting his voice drop to tell her that he missed her and loved her and wanted her. Right now. Not next week, or whenever it was she was coming home, but right now. Which had made her giggle, a soft chuckling sound that had made Jacquot draw in his breath with longing. She'd actually heard it, that gasp, at the other end of the line, that little intake of breath.

All that distance, an ocean between them, and yet . . .

And yet . . . she and Midou couldn't have been more wrong. Maybe it was just spending some time away from him that made him look so good. Because he certainly did. Good enough to eat.

And then she was letting go of the handles of her case and carrier bags, and straightening up, and she felt herself caught up in his embrace, almost lifted off her feet, his arms around her, hugging her to him, kissing her, a strange salty smell on him, mixed with a soapy pine scent that smelled of hot showers and careful preparation for this moment, for her return . . .

'You look beautiful,' he whispered into her ear, and she felt his hand on her belly. 'Both of you.'

She warmed to his words, the closeness of him, the wide spread of his hand, a fluttering of movement at the touch that she could feel but he wouldn't. The flutterings had started on holiday, and she was proud of them, longed to share them with him.

'And you, Monsieur, must have taken a lover,' Claudine replied, pushing out of their embrace, her lips stinging from the hard pressure of his.

At which he'd laughed, and after leaning down to take her case and bags he led her through the crowds to the Exit, then out to the parking lot, asking about her flight, and Midou, and the island. How good she looked . . . how tanned . . .

'I said, you must have taken a lover,' Claudine persisted, half as a joke, half in serious enquiry. There was something strange about him, something different, and she felt a tug of uncertainty. She'd been away too long. Or maybe it was just being pregnant, and feeling fat and frumpy and unattractive.

129

'Not a lover, *ma chérie*. But a woman all the same,' he finally admitted, stowing her bags in the boot of their car and opening the passenger door for her. Sliding into the driver's seat, a great deal more easily than Claudine remembered from the last time he'd driven her, he started the engine and turned out of the parking rank. 'Her name is Constance,' he said. 'But Constance can wait. First, I want to take you home.'

Jacquot had been hard at work. The house, she could see at once, was immaculate, smelled gently of aftershave and coffee, mown grass and garlic, the table in the kitchen already laid for lunch.

But first, as the *daube* simmered on the range, he took her upstairs, to the bedroom; windows open, shutters half-closed, sunshine slanting through the slats like leaning ladders of light. And the bed, freshly made, pillows plumped, the ceiling fan turning slowly.

'I should shower,' she said, turning towards him as he kicked the door closed behind them.

'Afterwards. Shower later,' he whispered, and with strong brown fingers he pulled the collar of her shirt away from her shoulder and laid his lips against the warm hollow of her throat.

'I want you right now. Like this.'

32

'*MERDE*, HE WEIGHS A TON,' said Léo.

The two men were no more than fifteen metres from their Toyota 4x4, still within the beam of its headlights, but the body was already slipping from their grip. And there were still another forty metres to go, off into darkness, over steep, rough terrain, before the slope levelled out.

'I'm losing him,' said Zach, Léo's companion, and they stopped, let the body slump to the ground. A stone, dislodged by the impact, rolled away down the slope.

Hands on hips, the body sprawled between them, the two men paused to draw breath. The night was still warm. An owl called its haunting two-tone somewhere to their right, and five hundred metres below them the narrow coast road from Théoule-sur-Mer to Mirabeau was unlit save for the occasional beam of passing headlights cutting through the night. Beyond the road, a dark, silent sea slapped against the cliffs, the glow of unseen lights from Fréjus outlining a distant ridge.

'He's so short you'd think he wouldn't be so heavy,' said Zach, taking in a breath of the night air and tipping back his head to look at the stars. Taller than Léo by a few centimetres, with a gym build and tight crew cut razored in an angry line around his ears and neck, Zach, sometimes known as Zak-Zak, was an ex-boxer who looked like he'd taken as many steroids as he had punches. 'Heaviest I ever had to do up here.'

'Short, sure. But he's built,' said Léo. 'Solid. Must have kept himself in trim.'

'Wasn't half this bad when we hauled him into the van back on Paradis.'

'Well, he wasn't dead meat then,' said Léo. 'There was movement, right? Momentum. Like ju-jitsu – you use your opponent's energy to your own advantage. So . . . you ready?'

'We could always drag him.'

Léo grunted. 'You say that every time. You and Dhuc and Milagro, you're all as bad as each other.'

'Well, who's to know?'

'It's not worth it. We got to carry. No signs, remember?'

'Then you mind if we swap? You take the arms?'

The two men changed position, Léo shaking his head, and together they bent down to retrieve the body.

'*Un, deux, trois* . . . hup-la!'

They struggled to their feet. This time they made sure their grip was solid, with elbows locked around the dead man's armpits and knees rather than taking his wrists and ankles. In this new position the head was now pressed against Léo's chin, and the bare feet felt as though they were actually walking behind Zach, one of the knee joints not so pliant, jerking and crunching with every step he took.

'You think he knew about the gold?' asked Zach, between breaths.

'If he did, a nine-millimetre in the ankle and kneecap would have had him squawking. You ask me, he didn't know a thing.'

'He didn't see it coming, did he?'

'They never do. Always think they're the ones who'll beat it.'

'That Didier's a cold one, isn't he? Gets the nod from the old man and I swear he smiles each time he pulls the trigger.'

'You don't mix it with Didier, that's for sure,' said Léo, who'd worked for the Famille Polineaux a few years longer than Zach and didn't like it forgotten. 'Looks like butter wouldn't melt, but you'd be wrong. There's plenty who've played him that way and paid the price. And with the old man fading, he's someone we better keep in with, if you follow my meaning.'

Grunting with the effort, Léo and Zach covered the remaining ground and dropped the body with sighs of relief. By now the Toyota's headlights were far enough back not to throw shadows.

'You bring the torch?' asked Zach.

For answer Léo switched it on and played the beam around them. They were standing on level ground, a few metres into the brush, at the foot of a rising face of red Esterel rock and just a few metres from where they needed to be.

'Why don't we roll him?' asked Zach. 'It's clear now and there's enough of a slope. No one comes in this far.'

'Suits me,' Léo replied, and the two of them, using their feet, pushed the body to the lip of a sinkhole concealed beneath the base of the rock wall. With a final kick from the two of them, it rolled over the side and disappeared. Léo switched off the torch and in the darkness they listened for the impact. It came seconds later, with a dull, distant thump from somewhere deep beneath their feet.

'*Voilà*,' said Léo. 'And good riddance.'

'We got time for a drink then?' asked Zach, as they turned back to the Toyota. 'There's that beach place in Théoule.'

'You got any money?'

'Enough, sure. No problem,' said Zach, quickly perking up. A few drinks, some good music, and those pretty waitresses. A nice way to end the evening.

And then, stepping out on to the track, Léo froze, held up his hand. He stopped so unexpectedly that Zach stumbled into him.

'Shhh! You hear something?'

The two men stood just outside the arc of the headlights and listened hard.

'Where? What was it?' whispered Zach, crouching down, reaching for his gun.

'I thought . . .' Léo played the torch through the thin low brush to the left and right of the track.

Zach followed the light with the muzzle of his gun.

'I don't know . . . I thought I heard something.'

They stood there for a minute, peering into the darkness, watching the shadows of brush and boulder shift and spring away from the sweeping beam of the torch.

'There's nothing there,' said Zach, straightening, slipping his gun back into its holster, anxious now to make it back to Théoule before the beach bar closed. 'It's nothing. A fox maybe. *Allons*.'

Zach pushed past him, but Léo stood there a moment longer. Playing the torch, looking, listening.

'I could have sworn . . .'

33

JACQUOT FELT A HUGE SENSE of excitement the following morning as he pulled out from the millhouse and set off down the lane. Beside him, Claudine watched the familiar fields spin past.

'You're being very mysterious,' she said. 'And I'm not sure that I like it.' Which was true. She didn't. Since Marignane, Jacquot had been maddeningly elusive, refusing to be drawn on who this Constance was. She had no idea what was in store, who she was about to meet. All she could really say was that she'd been warmed by his welcome home. But was it just a cover for something she might not like as much?

'Seat belt,' said Jacquot when they came to the main road, determined not to reveal anything about *Constance*. He wanted to play it like Salette. Lead her on. Let *Constance* do to Claudine what she had done to him. He was sure she would. Hoped and prayed she would. If Claudine took against *Constance* for some reason, pointed out the impracticalities, well, there'd have to be a reappraisal, some adjustments. After all, a boat could be a serious distraction, not to mention a serious, and unnecessary, extravagance – something she might feel didn't fit too well with the impending addition now only a few months off.

As they skirted through Cavaillon and headed for the autoroute, Jacquot wondered what he'd do if Claudine put her foot down and said 'no'. Sell the boat? Hand her back to Salette? After the time he'd spent with *Constance*, he wasn't sure how he'd feel about that. Well, actually, yes, he was. He knew exactly how he'd feel. He didn't want to sell her, or give her back to Salette. He wanted Claudine to smile with delight and wonder at their unexpected good fortune, and be tantalised by *Constance*, just as he had been. And say 'yes'.

An hour later, the two of them came up from the underground parking on Cours d'Estienne d'Orves and he led Claudine down Place aux Huiles to the port. It was a bright sunny day, the sky a high, distant blue, the air sharp and fresh with the scent of the ocean.

Waiting for the traffic on Quai Rive Neuve, Claudine slipped her hand into his. 'Where *are* you taking me?'

'You'll see,' he replied, and five minutes later, holding open the mooring quay security gate, he stood aside for her to pass.

'Constance lives on a boat?'

Jacquot smiled. Exactly the words he'd said to Salette. But he didn't reply and, securing the gate behind them, set off down the pontoon, steering Claudine ahead of him.

'If we carry on any further, I'll end up in the harbour,' she said, as they reached the end of the pontoon. And then her head turned to the left and Jacquot could see that her eye had been caught by the name of a boat. Just as he had planned it. She looked at the name, frowned, then turned back to him.

'Please don't tell me you've bought a boat?'

Almost the same words he'd spoken to Salette. But somehow they didn't sound quite the same coming from Claudine. Without replying, and just as Salette had done, Jacquot clambered aboard and made his way round the deck and wheelhouse, loosening the ties on the cover and hauling it off.

In the morning sunshine, *Constance* sparkled. The paint, the varnish, the brass and chrome trim, everything caught the sun and seemed to wink at him, as though they were in on the set-up together. Their little trick. As he hauled in the cover and folded it, Jacquot looked around proudly. All that hard work he'd put in had paid off. It was as though he was seeing the boat through Claudine's eyes. For the first time.

He glanced back at her, to see how she was taking it. She was still standing on the pontoon. There was no expression on her face, just a long thoughtful look, cheeks slightly sucked in, lips almost pouting. To fill the moment, Jacquot bent down to stow the cover in its seat locker. But in his haste, he failed to pack it away neatly. Which meant the seat top didn't close properly. Which annoyed him. He had wanted it to be perfect, and for a moment he considered taking the cover out, unfolding it, re-folding it and then stowing it correctly.

But he didn't. He caught Claudine's eye, and he left the cover as it was, the seat locker not quite closed. She'd crossed her arms on her chest and was tilting her head to one side, no longer considering the boat. Now she was looking directly at him. A stern, unwavering gaze. She didn't smile, and she certainly didn't look amused. Jacquot felt a lurch in his guts and found himself struggling to think of something to say – an explanation, a justification – something to fill the silence.

But she beat him to it:

'So tell me, Daniel . . .'

Another lurch in the guts. He recognised that voice. Its disbelieving tone. This did not sound good.

'Sure,' he grinned, managing somehow to keep the grin in place. A schoolboy's grin of innocence. Hard held. 'Tell you what?'

Claudine narrowed her eyes, pinned them on him even more tightly.

'Tell me how, exactly, did this . . . *Constance* come into your possession? And how much, even more exactly, did it cost?' she asked.

'I was left her,' he replied. 'A bequest. From an old friend of Salette's called Philo. And I only met him a few times. Quite extraordinary, isn't it?'

'So you're saying you didn't pay any money for her? Is that right?'

137

'Just the berth, the *notaire*, a few odds and ends.' Jacquot gave a shrug. '*C'est tout.*'

'And you're thinking of keeping her?'

'Well, that depends. Obviously, we'll need to discuss it. See what you think . . .'

'So I'm away just a couple of weeks and this is what happens? Is this how it's going to be?'

Jacquot shrugged. This was turning out to be a great deal more difficult than he had bargained for. He'd imagined that Claudine would fall in love with *Constance* at first sight. A boat. In the Vieux Port. It was a dream. And it hadn't cost them a *sou*. Surely she couldn't complain, or find fault?

But she still hadn't said what she really thought about it, what he wanted to hear.

'So what do you think?' he prompted, side-stepping her questions.

She looked around, taking it all in, started to shake her head.

'I think it's madness. And I don't believe a word of it. No one leaves someone a boat. Someone dies, the boat gets sold. That's it.'

'I promise you, it's just as I've told you.'

There was desperation in his voice now; he couldn't conceal it.

It was what Claudine had been waiting for. Very slowly, the trace of a smile slid across her lips.

'*Dis-moi*, is this where you're planning to bring your lady friends while I'm changing nappies at home?'

'Only the really important ones,' he said quickly, unsure of his voice, still not certain where this might be going. It might sound encouraging but he knew it wasn't yet a 'yes'.

'So do I get invited aboard? Or is this just a tease? I'm not one of the "really important ones" quite yet?'

'Just enough of one,' Jacquot replied, and helped her across from the pontoon and down on to the aft deck.

She looked around her: at the city, at the boats beside them, at the various cruisers and sailboats and ferries ploughing to and fro on the main channel, and up at the wheeling gulls and blue sky.

Then she stepped forward to the seat locker. Its lid was still ajar. She leaned over, prodded the offending fold with a finger and the lid dropped neatly into place.

'Here's the deal,' she said, sitting down on the seat now provided, crossing her legs and giving him a serious look. 'I want you to understand, right now, right here, that every single last franc you spend on this boat, you spend the same amount on me. And then some.'

The offer hung in the air, as Jacquot tried to make sense of it.

'So does that mean I'm not going to have to sell her, or give her back?'

She nodded, smiled and reached up for his hands.

'I should go away more often,' she said at last. 'And the kids'll love it.'

'Kids?'

Claudine's smile turned to a look of surprise. A frown stitched itself across her brow.

'Oh. Didn't I tell you?'

'Tell me what?'

She pushed out her belly, looked down at it proudly and then back up at Jacquot.

'They made a mistake. It's twins.'

34

THEY CAST OFF AN HOUR later, after opening a bottle and toasting Claudine's news.

'Are you sure you know how to do this?' she asked, sitting beside him in the wheelhouse as he steered out past the breakwater, between the buoys, and took a bearing on Cap Croisette.

'You forget, seamanship is in the blood.'

'You mean you've had a few lessons from Salette.'

He grinned, eased open the throttles and *Constance* surged forward, slicing through the rougher water, seaspray dashing over her bow. 'You're right,' he said. 'I've had a few lessons from Salette.'

If Jacquot could have dreamed up the perfect day, it would have been this day, in this boat, with this woman. The cool salty splash of the sea, a warm breeze and blue sky, a fridge filled with supplies and a cool box with wine and beer.

They were going for a cruise. Just as he'd planned.

'But I've only got what I'm standing up in,' she'd told him when he suggested it. 'I can't possibly . . .'

'Check the for'ard cabin,' he told her. 'I took the liberty of bringing a few things down. Swimsuit, toothbrush, some jumpers in case you get cold, that kind of thing.' He'd even brought her gardening hat and a headscarf so the wind wouldn't flick at her hair, or the sun burn her. All possible complaints planned for, all contingencies allowed for, in case he'd had to fight his corner. Not that he'd had to. Not that much.

And twins, confirmed during a routine check-up on the island. Not just one baby, but two. He could have laughed out loud with delight. So he did. Just a perfect, perfect day.

'There's got to be a catch,' she said now, pulling down the brim of her gardening hat. 'I can't believe things just happen . . . like this. I mean, a boat?'

'If there's a catch, I haven't found it yet,' said Jacquot. 'The papers are in order, the berth's paid for. It's . . . ours. If we want it.'

Claudine shook her head, as he had done with Salette, at the sheer impossibility of something like this. And then she stopped shaking it and her eyes widened.

'Aren't we getting a little close to that ship?' she asked, pointing ahead. A commuter ferry from Cassis was coming towards them, heading for La Joliette. Its horn blasted across the water.

'Maybe just a little,' admitted Jacquot, and he put the helm hard over, heart pumping fast.

It took the best part of an hour to reach Île de Riou and a further twenty minutes to cruise around to the south of the island where Jacquot brought *Constance* into a narrow, sheltered cove, its sheer limestone sides rising above them. The sea here was flat calm and a dazzling azure, clear enough to see fifteen metres down to a sandy bottom. Jacquot had prayed there would be no one else there, and his prayers had been answered. Midweek, at the tail-end of summer, the inlet was empty, belonged only to them. Jacquot killed the engine, went forward to drop anchor and when he turned back to the wheelhouse he was just in time to see a naked Claudine dive off the boat and into the water. He wasn't far behind her.

They had lunch on the aft deck, in the shadow of the wheelhouse – a cold chicken and potato salad he'd smuggled down that morning, and a dish of ripe Violettes figs from Solliès-Pont, Claudine's favourite. They had their own fig tree in the millhouse garden and the fruit it provided was sweet and succulent. But nothing came close to the black figs of Solliès-Pont which Jacquot had bought the previous week, hard and green and at great expense, from Traiteur Cigalle on rue Haxo. Now their skin was a deep purple, split at a touch, and the pipped pink flesh inside was soft and luscious.

'If that was meant to be a bribe,' said Claudine, pushing away the empty bowl and reaching for her wine, 'then it worked a treat. I could become seriously used to this kind of treatment.'

By now the afternoon was drifting away and the line of sunlight was working its way up the side of the cliff, leaving them in a dark blue pool of warm shadow.

'We'd better think about getting back,' said Jacquot, glancing at his watch.

'Do we have to?' asked Claudine. 'There's enough food to last, we've got bedding . . .'

She got no further.

Jacquot had leaned across and caught her up in his arms.

'I love you, my darling. More than I can say. And you. And you,' he said, tapping her stomach.

'You had better. You don't know how lucky you are.'

After clearing away lunch they swam again, they made love, and as the shadows darkened and stars broke out in the stone-framed splinter of sky above them, they left *Constance* and swam to a small sliver of sand at the end of the inlet, with a bottle and glasses, cigarettes and lighter, and some left-overs from lunch in a watertight grab-bag. Once ashore they collected scraps of splintered wood and sun-dried timber, lit a fire and sat by its flames, drinking their wine, picking at the food, and listening to the soft lap and slap of the water.

Just a perfect day, thought Jacquot, wrapping an arm around Claudine and drawing her close.

Just a perfect day, thought Claudine, resting her head against Jacquot's shoulder.

35

FIFTEEN KILOMETRES WEST OF RIOU, on the coastal slopes of the Sausset headlands, Claude Dupont kissed his wife goodnight, watched her climb the stairs, then retreated to his study. He closed the door, switched on the desk lamp and unlocked the drawer where he kept Lombard's folder. Reaching in he pulled it out, placed it on the desk and untied the cord.

There was work to do.

Claude Dupont did this two or three times a week, going through Lombard's notebooks, the various documents, the cassette tapes and videos, sorting through the Zip-lok plastic baggies, and deciding who to hit next: the city councillor who traded construction *permis* for cash? Or the union boss who dipped into union coffers to fund holiday breaks with his various mistresses? Or maybe the two small-time hoods in L'Estaque who skimmed every load of cocaine brought in by a dealer called Gonzalez? Or the judge and his fondness for rough trade? Or the doctor on rue Longchamps who liked to drug and molest his prettier patients? The list of the venal and the guilty went on and on, page after page. Names, dates, places. Everything meticulously recorded over the years by his client in Les Baumettes, and accompanied by a compelling range of evidence: from shell casings to bank accounts, from credit card records to expense receipts, parking tickets to shipping manifests.

And photos, of course – wallets of them. And tapes and cassettes. Everything neatly labelled.

All the documentation, Dupont had noted, was at least five years out of date, the most recent material dating back to a month before Lombard had been brought in for the Arab killing. But most of it was still as fresh and current as the day the various crimes and misdemeanours had been committed, and just as damning.

Of course, some of the people Lombard mentioned in his notes had died – one or two high-profile gangsters along the coast, a rapist in Villeneuve – while some had moved out of the area or were already serving time as guests of the Republic. But for all the blanks and dead-ends, it still made gripping reading.

When Dupont had first seen the contents of the case, he'd spent a couple of days wondering what to do with it all. His initial impulse had been to hand it all over to the *Judiciaire* – the notebooks, the documents, the gold, the money, the jewels – and let them sort it out. But he quickly realised it wouldn't have taken the police long to trace it all back to his client whom they'd immediately visit, asking questions, poking their noses in.

And that, he knew, would not serve.

Lombard would not be amused.

Even on his deathbed, in a prison, Dupont knew his client still had ways and means. He was not a man to fool with.

Of course, he could always wait until Lombard died – surely not long now – and then hand the material over to the authorities. Either anonymously, or perhaps as part of a last will and testament, final instructions he had been given by a client. But the more he thought about it, the more convinced he became that he had a professional and ethical duty to follow through on his client's instructions, despite being so thoroughly hoodwinked and upset by said client in the matter of his murder charge. In short, Dupont decided, it was a question of honour. And Dupont liked to think that he was an honourable man.

It was also, he came to realise, a cleaning-up operation, a chance to set the record straight, to see justice done outside the confines of a courtroom where so often justice was not seen to be done. And that appealed to him greatly.

And then, of course, there was the money. A great deal of money. The drugs – cocaine or heroin, he didn't know which – might have been worth more than he could imagine, but he'd already disposed of those, on the roadway above the house, the two packs torn open, their powdery contents given to the breeze, his hands scrupulously wiped clean. As to the rest, he knew that the gold bars and precious stones and assorted bearer bonds easily amounted to millions of francs. And then there was the cash, the wads of currency.

For now, everything rested in his safe, to remain there until he had properly worked out how to dispose of it. There was also the matter of his fees to consider, the work he had undertaken, the hours he could bill for. That, too, needed to be carefully calculated . . . well, not that carefully, he supposed. He was in his sixties, he had worked hard. It was time, maybe, to take things a little easier. And now he could.

But these were all attendant, almost secondary issues.

The main consideration at this early stage was what to do with the incriminating documentation that Lombard had provided, how to make it play to the best advantage, as his client had requested.

The trick, Dupont discovered, was matching documentation to recipient. To the best possible effect. Deciding who should be sent what. There was no question of him using it to blackmail someone; why would he want to take the risk of actual involvement? The fun and games were to be had by placing the incriminating information in the hands of the most appropriate recipient, then sitting back to see what happened.

That was what Lombard had wanted.

A little bit of mischief. Deadly mischief.

And that was what he had done.

And each time he went to his study, after Francine had gone to bed, the more fun it became. The stealth of it, the damning effectiveness of it. It was just as Lombard had promised, fun and games. And every time he sat there, Dupont felt a pleasing shiver of excitement. It was like playing God, dispensing justice. Three or four envelopes a week, posted from around the city or delivered by messenger. On a couple of occasions he'd even made phone calls, thrilled by the closeness, the intimacy of the disclosures. Tonight, sorting through the material, he decided to start with the British Ambassador in Paris, alerting him that his esteemed local consul in Nice had been selling off British passports for top dollar. Small time, sure, but still fun.

He had finished writing his standard covering note in short, sharp capitals, and was reaching for an envelope when he heard a noise in the hallway. The squeak of a door handle? A loose shutter? Francine coming down, looking for him, wondering where he was? She'd be cross, of that there was no doubt. He glanced at his watch – not too late – and then at his desk top. Nothing incriminating for her to see. Just work, some briefs to sort before next week, *chérie*. As he got up from his desk and went to the study door, he knew what words he would say to placate her.

But when he opened the door there was no Francine, just a man with a gun, raising its long, silenced barrel and pointing it right between his eyes.

36

IT WAS LATE MORNING WHEN Jacquot and Claudine arrived back at the millhouse after their night out on *Constance*. They had showered, changed their clothes and were finishing lunch on the terrace when the phone in the kitchen started ringing.

Jacquot took it. '*Oui*? *Allo*?'

It was Isabelle Cassier.

'I'm sorry to call you at home,' she began. 'But there's something you need to see.'

'Where?' asked Jacquot, as Claudine followed him into the kitchen with their lunch plates and glasses. She flipped open the dishwasher and slotted them away.

'Niolon, off the L'Estaque highway. We've got a nasty one.'

He gave Claudine a *do-you-mind?* look.

She pointed to the ceiling, put her cheek to praying hands. She'd told him over lunch that she wanted a rest. And that's what she was going to do.

'Give me an hour,' he said, and hung up.

Jacquot found the house easily enough, a scrum of squad cars, lights no longer flashing, crowding the driveway off the Niolon beach road. The coast here was steep and rocky and only a few brave villas perched on its slopes. Those that did were walled, private and expensive with spectacular views across the bay, to the distant smudgy sprawl of Marseilles, and to the craggy outlines of Cap Croisette and the islands.

Isabelle, wearing blue latex gloves pulled up over the cuffs of a cream blouse, was coming down the stone stairs from the first floor when Jacquot stepped through the front door. The place had been ransacked – books, magazines, papers strewn over the floors, furniture overturned, pictures snatched from the walls, broken glass crunching underfoot.

'Husband and wife,' she said, leading him down a long tiled hallway and into the main salon. The shutters were closed, curtains drawn and an overhead light was on, throwing shadows off the two bodies beneath it, facing each other, three metres apart, wrists and ankles wired to the chairs they sat in. Both were naked, shoulders slumped, heads hanging down. And of a certain age – loose wrinkled skin, grey hair, thin legs and arms. Judging by the sprays of blood and scattering of pale bone fragments on the tiled floor between them, they had been shot in the back of the head. And judging by the state of them, thought Jacquot as he walked around the macabre stage-set, that swift execution must have been a welcome release. Open knife wounds like scarlet lips on their skin, circular black burn marks so large that they must have come from the burning tip of a cigar, fingers bruised and bent. He noticed the blood on the floor had still to form a skin. They hadn't been dead long.

'Names?'

'Claude Dupont. A lawyer in town. Top firm. His own. And his wife, Francine.'

Jacquot knew the name. And the man. Though he'd never have recognised him from the body bound to its chair. More than once Maître Dupont had visited police headquarters to take instructions from clients being held there, or issue them to investigating officers with regard to his clients' rights and comforts. Only big name clients, as far as Jacquot could recall. Dupont did not appear to represent the lower criminal classes. Clearly the tactic worked. This house would be worth a fortune.

'The housekeeper found them when she came in this morning,' Isabelle was saying. 'By the time I got here, around eleven, the local boys from L'Estaque and Nationale were crawling all over the place.'

Jacquot whistled softly. 'Somebody wanted something pretty bad.'

Isabelle nodded. 'That's how it looks. More wounds on the woman, to make hubby talk I guess. Both shot in the head. No casings. And I'll guarantee no prints anywhere. A professional job.'

'Family? Kids?'

'We're still checking. But no photos anywhere, so I'd say childless.'

'Didn't the housekeeper know?'

'She's new. Just her second week.'

'So what have you got?'

'What you'd expect for a lawyer like Dupont. Out and about. A busy man. He kept a pretty meticulous diary. In his study. I'll show you.'

The study was as worked over as the rest of the house: every book swept from the shelves, pictures smashed, desk drawers emptied on the floor and cast aside. A desktop computer lay on its back, the keyboard smashed through the screen. As in the salon, the shutters had been closed and the curtains drawn. The overhead light, and four wall sconces hidden behind green pleated shades, had been left on. A book, a leather-covered business diary, lay open on the desk.

'And?'

'I flicked through a few pages. During the week, it's mostly professional engagements, given the names and places: meetings, dinners, drinks and receptions. Saturdays and Sundays it's just social: lunches, suppers, playing cards with friends. Workwise, he's been in court the last couple of weeks on the Belledaire case. Head of the defence team – and good luck on that one,' she added.

Jacquot had read about the case. A real high-profile one for the prosecution: 'Big' Tito Belledaire, 'big' in legitimate construction, and equally 'big' in less legitimate sidelines – whatever put money in his pocket. Everything rumoured, but never proven. Until now. Six months earlier he'd shot a motor-cycle cop on a sliproad off the A7. The cop had taken five bullets before Belledaire drove off. But he'd survived. And identified his assailant.

'You think there might be a tie-in with Belledaire?'

'Possibly.'

Jacquot went round the desk and leafed through the pages, a half-page a day. There didn't seem to be many days when there wasn't something written in – a mix of pen and pencil jottings, names, places, longhand and capitals, the slant of these vaguely familiar.

Jacquot turned to the last entry. He didn't have to bother reading it. Isabelle went through it for him, as though she knew it off by heart.

'Thursday. Going over "defence prep" notes in the morning. "T.B." Tito Belledaire. Lunch with his team in a private room at Mouche near the Palais de Justice. Afternoon in court, an early-evening drinks reception at the Opéra, then cards and supper with a couple called Rosseaux. We got the address from the wife's diary. Up in La Rove, not far from here. Laganne and Chevin are there now, having a word. The last thing he wrote was "500 francs", underlined, with a couple of exclamation marks. Probably winnings.'

'Anything torn out?' asked Jacquot.

'Nothing.'

'Any codes in the diary? Initials? Anything strange?'

Isabelle shook her head. 'Not that I can see. Pretty much what you'd expect.'

'So sometime between late last night and early this morning someone paid them a call. Or was waiting for them when they came home from La Rove.'

'That's how it looks.'

Jacquot noticed a phone on the floor beside the computer screen. 'Phone records?'

'I put in a request, incoming and outgoing, but I won't get anything until later.'

'Forensics?'

'On their way, apparently.'

Jacquot nodded, shot her a look.

'So what do I need to see? Looks like you've got all you need to start the ball rolling. Why bring me in on it?'

She smiled, pushed aside a desk drawer with her boot and reached down.

'Take a look at Maître Dupont's stationery.'

37

TYVEK. LUXEMBOURG.

Jacquot took the envelope from Isabelle and felt the same silky weave between his fingers that he'd felt aboard *Constance* when Isabelle had called by the previous week. He also remembered the words in the covering note, spelled out in capital letters: *SOMETHING I TRUST YOU WILL FIND OF INTEREST.* Slanting capital letters, like the writing in the desk diary.

A lawyer or a doctor, Jacquot had suspected. A professional man. Well-educated. And from all he knew of Dupont – vaguely recalled from shadowy interview rooms, occasionally coming up against him in court, and gleaned from the house he had lived in, the possessions he'd surrounded himself with – Jacquot was in no doubt that Maître Claude Dupont was the man who had written to a priest in Avignon and to Yves Guimpier at police headquarters.

He lifted the envelope, sniffed it. Nothing. No scent. But he was fairly certain that if he went to the couple's bathroom he would find something woody, something that smelled of coconut, an expensive soap.

'*Alors*, so I'd say we have our letter-writer. But a lawyer who keeps crucial evidence from the authorities? A man like Dupont?' Jacquot put down the envelope and turned out his lip, shaking his head. 'I don't think so.'

'So what do you think?' asked Isabelle.

'What I think is that somehow Dupont got hold of the tapes and the shell casings – maybe other things too – because he was given them. And, for whatever reason, he didn't surrender them to the authorities but decided to put them into service.'

'Then it has to be Lombard,' said Isabelle, peeling off her gloves and wiping her hands on her jeans. 'According to the phone tapes, he was the one who picked up the shell casings in La Caboucelle, and didn't throw them away, and it was clearly Lombard who recorded the subsequent conversations with Monsieur Suchet.'

'So what's the link between Dupont and Lombard, do you suppose? Lawyer, client?'

'Could be. Easy enough to check.'

'I'd put money on it. A prison visit?'

'Likely, too. I'll check.'

'But was Dupont killed for the shell casings – that missing fourth one, remember? Or for something else? Because we weren't the only ones to get an envelope.'

'The priest in Avignon . . .'

Jacquot nodded. 'And maybe others, too. Any of whom – and I'm including our own side here – might have been given good cause to come looking for him. But how did they find out about him? How did they track him down here? They get an anonymous envelope in the post, or maybe by courier, and they know it's Dupont? Too easy. Something like that would take time. Or inside information. And who were the killers? There must have been two or three of them to make this kind of mess. Which means someone sent them in. Someone big. Or someone with the kind of friends who don't mind doing this sort of thing to help out a pal. It'll be the former, if you ask me. Someone big. Someone who didn't like what he got in the post.' Jacquot cast around the room: the emptied shelves, the tossed drawers, the chaos of a ruthless, almost desperate search. 'And what were they after? The missing shell case, more tapes, or something else? Because they weren't here to teach Dupont a lesson. They wanted something he had.'

'And did they find it?' added Isabelle, following Jacquot's look around the room.

'If they did, it wasn't easily found.'

'You think Dupont held out? Even with them working over his wife, right in front of him?'

Jacquot shrugged, spread his hands. Questions, questions. It was always like this at an initial crime scene. Who? How? Where? When? Why? All you ever had were just a few loose pieces of a very large jigsaw . . . The trick was to find new pieces, and then fit them all together. Slowly to start with, then picking up speed.

From beyond the drawn curtains and closed shutters came the sound of vehicles drawing to a halt on the gravelled drive, sliding van doors and car doors opening and closing.

As Isabelle and Jacquot came out into the hallway the first forensic boys were coming in, already masked, their hooded Nyrex suits swishing, silvered equipment cases swinging. One of the figures, shorter than his companions, stepped over to them. Jacquot recognised the red bushy eyebrows a moment before Marseilles' senior forensics man, Dr Aristide Clisson, pulled off his mask.

'Jacquot . . . Daniel. What a pleasant surprise.' Clisson's voice was brisk, inquisitive. If he'd had whiskers, thought Jacquot, they'd have been twitching like a squirrel's. For that was what Clisson most reminded him of. 'A little off your beat aren't you?' Clisson continued, then glanced at Isabelle.

'I'm new,' she said, introducing herself. 'Chief Inspector Cassier from headquarters.'

'New, maybe, but familiar nevertheless,' said Clisson, shaking her hand, his eyes narrowing. 'You have worked in Marseilles before. I remember you.'

Isabelle gave a little smile. Jacquot could see that she was impressed, maybe even flattered, that he should remember her.

But Clisson didn't waste any more time. Releasing Isabelle's hand, he dug in his pocket and pulled out a pair of latex gloves, snapped them on. Down to business.

154

'So. Maître Dupont himself.' Clisson gave a grunt, looked around. 'Live well, don't they? Lawyers, I mean.'

'Not any more,' said Isabelle, and pointed to the salon at the end of the hallway where the forensics crew were setting up.

Clisson pulled his mask back on. 'I've been questioned . . . no, interrogated . . . by Maître Dupont more times than I care to remember. Absolutely lethal,' he said as he strode off towards the salon, striding as only short men can do. 'The coldest voice. Very low. Very precise. And sharp little eyes.'

One of his boys was already taking photos, the rest of the team standing back.

'Aaaahhhhh . . .' was all Clisson said when he saw the bodies.

38

'AAAAHHHHH . . .' SAID PATRIC POLINEAUX, STEERING himself into the main salon, the high electric whine from his wheelchair indicating full throttle. Didier and three of his boys – Léo, Zach and Milagro – all in black jeans, black tees and trainers, stood side by side in the centre of the room. On a table in front of them was a large black bag, the hold-all that Claude Dupont had retrieved from its locker at Gare Saint Charles.

'Good work, boys.' Polineaux brought his wheelchair to a stop, gave them each a nod. 'Didier, stay. You three . . . Go get yourselves some lunch, a drink, down in the kitchen.'

When they had gone the old man turned to Didier. 'So what have we got?'

'I think you'll be pleased, boss.'

He unsnapped the clasps, pulled open the zipper and dug into the case. Polineaux leaned forward, watching hungrily.

Didier started with the diamonds.

'Rough and cut,' he said, dropping the velvet pouch on to the table. It landed with a satisfying crunch. Then came the emeralds, the sapphires. A wad of bearer bonds. Various stock certificates and other documents, stacks of photos and a selection of video and audio tapes.

'That it?' said Polineaux, frowning, pushing at one of the gem pouches with a bent old finger. '*C'est tout?*'

'Not quite. There is, of course . . .' Didier reached into the bag, smiled, and heaved out '. . . the gold,' he said, placing two bars, one after another, in a line in front of the old man.

Polineaux's eyes widened and his jaw dropped open.

'Oh yes, oh yes, oh yes,' he whispered, almost trance-like, his voice thick and low with a kind of greedy hunger. He reached forward, tried to pick up one of the bars, but its weight and shape were too difficult for him to handle.

Didier knew better than to offer any help. Instead, he watched Polineaux slide the bar towards him, manoeuvre it off the table and cradle it in his arms.

'I knew it! I knew it! Those bastards . . . But where's the rest? Where's the rest of it, *hein*? And who's got it?'

Stroking the gold bar in his lap, Polineaux's eyes settled on the notebooks, the photos, tapes and cassettes. He looked at them carefully, thoughtfully, then hoisted the bar back on to the table. He reached for the cassette nearest to him, a video in a white cardboard sleeve. He read the title on the label.

'*Alors*, *on commence*. Didier, have Jarrive set up the television.'

39

IT WAS JUST AS JACQUOT had suggested. Lawyer-client. According to the records that Isabelle called up the moment she got back to headquarters Pierre-Louis Lombard was Claude Dupont's client. Said client currently residing in Les Baumettes, just a little more than eight kilometres from her office, the other side of the city. Two hours after leaving Dupont's house – with Jacquot following her all the way to L'Estaque before peeling off towards the autoroute with a flash of lights – she rang the bell at a guarded side-gate and entered another world, a world of straight lines, bright lights and electric shadows, distant echoes and soft murmuring, the rattle and clang of daily life in Les Baumettes Prison.

Warm rubber and stale cabbage. That's what it smelled like. That prison smell. Never quite the same, but never more than a few subtle notes either side of that still, rich base – a thick, airless stench that filled the nose and throat. Every visit she made to a prison – in Marseilles, in Paris – it was the smell she waited for, and always hated. One time she had dabbed Chanel on her top lip, but had earned a frown from one of the guards. A cop didn't wear perfume in prison. Now, not a minute past the stone walls and razor wire, Isabelle parted her lips and started breathing through her mouth.

'Monsieur Ranque, the assistant warden, would like a word when you're done,' said the guard, leading the way to the isolation ward. 'You won't be long in there, so I'll wait.' He unlocked the door, held it open, then closed and relocked it after her.

As the key was withdrawn from the lock, Isabelle looked around: a long room with a high ceiling and lino-tiled floor, windows barred and opaque, the first two metres of wall painted a green gloss that had long lost its shine, and the rest a flaky cracked cream. There were four beds along each side of the room, a line of fluorescent tubes hanging down on thick black cables, and a pair of ceiling fans, their green metal blades turning idly, more of a trot than a canter, as though they'd long given up any hope of clearing the air. If the rest of Les Baumettes had smelled of warm rubber and stale cabbage, the smell here was altogether different. She chanced a sniff. More disinfectant now, less rubber and cabbage. But this time the air was laced with a greasy, gamey scent that she could feel settling in her hair, stroking her skin, reaching into every pore.

There was only one bed occupied, the other seven just bare mattresses with a neat fold of blankets and slipless pillows on each one. When she got to Lombard, she stopped at the foot of the bed. The man appeared to be asleep, not disturbed by the sound of the door locks, or the tap of her boots across the lino, or the small cough she gave, or the introduction she made:

'Monsieur Lombard. I'm Chief Inspector Cassier, from police headquarters. I would like to ask you some questions.' She leaned forward, hands on the bedrail. 'Monsieur Lombard?'

There was no movement from the bed. No acknowledgement. Just a regular and rapid rumbling from the man's chest, like the distant sound of a train in a tunnel. The eyes were closed, mouth open, lips flecked with dry white spittle. A tank of oxygen stood by the bed, mask and tube wrapped around the control valve.

Isabelle had called ahead, been told of Lombard's condition, that it would likely be a wasted visit, that he was close to death. And it certainly looked that way. The only thing missing from this bedside, she decided, was a Curé in black soutane and purple stole, murmuring over his prayer book. But despite the warning, Isabelle had insisted on the visit, told them she would risk it. And when Claude Dupont's phone records were brought to her as she was getting ready to leave the squad room, she was glad she had. Three weeks earlier, Maître Dupont had received a phone call from Les Baumettes.

Isabelle was checking out the oxygen tank and what was on the bedside table when she became aware that Lombard's eyes were now open, and watching her. Or rather one of them was; the other rolling up to stare past the fans and fluorescent tubes. It was difficult to hold eye contact, so she smiled to cover herself.

'Questions?' The rumble from his chest turned into a throaty laugh, deep and laboured, that brought up from the depths a thick wad of phlegm. Turning his head on the pillow, Lombard spat it at the tank. It landed short, at the edge of the bed, sliding into a fold of the bedsheet. He didn't care. He turned back to her and his eyes roamed.

'Questions? Questions?'

'Monsieur Lombard, I appreciate you're under no obligation to . . .'

'*C'est vrai*,' came another phlegmy reply, his eyes swinging this way and that. 'No obligation.'

'I just want to ask if you know a man called Bernard Suchet? He's a . . .'

'Crook, to his polished fingernails, and you know it.' Each of the words came out on a panting breath, the last of them accompanied by a lip-curling grin.

'What makes you say that?'

'Find out for yourself, why don't you . . . ?'

'So tell me about your lawyer, instead. Maître Dupont, isn't it?'

'What of him?'

Isabelle waited a beat before she spoke again.

'He's dead. Murdered last night. His wife too. I saw the bodies. Did you know about that?'

160

Lombard didn't reply. Just licked his lips. Swivelled his eyes around the ward.

'He should have been more careful,' he said at last. 'A lesson to be learnt, *n'est-ce pas*? Now do me a favour, *m'petite*, and go fuck yourself.'

And that was the extent of her interview with Pierre-Louis Lombard. The wayward eyes closed, there was another grunt and throat-clearing, the results swilled round in his mouth as though another spit was on the cards. Isabelle stepped back from the bedrail in case it was sent in her direction, but this time it was swallowed, a scrawny Adam's apple bobbing with the effort.

Now she understood what they'd meant by a wasted visit. Not so much his condition, but his . . . personality.

As the guard locked the ward door behind her, she asked if there was a record of visitors, and if there was could she see it? A ledger was produced and she flicked back through the pages until she found the entry for Claude Dupont, visiting his client the same day he had received a phone call from the prison, and just a little more than an hour later.

40

AFTER LEAVING THE HOSPITAL WING, Isabelle Cassier was shown to the office of the Assistant Warden, Jules Ranque. He came out from behind his desk and greeted her warmly, professional to professional, offered her coffee and, as she took the seat he indicated, glanced swiftly into the top of her blouse. He seemed to be in his early fifties, with a bushy grey moustache that would have looked better on tanned skin, quick black eyes and a reddened nose as though he had a cold.

'Lombard made a request that his lawyer visit him,' Ranque explained, when Isabelle asked about the phone call from Les Baumettes. 'Not so much a request, more a demand,' he continued, crossing his legs and smoothing a hand across his wiry grey hair. 'Normally the *salaud* could have *demanded* as much as he liked . . .'

'Surely prisoners are allowed to make phone calls?'

'There is a schedule for these things.'

'Even in an isolation ward?'

Ranque smiled, spread his hands. 'This is a prison, first and foremost, Chief Inspector. There are rules. You know how it is.'

'He made the call himself? From the ward?'

'I made it for him,' Ranque replied with a sigh. 'Given his condition.'

'He does seem very ill. Should he not be hospitalised?'

162

'We are fully able to cope, Chief Inspector. You could class our medical wing here almost as an annexe to a main hospital. *En effet*, you probably get better treatment here than La Timone.' He pulled a handkerchief from his pocket, a garish paisley affair, and blew his nose. After a wipe and a further sniff, he slipped it back into his pocket.

'You were here, on that Sunday, when Claude Dupont visited Lombard?'

'Correct. Nothing out of the ordinary, I can assure you. There are no weekends for an assistant warden. It's always the second-in-commands who work the grindstone, *n'est-ce pas*?' The message was implicit. They were both in the same boat, both of them in that secondary, supporting role. Isabelle did not acknowledge this overture of familiarity.

'You met Monsieur Dupont?'

'I did.'

'And how did he appear?'

'Flustered, I would say. *Disconfortable*. He was not a regular visitor, you understand. But for someone like Lombard . . . ? I would say he really had no choice.'

'When you say "someone like Lombard" . . . ?'

Ranque gave her an indulgent look. 'Lombard is no ordinary prisoner, Chief Inspector. He is a powerful presence here in Les Baumettes. To all outward appearance quiet and unassuming, but beneath that façade is a . . . how to say it? A force to be reckoned with.'

'Even to his lawyer? Outside Les Baumettes?'

'Even to his lawyer. A word from a man like Lombard, even *in extremis*, and life for anyone inside or outside these walls could become very difficult indeed.'

Isabelle took this in.

'And you have no idea what they talked about? The reason for the visit?'

'None at all. They were lawyer and client. But I would suggest that Lombard called him in to make certain arrangements. Maybe

163

Dupont brought something with him. Something in his pocket. A document to be signed by Lombard. Some final instruction.'

'And after their meeting, when Dupont came out of the ward?'

'Relieved it was over, I would say. And anxious to be gone. As I said, Lombard is not a man to cross. Even behind bars. Even now. Right at the end, he takes no prisoners. As I'm sure you will have discovered.' A sly smile curled across his face, as though Ranque knew exactly what had happened at Lombard's bedside.

A silence settled between them then, but as Isabelle reached for her shoulder bag, preparing to leave, Ranque continued: 'May I ask about the police interest in Lombard? The reason for your visit?'

'You may . . .' she replied, returning his smile. Equally sly and conspiratorial.

It took Ranque a moment to get the message, then he nodded, waved a hand; he understood. He did not look at all put out.

So she told him anyway, leaning forward a little as though sharing a secret, just to see how he would respond. A business-like short-hand: 'Lombard's lawyer, Monsieur Claude Dupont, has been found dead, together with his wife. They were tortured, then murdered. The house had been ransacked. We believe that certain items might have been removed from the property. Something that might have belonged to Lombard, which was in Dupont's possession. Maybe something Lombard gave him on that last visit.'

Ranque started shaking his head before she had finished speaking.

'It was a few weeks ago now, but I am sure that Maître Dupont did not take anything away with him. They spoke for maybe ten minutes, that's all. And he left as he arrived. But, as I said, maybe there was some document, folded away in a pocket. Something I could not see.'

And that was that. A brisk farewell, handshakes, and she was shown to the door, an orderly summoned. The walk back to the gatehouse. The sliding of bolts, the turning of locks and the long electric buzz of release. Closing her mouth and breathing through her nose at last.

164

Afterwards, on her way back to police headquarters, Isabelle stopped off at her apartment, and ran herself a hot shower. Stepping into its beating pinprick heat she washed Les Baumettes from her body, thinking of Ranque and his bushy moustache, the bitten fingernails and the way he smoothed back his hair with his hand held stiff, like an iron. There was something strange about him, Isabelle decided, tipping her face to the spattering stream of water. Something not altogether wholesome. Whether it was professional or personal integrity he lacked she couldn't quite decide. But he'd seemed strained, uncomfortable, as though he wasn't being altogether straight with her, as though he might be holding something back.

But then, with the hot water beating over her, she thought of Jacquot instead.

Where he was.

What he was doing.

And she smiled.

So close.

41

JULES RANQUE SMELLED TROUBLE.

And that trouble had a name.

Pierre-Louis Lombard.

The two men – one of them with a title, the other with a number – had arrived at Les Baumettes in Marseilles' ninth *arrondissement* within a few months of each other. Ranque had come first, installed as assistant warden after six years at the Centre Pénitentiaire de Lyons, in time to see Lombard brought back from the city's Palais de Justice at the end of his trial to spend the rest of his useful life behind bars.

If Ranque had learned one thing in his prison service it was that those prisoners sentenced to the longest terms were often the hardest to control; they had nothing to lose. How did you punish a man who was in his sixties and facing a twenty-year term? Quite simply, you didn't. Isolation? Withdrawal of privileges? What kind of threat was that? Yet Lombard had settled into prison life without causing a ripple. Once inside he had kept to himself, did not appear to involve himself in any of the prison gangs, nor had he made any attempt to create his own little fiefdom. He just kept his head down and did his time.

But there are always whispers in prison, and one of the whispers that had reached Ranque suggested that, in Lombard's case, appearances really were deceptive. For it seemed that nothing happened in Les Baumettes without Lombard having some hand in it, knowing about it, being able to screw up even the best-laid plans if it so suited him or, if he was feeling magnanimous, being happy to provide whatever assistance was needed. Muscle, money, drugs, weapons . . . Whatever you wanted, Ranque's source told him, Lombard was your man. In just a few short years, without the authorities spotting it, he had become a major player in the prison community.

All of which seemed to fit in with the way he had lived his life before, working the quays and wharves of L'Estaque and La Joliette like a miner on the motherlode. Always in the shadows, low profile, yet somehow always in the middle of everything. Which was why Ranque had begun to watch Lombard – visiting the kitchens where he worked in the bakery, or the library where he loaded his trolley for the book run, or spying on him from a guard tower when Lombard shambled into the exercise yard.

And it hadn't taken long for Ranque to see that the whisper was good. Not five minutes went past in that yard without someone stopping for a chat, a cigarette, acknowledging his presence. If that was not a compelling enough argument for his importance and standing in the prison hierarchy, there was the discovery of Ranque's informant, just a week after that initial whisper, hanging in his cell. Suicide.

What particularly concerned Ranque was what Lombard might know of him. For Ranque had worked in the prison service long enough to realise that his State salary was never going to make him rich. It needed topping up. And Ranque had wasted no time in using his position as Les Baumettes' assistant warden to set up the scams he'd learned but never had the opportunity to carry out at other prison facilities. Tobacco, drugs, alcohol, even women. Anything could be arranged if the price was right. And at Les Baumettes, with multi-million-franc contracts for renovations and refurbishment up for grabs, there had been even more opportunity to line his pockets. A favourable word on behalf of a bidding construction company, or an electrical supplies outfit, or a security systems provider . . . The list of potential suitors was endless – all kinds of commercial interests keen to suckle at the State's swollen tit, all of them tendering estimates, all of them prepared to grease whichever palm was presented to secure their bid. And in pretty much every case, the palm presented was Ranque's.

But did Lombard know?

About the trafficking and supply behind bars? He had to, surely.

But what about the contracts and backhanders? Did he know about those too?

Because suddenly, on his deathbed, everyone wanted to see him. First the lawyer, Dupont, obviously taking some kind of instructions from his client. And now some hot little Chief Inspector snooping round, requesting an interview with Lombard then telling him that Dupont had just been murdered.

Ranque swung his chair round to one of the few unbarred windows in the great stone and razor-wire sprawl of Les Baumettes prison and gazed over the walls at a distant, sparsely wooded slope, thrown now into shadow.

On his deathbed maybe, thought Ranque, but Lombard was still breathing. And while he breathed, he might easily prove a significant threat to everything that Ranque had so carefully engineered for himself.

A man with nothing to lose.

Turning back to his desk, Ranque reached for the phone and dialled a number.

Fifteen minutes later there was a knock at the door. A guard first, a prisoner following. The guard was in a blue uniform shirt and black trousers, a ring of keys on his belt, the prisoner with his wrists shackled to a leather belt.

With a wave of his hand, Ranque dismissed the guard.

'But, sir . . .'

'That will be all, sergeant. I will call when I'm finished.'

Left alone, the prisoner looked around the governor's office. His name was Castel and he was short and fat, his pudgy pink fingers

168

clasped in front of him, dull eyes slow but watchful. The last time he'd stood there, eleven years earlier, he'd been confined to solitary for his own protection, and had been there ever since. He might not have been very visible but everyone in Les Baumettes knew who he was, and there were many who would have been waiting for him had he made an appearance. He wouldn't have lasted a night in the general prison population. Not after what he had done . . .

'I have a proposal to make,' Ranque began, picking at some lint on his trousers. 'It's a one-time offer, and it never happened. *C'est clair*?'

Castel's eyes latched on to Ranque. He smiled a coy little smile, nodded. What was clear was that he liked the sound of whatever was coming, even before he'd heard it.

'You look sick. Not well. Some time in the infirmary should do the trick.' Ranque gave a couple of short, sharp sniffs, cleared his throat.

'If you say so.' The man's voice was high and reedy.

'Isolation.'

Castel nodded again, waited.

'There is a man there. Very ill, *le pauvre*. A pillow should do it. To put him out of his misery.'

A silence settled between them, broken only by the soft metal crunch of Castel's chain links. Both men understood what would come next. A job had been offered and accepted; now all that remained was a price.

'There is a young man, just in,' continued Ranque, leaning forward to brush a smear of dirt from a shoe. 'Twenty? Twenty-one? Very beautiful. Mauritanian, I believe. Do your job and I'll have him sent to your cell. One night only. No interruption. Whatever you want. *Compris*?'

Castel licked his lips. 'Whatever I want?' Almost a squeak.

'Anything.'

Another coy smile. '*Compris*.'

42

ON THE TERRACE OF HAUTS des Pins, a blue cashmere rug wrapped around what remained of his legs, his skull-like features thrown into shadow beneath the brim of a favourite Panama, Patric Polineaux decided that fate had dealt him a fine hand of cards.

The diamonds, the sapphires and the emeralds had all gone off for sale within a day of Didier bringing them to the house. The family's gem man had come in and taken a look, peering through his loupe. Not the best quality, apparently. Poor colour, some significant flaws, inferior cutting. Fourth, maybe a few of them third-division stuff, he'd suggested, but nothing finer. Ten . . . maybe twelve million. Not as much as Polineaux had hoped for, but a good return on a single night's work. And there were still the bearer bonds and share certificates and property portfolio to consider. Another useful acquisition.

Only two things remained. The gold bars kept in his safe, back there in the main salon, and the concertina file with its bits and pieces strewn across the table beside him. The tapes, the videos, the various documents pinned down beneath an ashtray. A quite extraordinary treasure trove of information. A remarkable collection. Lombard had, indeed, been a very busy little bee.

Of course, some of it he knew about. But there was still so much more that was new, things he had never imagined: names he recognised, people he knew; the things they got up to. And if the documentation was sometimes beyond belief, photos and tapes and videos didn't lie.

Given all the familiar names, the closeness of it, what surprised Polineaux most was how little he himself featured in the haul. And if it was satisfying on the one hand – low-profiles always paid off – it was nevertheless annoying not to have learned more about that long-ago heist on the Col de la Gineste, and the current whereabouts of his gold.

His gold. His gold. His damn' gold.

The biggest goddamned heist in history.

And he was the one who'd dreamed it up, put it all together. On his own. And carried it off. It made Mesrine look like a school girl. A secret bullion shipment from Algiers, via Toulon, to Marseilles and Paris. Reparation? Investment? Who cared? Three tons of gold. In three security trucks. Two hundred and twenty-five bars. Seventy-five bars in each truck. Each bar at a delivery weight of over four hundred troy ounces or more than twelve kilos. Valued back then at a little over three hundred francs a troy ounce. More than thirty million francs.

And the plan had been a honey, practised a dozen times, polished to perfection. Fifteen men in three separate units. Three drivers, three four-man squads, each of them fit enough to deal with the opposition, and handle the transfer of bullion from the security trucks to half a dozen unmarked transports, waiting in Lombard's warehouse, down in the railyards of Le Canet.

A real Marseilles job.

Something to be proud of.

But someone had snitched. The *flics* were waiting for them at Le Canet. Two of the trucks were seized. But not the third. That one never arrived. It just vanished, disappeared for long enough for someone else to get hold of what remained of his gold.

Seventy-five bars. Just like the two in his safe. A little over a ton.

Just . . . gone.

But now, maybe, coming up for air.

Polineaux had a feeling.

And old man Polineaux had learned to trust his feelings.

43

WHEN THE MOMENT CAME, AT a dark, silent hour in the night, Pierre-Louis Lombard was too weak to do anything about it.

He'd recognised the man when they'd wheeled him in that afternoon, just by the size of him. The heaviest man in Baumettes. That *con* Castel. The butcher of La Bouilladisse. One of the living, breathing horrors from 'S' wing. Solitary. For their own protection. He was coughing, sharp and tight, holding a pudgy fist to his mouth as though to stop the spread of germs, limit the risk of infection. As if someone like Castel cared about something like that. But it made a good cover, Lombard supposed. At Baumettes, nothing surprised him.

Without raising his head from his pillow, Lombard watched the two ward orderlies and the two guards transfer Castel's bloated body from trolley to bed, heard the springs shriek at the load, and then the jolly rattle of the trolley's wheels, no longer burdened by that huge weight, as the guards pushed it out of the ward. Once the new patient was settled, the two orderlies followed the guards and the locks turned.

It was one of three things, Lombard decided. Either the man really was sick (in which case, how come he stopped coughing when the orderlies had gone?), or he was taking some time out from solitary, or he'd come to the ward because he had a job to do.

With a growing sense of resignation, Lombard decided that it was the third option he should go for. The man was here for a reason, and Lombard knew what that reason was. Deep inside he'd been expecting something like this. Either the AIDs would get him, or someone would finish him off first.

His days weren't numbered. They were over.

Dinner was brought in at 6:30. Ward door unlocked. Two trays wheeled in on a trolley. The orderlies lifted their two patients, plumped up pillows, settled them back and placed the trays on their laps. Usually Lombard was fed, but this time he elected to do the job himself, trembling hands reaching for knife and fork, dipping into the dark beef stew and pushing it into his mouth, chewing, watching the man opposite. He hadn't spoken since they'd brought him in, and he didn't speak now, not even a glance in Lombard's direction.

There was a reason why he had chosen, on this occasion, to feed himself. And when the orderlies came back to collect the trays and hand out their medicines, Lombard slid the plastic knife beneath his sheet, making a fuss as the tray was removed, cursing the orderly with croaking breaths, spitting out the pills they tried to give him, the missing knife overlooked.

Of course, it was only plastic. But if he held it close to the tip he knew it would be enough to do some damage, to gouge into the eyes of the man opposite when he decided to make his move. At least Lombard would have something to defend himself with. He'd go down fighting. The way it should be.

Once the orderlies had disappeared, the evening wore on, hot and stuffy, the fans above them barely moving the stagnant air, just the hourly check-ups from now till morning: water jugs topped up, temperatures taken, pulses felt for, the straightening of a sheet, nothing more. No conversation. Only the squeaking of the orderlies' plimsolls on the lino-tiled floor.

The fluorescent strips between the fans flickered out at ten, but there was still enough light from outside, through the line of windows, to see the layout of the room, the beds. Two hours later it was pitch black in there.

For the last twenty minutes, Lombard had lain still, putting out a gentle snore. At one o'clock, the door was unlocked and one of the orderlies made his rounds, flashing his torch, then left, re-locked the door.

And that's when Castel made his move.

The soft brush of a cotton sheet pushed back.

The gentle squeak of bed springs.

The slow sticky sound of bare, sweaty feet on lino.

Lombard couldn't see him, but he sensed him coming close. Sensed the heat of him. The way the air seemed to part, give way before his bulk.

Silently, he drew the plastic blade from beneath the sheet, pressed his thumb and forefinger against its tip and waited for the moment.

One second. Two. Three. Four. Five.

And then, out of the darkness, he smelled an odd mixture of hand cream and onions, and suddenly a pillow was over his face, pressing down, a knee brought up to pinion his right arm before he had a chance to strike out with the knife. Castel must have known, must have seen him hide the knife away. Or simply been cautious. Just in case.

Lombard tried to cry out, he tried to twist and turn, he tried to buck off his assailant like a wild horse its rider.

But in just a few moments, these tiny efforts exhausted him.

Suddenly there was no strength in his body.

Just a bitter will to fight back.

But there was no fight he could make.

The weight on him was too great.

Hot, sweaty, lumpy. Pressing his body down.

The pillow stifling his grunts, his breath.

He felt the knife slip from his fingers.

Tried to draw a breath.

Felt his face redden and bulge.

Felt his throat constrict and burn.

His lungs scream.

And then, in the darkness, there came a gradual easing, as though the pressure had somehow been lifted off him.

No longer any sense of weight or movement or struggle.

No smell of hand cream and onions.

Nothing.

Just a soft darkness.

44

IT WAS ALWAYS GOING TO be a night job. No alternative. For something like this, on rue Vandon, in the heart of Endoume, the cover of darkness was as critical as the Browning automatics that Beni and Jo-Jo carried in stiffened nylon holsters under their black leather jackets. With its shops and boutiques and the close proximity of a number of popular restaurants lining the busier avenue Galère, a daylight hit on rue Vandon had never been an option. There were simply too many people around, too many cars and vans and motor-cycles clogging up the single-lane, one-way, slightly sloping thor-oughfare between Galère and Fiolle.

But after the shops shut for the day the traffic eased, pedestrians and motorists alike, and it was a great deal easier finding a parking space, never more than fifty metres from the stepped entrance of Résidence Daumier, the six-floor block of balconied apartments half-way along the street where Jean Garnolle lived with his wife, Clara.

When Aris Moussa, René Duclos' fixer, had told them what the boss wanted, Beni and Jo-Jo had reckoned they'd have the job done and dusted in no time. A day scouting out the neighbourhood, and just the one night for the hit. A lot more fun than picking up dog-crap, Beni decided.

But it hadn't worked out like that. For the last three nights Jean

Garnolle hadn't shown his face. As though he sensed that someone was out there, waiting for him, and that he was safer staying inside.

Right on both counts, thought Beni, sitting behind the wheel of his Mercedes on the fourth night of their stake-out, the engine still ticking from the long evening drive into Marseilles from Toulon, parked close enough to Résidence Daumier to observe not just the entrance but the zig-zag fire escape that dropped down the side of the building into a shadowy sidestreet, the only ways into and out of Résidence Daumier. Here we are, waiting for you, and all you want to do is stay inside and watch TV.

For the last three nights, at about the same time that the street-lights had come on along Vandon, so, too, had the lights in the fourth-floor apartment where the Garnolles lived. And for the last three nights that's how they'd stayed until midnight when the lights were switched off, only the glow from a television set in what Beni reckoned had to be the couple's bedroom. Any other apartment block in Endoume, there'd have been no problem – just take the lift, knock on the door and show the Browning. But Résidence Daumier wasn't 'any other apartment block'. It was high-end, the kind of place that cost big money, with a rota of uniformed concierges on duty twenty-four-seven. Which would have meant making their approach through that marble hallway and waiting for said concierge to ring ahead. Not an option.

Across the road a movement caught Beni's eye: the Daumier's concierge coming out on to the step to take in the evening air. And twenty metres beyond him, there was Jo-Jo coming back up the slope with coffees and baguette sandwiches from Café Gente on the corner of Galère. As he closed on the concierge, Beni saw Jo-Jo settle his head in his collar and keep his eyes on the pavement. The concierge watched him pass, idly, not much interested. He might have been if Jo-Jo had crossed the road and got back into the Mercedes. But Jo-Jo didn't do that. He just kept on walking, with Beni watching in the wing mirror until he turned the corner into rue Fiolle. Good old Jo-Jo. No flies on him. Five minutes later, the concierge went back into the building and two minutes after that,

Jo-Jo was back at the Merc, sliding into the front seat with the coffees and sandwiches.

'Did he watch me?' asked Jo-Jo.

'All the way to Fiolle.'

'You think he's made us? The car? He's been on the same time the last three nights.'

Beni shook his head, sipped his coffee. 'Not a chance. Just stretching his legs, taking the air.'

It was then that the streetlights began to flicker on, starting at the bottom of the slope and working their way up to the Merc. Little orange globes that burned into life against the darkening night sky. And right on time, the lights in the Garnolles' apartment snapped on too.

But they didn't stay on.

As Beni balled up the sandwich wrapper and tossed it in the back and swallowed the last of the coffee, the lights on the fourth floor went out. A few minutes later, the time it would take for the caged lift to crank down four flights, Jean Garnolle pushed open the main door to the block and stepped out with his wife. The bald head, the big ears . . . Beni recognised him immediately. He had worked for Duclos long enough to have known the man down in Toulon, before he retired. Soft, lispy kind of voice he had, Beni remembered. Tight as a clam with Duclos, but kept himself to himself with the rest of them. Only spoke if he was spoken to, and then it depended on who was doing the speaking. He had a way of not seeing you, like he was looking right through you.

'It's him,' said Jo-Jo, dashing out his cigarette in the ashtray.

'The wife, too,' replied Beni. 'Couldn't be better.'

In the plan that Beni had hatched, the wife was crucial. When they made the hit, Garnolle had to be with the wife. If he wasn't, the chances were that he'd do something stupid. He knew who they were, he probably knew what it was all about. He'd try and make a run for it; there would be all kinds of trouble, and someone was sure to end up shot. In all, a fuck-up. And Monsieur Duclos didn't like fuck-ups.

Coming down the steps, the Garnolles turned right, linked arms and set off down the slope towards Galère.

'You ready?' asked Beni.

Jo-Jo nodded, and the two men got out of the Merc.

Keeping to their side of the road, they followed their targets to the corner, quickening their pace when the Garnolles turned right again and started out along Galère. They caught up easily enough, now just a few steps behind them, but both men knew it was far too busy to try anything here, still early enough for there to be people around: late-night shopping at the Arab grocer on the corner, at the kebab houses and roadside grills, the air laced with the charred scents of chicken and lamb on the spit. Hands in pockets, slowing their pace now, Beni and Jo-Jo kept a steady fifteen metres behind the Garnolles, walking past without a glance as the couple suddenly stopped up ahead and entered a small Lebanese restaurant.

Taking a table at a café across the road, the two men ordered beers and settled down to wait, keeping an eye on the restaurant opposite. The longer it took them to eat their meal, Beni decided, the happier he'd be. In a couple of hours the Arab grocer would close up shop, the street wouldn't be so busy and the way home would be quieter, hardly anyone about on rue Vandon.

It was closer to three hours, however, before the Garnolles reappeared, Jean Garnolle coming out on to the pavement and helping his wife with her coat. At the café Beni slipped some notes from his bill-clip but as he and Jo-Jo pushed away from their table another half-dozen people came out of the restaurant, all of them talking, laughing . . . and joining the Garnolles on the pavement. Not just an easy *diner à deux*. A party, goddammit. Beni's heart sank. If Garnolle or the wife invited anyone back to their place for a drink, they'd be fucked. Another night's stake-out down the pan, and old man Duclos would be wanting to know why the fuck such a simple job was taking so fucking long. If it didn't happen tonight, thought Beni, there was going to be some serious trouble back in Toulon.

But the Garnolles did not invite anyone back with them, or if they did the invitation was not accepted; thanks but no, it's late, another time. And when a cab with its light on cruised down Galère, one of the men stepped to the kerb and flagged it down, while another flourished his car keys and offered lifts. With final waves and calls of farewell – *bonne nuit, adieu, à la prochaine* – the group dispersed and the Garnolles set off, alone, for home.

Just as Beni had hoped, the strip was quieter now, the grocer on the corner closing up, and rue Vandon, when they turned into it, ten metres behind the Garnolles, all but deserted.

'You set?' asked Beni with a final look-around, checking the pavements, lit windows, feeling a light drizzle settle on his face.

'Set,' whispered Jo-Jo, and the two men pulled down the peaks on their trucker caps and reached into their leather jackets.

45

JEAN GARNOLLE WAS NOT IN a good humour. It was late, it was starting to rain, and he was ready for his bed. He'd spent the last three hours sitting with half a dozen people he hardly knew – Clara's friends – in a restuarant where the chairs were uncomfortable and the food not to his liking. Plate after plate of fiddly Lebanese *mezes* that tasted of lemon and breadcrumbs and chopped coriander rather than the tidbits of lamb and beef and prawns that they covered, the whole tedious meal made only bearable by a very creditable Château Musar. If it hadn't been for the wine, he'd never have lasted as long as he had.

But it was over. They were nearly home and he could put the whole ghastly evening behind him, pour himself a cognac and call it a night. In the old days, of course, working for Duclos, this would never have happened. He'd have been able to make an excuse back then. Tell the wife there was a meeting in Toulon he couldn't miss, he had documents to go through or accounts to complete, he'd be back too late. But he couldn't do that now. He was retired. He was trapped. There was no option.

'Did you enjoy yourself, *chéri*?' asked his wife, as they turned the corner and started up rue Vandon.

'I did, I did,' he lied.

'Isn't Jean-Marie just a riot? So amusing.'

'Jean-Marie?'

'Jean-Marie Artaud. Sitting opposite you. With the round spectacles. He runs EDC, did he tell you? The Experimental Dance Company on Cours Julien. I'll have to take you there. It's quite the . . .'

But that was as far as she got.

Just a few steps from their building, Jean Garnolle felt a hand grip his arm, a mouth at his ear.

'Keep walking or my friend will shoot your wife.'

'What's going on? Get off me . . .' he heard his wife say, her arm torn from his, staggering a little on her heels.

For a moment Jean Garnolle assumed it was a mugging, tried to shake off the restraining hand, thought about his wallet, his credit cards. But as he turned to his assailant he recognised the face, or more precisely the small white scar that seemed to divide the man's left eyebrow. Two eyebrows, one above the other.

He frowned, squinted. 'I know you . . .'

'Someone wants a word,' said Beni. 'Like I say, do as I tell you or your wife dies.'

Garnolle, in that instant, knew exactly who Beni was, and who it was who wanted a word. He went pale.

'Yes, yes, I understand. Of course.' He turned to his wife, still struggling in Jo-Jo's arms, just seconds away from giving out a good, wholesome scream. 'It's okay, Clara, don't fret, *chérie*. It's okay. Just do as they say and we'll be fine . . . Just act normal.'

'Let's go,' said Beni.

'But Clara . . .'

'. . . stays here with my associate. Just to make sure you behave. Come on,' he said, and tightening his grip on Garnolle's arm, he steered him across the road and up the slope towards the Mercedes.

Garnolle did exactly what Beni asked, holding out his wrists to be secured with duct tape and climbing into the boot of the Merc where a blanket and pillow had been put down. No argument. If he tried anything, he knew that it would be Clara who paid the price.

183

Starting up the Merc, Beni pulled out of the parking space and let the car roll down the slope, flicked on the wipers, slowing as he passed Résidence Daumier and coming to a halt where Jo-Jo and Clara were waiting, huddled together under an awning.

But Clara, as Beni and Jo-Jo knew, was simply the means to an end. Once her husband was in the car, once they had him where they wanted him, they had no further use for her. Left alive she could have raised the alarm, given their registration number to the police.

Beni nodded and Jo-Jo wrapped his arm round Clara's shoulder as though to give her a farewell hug. Instead he buried the muzzle of his Browning in her chest and fired three times, holding her as she jerked away from the gunshots, lowering her body down into the shop's shadowed doorway.

As though she was sleeping. Just a drunk.

She could be there hours and no one would bother her.

It was done.

46

POLINEAUX WAS RED IN THE face with fury. Delon, his nurse, would have had him back in bed and in the oxygen tent in seconds if he had seen him now. But Delon was not there. Just Didier.

'He's what?'

'Dead.'

'Lombard's dead?'

'He had AIDs.'

The old man quietened, frowned. 'AIDs? What's that?' he asked, in a scared, querulous tone.

The question took Didier by surprise. Didn't the old man know about AIDs? Or was it old age, this forgetting? Just a beat or two behind the action. It was happening so often these days.

'It's an illness,' Didier replied, carefully. His boss didn't like talk of disease and death, but he chanced it. 'Like cancer. You don't get better.'

Polineaux growled like an angry cat, deep in his throat. And then, 'You believe it?'

Didier looked puzzled.

'That he died naturally, I mean. Of this . . . AIDs thing.'

Didier registered another jolt of surprise. Perhaps the old man wasn't quite so slow after all. 'There's a whisper one of the prison staff might have been behind it,' he replied.

'Who? Do we know who?'

'According to Pisco, Lombard was in an isolation ward. Like solitary, except some schizo was put in there with him. Following morning Lombard's dead.'

'Who set it up?'

'Pisco says the assistant warden, Jules Ranque.'

'Ranque? Ranque?'

'The one we've been softening for the kitchen contracts. Couple of years now.'

'Ranque? That two-faced greedy little shit?'

'That's the one,' replied Didier.

Polineaux fell silent, tried to work it through. It wasn't easy grinding dentures; they cut into the gums. But Polineaux didn't care. He wheeled himself to the terrace balustrade and looked down into the garden.

'But why would Ranque . . . ?'

'Maybe Lombard had something on him. And the stupid fuck couldn't wait for this . . . disease to kill him. Maybe Ranque got scared.'

Polineaux shook his head. 'And just when I wanted to have a word myself.'

'You were going to talk to Lombard?'

'No, you were. To find out what's going on. If he knew anything, about the gold. He must have done.'

'Well, it's too late now.'

It was the wrong thing to say. Didier knew it the moment the words were out of his mouth.

Polineaux spun round, fast enough to set him rocking in his wheelchair.

'Of course it's too fucking late, you moron!' screamed the old man. 'The fucker's dead. What do you think I am, stupid or something? For fuck's sake . . .'

Didier took a step back, shaking his head, holding up his hands. '*Pas du tout*, *pas du tout*. Not at all, not at all.'

He might have been getting on in years, thought Didier, but the old bastard could certainly hand it out when he felt like it. And how. That spitting, screeching voice made the blood freeze.

Finally, Polineaux spoke again. More softly now, but still a little breathless, his flare of temper reined in.

'Ranque. I want him dealt with. Just for . . . fucking things up. Tell Léo. He can set it up.'

47

'WE HAVE A MATCH,' said Isabelle.

Jacquot was down in Marseilles for a final examination and sign-off with his doctor at La Timone, and had decided to check out *Constance* before driving home. Isabelle had dropped by as he was stowing the cover, on the off-chance he was there, she told him, and accepted his invitation aboard. A bottle of rosé was fetched from the fridge, a corkscrew found and glasses poured.

'The smudge on the parking ticket and my ID card,' she continued, kicking off her shoes, stretching out her bare legs along the seat and hooking her elbow over the side. The sun was settling over the slopes of Le Panier, and a compilation tape was playing softly in the cabin. 'The same prints. So your guess was right. Monsieur Bernard Suchet.'

'You paid a call?' asked Jacquot, taking the other locker seat. He raised his glass, sipped the wine, and took in the long brown legs, the fluttering open collar of Isabelle's blouse. He was pleased she had dropped by. Claudine was having dinner with her best friend, Gilles, telling him all about her stay on Guadeloupe, so there was no huge rush to get home.

'We would if we could,' said Isabelle.

'Meaning?'

'Monsieur Suchet is missing.'

'Missing, or just taken to his heels?'

Isabelle shrugged. 'Could be either. All we know is that Madame Suchet reported him missing after we paid him a visit.'

'Any ransom demand?'

'Nothing yet.'

'What about Madame? Where was she?'

'Down the coast with their daughter. Saint-Tropez . . . the family yacht. They came home for a dinner party and Suchet's a no show. Madame got in touch with the police in Aix, where they live, and they contacted us because this is where he has his head office. It would appear that you and I were probably the last people to see him. He'd arranged a pick-up that evening with his driver at the Mercure but never showed, hasn't been back to the office and off air ever since. *Pas un mot.* Not a word.'

'How's she taking it?'

'The wife? I think she's worried.'

'You think?'

'It's hard to say. She's a toughie. Doesn't let anything show through. But I'd say the woman's . . . distraught inside. Just keeping it all together for her daughter who really has taken it badly. There's a wedding coming up. If you read the magazines you'd know about it. Prospective son-in-law said to be a fast track Chirac boy. True love. But Suchet must have been thrilled all the same. Same for the mother, I'd imagine.'

'Anything missing from the house in Aix? Clothes? Money? Passport?'

Isabelle shook her head. 'Not a thing. Passport and cash in the safe. Suitcases accounted for. No clothes missing.'

'Office?'

'According to his PA, Monique Berthelot, his desk was just as he'd left it. She had strict instructions that his desktop should never be touched. Tidy or in a mess. In this instance, it was tidy.'

Jacquot fell silent, remembered Suchet stepping out of his building: short, bullish, wrapping that scarf round his thick neck as though he needed it, as though there were a chill in the air.

And he remembered something else, the image just popping into his head: the van, coming up behind Suchet as he approached the corner of Grignan and Paradis. A black van, dawdling along, then speeding up, going against the traffic lights.

'He's been taken,' said Jacquot quietly, certain of it. 'Out on the street. And you and me? We saw it happen.'

Isabelle looked at him, frowned. 'How so?'

'When we were following, remember? He was across the road from us, going up Grignan, heading for Paradis? And there was that black van . . . slowing for the lights so we couldn't see him, and then speeding off. And Suchet had vanished. Just gone. We assumed he'd turned the corner into Paradis. We were wrong.'

'So where do you think he was headed, on foot? Some shopping maybe? Something for his wife? For the dinner?'

'Possibly. Or meeting someone?' Jacquot suggested.

'A pay-off? Maybe he'd received one of Dupont's envelopes, with a ransom demand. Pay up or I'll spill the beans about that parking garage, La Caboucelle. And Barsin.'

'Not blackmail. Not Dupont. But maybe someone else. Maybe the same people who called on Dupont. You could always check it with his PA, show her one of those Tyvak envelopes. See if she recognises it.'

Isabelle shook her head. 'Done it already. I asked her to look, but she couldn't find anything.'

A pair of quarelling gulls swooped overhead and Jacquot watched them wheel away between the masts, marvelling at their agility.

'*Dis-moi*, you said he had a driver?'

'That's right. Monique told me he'd asked for his driver to pick him up outside the Mercure. According to the driver, he never showed.'

'The driver didn't think that strange? A man like Suchet?'

Over Isabelle's shoulder, Jacquot spotted Gala coming down the pontoon towards them. When Gala saw he had company she turned on her heel and went back to her own boat. A good girl, thought Jacquot. How many others would have come sniffing, curious to see what was going on?

190

'Apparently it happens quite often,' Isabelle was saying. 'He has the driver go somewhere to pick him up and he doesn't show. *Tant pis*. Who cares? He's just a driver. Let him wait.'

'What time did Suchet want the pick-up?' Jacquot reached across with the bottle and topped up Isabelle's glass. He was pleased they'd met up. It was good having her there, the company, and bringing him up to speed. And he realised he was enjoying himself. Being in the loop, but not having to do any of the legwork. Just make a few suggestions, talk things through, maybe gently direct Isabelle's path of enquiry. It really didn't get much better than that.

'Eight forty-five,' said Isabelle, raising her glass in thanks. 'The driver hung round for an hour then went home.'

'So Suchet leaves the office late afternoon, to go somewhere until, say, eight o'clock. Enough time for him to get to the Mercure from wherever he's been, whoever he's been seeing.'

'He could have been having a meeting in the Mercure?'

'Possible, but I doubt it. Not Suchet. The Nice Passédat, yes. Maybe even the Sofitel. But not the Mercure. Not his style at all.'

And then he gave Isabelle a knowing look. She caught it.

'What? What are you saying?'

Jacquot spread his hands.

'I remember the way he looked at you, that's all. Maybe he was . . . hungry.'

It took her only a second or two to catch on. 'You're kidding?'

'No, I'm not. Remember the time. A hard day at the office. He needs to unwind before he goes home. Some afternoon delight. *Cinq à sept*. Or as near as dammit.'

'A mistress?'

'Or a hooker. He had that look about him, didn't you think? And for a man like Suchet a mistress could be difficult. A hooker's a whole lot less trouble.'

Isabelle gave it some thought. 'We could go through his address book, see if there's . . .'

Jacquot shook his head, smiled.

'Those are not the kind of numbers you write down, Isabelle. You know them by heart.'

'Is that so?'

'I think so.'

'And you'd know?'

He spread his hands. 'Call it a man thing.'

'A dirty old man thing, if you ask me.'

'Talking of which . . . any news on our priest?'

'Nothing significant. All we've got is Saint-Ignace church, off Kléber. He was there for a couple of years, back in the eighties. But we can't identify any of his . . . companions. And even if we did . . .'

And so it had gone, that unplanned evening on *Constance*, the two of them chatting about the investigation, going over the possibilities, Isabelle telling Jacquot about her visit to Les Baumettes and her interview with Lombard, what he'd said about Suchet and Dupont.

When the first bottle of wine was finished Jacquot opened a second, prepared a tray of bread and pâté and olives which they ate on deck, watching the sky turn through orange to purple, until the stars started to twinkle above the sulphurous glow of the streetlights.

After clearing away the dishes and tidying the cabin, Jacquot came topside with his jacket over his shoulder.

Isabelle felt a twist of disappointment.

'I'd love to stay and open another bottle, but I have to be getting back,' he said, turning to lock the wheelhouse hatch. 'Can I give you a lift somewhere?'

'No, no. That's fine,' replied Isabelle, picking up her own jacket, slipping on her shoes and reaching for her bag. 'I can walk it from here. And I do have my friend.' She tapped her holster.

'You live close by?' he asked, stowing the seat cushions.

'Le Panier. A ten-minute walk.'

'I used to have a place up there. Rent it out now.'

'I know.' She gave him a look. 'I helped you move, remember?'

'*Mais, bien sûr.* Of course you did,' he replied, a little shocked that he had forgotten. How Isabelle had helped him move out of the apartment, out of Marseilles after the Waterman case, and up to Cavaillon. To another life. And another woman.

Up on the quayside, Jacquot reached for his car keys. The traffic was loud here and they had to draw close to hear each other speak.

'It was fun,' said Isabelle. 'Thank you.'

'I enjoyed it too. Like being back at work. In the thick of it again, without any of the hassle. And thanks for keeping me in the loop,' he said, and leaned forward to kiss her cheeks. She held his elbow as she returned the kisses, then stepped back.

'*À la prochaine,*' she said. 'Until the next time.'

'*Oui. À la prochaine,*' he replied.

48

JEAN GARNOLLE KNEW THAT HE was going to die.

What he didn't know was when or how, his one real fear the level and extent of the pain that he would experience in the minutes or hours or days leading up to that sweet release. René Duclos was not the forgiving type and Garnolle wondered just how much, and for how long, his old friend would make him suffer before that obliging bullet in the head.

Garnolle knew why they had come for him.

Twenty-seven years may have passed but he knew why he was there, in his socks and underpants, wrists bound, roped to a hook in the ceiling. The only thing he had ever done that he shouldn't have. The one single action in his life that had, in the intervening years, turned dreams into nightmares.

Just a small job.

Call it a favour.

A one-off. No one need ever know.

Had it been worth it, he wondered now? As he hung there, alone in the darkness, he decided it had not, and he knew that now he was going to pay very dearly for that little indiscretion. And knew, too, with an absolute certainty, that he would never see daylight again.

He'd known it the moment they bundled him into the boot of the Mercedes. And if, for a moment, he'd doubted it, the three short, sharp shots – pop, pop-pop – that he'd heard from the boot's swaying darkness left no room for doubt. There was no mistaking that sound. They had killed Clara. Right there, in the street where they'd lived for more than twenty years, just a few metres from their front door. And if they were prepared to kill her on the street, there was no doubt that he was facing the same prospect. At least her death had been quick. He hoped he was as fortunate.

It must have been well past midnight when they arrived back in Toulon, and as soon as the boys opened the boot he'd smelled that sharp, familiar scent from the Pesquiers salt pans across the bay, and had seen through the trees the columned stucco façade of the Duclos mansion. But this time he'd been taken to the basement rather than the summerhouse annexe where his old office had been, stripped, strung up and left alone in the darkness.

It was difficult to tell how long he had been there. An hour? Less? More? His arms and shoulders had started to ache, that was for sure, and his wrists to chafe. But then he was in his sixties. This was not something he was used to. And though it was warm and close in that darkened room he had started to shiver – the expectation of confrontation, the chill of fear.

Knowing his life was as good as over.

Just a last few hours to go.

If he was lucky.

He'd already decided that he would answer every question he was asked, that he would volunteer as much information as possible, as quickly and as accurately as he could, leaving nothing out, to avoid any unwanted physical encouragement. He'd also decided that if he didn't know the answer to a question he would make up some credible answer. You didn't say 'I don't know' to René Duclos.

Some time later, maybe another thirty minutes, Garnolle heard footsteps come down the passage. The rubbery squeak of trainers, the clip of leather soles. The door opened and the two men who'd brought him here came in. The taller of the pair, Garnolle remembered, was called Beni, but the other one he didn't recognise. The

195

one he didn't know, the shorter of the two, the one who had shot Clara, switched on an overhead light, and Beni, a wad of gum in his mouth, came over and checked his bindings. Then, from the hallway, came a familiar sound, the scampering click of tiny paws.

Salome, the dog.

Which meant that Duclos would not be far behind.

Garnolle took a deep breath, and tried to control the shivering. It didn't work.

Salome came in first, darted around the room, poked her snout into every corner, then found what she was looking for and squatted down to pee. She seemed excited to be there. She had finished her business and was sniffing around his feet when Duclos finally appeared.

There had been no sound of footsteps, no sense of his approach. Suddenly he was just there. In the doorway, pausing before entering, as though unfamiliar with the lay-out of the room.

The dog went to him, pranced around him, then came back into the room. Duclos followed. As he stepped into the light Garnolle could see that he was dressed in evening clothes, a silk scarf round his neck, one hand in his jacket pocket, the other holding a half-smoked cigar. His thin grey hair was slicked back, his eyes bright and sharp, but the face was creased and heavy with wrinkles, the neck stretched and scrawny, the fingers clamping hold of the cigar gnarled and claw-like.

There was no greeting. No sound save the scrape-scrape of a match, a soft flaring and a lazy puff-puff-puff as Duclos drew on the stub, its ashy tip glowing into life, smoke coiling around his head and drifting upwards.

When he was satisfied the cigar was properly alight, Duclos pocketed the matches and, for the first time since entering the room, he flicked his eyes at Garnolle, as though he had just noticed him.

'So tell me about Jéromes Frères,' he began, without any preamble. 'You know the ones, Jean. Those gold dealers in Zurich.'

49

'IT WAS BARSIN. THE COP. He was the one set it all up.'

'In Marseilles, you said?'

'That's right. And that low-life Lombard. He was in on it too. The one they call The Seahorse. A real player on the docks.'

'I know all about Lombard,' said Duclos quietly. 'But it was this Barsin, the cop, who brought you in?'

'That's right. Like I told you, I didn't know him, I'd never seen him before.'

'Why you?'

'He'd heard about my connections, he said. In Switzerland. Seemed to know what I'd done for you.'

'He knew about me?'

'That's how it sounded.'

'Who from? How did he know about me?'

'Lombard, I think. Lombard seemed to know everything about everyone.'

'So this cop, Barsin, came to you and asked about selling gold bars?'

'That's right.'

'How many gold bars?'

'Nine. He said they had nine to get rid of.'

'They?'

'Barsin and Lombard, I suppose.'

'You knew where the gold came from?'

'Of course. It had been in the papers. The hold-up. I'd read about it. One truck missing. Seventy-five bars. Ten, twelve million, give or take.'

'And he said they had nine? Just nine bars?'

'That's right. Just the nine. I told you.'

'What about the rest?'

'It went missing, that's all I know. Barsin said someone had done a switch and they got there too late. Just the nine bars left.'

'And the "someone"?'

'He didn't say. I got the impression there was the original heist, and then a couple of groups who didn't know about each other trying to get some for themselves. An inside job. One of them got the gold and the others were left with the crumbs – the nine bars.'

'And you knew this Barsin was a cop?'

'Not at first. I thought he was one of the gang.'

'The boys that pulled the heist on Gineste?'

'Either them or one of the freelancers. That's right.'

'So who was pulling the strings? The original heist. Whose boys?'

'Lombard said it was Polineaux.'

Duclos nodded to himself, as though he'd suspected this all along.

'So how did you find out Barsin was a cop?'

'Lombard again. He warned me not to mess with him. Said to do as I was told, or there'd be trouble. For me. For you.'

'And your job was to trade the gold?'

'That's right. Get the best price. Legit. What they wanted was a spread of dealers. A bit here, a bit there. They were thinking of melting it down – no trace. The story was going to be it was Nazi gold, like unmarked treasure trove. Pulled out of some lake in Austria. Not that the Swiss would have cared.'

'And you agreed?'

'I had no choice.'

Duclos frowned. 'They had something on you?'

'Lombard did. That's how it all started.'

'So what did he have on you?'

'I was having an affair. He had photos. Said if I didn't help, he'd send the photos to Clara.'

Duclos gave a grunt. He was leaning against the wall. Salome sat beside him, tongue out, panting. He took a last draw from his cigar and handed the butt to Beni.

'So what happened then?'

'He gave me a bar to trade.'

'Barsin?'

'That's right.'

'And when was this?'

'A few weeks after the heist. Just before Christmas.'

'Melted down?'

'No. Still with all the markings. Banque Nationale d'Algérie. That's when I knew for sure what it was. The hold-up on Gineste.'

'And where was the rest of the gold being stored? The other eight bars?'

'Barsin said that Lombard had it some place safe, that's all I know.'

'And Barsin had this one bar for you to trade?'

'That's right. A tester, he said. To see how things worked out.'

'And?'

'I was to take it to Zurich, to establish value and negotiate a trade.'

'Jéromes Frères?'

'And some other traders.'

'But you didn't go to Zurich?'

'Not then. A couple of days after Barsin gave me the bar he was shot. In Marseilles. I read about it in the papers. So I didn't do anything.'

'Who shot him? Lombard?'

'I don't know. But that's my guess.'

'So what happened then?'

'A few days later Lombard got in touch, told me to go ahead and make the first trade. So I passed on the bar. To Jéromes Frères. Got a price.'

'And told Lombard?'

'That's right. Gave him all the documentation.'

'And what did he do?'

'Told me to go ahead. Gave me one bar at a time. A spread.'

'All nine bars?'

'Just seven in the end.'

'What happened to the other two?'

'Lombard kept them, told me he was going to trade them through someone else.' This was the first time that Garnolle had lied. The truth was he didn't know why he'd only been given seven bars and not the nine. Lombard hadn't said anything. The gold just stopped coming.

The lie seemed to work.

'So far as you know . . .'

'That's my best guess.'

'And what did you get out of it, Jean?'

'Lombard gave me the photos he was going to send to Clara.'

'Any money?'

'Just the commission from Jéromes Frères.'

'Did Lombard know?'

'Maybe he guessed. Like he knew. But he never said anything.'

'What was his take?'

'A million plus, thereabouts.'

'That's what you got for the bars? In Switzerland?'

'That's right.'

'And how long did the trading go on for?'

'Maybe six months.'

'And without Barsin, Lombard got to keep it all?'

'Unless there was someone else involved I didn't know about.'

Duclos seemed to consider this.

'And all that time . . . not once, not one single time, did you think of mentioning this to me. That you knew about the gold. That

Polineaux was behind the heist. And that you'd been brought in to trade.'

'I'm sorry. I was wrong. I can see that now. But like I said, it was just seven bars.'

'And you expect me to believe that? Good old Jean just brought in at the last moment by some dockie shit and a bent cop. To get rid of a few measly gold bars.'

'That's the truth. That's how it was.'

Garnolle felt a sudden, desperate twist of fear. So far the interrogation had gone without Duclos' thugs doing him any harm, but something had changed; there was a sense now of things coming to a head.

And a chilling realisation that Duclos had not believed a word he had said.

'So let's go over it one more time,' said Duclos quietly, sliding another cigar from his breast pocket and biting off the tip, spitting it on to the floor. 'And this time, your old friend Beni here is going to try to help you remember . . .'

201

50

IT WAS FOUR DAYS BEFORE Jacquot spoke to Isabelle again. Every day he expected to hear from her. An update. Testing a theory on him. Asking for an opinion. But she didn't call. Of course it was good to have the time to spend with Claudine, and catch up on work around the millhouse, but he missed that sense of being a part of something – beyond the millhouse.

In a couple of months his convalescence would come to an end and he would begin that morning drive into town, sitting at his desk overlooking the railed garden of Église Saint-Jean, and giving his assistant, Brunet, a hard time. As the days passed it was something he started to look forward to, and as he worked in the garden, or tended his plants in the vegetable patch, or got to grips with an argumentative boiler in preparation for winter, Jacquot found himself wondering what was going on down south, not a hundred kilometres away in Marseilles.

In the end he phoned Isabelle, just a friendly call, and left a message.

Twenty minutes later Claudine came on to the terrace from her studio, called out to him. A Chief Inspector Cassier on the phone.

When Jacquot came into the kitchen, Claudine was back in her studio. She was pinning up a series of holiday photos on her corkboard – what looked like dozens of studies of island vegetation – that she would soon start sketching, before turning the sketches into canvases. He pulled out a kitchen chair and picked up the phone.

'I hadn't heard from you . . . I thought I'd call, see how the Dupont case was . . .'

'Busy,' said Isabelle.

'That's good,' replied Jacquot, recognising the excited lilt to her voice. 'Busy' was department shorthand for 'developments' and rue de l'Évêché loved developments. An investigation lived and breathed on developments. Without them everything slowed, tempers frayed and, on occasions, heads rolled.

'We've found Suchet.'

'Found' was another emotive word. It meant, usually, that a body was involved, rather than someone alive who had been tracked down and apprehended.

'Where? When?'

'Last week. In the Esterel. You wouldn't believe it. And there's more.'

'What? Tell me.'

'It'll cost.'

'Cost what?'

'Lunch. On you. Or dinner, on *Constance*.'

'I'm coming down Saturday. If I leave early enough we could meet for lunch?'

'If it's Saturday it'll have to be an early supper,' she replied. 'I'm on call most of the day.'

'Come over when you finish. I'll be there.'

When he put the phone down Claudine came out of her studio, pulled open a kitchen drawer and rummaged around for another box of drawing pins.

'Don't tell me,' she said, finding the pins and closing the drawer. 'I'm six months pregnant and you're having an affair.'

'Just the one. And only weekends,' he replied. 'The rest of the week I'm yours.'

She came over, pressed her swollen belly against his shoulder and then leaned down to kiss the top of his head.

'Is this the one you had while I was away? Or another one?' she said, sliding her fingers through his hair.

'A new one.' He felt her tug his hair, playfully. But only just.

'And I suppose you expect me to let you slink off every time your lady friend calls?'

'I told you, it's just an affair. What's the harm?'

'Tell me she has the face . . . and the body . . . of a wrestler.'

'A retired wrestler. Put out to seed.'

'That's all right then. You can go. And I suppose you'll want to stay over?'

'There are some things I need to do.'

'So long as it's just *Constance* you need to do them to,' she said. And with a final, deliberate bump of her belly against his shoulder, as though to remind him of his new obligations, Claudine returned to the studio with her box of pins.

51

JACQUOT ARRIVED IN THE VIEUX Port and boarded *Constance* for the first time in a week. It was good to be back, and he spent the afternoon finishing off a few odd jobs left over from his last visit before heading off to the stores for some supplies. An hour after getting back on board he spotted Isabelle coming down the pontoon. She waved and he waved back. She had clearly been home. Her hair was wet from a shower and she'd changed from her work clothes into jeans and a loose white T-shirt, a long grey belted cardigan, feet bare and deckshoes in her hands. He helped her aboard and as she stepped down on to the aft deck she came close enough for him to catch the familiar musky scent he knew so well.

No wrestler this, thought Jacquot, and somewhere a small alarm started to ring. He remembered the look Claudine had given him when he'd set off that morning, and the teasing smile that had accompanied it. 'Take care,' was the last thing she'd said. He hoped he wouldn't have to . . . or rather, he knew he wouldn't have to. There was nothing more in store than an easy supper with an old friend – albeit a one-time lover – and colleague. A catch-up chat. It was, after all, four years since they'd split up, gone their separate ways. Nor had he forgotten that it hadn't been him who had ended it. It was Isabelle who'd thrown in her cards, called it quits. There was no unfinished business here, he was certain of it.

'Whoosh, what a day!' she said, dropping her tote on the deck and loosening the belt of her cardigan. She unclipped the holster and gun from her belt and stowed them out of sight in the wheelhouse. It was as if she was coming home after a hard day in the office, Jacquot thought. He couldn't help but smile.

'What?' she asked, with a smile of her own, taking a glass of wine from him and her favourite seat looking out over the water at the square tower of Fort Saint-Jean.

'You look at home. It's nice to see that you like it so much.'

'What's not to like?' she replied, sweeping a hand towards the forest of silvery masts, the blue sea and sky and the rising heights of Le Panier across the harbour. She drew in a breath and let it out slowly. 'Mmmmhhh, *délicieux* . . .'

But Jacquot was keen to hear about the investigation, to be brought up to speed.

'So,' he began. 'Suchet.'

'Dead,' she replied, getting down to business. 'Just his underpants and a bullet in the back of the head. And knee. And ankle. Dumped in a sinkhole in the Esterel. Twenty metres down. Up above Miramar on the Cap Roux.'

'A sinkhole?'

'Like a mineshaft. Or well. But natural. Something to do with lava flows millions of years ago, Clisson said.'

'That's the kind of thing Clisson would know.'

'And he wasn't alone. Suchet, I mean.'

Jacquot gave her a puzzled look.

'A couple of dogs, cats, a fox, some rabbits . . . and eleven other corpses in varying states of decomposition. Three of them women, but all eleven known names, associated with the *Milieu*. It's like a gangland dumping ground up there. Step on someone's toes and it's sinkhole city.'

'How do you known they're all names?'

'There was a stack of personal information with the bodies:

wallets, credit cards, driving licences, you name it – as if whoever dumped them didn't care about identification, what was in their pockets, or didn't imagine they'd ever be found. There's so much to get through that Clisson's called in help from Aix and Avignon.' She took another sip of her wine. 'And whoever's doing the dumping must have been doing it for years. Right at the bottom, the last body brought up had a pair of tickets for the Olympique Coupe de France final in 1969.'

'So whoever he was,' said Jacquot, 'he wasn't dumped there by a football supporter.'

Isabelle frowned.

'An Olympique fan would never have let those tickets go,' Jacquot explained with a wink. 'Worth their weight in gold.'

Isabelle gave him a look. 'If you say so, but it hardly narrows the field . . .'

'So who found the body?' asked Jacquot, reaching for his cigarettes. 'Up there, it's wild country.' He lit one, drew in the smoke and then let it out in a long plume.

'A couple of hikers doing the Chemin d'Esterel. Dutch. It was their second day out from Fréjus and they'd camped on the ridge above the sinkhole. Around midnight, they were woken by a car coming up the slope. One of them, the husband, left their tent to see what was happening and looked over the edge. And there were these two guys hauling a body up the track. He watched the whole thing, till they got to the sinkhole directly beneath him when he couldn't see what was going on.'

'At night? How could he see at all?'

'Whoever it was had left the car headlights on, so they could see what they were doing.'

'And?'

'The following morning the hikers went down to Miramar and reported it. What they'd seen. After that . . .'

'He get a vehicle registration? The husband?'

Isabelle shook her head.

'Too far away. But close enough, apparently, for the killers to hear him. A rock dislodged from the ridge. One of the men heard it, stopped, flashed the torch around. For a minute or so the husband thought he was done for.'

'But he lived to tell the tale.'

'He did indeed. Except it took a while for the local boys to get a handle on it and organise themselves. To get up there, take a look, bring in someone to rope down into the sinkhole. The usual thing. The first body, Suchet's, was hauled out two days later. Which was when they discovered the others.'

'Time to have another word with Lombard, I'd say. See if he knows anything about sinkholes in the Esterel.'

'If I could, I would. Monsieur Pierre-Louis Lombard is dead.'

'Natural causes? Didn't you say he had AIDs?'

'That's how it was recorded. But when I heard about it, I asked Clisson to have a quick look at the body.'

'And Clisson told you to take a ticket and get in line?'

Isabelle flashed Jacquot a coy smile. 'No, he did not. As a matter of fact he was most helpful. He didn't have time to cut, he said, but he offered to do a quick once-over. It took him about ten minutes. Not natural causes. Smothered was his opinion. Not conclusive, of course. A more thorough examination . . . blah, blah, blah. But judging by the broken blood vessels in the eyes and bite marks on Lombard's tongue and the inside of his lips . . .'

'Anyone in the frame?'

'As soon as I heard, I called Jules Ranque, the assistant warden at Les Baumettes, to find out more. Apparently Lombard wasn't the only patient in the ward. He was alone when I visited, but another prisoner had been sent up to isolation soon after. You'll know him. A man called Castel. "S" wing. Category One abuser.'

'Castel? Oh, yes, I remember him,' grunted Jacquot.

An image leaped into his mind. The first time he'd seen Castel, after a three-month manhunt: in the back of his butcher's shop in La Bouilladisse; his latest victim bent over a wood-block chopping table; ankles and wrists tied to its legs; an assortment of butchery tools to hand. One of the reasons Castel got away with the killings for so long was doing the deed in his butcher's shop. Blood and guts easy to conceal there. The victim, a seventeen-year-old Arab boy, had not survived Castel's loving attentions. At his trial, Castel's lawyer had pleaded insanity but the defence had fallen on deaf ears. Castel had gone down full-term with no parole. He would never leave Les Baumettes.

'What was he doing in the isolation ward? What was wrong with him?' asked Jacquot.

'Interesting you should ask,' replied Isabelle. 'According to the prison doctor, Castel had complained of intestinal pain. He'd soiled his bed. Diarrhoea. It was enough for Ranque to order him to isolation despite the doctor's reservations.'

'Reservations?'

'Apparently a spell in the hospital wing was considered something of a holiday for loners, the boys on "S" wing.'

'You spoke to the prison doctor?' he asked.

'After speaking to Ranque . . . just routine, to double check. The doctor agreed with Ranque that there's nothing worse than a gastric infection raging through a prison, but he hadn't been altogether convinced by the symptoms presented.'

Easy enough to fake, thought Jacquot. Just mix a healthy stool with water, smear it around, clutch your belly and groan. There was a kid at the orphanage Jacquot had been sent to, after his mother died in an anarchist bomb blast, who did it to get off the work rota.

'Did Castel have anything to do with Lombard? asked Jacquot. 'Did the two men know each other?' He finished his cigarette and dropped it into an empty soda can; he'd stopped flicking his butts into the harbour after being told off by Michel Charbon.

Isabelle shook her head. 'Castel was kept in solitary, away from the general prison population, so their paths wouldn't have crossed. And it seems unlikely they'd have known each other outside. As far as Ranque and the prison doctor were concerned, Lombard died of natural causes. They'd been expecting it.'

'Did you tell them about Clisson's findings? The bite-marks?'

'Just Ranque. He's promised to look into it, but he did say that there's not a lot he can do. Castel is hardly likely to confess anything – why should he? And how much time can one man serve, when he's already in for life and no parole? He'll die in Les Baumettes.'

'Tell me about Ranque.'

Isabelle sighed, played with her wine.

'Slimy. You know the sort. Slick, smart and charming on the outside, but underneath . . .' She shook her head. 'I didn't like him.'

'How well do you know him?'

'I've met him just once. When I went to see Lombard.'

'He was there? With you?'

'No, he asked to see me after the visit.'

'Was he there with Dupont, do you know?'

'Not with him. Lawyer-client privilege, he told me. But he was waiting outside. I remember in his office, he was keen to know what was going on. The interest in Lombard. First his lawyer, then the police, just weeks apart.'

'Did you tell him about Dupont? That you believed he'd been given something by Lombard. Something he'd likely been killed for.'

Isabelle nodded.

'And how did he react?'

'He didn't really. Just . . . interested.'

Jacquot took this in.

'Why?' asked Isabelle. 'Do you think Ranque might be involved? In the Dupont thing, with Lombard?'

'Who knows?' sighed Jacquot. 'But it all feels just . . . too close, too comfortable.'

And then the mood changed.

'So what's a girl have to do to get some food around here?' she began. 'Or are you going to take me to Mirador?'

'Not quite the Mirador, but pretty close,' replied Jacquot.

52

WHILE ISABELLE STAYED ON DECK with her wine, Jacquot went below and prepared some food, handing up a dish of sliced hams and salamis and a tub of *rillettes* from Charcuterie Brignolards on rue Cevennes, a green pepper salad, three different cheeses from Fromagerie du Port on rue Cartone and a *grande rustique* from Chamère, the boulangerie just a block back from the harbour. He could have set up the trestle table he had bought and kept stowed in the for'ard cabin, but he spread out a rug instead, took the cushions from the seats and laid everything out picnic style. Hunkered down like that all you could see were masts and sky and the top floors of the buildings along Quai Rive Neuve, the rising slopes of Le Panier and the spotlit spire of Les Accoules.

'I forgot to tell you,' she began, pulling a cork. 'I saw you on TV the other night.'

Jacquot groaned. He knew what was coming. With the Rugby World Cup fast approaching, the sport channels had started running old footage of the French national squad. Great tries, great victories. In recent years there had been few to compare with Jacquot's own try, the length of the pitch at Twickenham. A Five Nations final. Against the English. The winning try, with just minutes to go to the final whistle. It was the first and last time Jacquot had played in the blue strip, with the gold *coq* on his chest, seen off the pitch with a snapped Achilles tendon just weeks after that debut appearance. Twenty years on, it seemed like another life, another person, but even without the ponytail he wore back then, there were people who still recognised Jacquot, the size of him, the broken nose, the name. For some, that's all it took before a drink came his way, or a hand slapped his back, or someone caught his eye, gave him a nod of recognition.

That's what his life had been back then. The rugby. Playing for club and country. Sometimes it was difficult to escape, impossible to forget.

'You looked very young,' she said, filling their glasses.

'*Looked*? I haven't changed a bit.'

She laughed. 'It was a fantastic try. I never thought you'd make it.'

'Nor did I,' said Jacquot. 'The longest seventeen seconds in my life.'

'I knew you'd done it, of course. I'd heard the stories around headquarters. But I'd never seen it.'

'They'd only just invented TV back then. The footage must have been black-and-white.'

'That Englishman got so close. Catching you up. And then, when he went for the tackle, my heart was in my mouth.'

'If it hadn't been for the mud, I'd never have crossed the line. I just slid the last few metres. The great sliding try. I had more mud up my nose than on my boots.'

Somewhere a police siren started up, a distant, rising whooh-whooh-whooh over the drone of harbour traffic. As they worked away on their supper, they listened to its pulse soften and disappear. When it had gone, they caught each other's eye and laughed, hunkered down on *Constance*'s rear-deck like naughty children hiding from their parents.

'The commentator said you never played again,' Isabelle continued.

'Not for La France. And only once more at club level, just a couple of weeks later. One of the scrum, a big fellow from

212

Béziers . . . my own side, would you believe? . . . dropped himself on the back of my leg. My foot was pointing in the wrong direction. Snap.' Jacquot flicked his fingers.

'And that was that?'

'That was that.' He passed her a basket of the bread and watched her break off a wedge, wipe it through the remains of her salad.

'Do you miss it?'

Jacquot sighed, not sure how to answer truthfully. It was something he often wondered, as the years passed and he grew older. 'Not the playing,' he began. 'I'd be dead meat on a field now. But watching it is wonderful. Sometimes, at the end of a match, my legs are aching from all the running.'

'So tell me about your wife. Claudine, isn't it?'

It was an ordinary enough question, but coming so close after the rugby it threw Jacquot a little. He put aside his plate and reached for his cigarettes.

'Not my wife. We're not married. I asked her once but she said "no".' Jacquot lit the cigarette, blew out a column of smoke over their heads and gave a light chuckle.

'She has a lovely voice.'

'That's exactly what she said about you. I had to tell her you looked like a wrestler.'

'Well, thanks for that,' laughed Isabelle. 'So when did you meet? Tell me all.'

The telling made Jacquot feel comfortable: the Gallery Ton-Ton here in Marseilles, Claudine's first exhibition, the canvas with the lemons, the hotel in Luissac. It allowed him to construct a wall, to let Isabelle know in the kindest, most complete way that he was happily involved.

'Does she come here much? To the boat?'

'She's been a couple of times, but boats and pregnant women don't really mix.' It wasn't altogether true but it served its purpose, given the circumstances; letting Isabelle down gently, in case she had anything other than friendship or professional matters on her mind.

'She's pregnant? You didn't say. I didn't know. But that's great. When's the baby due?'

'Christmas. The New Year,' replied Jacquot, deciding to hold back on Claudine's latest news about twins.

'A new century baby, how lovely! Boy or girl? Do you know?'

Jacquot told her they didn't know, hadn't asked, didn't want to know. They'd deliberately kept it quiet, he told her, and he hoped she wouldn't say anything at headquarters. Not yet anyway.

'So what's it feel like to be a dad?'

'Frightening,' said Jacquot, with a nervous laugh.

'I bet,' said Isabelle.

And that's where their supper ended. When Jacquot dropped his cigarette into the soda can, Isabelle glanced at her watch, said it was time to go, that she mustn't keep him. She offered to help with the clearing up but he waved the offer away. She didn't press it, for which he was thankful. Instead he walked her along the pontoon, and saw her through the security gate.

'Let me know how things pan out. Anything I can do.'

'You can count on it,' she said, and with a parting kiss, a smile, she turned and walked away along the streetlit Quai Rive Neuve.

53

ISABELLE CASSIER HAD TAKEN THREE lovers since she
and Daniel Jacquot had parted company four years earlier. The last
of these had been her superior officer at Police Headquarters on
Île de la Cité in Paris. They met at least twice a week in a small
pied-à-terre he rented for just such assignments off place Joubert
in the Latin Quarter. It was up in the eaves of an old house overlooking a corner of the Luxembourg Gardens. There was a small
sitting room with a bed that came out of the wall, an electric kettle,
a one-ring camping stove, and a cramped, windowless shower-room
with a sink, bidet and lavatory. They rarely used the stove or kettle.
If they were hungry, they stopped for a coffee and Danish in the
small café on the ground floor.

At first, Isabelle had found it exciting and sexy but she soon
tired of it, just as she tired of the five floors she had to climb every
time he left a note on her desk. The same note. Just two words.
Rue Cayenne. And the time – anything between breakfast and
supper.

When, eventually, the officer's wife found out about their liaison,
she had reported them both. It was in the way of these things that
Isabelle had been the one disciplined, a transfer hastily arranged
to a posting of her choice. She had asked for Cannes or Biarritz;
somewhere far from Paris but close to the sea. So they gave her

Marseilles. No choice. No argument. No room for manoeuvre. The last time she saw her lover, he was putting a note on his new secretary's desk. After he'd left the building she stopped at the girl's desk, took a look at the note. Just two words. Rue Cayenne, 2:45. She'd changed the time, the two to a three. Let the bastard wait. It was a small revenge, but it made her feel better.

Back in Marseilles once more, Isabelle had been surprised how often she found herself thinking of Jacquot, how far he strayed into her thoughts. He might have moved to Cavaillon but at police headquarters on rue de l'Évêché, up in the squad room on the third-floor again, he was everywhere. The ghost of him. And despite herself she regretted that she had let him go so easily, calling him from the very desk she now occupied to tell him that she could not continue with a man who did not feel the same for her as she felt for him.

For that was what it had been.

That was what had come between them.

Jacquot was a great cop – intuitive, focused, almost magically talented. And he had been a caring, glorious lover. But from that first night in Marseilles – the dinner at Mirador, the house *bourride* and lemon soufflé, his wide bed beneath the rooftiles in Le Panier – his heart had not been in it.

A reluctant lover, marking time.

And now, four years later, soon to be a father.

The news had stunned her. But as she cut up past the spotlit Hôtel de Ville into the stepped warren of Le Panier she decided that it was not necessarily an obstacle.

Because there was still something there between them, she was sure of it.

Maybe she had been wrong four years ago.

Maybe she had just misread it.

Maybe his heart had been in it.

And maybe now was the time to win him back.

54

PATRIC POLINEAUX LAY ON HIS bed and looked the girl over. She was young, mid-twenties he guessed. A blonde, as requested, in a flower print dress, a red scarf tied bandeau-style across the top of her head, knotted at the back of her neck, lifting the wavy curls just so.

'Go to the window,' he growled. 'Open the shutters.'

The girl did as she was told. Crossing the room she flipped the latches and pushed the shutters open, pressing them back against the outside walls, moonlight spilling over her, turning the blonde hair a silvery white.

Polineaux sighed. So like her. Every movement, from the swirl of the dress down to the bare legs and tip-toes as the girl leaned out of the window to secure the shutters.

'Now rest against the window ledge, look out into the garden, and touch yourself, your breasts. Just softly. Nothing more. As though you are dreaming of your lover.'

Again the girl did as she was told, everything going as the younger man who'd greeted her had said it would. A bit of a hulk, she thought as her fingers slid between her breasts. Didier was his name. She'd like a bit of that, she thought. Instead she was here with the old man, her first time.

'Just do whatever he tells you,' Didier had told her, taking her

217

coat, looking her over, then leading her up the stairs to the old man's bedroom. 'There's nothing to be frightened of. It's really very easy.'

'I know who he is,' she whispered. 'Madame told me.'

'And what did Madame say?' asked Didier.

'She said he was a dangerous man. A real *parrain*. And to do as I was told or else.'

'So there you are. That's all you have to do. And it's nothing that you can't handle. Now then,' he said, coming to a stop outside Polineaux's room, his voice dropping to a whisper. 'Take off the shoes, you have to be barefoot. And remember, don't speak to him, don't say a word.'

And then he'd knocked softly, opened the door for her, and slipped away.

Down in the gardens a frog croaked over the swish-click, swish-click of the *arrosage*, the lawns drenched and sparkling in the moonlight. She wondered what it would be like to walk over that wet grass, feel it spongy and soft underfoot. To live in a house like this . . . Some people had all the luck.

'Undo the buttons,' she heard the old man say, just a shadow on the bed in the silvery darkness, his voice a little croaky, his hand waving in the air, spinning a finger, like a conductor. 'Slowly, slowly,' he added as she set to on them, a little too swiftly. 'That's better. That's better. And when you reach the waist just open the front of your dress, slip it from your shoulders.'

When she'd finished with the buttons, the girl used both hands, left hand to right shoulder, then right hand to left shoulder, fingers slipping beneath the silk, lifting it, pushing it away. Shrugging out of it. Letting the top of the dress slide down her arms, to fall around her waist.

She heard the sigh across the room, over the croaking of the frog and the swishing of the sprinklers. A long, drawn out sigh. Had she done enough? she wondered. Had he finished already? Money for old rope if he had, she thought; if that was all it was.

'Move away from the window, *ma chérie*, but stay in the

218

moonlight,' she heard him say. '*Voilà*, just there, that's perfect. Now slip off the dress . . .' which she did with a coquettish wriggle, '. . . that's right, and now raise your arms, like a dancer . . . untie the scarf, let it drop . . . and tip back your head, shake out your hair . . . *Parfait, parfait.*'

She did exactly as he told her, beginning now to enjoy the performance, being directed like this, not having to think. And far enough away from the bed to feel safe, unless he had a gun to hand. She stiffened at the thought, felt a shiver race across her shoulders.

He must have noticed. 'You're cold, *chérie*, come to the bed, sit beside me, with your back to me.'

She did as she was told. The bed was hard and she could smell him now, a spray of cologne not strong enough to cover the scent of embrocation, bad breath, of those hidden places. Old man smell. And this one with no legs. She prayed he wouldn't want to kiss her.

That's when she heard the rustle of the sheet that covered him, sensed the give in the mattress and felt his fingers on her back. Long, soft strokes, the backs of his knuckly fingers.

'In the bedside drawer,' he said, 'you'll find a pack of cigarettes. Light one, smoke it.'

She leaned forward, slid open the drawer, found the cigarettes, a lighter. She put one to her lips and raised the lighter. Lucky she smoked, she thought.

'Turn away when you light it,' she heard him say, and she did as she was told. Flick, flick; the flame held and she touched it to the cigarette, inhaled. Menthol. They were menthol cigarettes. She hated menthol. But she smoked it, breathing it in, softly whistling it out.

'Where are you, my love?' she heard him whisper, softly, wistfully, almost under his breath. 'Where did you go? Why did you leave me?'

She wondered what to do, whether she should respond in some way. She'd been told not to speak but it seemed wrong not to answer.

What to do? What to do?

And what should she do with the cigarette?

Where should she put the ash?

And then, from nowhere, out of the moonlit darkness, came the slap to the side of her head, a massive weighty blow that snapped her teeth together, rocked her head on her shoulders, and sent stars spinning across her eyes. The cigarette spun from her fingers, skittered across the tiled floor.

'Bitch!' he screamed. 'Bitch, bitch, bitch!' And she felt his fingers wrap round her arm, pull her to him, shake her. And another mighty slap followed the first, to the other side of her head this time, as she struggled to get away from him, sliding off the bed, knees on the floor, her arm still held by that clawing grip, desperately trying to pull free, too stunned to cry out, to fight back.

'Whore-bitch. You whore-bitch,' he swore, gripping her arm with one hand, swiping at her with the other. 'How dare you do that? How dare you do that? To me. To *me*.' One dizzying blow after another, punctuating the words, until she was aware of light from the bedroom door, light from the hallway, and Didier hurrying towards her, loosening the old man's grip, pulling her away, scooping up her clothes, dragging her across the room, out of the door, the old man still swiping at thin air, ranting like a madman.

'He's crazy,' she screamed, tasting blood on her lip, wiping it away. 'He's fucking crazy.'

'There, there,' said Didier. 'It's fine, it's fine. Everything's fine now. There, there . . .' And he held her to him until the shaking stopped.

55

IT WAS CURIOSITY. NOTHING MORE. The cop's curse, thought Jacquot as he selected three of Philo's books from the main cabin – a Maigret story by Simenon, a Dumas, and a Balzac – and set off the following morning at a steady amble for rue Céline.

Just a couple of blocks from the Opera House, rue Céline and its neighbouring thoroughfares were a night-time favourite with ladies of a certain age and straitened means. As soon as the sun had set and the shops on Céline had brought down their shutters, these colourful exotics took up residence in doorways, under street-lights, and on corners – where the trade was always brisker. The area was safe for what they had in mind, and central, and close to their homes in Réformé and Belle de Mai and Breteuil, and a number of short-time, ask-no-questions hotels were close at hand to serve their requirements.

In daylight there was nothing but the occasional neon hotel sign still flickering above a doorway to suggest these streets might serve another role after dark. Now, at a little after 9 a.m. on a weekday morning, there was a busy hum of activity on Céline: cars sliding carefully between the bollards that marked out pavements in these narrow streets, shoppers with their bags and prams, pigeons pecking and strutting. There was a mixed scent of ripe fruit and coffee, baking bread and the sea, and the morning sun cut along its length like a slice of butter.

At this time of the morning, the sun had yet to strike Librairie Santal, its awning still rolled, a line of trestle tables set out on the pavement and laden with wooden boxes, each crammed with books, spines to the sky. Jacquot pushed in through the glass door, a bell on a spring announced his arrival, and the smell of ancient leather filled his nostrils. The books on display outside the shop might have been used paperbacks but the shelves inside were lined with books of a different character. Coffee table tomes on art and architecture, travel and fashion, scholarly works on science and history, biography and the classics, all of them second-hand but all in excellent condition. As Jacquot went deeper into the shop the darker the passage way between the bookshelves became, the dustier and more valuable the stock: leather-bound collections, fine gold lettering on scarlet squares, spines ribbed and rubbed, the dusty scent of the centuries.

At the very back of the shop, sitting at a roll-top desk stuffed with papers, was an overweight gentleman in brown cords, a plain blue shirt and extravagantly dotted bow-tie. With a pair of tortoise-shell spectacles on the point of his nose, he had the look of a university professor, Jacquot thought, and glanced at the jacket on the back of his chair to see if the sleeves had patches. They did. Suede.

The man looked up at Jacquot, as he would any browser, smiled briefly and went back to the auction catalogue he was reading. When Jacquot failed to move on, the shopkeeper looked back, removed his glasses, put down the catalogue and gave another longer smile.

'M'sieur, *bonjour*. Can I help you?'

'I hope so,' said Jacquot, and he offered the books he had brought with him, tucked under his arm.

The bookseller – Santal, Jacquot assumed – reached out a weary hand, took the books, and slipped his glasses back on.

'Ah, Honoré,' he said, when he came to the Balzac. He riffled through the pages like a card sharp. One of Philo's bookmarks spun out and landed in his lap. Santal picked it up, glanced at it, then jammed it back in the book. 'The great realist, *n'est-ce pas*? Proust? Zola? Flaubert? All of them in de Balzac's debt.'

Having thus established his credentials – not just a shopkeeper, but an authority on his stock and subject – Santal put down the book, took off his spectacles again, and looked back at Jacquot.

'So? What can I do for you? You want a price? Ten francs the three.' He smiled, slipped his spectacles back on.

An offer made, to be accepted or not.

Nothing further in this transaction.

'I regret that they're not for sale,' Jacquot said, with a sad smile. 'But I believe they came from your shop . . . Monsieur Santal?'

'Santal, that's right. Emile Santal. *C'est moi*.' He flicked the cover on each of the three books until he came to the Santal stamp. 'Ah, yes. At least one of them, it would appear. And the Dumas and Simenon do look familiar.'

'I wondered if you remembered the man who bought them?'

Santal gave Jacquot a look, over his spectacles, and chuckled.

'I may not get much custom, Monsieur, but enough, I assure you, not to be able to remember everyone who walks through that door.' He nodded past the crowded bookshelves, to the front of the shop.

'His name was Philo. His friends called him The Scholar.'

Santal started shaking his head.

'An old man, about so high . . .' Jacquot continued, holding a hand level with his upper arm. Wondering why he was bothering with this charade. This was going nowhere. And then he remembered the name that Salette had mentioned. 'Perhaps you might recall his proper name. Emanetti. Niko Emanetti.'

'Ahhh, Monsieur Niko,' said Santal, with the same warm familiar affection that he'd shown just a few moments earlier for Honoré de Balzac. '*Mais oui, bien sûr*. Of course. Of course. You should have said. So how is he? How is he?'

And that was the moment Santal's expression changed, a bright smile of recognition reduced to a sudden frown, his eyes fixing on Jacquot.

'He's all right, isn't he?'

'I regret, Monsieur, that Monsieur Emanetti has passed away.'

'Oh, I am so sorry,' said Santal, the breath almost snatched from him. *'Mais c'est affreux. Affreux. Quelle tristesse.'*

Jacquot was surprised to see how badly, how genuinely, Santal had been affected by the news.

So not just any old customer, then.

'Is there a funeral?' he asked. 'I must go. *Il faut respecter . . .'*

'Again I regret . . . He was buried some weeks ago. At sea. Only close family.'

'At sea? Monsieur Emanetti?'

'Alors, he was a sailor after all.'

'A sailor? Then it must have been a shipping line he owned.' Santal chuckled again, deep and throaty. Then he frowned, gave Jacquot a long look. 'And you? You are family. His son, perhaps?'

Jacquot shook his head. 'I was . . . left his books.'

Santal held the look a moment longer. 'Then you are a lucky man, Monsieur. It is a truly wonderful collection.'

Now it was Jacquot's turn to frown – still pondering the 'shipping line' comment – and thought of the books on *Constance*. They were well kept, and they represented a wide range of writers and subjects. But apart from a few volumes, like the ones he had brought with him, they were mostly paperbacks. Nothing he had seen was of any obvious worth.

'You have spoken to Joubert, of course,' continued Santal.

'Joubert?'

'Philippe Joubert. Senior curator at the Musée Bibliothèque in Aix. The bulk of Monsieur Emanetti's collection is kept there, but only on loan, I understand. They could be taken back very easily, although Joubert would have something to say about it, I can assure you.'

'You said "the bulk" of the collection?'

'The good stuff. The jewels. The rest, call it the second division

224

– the folios, the prints – well, I assume, Monsieur, that they are at his home.' He looked at Jacquot as though Jacquot should know that.

'In Madrague?'

'Madrague? *Non, non, non*. In Roucas Blanc.'

'Ah, the Roucas property,' said Jacquot, nodding but trying hard to keep up.

'Les Étagères. Rue Savry. A sense of humour, Monsieur Niko. Always cracking a joke.'

Les Étagères. Shelves, thought Jacquot.

'I went there once,' continued Santal, fondly now. 'To deliver an order.'

'You supplied his collection?'

'Sometimes, if I found something of interest. If I knew he was looking for something.' Santal frowned. He had realised he didn't know who he was talking to. 'And you are, Monsieur . . . ?'

'Jacquot. Daniel Jacquot. Niko was my uncle.'

Santal's eyes narrowed. Either he recognised the name, thought Jacquot, or he'd smelled the possibility of making some more money.

'Did you know Niko long?' asked Jacquot, lying casually, sensing he'd get more from this man if he continued to present himself as a family member and not a police officer. He was pleased to see that the reference to his 'uncle' had worked its magic.

'A good twenty years now,' replied Santal, not even needing to think about it. 'Without question, my longest, my most loyal and best customer.'

'Do you remember when he last visited?'

'Maybe six months ago. The start of summer. I had found him a near perfect sixteenth-century first edition of Cristoforo da Messisbugo's *Banchetti, composizioni di vivande e apparecchio generale*. He had been searching a long time for it.'

'Did he buy it?'

'A Messisbugo? *Mais oui*. An edition like that? In that condition? It was an opportunity not to be missed.'

'A cookery book, if I'm not mistaken.'

'But for some, like Monsieur Niko, *the* cookery book.' Santal paused. 'You are a collector yourself, Monsieur Jacquot?'

'I take an interest, certainly, though my uncle was the expert.'

'Well, Monsieur Jacquot,' Santal continued, somehow managing not to rub his hands together at the sudden and pleasant prospect of resupplying or selling the collection on the estate's behalf, and taking his commission, 'if there is anything that Librairie Santal can do to help, in terms of looking out interesting items . . . ?' He tapped the catalogue on his desk. 'Or if any sale must be effected . . . ?'

'Then I will certainly be in touch,' Jacquot replied, anxious now to be gone.

To Les Étagères, in rue Savry, Roucas Blanc.

At the earliest opportunity.

It was then that he remembered the other reason he had called.

'Ah, I had almost forgotten,' he began. 'In those other two books – the Dumas and Simenon – there's an ex-libris label and another stamp.'

Santal flicked open the covers, read the names, then handed the books back.

'Lycée Simon? Long gone. Over in Belle de Mai. I cleared it myself.'

'And Edina?'

Santal gave a grunt, lowered his head and peered at Jacquot over his spectacles. 'You didn't know Edina?'

A trap sprung. A nimble sidestep required. All he could assume was that whoever Edina was, she was no more.

'I didn't know she collected books, too,' said Jacquot, hoping for the best. The deception seemed to work.

Santal tapped the book with Edina's name inside, nodded with an indulgent enthusiasm.

'She loved her Simenons, did Madame. The *policiers*, the whodunits. Jules Maigret was her favourite, but no surprise in that. The master, *hein*? No one comes close. Not even now.' Santal

226

sighed. 'But that is as far as it went. Really, she was very patient with Monsieur Niko and his esoteric, expensive tastes.'

And with that, not wishing to risk another careless question about Edina, Jacquot took his leave, putting the three books from *Constance* under his arm, and shaking Santal's hand.

He would find out what he wanted to know soon enough.

And if he didn't, he could always have Isabelle call back in a professional capacity.

56

IF JACQUOT HAD EXPECTED Les Étagères to live up to its name, the house lined with bookshelves, he was sorely mistaken. There was not a book to be seen.

Les Étagères was one of only three properties on rue Savry, a narrow, tree-shaded *impasse* in the prestigious Roucas Blanc district of Marseilles. Occupying a series of wooded ridges between the city centre and the beaches of Prado this sixth *arrondissement* is quiet, secluded and thickly planted with cypress, palm and spreading pine, the homes within it high-walled and gated, only their upper floors and tiled gables visible from the street. Security cameras top the gates of most of these properties, but Les Étagères boasted no such adornment, its wrought-iron gates set between stone pillars and left invitingly open to the road.

The house was not the grandest that Jacquot had visited in Roucas Blanc – the old Cabrille mansion just a few blocks away probably took that prize – but Les Étagères was still a valuable slice of real estate built on the coastal side of a hill, with tantalising views of the islands beyond the Corniche road. Judging by its low, rounded stone balconies and its metal-framed windows Jacquot decided the house had probably been built in the early thirties, an Art Deco seaside villa for a wealthy *Marseillais* businessman. Large spikey aloes lined the drive and forecourt where Jacquot parked, and the half-dozen front steps were wide enough to accommodate a pair of glazed terracotta pots on each, tumbling with sweet smelling purple georgettes.

Jacquot had rung the doorbell, had picked up the buzz somewhere inside the house, and was waiting for the door to open when he heard a voice behind him.

'Monsieur? *Bonjour*.'

Jacquot turned. The woman was in her late thirties, he guessed, slim and gently tanned, with a tumble of blonde hair bound in a cream bandeau. In her Capri pants and man's shirt, its tails knotted at her waist, a basket of fruit on her arm, she looked almost Nordic.

Coming back down the steps, Jacquot reached out a hand and introduced himself as Chief Inspector Jacquot of the *Judiciaire*. He was technically off his beat and he hoped she didn't ask for more detail. She didn't.

'And I am Madame Jeanne Vaillant,' she said, hardly glancing at the badge that he showed. 'So how can I be of assistance, Chief Inspector?'

'I am trying to locate a Monsieur Niko Emanetti,' Jacquot began, wanting to limit the detail, to see what she might know. 'I understood that he lives here.'

'Not any more. He moved out two years ago, when my husband . . . my ex-husband . . . made an offer on the property. Somewhere to hide me away, it turned out. Though I didn't know it at the time.' She gave a small, brittle laugh, but her eyes twinkled.

'Two years ago, you say? The house was on the market?'

'Around here, nothing reaches the market, Chief Inspector. You have to know the right people. People like my ex. Please . . . I was just about to have coffee. Will you join me?'

Before Claudine, Jacquot would have recognised the look that Madame Jeanne Vaillant gave him then, and would have either acted on it or not. The gentle smile, the tilt of an eyebrow, the flicker on her lips – a whisper of promise so subtly delivered that

229

it hardly registered as she brushed past him, indicating that he should follow her.

Catching a faint trail of Chanel, he followed her into the house, across a tiled hallway, into a salon carpeted in frayed and worn kelims, and through a pair of arched french windows on to a wide balustraded terrace. From front door to terrace there was not a shelf or a book to be seen.

'You make that sound ominous . . . knowing the right people,' Jacquot said, as she showed him to a table, put down her basket and wiped a sleeve across her forehead. A maid appeared with a china pot of coffee, as though Jacquot had been expected. But there was only the one cup. A second was asked for and swiftly brought. Making himself comfortable Jacquot took in the view, the slope of the land, the terraced lawns, the cypresses that marked out the property and the sparkling blue sea that glittered distantly between their spear-tip points.

'Ominous? You're right. It is,' said Madame Vaillant, pouring him coffee, beautifully manicured fingertips holding down the lid of the pot. 'But that's how it works. Someone knocks on the door, sees that you're old, and persuades you that a smaller apartment on Prado might be a more sensible alternative, and just think of the capital released . . . Nine times out of ten you are sent on your way, but all it takes around here is one hit. And my husband is one of the best when it comes to sliding his foot into a door. All along the coast. From here to Menton. He has his own company. Basle et Cie, with a head office in Zurich. Apparently Basle is a more comforting name than Zurich – less threatening, less intimidating.'

Jacquot admitted that he didn't know the name, though he could easily imagine the kind of man she was describing and the type of operation he ran. Claudine's second husband had been like that. A property speculator, he called himself. Swindler would have been a more fitting description.

'And that is what he did with Monsieur Emanetti?'

'It just so happened that he wanted to sell. Had been thinking of getting in touch with a local *immobilier*.'

230

'Did you meet him?'

'Oh yes. A dear old man. A widower. His wife had died and he lived here alone. Such a big place.'

'As your husband would have pointed out, no doubt?'

Jeanne Vaillant smiled. 'Ex-husband, remember. And yes, more than likely,' she admitted. She glanced at Jacquot's shoes. 'You look as if you've been fishing, Chief Inspector.'

He looked at his Docksiders and caught the glitter of fish scales.

'You'd make a good detective,' he said.

'Oh, I don't think so,' she replied, tucking a stray blonde curl back beneath the bandeau. 'I was never really cut out for work, if you know what I mean?'

He smiled, considered the woman sitting across the table. No, you probably weren't, he thought. But he guessed that whatever Jeanne Vaillant had done to end up in a house like this, she had probably done it extremely well.

'You said his wife had died?'

'That's correct. Shortly before we met, before the sale. But there were photos of her, of the two of them, all over the house. And paintings too. Portraits. She was a beautiful woman.'

'Do you happen to know how she died?'

Madame Vaillant shook her head.

'I didn't want to pry, Chief Inspector, and he didn't volunteer any information. But it was clear that he had been deeply affected by the death. It was as though he didn't want to be in the house any longer than he had to be. Memories, I suppose.'

'Did you see much of him?'

'When the sale had been agreed and contracts were being drawn up I used to pop round – taking measurements, all that kind of thing. He was always very welcoming. *Très sympa*. Nothing was too much trouble. Once he prepared lunch for me, out here on the terrace. Great hunks of bread and hard cheese and pâtés that had seen their finest hour . . .' she chuckled at the memory '. . . and the roughest, roughest white wine – you wouldn't believe. Such a strange person. On the one hand a knowledgeable, cultured man,

231

something of a scholar one might say – the books, the paintings – but on the other, *à table*, for example, well . . . not to put too fine a point on it, he was . . . *un paysan*. Oh, and the most outrageous flirt, Chief Inspector. He must have been in his late seventies but sometimes, when he looked at me . . . well, let's just say I could feel his eyes all over me.'

'This may seem a very strange question, Madame, but . . . did he have teeth?'

'Dentures. Sometimes he shifted them in his mouth. It was quite disconcerting and somehow . . . well, suggestive.' She chuckled again. 'The way he did it, the way he looked at you when he did it.' She raised a hand to her face, fanned her cheek. '*Ooh là là . . .*'

If she could have blushed, Jacquot was certain she would have done. But a woman like Madame Jeanne Vaillant, he suspected, was long past blushing.

'He liked his books, I understand.'

'Books everywhere. Good books, too, by the look of them. Leather bound. Shelves in every room. It took days to dismantle them all, get them out. And the space without those shelves, Chief Inspector, you wouldn't believe. The house was so dark when I first came here.'

'And the paintings? You said he had paintings.'

'Apart from the portraits of his wife, his preferred subjects were nautical. Every single one. Ships at sea, in storms, in battle. You know the sort of thing.'

'And do you have any idea where he went, after the move?'

She shook her head. 'I'm sorry. He left no forwarding address. When I asked about mail, that sort of thing, he said I was not to worry. His lawyer would take care of everything.'

'Do you happen to remember the name of the lawyer?'

'A firm in Avignon. Cluzot Fils. I don't have a number, I'm afraid, and I no longer have the address, but I'm sure they're in the book.'

Jacquot finished his coffee, and pushed away from the table, got to his feet.

232

'Are you leaving? Is there anything else . . . ?'

'Madame, you have been most helpful.'

'Tell me,' she said, also getting to her feet and indicating the garden steps, 'has Monsieur Emanetti done something dreadful? Is he a wanted man? Will I have to dig up my terraces?'

'At the moment it's nothing more than a general enquiry. Another investigation. His name cropped up.'

'Well, if there's anything else I can help you with, Chief Inspector . . . don't hesitate to drop by,' she said, as she led him along a gravelled garden path, back to the front of the house.

'You can rely on it, Madame.'

57

NEIGHBOURS. NEIGHBOURS WERE ALWAYS A good bet. Even within the guarded, private estates of Roucas Blanc, people saw things, people heard things. The people who lived in these privileged suburbs, and the people who worked for them, coming in from the narrow alleyways of Le Panier across the harbour, and the concrete blocks of the *projets* in the city's northern suburbs.

After leaving Madame Vaillant, Jacquot drove through her gates and parked fifty metres further along rue Savry. The next house he tried, its gates closed, its grounds enclosed by high stone walls draped in morning glory, showed shuttered windows on the second floor, and despite three long buzzes on the entryphone there was no answer to his call.

At the third house, across the road, a smaller property with no view of the sea, he had more success and took another coffee with the old lady who lived there. A widow. Madame Nallet. She was plump and friendly, and clearly pleased to have some company. Her hair was tightly permed, like a bouffant helmet, creamy white with a rose shadowing, and thin enough to show the shiny skin on her scalp. As she led him into the house, a pair of dachshunds yapped at his heels and skidded around him on the tiled floor. She shushed them but they paid no attention.

'Nelli and Maria. After Melba and Callas,' she told him. Her late husband, she explained, had been music director at the Opéra Garnier in Paris, before retiring and coming south. It had been his little joke, she explained; such shrieky little barks.

In the small salon where they settled the walls were covered with old black-and-white photos of a younger Madame Nallet on the arm of her husband – in gowns and tails, at first nights and at fancy restaurants – and the polished top of a grand piano in a corner of the room was similarly crowded with signed and silver-framed photos of the pair of them with famous operatic stars: Domingo, Caballé, Pavarotti, Luchese and the aforementioned Callas. Above the hearth was an oil painting of a maddened Othello beside a clearly deceased Desdemona. He held a hand to his heart, an arm flung out, the whites of his eyes rolling in a black face, his mouth a twisted rictus of despair.

'Did you sing, Madame?' asked Jacquot. She certainly had the build and bearing of an opera singer.

'I was in the orchestra. I played the cello.'

Jacquot nodded.

'Charles, my husband, used to tell people: "She played cello. What can I say? I married her."' Daringly, to show him what she meant, Madame Nallet parted her knees and pushed her skirt between her thighs to mimic the placement of the cello. '*Voilà*,' she said, rearranging herself, and the chuckle turned into a fond laugh. 'So, Chief Inspector. How can I be of assistance?'

Jacquot crossed his legs, remembered the fish scales, uncrossed them and tucked his shoes under his chair. He began by asking about Philo – Niko Emanetti – but there wasn't much she could tell him.

'He was never really around. At least, that's how it seemed. I'd see him every now and again, but I never really . . . got to know him. Short, wiry, brown as a nutmeg. He had the look of an old fisherman . . . a bit of an eccentric, if you ask me. Must have been in his late sixties, seventies when we moved here, but still with the magic, if you know what I mean? The odd occasions we met, well . . . he had it. The way he looked at you. Must have been a naughty boy in his time.' Madame Nallet chuckled again at the thought.

'What about his wife? Edina?'

'Oh Eddie! Yes, I knew Eddie. Far better than I knew him. What a beauty. Much younger than him, of course. But not his wife, Chief Inspector. They wore rings, but . . .' Madame Nallet shrugged, as though such a thing was of no importance. 'She'd been married before, you see? I don't know to whom, she never mentioned his name, but she told me about him. Like Monsieur Emanetti, he was older than her. I gained the impression she preferred older men. Some of us are like that. And pay the price with a lonely old age.' She waved her hand as though to dismiss such a self-pitying thought and her lips tightened around a sad smile. 'But this one, the one Eddie was married to, was a bully. Early on it had all been wonderful, she told me, but after they married, it changed. So what's new, *hein*?'

Jacquot nodded, agreed that, sadly, that was often the case.

Was offered more coffee, but declined.

'He beat her up,' Madame Nallet went on. 'Any excuse. Jealous. Jealous. Jealous. And she grew to be terrified of him. He sounded like a real low life. But rich. A lot of money. A gangster, that's what he sounded like. Some horrible *gorille*, if you'll pardon the expression. She was well rid of him, if you ask me.'

'There were children?'

'Not that I know of. She never said.'

'They divorced?'

'Oh no! *Mais non*. No divorce. He'd have killed her before they got to the lawyer's office. That's what she told me. She simply ran, she said. Left him. Jumped in the car and was gone. Disappeared. But, of course, she had Niko. The love of her life, she said. He helped her. He set her up, took care of her. Moved her from Nice. Brought her up here. But Nice is still close, *n'est-ce pas*? She didn't go out much. They kept to themselves. Except for the holidays, of course.'

'They travelled a lot?'

'Always away somewhere. Four or five times a year. At least. America, which they both loved. The Far East. Africa. Always off on some jaunt or other.'

'And how long did they live here?'

Madame Nallet gave it some thought. 'A long time, long before Charles and I arrived from Paris.'

'*Dites-moi*, Madame, did Monsieur Emanetti work? Did he have a job?'

'I understood that he had family money. That's what Eddie told me.'

'It sounds as though the two of you were great friends.'

'I suppose we were. She was such a sweet thing. You couldn't help but love her. So full of life. So gay. Yet underneath, a sense of fear, you know? Always there. As though she was afraid that brute of a husband would find her. Afraid of what he might do. To her. To Monsieur Niko.'

'I understand she died? Not so long ago.'

'Ah, so sad. So, so sad. So young, too. In her fifties. She can't have been more.'

'And how, exactly . . . ?'

'Cancer. It had spread. She went down very fast. Here one day, gone the next. I hadn't seen her for a few weeks, thought they might be away on one of their trips. Then she called, asked me round. She was on a day bed in the salon, facing the sea, propped up. I took one look and knew at once that she was doomed. There was no chance. *La pauvre.*'

'And how did Monsieur Emanetti take it? Her death.'

'He was brave. But you could see it hurt. Hurt terribly. The light went out in his eyes. Soon after, the house was sold and he was gone. I have no idea where he went.'

Madame Nallet gave Jacquot a look. He knew what she wanted to ask, what she suspected.

'I'm afraid Monsieur Emanetti has died, too, Madame. A couple of months ago.'

'Of a broken heart, *je suis certain*. He was devastated. *Si désolé.*'

'I understand the house is now owned by a Madame Vaillant,' said Jacquot, not wishing to let Madame Nallet know that he had already called on her. It would be interesting to hear what she had to say.

'Is that her name? I didn't know. We haven't met.'

Jacquot sensed a certain shortness in the tone. He wasn't surprised. He doubted the two women would have had much in common. He said nothing, waited.

'There are parties, Chief Inspector. Late at night. A lot of noise. A lot of visitors. It is not . . . considerate, you understand.'

'Quite so,' replied Jacquot. 'Well, Madame. Thank you for your time. And the coffee.'

Sensing a movement, Nellie and Maria scrabbled to their feet, and started up their yapping again. Despite her admonishments, the two dogs kept it up all the way to the front door. They only fell silent when he turned out of the gates, with a final wave from Madame Nallet.

58

THAT EVENING, WHILE CLAUDINE BAKED the plump, silvery sea bream that he had brought back from Marseilles' Quai des Belges fish market – stuffed with fennel, doused in Vermouth, coated in rough sea salt and wrapped in foil – Jacquot phoned Philippe Joubert.

Like Santal, the senior curator at the Musée Bibliothèque in Aix had not heard of Philo's death. He sounded just as shocked as Santal, and for much the same reason, Jacquot suspected, more concerned that his collection might be removed than by the passing of its owner. Playing the same role that he had played with Santal, nephew as executor, Jacquot established that Joubert had met Philo on a number of occasions.

'Such a wonderful, dare I say, eccentric gentleman?' Joubert had spouted. 'A bibliophile to the very tips of his fingers. Not to mention a hugely generous patron of the Museum.'

Jacquot had picked up on the eccentric. 'How so?' he asked, trying to put a face to Joubert. Longish hair, he decided, parted in the middle. A cardigan. Moroccan slippers.

'Oh, so many things,' Joubert began. 'One time, at a reception, he turned up dressed like a fisherman. Can you imagine? The great and the good of Aix and Avignon and he turns up in a hat with a gold anchor on the brim, a big roly-poly fishermen's jumper, rough cotton ducks and down-at-heel espadrilles. He was always playing these little tricks. Always a glint in his eye.'

'Did my uncle tell you how he acquired the collection?'

There was a pause down the line, and a cautious, quiet '*non*', as though he was about to learn something he didn't want to hear. 'He just said that he had loved books since childhood, had been collecting for years.'

'Quite true,' said Jacquot. 'I never saw him without a book in his hand. A real scholar, despite appearances. So tell me, Monsieur, how long has the collection been with you?'

'A little over two years. Monsieur Emanetti said he needed more space, that the insurance was becoming . . . burdensome.' Joubert gave a chuckle. As if . . .

'I wonder, could you put a price on my uncle's collection?'

Another pause. 'That's difficult to say, without a proper audit . . .'

'Roughly. For tax, death duties, you understand. I will need to make proper declarations.'

'Of course, of course. Well, let's see. Maybe . . . somewhere in the region of . . . say, three, maybe four million francs.'

If Jacquot could have whistled, he would have. Books worth four million francs? A house in Roucas Blanc? Was there any possibility he was mistaken, that Santal had got it all wrong, sent him off on the wrong track, that the Niko Emanetti they were discussing had nothing to do with the Philo whose motor cruiser he now owned? But there was no chance of that. The evidence from Jeanne Vaillant and Madame Nallet was all too compelling. Right down to the dentures.

'Thank you, Monsieur Joubert. You have been most helpful.'

'I am only too happy to have been of assistance,' he replied. 'And so sorry for your loss.' Then, a little tentatively: 'And the collection?' he asked, finally summoning the nerve to ask the only question he really needed an answer to. 'What do you suppose the estate will want to do with the collection?'

'Unless you hear otherwise, I have no doubt that it will remain with you for some time, Monsieur Joubert.'

Breaking the connection, Jacquot called the number he had found for Maître Cluzot of Cluzot Fils in Avignon. The office was closed but his call was redirected to an out-of-hours answering service. After Jacquot mentioned the words 'Chief Inspector' and '*Judiciaire*', the woman at the end of the line was quite happy to pass on Cluzot's home number.

The lawyer, Jacquot decided when he heard the voice, sounded fat, prosperous and heavily jowled, a little breathless too, probably from carrying around too much weight. Like Joubert and Santal, he was unaware that his client had died.

'Funny little fellow,' Cluzot admitted, after passing on his condolences. 'Played havoc with the secretaries whenever he called by. A wink, a pinch even. But they all adored him. And he was hardly a picture, Chief Inspector.'

'I believe you acted for Monsieur Emanetti in the sale of his home?'

'That is correct.'

'It was sold to a Monsieur Vaillant, I believe?'

'*En effet*, to a company called Basle et Cie.'

Made sense, thought Jacquot. He wondered if Madame Vaillant knew who owned her home. He had a feeling she didn't.

'And the price?' he asked

'I don't have the figures . . .'

'Roughly,' said Jacquot, just as he'd said to Joubert.

'After the various taxes and fees, Chief Inspector, a little over twelve million francs.'

Jacquot had been expecting something substantial; he wasn't disappointed. But there was more.

'As for the contents,' Cluzot continued without any prompting, 'the house was cleared of all but a few personal possessions by an auction house here in Avignon. After the various sales, the cheques started coming in, to be added to Monsieur Emanetti's account.'

'And the proceeds of those sales? The contents. How much?' Jacquot was thinking of the 'second-division' book collection that

Santal had mentioned, the portraits and nautical paintings that Madame Vaillant had told him about, along with the usual furnishings, fixtures and fittings.

'A little in excess of four million francs,' said Cluzot. 'The money from Basle et Cie, and from the various auction houses, was paid into our client account.'

'What about his bank?'

'If he had one, I didn't know about it.'

'So what happened to the money? From the house sale and the auctions?'

'A number of disbursements. Bequests.'

'All of it?'

'Every last *sou*, all drawn on our firm's account. I arranged payment on the last one only a few weeks ago.'

'To whom?'

'A refuge in Marseilles. For abused women. Run by nuns. A cash settlement. Anonymously. Like all the rest.'

'Why the delay getting them the money?'

'There were many bequests, Monsieur. And many of the designated beneficiaries were hard to find.'

Cluzot heard the silence, and quickly continued: 'Of course, all earned interest to the date of disbursement was apportioned equally amongst said beneficiaries. As I said there's not a *sou* left. The account was closed after that final payment.'

'Who else benefited? The other beneficiaries?' Apart from me, he thought.

'Oh, there were so many. A sailors' mission in Genoa. The Musée de la Mer in Sanary. An old cinema in Nice, scheduled for demolition. And to make matters more complicated, many of the recipients were overseas: a wonderful charity digging water wells in remote areas of India; farm collectives in Kenya and Malawi; a school for blind children in the Philippines. Apparently most of the children were blinded while suffering from measles. That's what he told me. The strong sunlight, you understand. The parents didn't realise . . .' Down the line Jacquot heard Cluzot sigh. 'The list,

Chief Inspector, was extensive. But we did it all. As instructed by our client. Everything above board.'

Jacquot remembered the holidays. Africa, India, the Far East, Madame Nallet had told him. It all made sense. A remarkable kind of sense. But where had all the money come from?

Over by the oven, Claudine was unwrapping the bream. A cloud of steam billowed from the opened foil and the warm scent of aniseed filled the room. She caught Jacquot's eye, tapped her watch.

'*Alors*, Maître Cluzot, you have been most helpful.'

'*À votre service*, Chief Inspector. If there is anything else I can help you with?'

Jacquot assured him that he would be in touch if that turned out to be the case, and with further thanks he brought the call to a close.

'That looks wonderful,' said Jacquot, replacing the phone.

'You don't deserve it,' Claudine replied, trying to dodge the kiss he was intent on placing on her neck. 'On the phone all night. You're on sick leave, remember?'

'This is not police business, my darling,' he replied, managing to place his kiss, then taking his seat at the kitchen table.

'And my name is Jacques Chirac.'

'*Alors*, if that's how you want it, Monsieur *le Président* . . .'

59

JULES RANQUE WAS BADLY LATE. His wife would not be
amused. They had agreed to meet at Mirador on the old port at
eight-thirty, and it was already well past that as he spun down Quai
Rive Neuve looking for somewhere to park. He had booked the
table a week before. It was their anniversary, twenty years together,
the only blight in their time together their inability to have children.
Ranque wondered how much money they must have wasted on
IVF treatment, and wondered, too, how much longer he could
sidestep the increasingly broached subject of adoption.

Jesus Christ, over his dead body, he thought. He knew the way
the system worked. They'd fill in enough forms to clog up an entire
government office, and their backgrounds, the lives they led, the
friends they kept would be picked over with a fine-toothed comb.
And he couldn't even pull any strings. When it came to adoption
the authorities were rigorously inaccessible. Not that he would have
tried to twist any arms, though his wife had suggested it on more
than one occasion.

Because go the adoption route and what did you get? What was
on offer? Nothing white, that was a sure-fire goddamn' certainty.
Black, or yellow, or Arab, or soft in the head, or in some other
way disabled. Certainly disadvantaged. And the Lord alone knew
what kind of genes – some low-life loser getting another low-life

loser pregnant. Not that his wife seemed to mind. Anything would do so long as she could hold it and cuddle it and dote on it, and pretend it was hers.

Nature not nurture. That was what Ranque had learned after twenty years in the prison service. It didn't matter how damn much you cared for the little bastards and loved them, the money you spent on them, the schools you sent them to, the home life you provided. Ten, twelve years down the road, something clicks in and the kid goes wrong – after all you've done, all the money you've spent. The genes win out. No argument.

Tucking the car into a space off place Sadi-Carnot, Ranque switched off the engine and reached for his wallet, slid out a small paper wrap and looked around, checked the wing mirrors, rear-view mirror. No one about, the pavements empty both sides of the street. A couple of lines left, he estimated, carefully opening the wrap. Might as well do a big one, he decided, and tapped the remaining white powder on to the back of his left hand. With his right hand he took a Biro from his inside pocket, flipped off the cap and with his teeth pulled out the ink tube. A perfect funnel.

With a finger on one nostril, and one end of the tube in the other, he held the tip of the Biro over the coke and hoovered up the pile in a single take, just the one nostril. A lick of the hand to pick up the dust, a few stinging sniffs, and he waited a second or two for the first numbing lump of snot to slide down the back of his throat. Which it did, like a sweet, silvery snail. Swallowing and savouring the slippery wad, he pulled down the sun visor and checked himself in the mirror. Wetting the tip of his finger, he removed a few white crumbs from his moustache and licked them up, then wiped a handkerchief over his nose and mouth.

There, he thought. Much, much better. A drink, a good meal, a subtle steering of the conversation away from adoption, and the prospect of a table at Mirador, even with the wife, seemed to shine on the horizon like a golden light. He was home free.

Opening the car door, he struggled out and stooped down to lock it, fumbling with the key, his hand shaking as the coke hit.

Ranque didn't hear the motorbike, or if he did he paid it no attention. Not even when it slowed, came to a gurgling halt beside him, as though the rider was about to park or ask for directions. As he straightened up, pocketing his keys, he turned to see the pillion rider dismount, pull something from his jacket, and saw the driver rev the engine.

The next thing he knew, the pillion rider had wrapped an arm around his shoulder and was pressing something hard and cold into his ear . . .

And then, nothing.

Part Three

60

'*ALORS*, LOOK AT YOU,' SAID the waitress, Josette, as Jacquot stepped out of the midday glare into the shadowy darkness of La Marine. 'Much, much better. Put on some weight, hardened up, if you'll excuse my French. Looks like you found yourself the right woman,' she teased. 'Last time you were here, you had the stick, that painful walk. It hurt me every step you took. Now look at you.'

Jacquot thanked her, confirmed that, indeed, a good woman had been looking after him – Josette gave a playful moue of disappointment – and asked if his friend Salette, had arrived.

'The usual table, *chéri*. Pastis, like the old man?'

Jacquot gave her a nod and a smile and made his way into the back of the bar where he found Salette.

'You're late,' the old harbour master grunted.

'Good to see you, too,' said Jacquot, pulling out a chair and sitting down. There was a basket of bread and a bowl of wrinkled black olives between them. Jacquot helped himself.

'Feel free,' said Salette, folding away the newspaper he'd been reading. 'So how's the boat?'

'Intriguing,' replied Jacquot.

Salette frowned. 'Something wrong with her?'

'No, something wrong with the previous owner.'

The frown deepened.

Salette was about to say something when Josette arrived with their drinks, set them down and asked if they wanted some lunch, recommending La Marine's *plat du jour*.

'What is it?' growled Salette.

'*S'il te plaît* . . . the magic words.' Josette tipped a wink at Jacquot.

'What is it, *s'il te plaît*, Mademoiselle?' Salette repeated through gritted teeth.

'A *bourride*. Made by Raymond's mother.' Raymond was La Marine's chef and *propriétaire*. He was a good cook but his old mother was better.

'*Bourride* then,' said Salette. '*S'il te plaît*.'

'And the same, thanks,' said Jacquot. He'd smelled the *bourride* coming in, had been keeping his fingers crossed there'd still be some left. A good *bourride* went fast.

'So, Philo,' began Salette, when Josette had gone. 'Some problem?'

'I'm not sure you've been straight with me,' began Jacquot.

'Not again,' groaned Salette. 'I told you. It's a done deal. Philo left me the boat with clear instructions to pass it on to someone appropriate. You're that appropriate person. You signed the papers. You're the owner. *Finis*.'

Jacquot nodded. 'I know that, thank you. But did *you* know that Philo was married? Well, not exactly married. But closely involved with someone . . . lived with her for more than twenty years. A woman called Edina. Eddie.'

'No, I did not. Because he was not. Married or . . . otherwise. To Edina or Eddie, or anyone else for that matter. And I should know,' Salette said, tapping a finger on the table.

Jacquot nodded, as though taking this in.

'So what about the house on rue Savry in Roucas Blanc? And his collection of books at the Musée Bibliothèque in Aix? I suppose they're not real either?'

Salette gave him a look. 'You've been drinking, boy. Or had too much sun.'

Jacquot sighed. 'J-P, believe me, it's true. All of it. The girl, the house, the books. No mistake.'

But Salette was adamant, just as Jacquot had known he would be. 'I was his executor. I'm the one who knows. Twelve hundred francs in a current account. Three thousand in a savings account. At his bank. Credit Agricole on République. I closed it all up for him. Then there was *Constance*. A few personal belongings. *C'est tout*. I told you. He was a fisherman.'

Jacquot was shaking his head. He reached for another olive, a square of bread and popped them into his mouth.

'Maybe once, sure. But not for the last twenty odd years. I know. I've checked.'

'You're dreaming. All of it. There was no woman in his life that I know about, and he sure as hell didn't have a house in Roucas Blanc, or some book collection in a museum. Just those old paperbacks. And I would have known if he was up to something,' said Salette, taking a sip of pastis. 'I knew the man more than fifty years, Daniel. Out there,' he said, nodding to the harbour and the ocean beyond. 'Fair weather and foul. You learn a lot about a man in that time. Believe me.'

At that moment, Josette arrived with their *bourrides*. Cutlery was placed, a bottle of Bandol white opened and tasted – 'with the compliments of Raymond's mother,' Josette told them – and napkins flourished and laid across laps.

'*Merci*, Josette,' said Salette, with a growl.

'*De rien*, J-P,' and wishing them, '*Bon appétit*,' she tucked her tray under her arm, readjusted her superstructure and spun away.

In silence now, the two men took their first spoonfuls, blowing across the soup to cool it. It was rust coloured and lumpy, thick as a bad cold, and the garlic hit like a peppery grenade.

'So who told you all this?' asked Salette, still not convinced, breaking off a hunk of bread to push into the soup. 'Who did you check with?'

'A rare book dealer here in Marseilles, Philo's neighbours in Roucas Blanc, a museum director in Aix, and his lawyer in Avignon.'

251

'A lawyer now? An Avignon lawyer?'

'He acted for Philo in the sale of the house in Roucas Blanc, and with various bequests.'

'And this lawyer, and the others, they confirmed his identity? You showed them a photograph?'

Jacquot admitted that he had not, but that there was no doubt about it. Then he changed tack.

'*Dis-moi* . . . What did Philo do after the fishing stopped? When he was too old to go out? You, you moved to the *Capitainerie* here in Marseilles, got to be harbour master. And Bruno, harbour master at L'Estaque; Laurent, repairing nets in Madrague and running that chandlery in Pointe Rouge. But what did Philo do?'

Salette raised a hand, waved at Josette. She came over with the soup tureen and ladled more *bourride* into his bowl, the tureen pressing against her breast, swelling it, deepening her cleavage with every dip. The view settled him, and Jacquot could see he was thinking, giving consideration to the question.

'For you, *chéri*?' asked Josette.

Jacquot pushed his bowl in her direction. 'Delicious. Of course.'

After she had gone, Jacquot pressed his point. 'Well? He must have done something.'

'He took a job with an outfit called Tours d'Azur, out of Cannes. Long gone now, of course. Private charters, that sort of thing. The calanques. The islands. Did it maybe ten, twelve years. On and off.'

'On and off,' repeated Jacquot. 'So how often did you see each other? You and Philo. After the fishing. When he was skippering and you were harbour-mastering.'

'*La Fraternité* mostly. That's how we kept in touch. That's why we started it.' The Brotherhood was a group of old sea salts like Salette who met up every now and again for a good lunch. Sometimes it was once a week, other times, Jacquot knew, months would pass. 'And then there was *Constance*. Sometimes we'd meet up there . . .'

'And outside the Brotherhood? And *Constance*? How often?'

252

'Now and again. Nothing regular. *Alors*, we all had our lives to live.'

'Exactly,' said Jacquot. 'And in Philo's case, a life none of you knew about. A double life. Like the man who marries two women, supports two different families, in two different towns. It happens all the time. Sometimes they get found out. And sometimes they don't.'

'So he's a bigamist now . . .'

'J-P, I'm not saying you didn't know your friend, but there's more here than a good run of cards and luck with the ladies. A great deal more. Your friend Philo was a wealthy man. Very wealthy. What I'm saying is that you knew only what he wanted you to know.'

Salette spooned up some soup, pushed bread into his mouth, shook his head. Jacquot could see that he was getting tetchy. Salette was not a man who liked to be crossed, to be caught out. He reached for his wine, took a swallow.

They ate in silence for a moment. Jacquot re-filled their glasses.

Then he began again: '*Dis-moi*. Was Philo a kind man?'

'You've got his boat. You tell me.'

'I mean, generous. To his friends. Helping them out, maybe. Financially. Paying off debts, that kind of thing.'

Salette gave it some thought. 'He was always the first with his hand in his pocket, if that's what you mean. Never one to miss his round.'

'No. More than that. More than the price of a drink. Bigger money.'

'*Boufff* . . . He was a fisherman. What money he had was just enough. For his place in Madrague. For the skiff. Food and supplies.'

'And *Constance*.'

'And *Constance*. *Oui*. Of course.'

'So when did you first see *Constance*?'

'You are asking a lot of questions. Why?'

'I just need to square things, J-P. In my head. I'm a *flic*. I need to understand.'

253

Salette finished his soup, reached for his glass to wash it down.

'Well, I can't help you. About *Constance*. I really can't. I can't remember exactly. He just had it. Twenty years, maybe more. It was his little escape.'

'Who owned it before him?'

'I told you. The coastguard, down in Toulon. Then Customs. I know it was auctioned off. That's what he told me. Got it for a good price, he said. And knowing Philo, I don't doubt it. He could drive a hard bargain.'

'And then, presumably, he spent money doing it up. Like you said, it's been kept in pristine condition.'

'That's passion, not money. There were only two things Philo loved and that was reading his books . . .' Salette waved a hand to the door of La Marine, and out to the harbour, '. . . and the sea.'

'And women.'

'And women.'

'So tell me about his women. Who were they?'

Salette pushed away his plate, licked his finger and picked at the crumbs on the table cloth. 'I can't recall,' he said at last.

'Did you ever see him with a woman?'

Salette shrugged. 'Back in the day. They came and went . . .'

'So tell me about the place in Madrague. Is it sold? Rented out?'

'It's not the kind of place you'd put in an *immobilier*'s window. Word'll get round the port. The landlord will find someone. That's how it works.'

'Do you have a key? Like *Constance*?'

'Yes, I do.'

'And his possessions? Do you have them too?'

Salette gave Jacquot a sly smile, then pinched the soup from the corners of his mouth.

'And I suppose you want to take a look?'

'Correct.'

'The keys, too?'

'Also correct.'

'Will it stop all this nonsense?'

It was Jacquot's turn to shrug. 'We'll see.'

'Well, you can have the keys now,' he said, reaching into his pocket and handing Jacquot a metal ring. 'The address is on there. Rue Tibido. As for his possessions, your millionaire left a single shoebox,' he continued, as though this illustrated better than anything the fact that Philo was not the man Jacquot imagined him to be.

'If it's just the one box, I'll go through it at your place, and you can supply the refreshments.'

'*Boufff* . . . there's so little to see, there won't be time for a drink,' replied Salette, determined to have the last word. 'I'll drop it off, the next time I'm passing.'

61

OVER CAP FERRAT THE SUN was high and bright, almost white in a pale, milky sky, a warm, shifting sea-breeze ruffling the slim, green brush of the cypress trees that bordered Hauts des Pins. Shutters on every side of the house had been half-closed, their louvred slats angled to catch the breeze and keep the interior cool. On the terrace the awnings had been rolled out to their maximum reach but no more than half the terrace was shaded, the lawns below, dropping down to a distant rocky shore, crisp and brittle with heat, waiting for the cool, tapping spray of the evening *arrosage*.

Jarrive, the butler, and Delon, the old man's nurse, sat in the salon watching TV, occasionally casting an eye towards the terrace where Patric Polineaux sat sleeping in his wheelchair. An hour had passed since the old man had pushed away his *omelette nature* and salad, most of which he'd left, to continue leafing his way through the pile of photo albums that he had had Jarrive bring out to him, flicking through the stiff board pages, tilting the books to the light to see more clearly. Then he'd laid the last of them back on the table and drifted off, his head tipping back to the headrest, lips parted, mouth ajar. Neither the butler nor the nurse was keen to disturb him. So long as the breeze lasted, so long as the awning kept the sun off their boss, they would leave him as he was. He was always easier when he woke by himself.

Maybe it was those albums, memories of times past, that made Patric Polineaux dream. If either Jarrive or Delon had drawn close, they would have seen the old man's eyes moving behind closed lids, caught the jerk and twitch of a hand or a finger, heard a whispered catch of breath.

In that old head of his, under stray grey wisps of hair caught in the breeze, it was more than thirty years back. So distant now. Yet so close.

Like flicking through a journal – if he'd ever kept one.

Pages, dates. People, places.

Two years still to endure in a thankless, fruitless marriage, the cow he'd married, Cristina d'Angelo, as much an angel as a five-headed viper. Just as his father had warned him, which had made it even worse. And barren to boot, the bitch. Barren as a Bellecaire back lot. Twenty years he'd wasted on her – time and money both. And no kids. Not a one.

Thirty years back. When he still had his legs.

Thirty years back. With money in his pocket and a fearsome reputation. At the top of his game.

Thirty years back. When he first met Eddie.

Eddie Cassin. Edina. The love of his life.

Their cocktail waitress at Studio Cent. Him and the boys, celebrating someone's birthday. Wives left at home; the way it was back then.

Opening night. Down on the beach, in a corner of the bay, where the Promenade des Anglais skirts up to the port.

The way she bent her knees to serve the drinks, back straight, those long arms, long fingers, that smile. The girls they'd brought with them just paled beside her.

In the dream it was all so clear. So sharp. So particular.

It could have been happening right then. Thirty years later. First time round. That fresh.

Everything about her.

The Marilyn Monroe hair, blonde curls tumbling over those eyes, the mouth, the lipstick, that pouting smile. The way she moved – slow, effortless. That easy, carefree swing of her. Close enough to touch, but just out of reach.

He couldn't take his eyes off her. None of them could.

The way she laughed, throwing back her head, platinum curls sliding, shining.

And in his dream he saw her now, naked, as she opened the shutters in that little apartment he'd found for her on rue Sainte Reparate, a block or so back from the flower market in the old town, close enough to smell the blooms in the early morning, when the streets were in shadow and still wet from the cleaning wagons.

Beams in a low, warped ceiling, a sloping wooden floor, the topmost balcony, up with the pigeons, overlooking a landscape of tilting terracotta roofs baking in the heat.

The way she'd turn back to the bed, with the lace curtains shifting behind her. Her breasts, full and tight; the swell of her hips; the long, elegant turn of her leg; the warm smoothness of her thighs.

And always, in the bed, beside him, beneath him, above him, her sweet, secret wetness.

The way she panted, and whispered, and begged, and groaned, and made the bedsprings screech, loud enough, it sometimes seemed, for the whole neighbourhood to hear, which thought had always pleased him.

And afterwards, her plump lips bruised from their fucking, lighting his cigarette, passing it to him, a nipple grazing his chest, settling beside him, heart still pumping.

Or making coffee, wrapped in that green satin dressing gown, an embroidered dragon coiling up its back. Scarlet and blue.

The fridge in the kitchen with the squeaking door.

The candles in the bathroom where she liked to bathe him.

The day he took her to the races at Borély, and all three of the tips he had given her had come in.

The day they went sailing, out to the islands, just the two of them. Lunch on the beach. Making love in the shallows.

The day his divorce came through and he drove her along the high Corniche from Nice to Menton in his old English roadster, the wind in her hair, engine howling, the car's interior filled with the smell of petrol, leather and scent.

And on the terrace of Les Moulins, in that summer frock with the flower print, bare legs, blonde hair . . .

The day he asked her to marry him.

And she said yes.

But then, as always in his dreams, fast-forwarding through the fights and skirmishing that followed, to that haunting grand finale.

Just a few years later.

The last time he hit her.

The last time he ever saw her.

Watching her run to the car he'd given her as a wedding present, that old roadster, and drive away from Hauts des Pins.

Old Polineaux stirred then, as the *arrosage* started up its first spurting hiss and gentle tap-tap-tapping and a bold cicada answered from the fig trees. On the balustrade a gecko skittered over the stone. Paused. Skittered on. Disappeared over the edge.

Tiny sounds, tiny movements, but they were enough to alert Jarrive and Delon. Switching off the television, the two men came out from the salon, moved a day bed at the far end of the terrace, making its metal legs scrape on the stone, just loud enough for Polineaux to rouse himself without either of them having to come too close.

An old trick.

But this time it didn't work. He woke in a foul mood, as though one of them had shaken his shoulder, woken him from a wonderful dream.

'Bitch, bitch, bitch,' was the first thing he said. A soft, bitter whisper, blinking in the sunlight, swivelling his lizard neck to left and right as though not quite sure where he was, but his eyes fixing at last on the table and the albums, then narrowing as he remembered his dream, one arm lashing out to sweep them off the table.

'The bitch. The *bitch*. God damn her! How dare she?'

259

62

'HE WOULDN'T HAVE FELT A thing,' said Christophe Labeau, one of the clinical pathologists working at the Marseilles Centre d'Examination Forensique in rue Calliope just a few blocks from La Timone hospital. To demonstrate, he tilted the head to the left and right. 'Entry wound here,' he said, pointing to a blackened left ear. 'Exit wound here, as you can see,' he continued, pointing to what remained of the right ear. 'No shell, or shell casing, has been found, of course, but I would say a nine-millimetre slug, fired close enough to leave scorch marks on the skin.'

Isabelle Cassier, in a gown and mask, looked at the body on the mortuary draining table. The man was naked, arms by his sides, palms down, the legs thin and slightly bowed, large feet daintily turned out, one big toe tagged. The chest was oddly sunken, the nipples an unnervingly pale pink and the genitals all but hidden under a great curling brush of black hair. A livid, y-shaped scar, roughly stitched, stretched from the points of the narrow shoulders to a little below the navel.

Without the crumpled linen suit, a naked Jules Ranque looked oddly unfamiliar. She had only the face to work on, or more precisely the thick grey moustache, for the slack expression, the drawn, open lips with the lower teeth just showing, the closed eyes and matted hair, took longer to place. The last time she had seen him, in his office at Les Baumettes, he'd been alive, at his desk, legs crossed, a stiff, saluting hand sliding across his hair. She looked at the hand closest to her, registered the bitten, stubby fingernails. She took a breath and was grateful for the mask. She had pulled it on before going into the main autopsy theatre and knew that she had no more than a few minutes before its fresh hospital scent wore off and the real odours in that room worked their way through its fibrous cover. She'd be breathing through her mouth by the time she left the room.

'Anything else?'

'Oh, yes.' Labeau looked pleased with himself.

'And?'

'We don't have the toxicology results back,' he said, pulling the sheet over the body, 'but I can tell you one thing for sure. *Notre ami* used cocaine. A lot of it. I'd say almost industrial quantities, certainly enough to seriously compromise the nasal septum. Another year or two and there wouldn't have been much left to separate the left and right nostrils. Funny how a lot of real cokers favour a moustache, don't you think? It hides that red top lip they often have. He was a drinker too. The liver was in a poor state.'

Isabelle remembered the sniffing, had thought it a nervous affectation. She had done her time working in vice and drugs, but had failed to spot the giveaway sniff, the frequent blowing and wiping of the nose. She knew why. You didn't expect the assistant warden of a correctional institution to be an habitual drug user, so you didn't consider it. She wondered where he got his supply. A dealer? Or one of his inmates? Or maybe he was dealing himself?

'Anything else?' she asked. She was aware of a sour smell, an odd mix of chemicals and gamey meat. It wouldn't be long now.

'That's it. You'll get a full report when all the results are through, but I doubt there'll be much more.'

'There's enough to be getting on with,' said Isabelle, and with a nod of thanks she left the room, waiting until the sealed doors closed behind her before pulling the mask from her face.

God, how she hated these places. It didn't matter how many times she visited, she'd never really got used to them.

63

YOU'RE WASTING YOUR TIME, SALETTE had told him. *There's nothing there, nothing to see.*

Probably, thought Jacquot, as he parked his car off rue Tibido three blocks back from Madrague's pocket-sized port. But given everything else he'd found, it would have been foolish not to follow up. Just on the off chance.

It was early afternoon and the sun was already high above Montredon, spilling across its rising, rocky slopes and slanting down into the port's narrow streets, a cooling sea breeze, sharply scented from the drying nets and traps and wired lobster pots stacked around the small harbour, whipping up a fine dusty sand from the roads and pavements. There was the normal market day bustle, the quayside stalls covered in striped awnings, the local community bolstered by intrepid tourists who'd seen what they needed in Marseilles and were now ranging further afield. Not that Madrague was any kind of tourist destination. It was a small working port with not much to recommend it beyond a flagged memorial to those who had fought and died for their country, a terraced bar and restaurant overlooking the harbour and a single small gift shop selling toy wooden fishing boats, knotted rope key-fobs, striped nautical T-shirts and fishermen's sweaters in roughly-knitted wool.

But there was, thought Jacquot, as he locked his car and set off down rue Tibido, a certain charm in the clustered busyness of the place, a large proportion of its residents employed, just as Philo had been, in one or other aspect of catching and selling fish.

When the idea of taking a look at Philo's old apartment had first lodged in his head, it had proved impossible to shift. It nagged at Jacquot. Nibbled away. He had seen the house in Roucas Blanc where Philo had lived with Edina; now he wanted to see the other side of the old fisherman's life. The home he'd retreated to when Edina died and Les Étagères was sold – the only home he'd had according to Salette.

Philo's apartment was on the top floor of a three-storey block built in the fifties on the site of an old drying shed burned down by the Germans. Back then, Madrague had been as rife with *résist-ants* and simmering insurrection as Le Panier, the hilltop warren of streets and alleyways overlooking Marseilles' Vieux Port where Jacquot had grown up. In Le Panier, the German occupying forces had given the residents twenty-four hours to move out, before the boys in *feldgrau* moved in and laid charges, blowing up a large part of the *quartier*. In Madrague, only the drying shed had been destroyed in an attempt to smoke out a small band of troublemakers.

Pulling out the set of keys that Salette had given him, Jacquot unlocked a planked wooden door set between two buildings and stepped into a shadowy passageway. It was cool here after the sunlit shadowless street and little more than shoulder width, its stone flagged path tilting and cracked, with blank side-walls rising up either side of him. Ten metres on, this passageway opened into a small paved courtyard, just as Salette had told him, and facing him, on the far side of this courtyard, was Philo's block, two ground-floor apartments with two balconied floors above, two apartments a floor. One of the courtyard doors was open, a beaded fly-strip curtain cinched back to the doorframe, its doorstep crowded with pots of geranium and cactus, its windows lace-curtained. The adjoining apartment was no different – the same pots and curtains – but the door was closed. No one in, just a large black cat on one of the window sills who settled his eye on Jacquot and watched as he crossed to an outside flight of stairs leading to the two balconied levels above.

On the first balcony there was no sign of life beyond a line of washing, the smell of spicy food and, from one of the apartments, the muted sound of a radio. Giving it just a glance, Jacquot climbed on until he came to the top floor. After the narrow passageway and tiny courtyard there was suddenly a freshness in the air, the salty scent of the sea, and, he could just make out, the sound of waves slapping against the breakwater just a few blocks away.

The number six on Philo's front door was brass and well polished, and Salette's key slid into the worn old lock with a familiar glide. Jacquot pushed the door open, stepped inside and closed it behind him.

Four rooms, two on the balcony side, two at the back, with a splinter of harbour glinting between the buildings in the next street.

The place had been stripped to its neat, serviceable parts. A Formica kichen table and two metal-legged plastic chairs. Sink, stove, cupboards, fridge. Sitting room – two beaten-up sofas pushed against the wall and a coffee table. Bathroom – just a shower, basin and bowl. Everything clean, but sterile too. No evidence of the previous owner, and nothing yet of the next. A kind of waiting limbo, thought Jacquot in the bedroom, sitting down on the side of the bed and looking round. He got up. Opened a window and let in the ocean – the smell of it, the soft, restless, distant sound of it.

A good place for an old fisherman to live.

And as good a place as any for him to die.

64

LOCKING UP PHILO'S APARTMENT, JACQUOT stopped at
every door on his way down to the courtyard and knocked or rang
a bell. No one answered, even in the flat with the radio playing.
Someone's idea of home security, Jacquot thought. There's a radio
on, someone must be at home. But there wasn't. In the courtyard,
he tried the closed door, then stepped between the geranium pots
and tapped his knuckles on the doorframe of the open door.

'*Il y a quelqu'un là?*' he called out into the dark interior.

'*Oui, oui, attend, s'il vous plaît.*' The voice was a woman's,
weary, broad and raw, the *oui-oui*s pronounced '*weh-weh*'. A fish-
stall voice, used to shouting the catch and the price per kilo.

Jacquot saw her rise out of the shadows and bowl down towards
the door, a round, wide-hipped shape rocking on her trainers,
whatever else she was wearing – a skirt or dress – concealed beneath
a flowered housecoat grimy at the waist from the kitchen range.
She came to a stop in front of him, a potato in one hand, a peeler
in the other. Both were dwarfed by her meaty fists. Her hair was
wrapped in a scarf, cheeks ruddy and pitted, her lips sucked in
over toothless gums.

'Smells good, Madame,' Jacquot began, raising his nose to sniff
appreciatively, nodding behind her towards the kitchen she had just
left.

'Bouillabaisse, my way. Not like Fonfon's. Or Michel's. Or Le Rhul's,' she said, reeling off a list of the best bouillabaisses to be had along that part of the coast. 'As good as it gets, even if I say so myself. So long as you don't mind turmeric for saffron.' She took a step back and looked him up and down. 'So, what can I do for you?'

'Monsieur Emanetti. On the top floor. Number six . . .'

'And? What of him?'

'Did you know him?'

The old girl gave Jacquot a skewed look. 'And you are?'

'His nephew.'

She lowered her head into a wide, bouncy concertina of chins and the skewed look turned suspicious.

'Never heard him speak of any family. Any nephew.'

'Jean-Pierre Salette gave me the key. Said I could call by.'

The name had an immediate effect.

'Ahhh . . . Salette? You know Salette?'

Jacquot said that he did.

'A rogue. A scoundrel. A naughty boy. So what did you want to know?'

Jacquot shrugged. 'About Philo. He lived here long?'

'As long as me. Longer. Too long to remember.'

'You must have known him well?'

'As well as anyone could – as well as he would allow.'

Jacquot frowned.

'When he was here,' she added.

'Meaning?'

She worked her lips, sucking and blowing, beady black eyes never leaving him. 'He came and went, did old Philo. Here a week, gone for three. Sometimes longer. Last couple of years he was here most of the time, but the old coot kept his own company. Had a boat, he told me. Stayed there, too, he said. But I never saw it.'

'He didn't have visitors?'

She shook her head, still suspicious despite his mentioning Salette. 'Like I said, he kept to himself.'

266

'Any girlfriends?'

The fishwife grunted. 'None as I saw.'

Jacquot nodded, and knew he'd come to the end of his questions. Nothing more for him here, just as Salette had said.

'You've been very helpful, Madame. Thank you.'

'*De rien*. It's nothing. My sympathies. Your uncle was a good and kind man.'

Jacquot had been about to turn away, but now he paused.

'Kind?'

She gave him another look, more curious than suspicious.

'What I mean is . . . Old Philo . . . he was always interested, you know? How things were going. And if you ever needed a few francs to see you through, he was the first with his hand in his pocket.'

'Just a few francs?'

She shrugged, waved her potato and peeler. '*Alors*, maybe some of them took more. Me, he covered the rent a few times, I'll admit. Always paid back, mind you. No debts, me.'

'What was the most he gave that you ever heard about?'

She gave the question some thought. 'Cotillon, I'd say. Old boy the other side of the port. Long gone now, but a good sort. Wanted a van for his son, to get the fish into town. Times were hard back then . . . ten, twelve years now. Old Philo gave him the money. No questions asked.'

'Gave or lent?'

'He never lent money. He gave it. Anyone in trouble; some not. But he never ever asked for any of it back. Just sort of, "*Here-you-are-take-this*." My opinion, if you paid it back it was a loan, right? If you didn't, it was a gift. Whichever you felt comfortable with. *Compris*?'

'So where do you suppose the money came from? The money he gave away. He was just a fisherman.'

'Cards . . . the gee-gees out at Parc Borély. "Never play him at cards or backgammon, he always wins." That's what Cotillon used to say. And that old coot would have known. Gambler to his holed socks.'

267

'You've been very helpful, Madame. Enjoy your bouillabaisse.'

'Come back tonight, why don't you? It'll be the best you ever had.' She gave him a wink. 'And the bouillabaisse is pretty good too.'

65

THE OLD LADY WAS STILL cackling as Jacquot crossed the yard and started down the path. Up ahead he heard the click of a lock and saw the gate swing open. Given the length of the passageway, and the fact that it was a tight squeeze for one person, he took a few steps back to the corner of the yard and waited.

Jacquot knew *gorilles* when he saw them and the two men who came through the gate – black jeans, blue jeans, white T-shirts, black leather jackets – could only have been 'family' men. Runners or hitters, whichever they were, hard boys both, doing whatever they'd been asked to do by the boss – whoever he might be. Falling in one behind the other, angling their shoulders to fit the space, they came down the passage towards him. The first man, chewing gum and carrying a knapsack over his shoulder – dark-haired, flat-faced, with a scar through his left eyebrow – passed without even a nod of thanks, as though Jacquot hadn't even been there, but his companion, with the matchstick in his mouth and the thin moustache, gave him a good once-over as he stepped past.

Jacquot was glad he was wearing his shorts and T-shirt. He looked like a fisherman on his way to the port, not worth a second glance.

'Messieurs,' he muttered, but there was no response as the two men crossed the yard and jogged up the flight of steps. Heading into the passageway, Jacquot looked back and saw them reach the top balcony, stop at Philo's door. Pausing in the shadow, he leaned out to watch the door open, the men go in, and the door close.

Letting himself out onto the street, Jacquot stooped down and checked the lock. He couldn't see any scratches on the lock itself, but there was a wedge-shaped indentation, probably made by the blade of a knife or a screwdriver, in the door's wooden frame. Easy enough to force a lock on such a weathered, splintered gate, thought Jacquot, turning to look along the street, the parked cars. Nothing stood out, nothing caught his eye, so he crossed the road and took an outside table at the café on the corner. He ordered a coffee, picked up a newspaper left on the other chair, and settled down to wait. Whoever they were, and for whatever reason, they were clearly interested in Philo. And Jacquot intended to find out why.

He didn't have long to wait. A double espresso, a cigarette, and the gate was opening, the two men out on the street again, job done, whatever it was. Jacquot watched them turn right and head up Tibido, turning into Pélanne where he had parked his own car. Leaving the café, he started up the street and a few metres from Pélanne heard a car engine start and catch. There was a clash of gears, a squeal of tyres and Jacquot reached the corner in time to see a dark red Mercedes brake at the bottom of the street and swing left.

It took him less than a minute to reach his own car and start after them. Down Pélanne, into Moulin and up to the Mont Rose crossroads on the edge of town. They were already a good way ahead, slowing now to make a left turn along the coast. Since there was only the one road out of Madrague, Jacquot resisted the temptation to catch them up. Instead, he kept his distance, turned into Mont Rose and saw the Mercedes a hundred metres ahead. With no traffic between them, Jacquot held back – along Montredon, past the marina at Pointe Rouge. He decided they were heading for Marseilles, but changed his mind when the car took a right at the first Prado roundabout. Other traffic, coming towards them from the city, also made the turn and by the time Jacquot swung into Boulevard Jourdan-Berry he was three cars back from the

Mercedes. By Jacquot's reckoning the two heavies were either heading for the north of the city, up towards Allauch or Aubagne. Or they were going to hit the D559 and take a right on Tassigny, out towards Cassis and La Ciotat.

A right it was and ten minutes later the line of cars was heading up into the Col de la Gineste, twisting up into the chalky highlands before dropping down towards Cassis. By-passing the town, the Mercedes headed on, staying close to the speed limit, now just a single van between them, both vehicles indicating for the autoroute and the fast way to Bandol and Toulon. Jacquot checked his gas. Just so long as they didn't go any further than Toulon; stopping for petrol was no way to handle a chase.

Thankfully, they didn't. Instead the Merc came off the autoroute in the north of Toulon and took the coast road to Cap Brun.

And that was where, much to his irritation, Jacquot lost the Mercedes, somewhere between Le Morillon and the Cap. One minute they were just three cars ahead, and then a lorry started out from a side road. The first two cars got by, but the one in front of him slowed, gave way, let the lorry out. By the time it had reversed a couple of times after making a bad hash of the tight turn, and pulled out ahead of him, the Mercedes had vanished.

And thanks to its skirt of mud and dust, he hadn't been able to read the registration.

66

AS HE DROVE OUT OF Toulon, back the way he had come, it was now abundantly clear to Jacquot that he wasn't the only person interested in Philo.

But why? And why now? At exactly the same time that Jacquot was following his leads and making his enquiries?

If the two *gorilles* in the red Mercedes had hoped to speak to Philo, for whatever reason, or to find something in his poor lodgings, then they would have been disappointed. The old man had been buried at sea weeks before and, as Jacquot had already discovered, his lodgings had been effectively stripped in preparation for the next tenant, as bare and chaste as a monk's cell. But the fact that these two heavies had made the effort to track him down and pay a visit suggested that Philo was of interest, that he had something, or had done something, that required them to come calling. Either on their own account, or because they had been told to.

In Jacquot's opinion, given what he'd found out about Philo, there could only be one reason for the visit. Money. And the money in question was undoubtedly the money that had underwritten the old fisherman's double life, the money that he had invested in his precious book collection and the money that had bought the house in Roucas Blanc, the last of which, as the lawyer Cluzot had confirmed, had now been dispersed among a number of worthy causes.

Someone was not going to be pleased.

But what Jacquot wanted to know was, where had the money come from in the first place? It was a fair guess that the heavies probably knew, but he didn't. At that moment it was their only advantage.

Given what Jacquot knew of Philo it didn't seem likely that the old fisherman had robbed a bank, or been part of a gang. If he had had any shady friends or associates, or indulged in any form of criminal activity, then Salette would surely have known about it. Which meant that whatever money had come Philo's way – a great deal of it, as Jacquot had established – had come to him in some other way. He certainly hadn't earned it as a fisherman, or a pleasure-cruise skipper, or over a gaming table or at the horses. But he had got hold of it somehow, concealed it and succcessfully run a double life to disguise it.

Or maybe it came from the woman. Eddie. Edina. The woman he'd lived with for so many years, the woman no one knew about except his neighbours in Roucas Blanc.

Had Eddie been the wife of someone important, as Madame Nallet had hinted? Someone Philo had taken her away from?

But Eddie had come from Nice, that's what Madame Nallet had said, not Toulon.

Maybe it was she who had provided the money? Stolen or otherwise.

Were the *gorilles* searching for Eddie and not Philo?

Or for Philo as well?

And did they know that the two of them were now dead?

Whatever else, Jacquot decided, as he parked in rue Pélanne and walked back to Philo's lodgings, this was all getting very interesting. And the more he found out, the more determined he was to get to the bottom of it all.

It was only late afternoon but it was already dark when he stepped out of the passageway and into the courtyard once more. The sun hadn't set, the sky was still a jigsaw piece of deep rich blue between the rooftops, but Jacquot could already feel a chill in the shadows, a soft dampness in the air.

And the place was still deserted. The same closed doors and curtained windows, a sense of residents still to come home from work – to have supper, watch TV, go to bed. Even the fishwife's door was closed. Certainly there were no families here, with children, thought Jacquot. School was long over; by now any kids would surely have been playing here in the yard.

Crossing the sunless courtyard, Jacquot climbed to the second floor and walked down to Philo's door.

He wasn't surprised to find what he did. There were splinters of wood on the ground and the door was ajar. Another forced lock, less tidy up here, out of sight, than on the street.

What did surprise him was the interior.

In each of the four rooms, the lino floor covering had been stripped off the floorboards, and every fourth one wrenched off its joists, tossed aside on to the folds of crumpled lino, or left at a gaping angle, to expose the space beneath. The two sofas and bedroom mattress had been sliced into foam-rubber shreds, the stove and fridge heaved out from their recesses, cupboard doors thrown open and drawers strewn in a jumble across the floor. They'd even set to work on the ceiling, opening up gaps in the plaster and lathe.

It must have been a noisy job, but with no one nearby to hear them, no near neighbours at home, they'd had nothing to worry about.

As he stepped through this mess of destruction, plaster crunching underfoot, it struck Jacquot that so far he was ahead of the game. He'd got here before the two *gorilles*, he'd watched them and followed them without being spotted, and he knew there'd have been nothing here for them to find, that they'd have left empty-handed.

And given that neither Madame Nallet nor Jeanne Vaillant had mentioned anyone else asking the same questions that he had asked, he also knew that they, or their employer, had not yet found out about rue Savry.

But he was only ahead by a narrow margin.

And possibly a narrowing margin.

67

BACK IN THE COURTYARD THERE was now some sign of life. The old fishwife was at her front door, with her back to him, bending over to water her plants, pouring what looked like dishwater from a bucket into the various pots.

When she'd emptied the bucket, she heaved herself up and was turning towards her door when she noticed Jacquot coming towards her.

'Back for my pot, *chéri*? Or is it the fish stew you're after?'

'I'll take a bowl, if you're offering,' he replied, and reached out a hand. 'My name's Jacquot. Daniel Jacquot.'

The old lady looked at the hand and then at Jacquot. For a moment she seemed surprised that he should have accepted her offer, and a little uncertain too. Then she reached out and took his hand, her own hard and wet and strong.

'If you're going to eat at my table, Monsieur, let's get one thing straight. You're not Philo's nephew are you?'

'No, I'm a cop.'

'I'll give you one thing,' she said, finally releasing his hand after a good wringing, 'you don't look like any *flic* I've ever seen. And seems you're an honest one, too. Marvels will never cease.' She gave him another look over. 'Well, you'd better come in then. The name's Clem. Clémentine, if you must know.'

The apartment was low and dark, with exactly the same layout as Philo's two floors above, except the kitchen was at the back and not the front, looking over a small slope of bare ground, an unused back garden in the next street. The only thing that made the view bearable was an old olive tree, bent and gnarled with the years but laden with leaves and berries, as healthy a tree as Jacquot had ever seen. And in such an unlikely spot.

Pointing him to a kitchen chair, Clem went to the range. She lifted a lid from a large stockpot and a cloud of fishy steam billowed up through the strings of onions, woven strands of garlic, white-husked loops of sausage and tied bunches of herbs strung out from wall to wall. The scent of it, in that low dark kitchen, was almost overwhelming, enough for Jacquot to know that what he was about to eat would be, just as she'd boasted, among the best he'd ever tasted. This was clearly a woman who liked her food, and knew how to cook.

'Seems *les flics* aren't the only ones interested in old Philo,' she began. 'First you, then those other two came right after. You must have passed them in the alley.' A bowl was fetched from a cupboard, a ladle lifted from a drawer. Dipping the ladle into the pot, she drew out a bowlful of the steaming sea-scented broth.

'You saw them?'

'Difficult not to. After they'd been up to Philo's they came knocking, just like you. Except not so politely.'

'You know that's where they went? To his apartment?'

'I didn't see them go up. But I heard the racket.'

'Have you seen what they've done up there?'

Clem shook her head as she put down the ladle and brought the bowl to the table.

'None of my business. Stayed where I was, me,' she said. '*Et voilà*, Monsieur Daniel Jacquot, *et bon appétit* . . . Ah, you'll need a spoon.' One was brought, then a dish of grated cheese, some croutons warm from the oven and a second, smaller bowl of rouille, rust-red and reeking of garlic and pepper, thick enough for a teaspoon to stand up in it. Having set them around his bowl

277

with red chubby fingers, she sat herself down with an 'Oufff . . .
alors.'

'What did they want?' Jacquot asked, breathing in the sweet,
salty scent of the soup and the stronger rouille.

'They were looking for Philo. Wanted to know where they could
find him . . .' She stopped, frowned at him. 'Don't sniff it, man,
eat it. There's nothing wrong with it.'

'And?' he asked, picking up the spoon. The broth was a creamy
yellow, puddled with darker globs of oil, broken with thick flakes
of fish, like icebergs, and the more treacherous blackened tips of
mussels. He took the broth first, a spoonful of the liquor, blew on
it and then tipped it into his mouth. The ocean, that's what it tasted
like. Fresh and hot and sweet, the flavour filling his cheeks.

'Told 'em he'd moved out. Up to Aubagne. A couple of months
back.'

'Did they say why they wanted him?' he asked, reaching now
for the rouille, dropping a spoonful into the soup along with some
croutons and cheese.

She shook her head.

'And they were happy with that?'

'As happy as two men like that ever get,' she replied, helping
herself to a crouton and dipping it into the rouille. 'A pair of low-
life *Mokos* and no mistake.'

Jacquot noted the old slang for someone from Toulon.

'Did you recognise them? Had you seen them around?' He knew
it was unlikely, having followed them all the way to Toulon, but
it was worth a try.

She shook her head. 'Like I said, not from around here. Never
seen 'em before. And never want to again. While they were standing
there, out in the hall, it was like they wanted to hit me, you know?
Beat me up, just for being me, for being here, answering the door
to them. I don't know how they stopped themselves. It was nervy,
I'll tell you.'

Jacquot understood. She, like him, had recognised what kind of
men these were, what they could do – and without a thought.

278

He fell silent for a moment as he worked on his bouillabaisse: a firm, pearly-white wedge of rockfish, then a mussel sucked free from its shell, more rouille, more croutons, cheese – with Clem watching every move.

'So how's the broth?' she asked.

He waved an empty spoon at the bowl, spoke with a full mouth. 'You were right, Madame . . . Clem, I mean. This really is very good indeed.' He swallowed the mouthful and gave a little chuckle, at his good fortune, at the improbability of it. 'Like you said, forget Fonfon and the others.'

'Cheaper, too.'

He tipped the bowl for the last of the broth.

'Tell me, do you live alone?'

'By necessity,' she replied, folding her arms across a voluminous chest. 'Never married, *chéri*. Not the sort. Preferred the girls, I did, and back then you couldn't do that.' She jabbed a finger into his arm. 'Just in case you had any ideas.'

When he put down the spoon, wiping his lips with the backs of his fingers and thumb, she took the bowl from him, got to her feet and went back to the stove. No need to ask. Another ladleful was poured into it. She rattled the lid back on to the pot and returned to the table. But Jacquot could see that her expression had changed. There was something on her mind.

'I was lying this morning,' she said at last, settling at the table. 'Just like you, Monsieur Nephew.'

'You lied?'

'You asked about girlfriends. Any women?'

Jacquot nodded.

'There was one. Years ago. And just the once I saw her. I was coming back early from the quay and there they were, coming out of the gate and me about to go in.'

Jacquot waited, started into his second helping.

'She was younger than him. Quite a lot younger. And beautiful. Curly blonde hair, and not a scrap of make-up. Natural, like. She didn't need it. He's got lucky, I thought. One of his charter passengers, she looked like. Going for a bit of rough, you know? But close up, I could see they were tight. The way she looked at him, held his arm. I remember there were little studs in her ears. Diamonds. They sparkled. Never seen anything like them.'

'Did he introduce her? Did you find out her name?'

She shook her head. 'Just nodded, smiled, *"Bonjour, ça va?"* That was it. Didn't expect no more.'

'And you never saw her again?'

'That was it. Just the once.'

'Did he ever say anything about her? Afterwards?'

'Nothing. Not a word. Like it had never happened. Like it wasn't important.'

But it was important, Jacquot knew.

'You said you saw more of him, the last couple of years.'

'A lot more. Pretty much every day. I'd come back from the shops, or pegging out washing, and there he'd be, sitting out on his balcony, reading some book. Sometimes I shouted up at him, "Get your old bones down here for a bite," you know – or I'd just wave, pass the time of day.'

'And what did he talk about? When he came down. Anything special?'

'The old days, what else? You get to our age and it's all that's left, the past.'

'Not if you can make soup like this,' said Jacquot, putting down his spoon.

'A silver tongue and honey lips. You'll go far, young man. If you haven't already. So what's he done? Why all the interest in old Philo?'

Jacquot sat back in his chair, felt a warmth and fullness in his belly, and sighed.

'I think our old friend might have been a naughty boy.'

'Those sailor boys, Salette and the rest of them . . . they're all naughty boys. That's what's so good about them.'

And the old girl slapped the table and cackled.

68

IF THERE WAS ONE THING that the butler, Jarrive, knew with an absolute certainty, it was that his boss could be a difficult son of a bitch, with a chilling temper and a cold heart. On Polineaux's seventieth birthday, Jarrive had watched the old man slide a knife into another man's chest and hold him till the jerking stopped; had seen the lazy way he dispatched a bungling subordinate, pressing his Walther automatic into the man's eye and pulling the trigger; and how he had used the same Walther to pistol whip a call-girl that his fixer, Didier, had brought in, for glancing at her watch while she fellated him. And on all three occasions he'd been confined to his wheelchair. Patric Polineaux was a dangerous man to cross.

Ruthless. Cold. Deadly.

And, it seemed, increasingly frustrated and temperamental. Less able to do what he wanted, when he wanted – as maddened by the restrictions imposed by his disability as he was by the advancing limitations of old age. Most of the time he sat in his wheelchair and looked down at the garden, seeming to dream the hours away, only really settled and alert when he had a cigar between his knuckly fingers and a drink at his elbow. Jarrive knew, for instance, that his boss rarely had any idea what day of the week it was, let alone which month, and on occasion had a way of looking at him as though he couldn't quite place him. More than thirty years working at Hauts des Pins and he might just as well have knocked on the door that morning, come to sell something. A slow but steady descent.

It wouldn't be long now, thought Jarrive, as he stepped out on to the terrace with a fresh jug of water and a plate of biscuits. As usual Polineaux was hunched over the table, its glass top, his rug-covered lap and the tiles around him littered with photos. Since Didier had brought in that case, the old boy had been through its contents a dozen times, laboriously matching notes with photos, sorting everything into a kind of order, getting him to fetch a magnifying glass, or have him read something, or set up the video player.

'Who's this *mec* in the white T-shirt?' asked Polineaux, without looking up as Jarrive came towards him. 'The little fella with the big smile. Looks like a sailor.' Polineaux was holding out a colour photo, drawing it close to his eyes, pushing it away, trying to get a focus on one part of it.

'I believe the names are on the back, Monsieur Patric.'

Polineaux flipped the photo over, peered at the name.

Emanetti.

'Who the hell's this Emanetti? Never heard of him.'

'If I may, Monsieur Patric?' Jarrive put down the jug and plate and took the photo, looked at it.

Seven people, standing on a quay. Five men and two women. Summer clothes. Bare feet. They were either going on a cruise or coming back from one. A gay, excited bunch. There was a wicker basket at their feet. Towels under their arms. Hats, sunglasses. Some of the faces were shadowed, hard to make out. Jarrive turned the photo to check the names.

'It looks like a trip out to the islands, or along the coast. It's difficult to tell,' he said. 'That's Monsieur Ballantine with his foot on the hamper; that old friend of yours, Hugo; and Hugo's son, Philippe, who got shot in the casino, remember? I seem to recall that the lady with the dark hair was Philippe's girlfriend. Then

282

there's Monsieur Pierre who looked after things for you in Antibes . . .'

'Run down, wasn't he?' interrupted Polineaux.

'In Paris, that's right.'

'Never knew if it was a hit or an accident. *Bouf*. So who else?'

'Then there's your wife, Edina, with the hat there, waving at the camera, and that Emanetti character, on the far right, standing a little apart, looking across at her. I seem to recall he was in one of the videos,' Jarrive continued. 'One of the SuperEight transfers. But he doesn't appear to be a part of the group. Just hanging round the edges. Maybe he skippered the boat.'

Polineaux's eyes narrowed, and something grim and cold and terrifying stirred in his guts.

'Show me the video. Fetch it. Now!'

69

TWO DAYS AFTER HIS TRIP to Madrague Jacquot drove to the railway station in Cavaillon to pick up Claudine's sister. Five years older, not as pretty, a journalist with *Le Monde* in Paris, Delphie was the woman who, four years earlier, had steered him towards her little sister. For which act, Jacquot would be eternally grateful. Indeed, he was as excited as Claudine at the prospect of having Delphie come to stay. When Jacquot saw her step from the carriage he hurried over, hardly aware any longer of the gentle complaint from his hip.

They embraced, exchanged the usual pleasantries ('You smell of the sea and sun cream, it's not fair,' was the first thing she said as he released her from his hug), and then Delphie sent him back into the carriage to drag out three large suitcases from the baggage racks.

'How did you get them on in Paris?' he asked, hauling out the last case, the gentle complaint from his hip a little more insistent now.

'A kind man, just like you, helped me. Unfortunately he got off in Valence. So there you are. Now, go and fetch a trolley, there's a good boy.'

There was no need for Jacquot to ask why Delphie had arrived with three large suitcases, in addition to her own bags. Claudine had explained everything. Big sister was coming down with baby clothes, everything that she and her quite wealthy husband had bought from some of the finest boutiques in Paris for their own two children. Since neither Claudine nor Jacquot had wanted to know the twins' sex, Delphie had had no option but to bring down everything, both her son's and her daughter's cast-offs. To cover the bases. The trip had been agreed a week earlier, but in the last few days it had still not been decided whether Delphie should drive, or fly, or take the train, given the large amount of clothes she was threatening to bring. She had finally decided on the train, and *voilà*, she had arrived. Everything in one piece.

Jacquot got on well with Delphie. She was just as fiery and feisty and flippant as her little sister, often even more so, and Jacquot relished the challenge the two of them presented. A man had to have his wits about him when the two Eddé sisters were on form, and that evening the dinner table was the usual battlefield: Chirac's rumoured light touch with government finances; the neo-Gaullist leader Sarkozy's political future after a poor showing in that summer's European elections ('But he'll be President one day,' declared Delphie, 'just you wait and see'); the end of the franc and the coming of the euro; the scandalous affair between a presidential advisor and a high-class call girl; not to mention all the latest books and films ('Enough Hollywood. Enough, enough, enough!' Delphie again.) As they worked their way through Claudine's signature *blanquette de veau* no subject was off-limits and blood, as usual, was spilled, their other dinner guests either brave enough to join in the fray, or content to sit back and watch the bloodletting. It was a loud and raucous evening and it ended late.

But sorting baby clothes was not on Jacquot's agenda. Normally he'd have been at his office in Cavaillon, or lying in the hammock, or doing some odd job round the house. But now that he had *Constance*, Jacquot had swiftly identified an opportunity to spend some more time in Marseilles without leaving Claudine on her own, not to mention the opportunity to further pursue his enquiries into the activities of Niko Emanetti and Edina . . . whoever she was.

285

A quick phone call to the lawyer, Cluzot, in Avignon, had provided two possible leads, and it was these that Jacquot was keen to follow up as he prepared to drive south the following afternoon, head still a little thick from the night before, promising to have *Constance* comfortably appointed for when the two sisters arrived for an overnight visit later in the week. Enough time, they had decided, to catch up on all their news and gossip, to have a few long lubricated lunches and, at some point or another, to sort through the caseloads of clothes.

'*Foie gras*. Don't forget I like *foie gras*,' Delphie had called after him as he turned the car and headed out of the drive. 'And a good Meursault to wash it down.'

'And make sure the sheets are clean,' added Claudine who, with Delphie's encouragement, had teased him unmercifully about the lover he had taken during her holiday in Guadeloupe, and whom he secretly entertained on *Constance*.

But Jacquot didn't go to the old port in Marseilles. Instead, an hour after leaving the millhouse, he was parking on rue Clermond in Belsunce, where, according to Maître Cluzot, he would find what he was looking for.

70

POLINEAUX SAT IN THE SMALL loggia beside the swimming pool and watched the dragonflies skim and hover over its surface. Delon had wheeled him out after lunch, set him in the shade and left him with the alarm to use if he needed anything. Both Jarrive and Delon knew that their boss preferred his own company, and could become fractious if they hung around. So there the old man sat, letting his eyes drift from the pool to the gardens, a sweep of lawn edged with Aleppo pine and cypress, and back to the house, its elegant Belle Époque lines cut against a sky as blue as the sapphires they'd found in Dupont's case.

And as he surveyed his estate, his thoughts, inevitably, began to wander back to the time he had spent here with Eddie.

She'd still be alive, thought Polineaux. Somewhere. Wherever she was. In her fifties now, getting on like all of them, but still a beauty. He was sure of it. She wouldn't have lost her figure, her looks. Just . . . older. Elegant, quiet . . . And sexy. She'd still be a sexy woman, he was certain. Under the surface. That look in her eye. Wrinkles didn't conceal that kind of truth.

But all those years ago she had walked out of the front door and never come back.

Vanished. Gone. No trace.

And for what? Just the lightest slap to her cheek, the mildest threat.

287

You had to keep these women in order or they'd run roughshod all over you. That's what his father had told him, his friends too, and that's what he'd always done. Cristina, Eddie . . . it didn't matter. Let 'em know who was boss. Right from the start.

So when he saw her jump into the Jaguar and spray gravel from its tyres as she accelerated down the drive, he had given it no thought. She would be back. Just as she always came back, sorry or still defiant. Sometimes defiant enough to earn another slap, or a push, or a kick, or whatever other small humiliation he might dream up.

Whether she returned because she somehow enjoyed the power he exercised over her and was aroused by his harsh treatment, or simply because he kept a tight rein on her spending money, he never really knew, never really cared. What he had known that long ago day, was that sooner or later she would be back. And given that it was her birthday in just a few days, he'd guessed it would be sooner.

Her thirtieth. She would never miss that.

But she did.

Three days later there was still no sign of her and with gritted teeth and a snarl of irritation, he'd had to cancel the caterers and the guests and suffer their silent pleasure at his discomfort.

For which the bitch would pay.

The very next day he'd sent out some of his boys to track her down but they'd come back with nothing. He called his bank to check her account and found that she had taken everything, a little over twenty thousand francs left from her monthly allowance. She wasn't going to get very far on that.

But then he remembered that she had the car. *The* car. A 1954 Jaguar XK120M roadster.

She wouldn't dare, he thought.

Not the Jaguar.

His wedding present to her. Worth a small fortune.

But she had. She'd sold it.

And he was the one who found it.

Three weeks later on the front lot of a classic car dealer in Antibes.

He'd been on his way to a meeting in Marseilles with Lombard when he'd driven right past it. He'd had his driver pull over and had stormed into the showroom. That car's mine, he'd shouted at the manager, waving at the Jaguar in the lot.

But of course it wasn't.

When he'd given Eddie the car as a wedding present, he'd had the registration papers changed to her name – a thoughtful touch at the time, but in retrospect a foolish thing to have done. And it was these same papers that the man had produced from a desk drawer, proving his ownership of the vehicle, along with details of the purchase – a ridiculously small amount compared to the two hundred thousand francs the man was now asking for *his* Jaguar.

So Polineaux had bought the car, then and there, without haggling. He'd taken the keys and had his driver follow him to the top most Corniche road where he had once driven with Eddie. And there, on a corner of Avenue des Diables, a thousand metres above Cap Ferrat, he had got out of the car, released the handbrake and let the Jaguar slide over the edge. A hundred metre drop before the rocks below crumpled that streamlined body into a tangled mess of metal, the petrol tank exploding a few seconds after the car came to a stop, wedged between two pines.

When he drove on to Marseilles, his anger was cold and deadly.

She would die, he decided – just as he might decide that he needed a new suit or a pair of shoes – for daring to leave him, for humiliating him, for selling the car, and for being the reason he'd had to destroy it.

But it never happened. He never got the chance.

She had simply vanished, and the weeks had turned into months, and the months into years. And now all he had was the memory of her. As clear and undimmed as ever.

A swallow skimmed the pool and left a wake where its beak had dipped into the water. Polineaux watched it go and as it darted between the Aleppos a sudden thought occurred to him, an awful, icy, gut-numbing thought.

The gold! The gold . . .

Had she been involved?

Had she somehow hijacked his plans and taken the gold in that third truck? The one driven by that retard, the slow one with the quick hands and the heavy foot, as Polineaux had always joked. The one whose body the cops had found on that quayside in Madrague.

She'd certainly have known about the plan, the heist. In the months before she left he'd held all kinds of meetings setting it up. And if she really had had that bastard retard on the inside then there was no telling what she could have done.

With the money to set it all up.

The price of a Jaguar.

The money to buy the boat that the gold had been loaded on to, speeding away under cover of darkness.

It was then, as he tried to reason it all out in his head, that he saw Jarrive come from the house, cross the sloping lawn, and walk around the pool towards him. He was carrying a telephone and extension lead.

'A call for you, Monsieur Patric,' the butler said, plugging in the phone and putting it on the table in front of him. He felt the old man's eyes flickering over him, narrowed with venom. Before he could say anything, Jarrive continued, 'A Monsieur Duclos on the line. I thought you might want to take the call.'

71

THE REFUGE WAS IN AN old soap factory, a high-walled compound in a part of town where Jacquot knew it was wise to keep a low profile after dark. When he'd worked homicide for the Marseilles *Judiciaire* this neighbourhood had been a regular night-time stop – small-time gang stuff, drug busts, the odd body. It wasn't much better in daylight, a scrubby, unloved, down-at-heel grid of streets and alleys where the few shops that there were had bars on their windows and roll-down metal screens at night. There were weeds sprouting between the paving slabs, torn posters and lurid graffiti on any flat surface, and wheel-less cars abandoned on brick supports.

There was no sign at the gates to indicate the presence of a refuge for abused women – which probably made sense, Jacquot reasoned – just a security camera on the wall and an entryphone. A woman answered his call and, when he held up his badge to the small camera, the gate creaked open.

'How can we be of assistance, Chief Inspector?' asked Sister Mercy, leading him down a lino-floored corridor that smelled of polish, distant food and candle wax.

'I'm looking for some information on a Monsieur Niko Emanetti,' said Jacquot, as the nun showed him into her office, sitting where she indicated, taking in the large crucifix behind her desk and the polychrome prints of Jesus Christ and the Virgin Mary to either side of it. 'I believe you know him.'

'I'm afraid that I don't,' replied Sister Mercy, her face chubby from the press of her wimple, cheeks red, eyes clear. 'I regret to say the name is not at all familiar.'

Which threw Jacquot just a little. According to Cluzot, a considerable amount of cash had been sent by his office to this address, the last of Niko's bequests.

'Monsieur Niko Emanetti, of Roucas Blanc? Some people knew him as Philo?'

The sister shook her head, gave him a bright smile.

'As I told you, I do not know the name, Chief Inspector.'

He decided to come at it from another angle. 'I understand that recently you received a sum of money. A contribution.'

The sister coloured. 'We receive many donations. It is how we survive.'

'This was quite a considerable sum of money.'

She narrowed her eyes, nodded. 'Then you are correct. There was such a contribution, yes.'

'For your information, it was Monsieur Emanetti who made that donation.'

Sister Mercy sighed, spread her hands. 'If he did, then we are most grateful for his generosity,' she replied. 'But that does not mean I have to know his name. There was no note with the money. *Tout à fait anonyme*.'

She folded her hands on the desk top and smiled. There was no intention to deceive, Jacquot was certain. The good sister really didn't know the name. And why should she lie?

'I believe he was married,' Jacquot began again, feeling his way. 'Maybe his wife was responsible for the donation?'

'If I don't know your Monsieur Emanetti, it is unlikely I would know his wife.' Another beatific smile. And a discreet glance at her watch.

But Jacquot persisted. 'Her name was Edina. Perhaps . . .'

The response was immediate.

'Edina! Oh, but of course,' said Sister Mercy, throwing up her hands. 'You should have said. We knew her well. She came here often. But I didn't know she was married.'

'She came here? To the refuge.'

'*Mais, bien sûr*. She read about us in the newspaper, when we first opened.'

'And that would have been?'

'Eight or nine years ago. That's when we started up.'

'And the reason for her visits?'

'As I said, she had read about us in the newspaper, the work we do here, and she wanted to volunteer her services . . . offered to help with the children while their mothers worked. That sort of thing. Happy to do whatever we asked. I suspect,' Sister Mercy continued, 'that she might have been abused herself, by a husband or a father. I can't say for sure, you understand. She never actually said.'

'It wouldn't have been Monsieur Emanetti,' said Jacquot. 'Could she perhaps have been married before?' he asked, knowing she had been.

'Possibly. Who knows? Edina was always very quiet, not at all forthcoming. But a beauty. In looks and in character. There was a kind of . . .' Sister Mercy looked lost for words '. . . a kind of brilliance about her; she seemed to shine. And that smile . . . Oh, just . . . luminous. And the children adored her. Always such a commotion when she arrived, laden with gifts for them – toys, sweets. She quite spoiled them.'

'You knew that she had died?'

Sister Mercy sighed, nodded. 'We received a card, asking us to pray for her. She suffered an illness.'

'She had written the card?'

'I do not know. I never saw her handwriting.'

'And then?'

'A few months later I received a phone call from a man. He was sorry, he said, to pass on bad news but . . .'

A sadness settled on Sister Mercy's face. It was clear to Jacquot that there had been a real affection for Edina at the refuge, and in particular from this woman sitting beneath the crucifix, and real sorrow at her passing.

'Did Edina ever say where she had come from? Where she had grown up? Anything like that?'

Sister Mercy frowned, then brightened as though at something suddenly recalled.

'Nice. I believe she came from Nice.'

72

THANKS TO MAÎTRE CLUZOT AND Madame Nallet, Nice was already on Jacquot's list. But as he drove away from rue Clermond and Sister Mercy's refuge, he decided it was too late in the day to make the journey. He would go in the morning, do what he needed to do, and stop for lunch at his favourite bistro in the old port. It was a long time since he'd been there, to the city and the bistro, and he was looking forward to it. The brief delay would serve to increase the pleasure.

Down in Marseilles' Vieux Port, Jacquot walked along the pontoon towards *Constance*, a rucksack filled with provisions from the millhouse slung over his shoulder. There was a warm gusting breeze out in the harbour that he hadn't really felt ashore, and a chop to the water that sucked and slapped at the pontoon.

'They say it's going to howl tonight,' called Gala, as Jacquot passed her mooring. 'Batten down the hatches. Pull a cork. Talking of which . . .' She waved a bottle. 'I was just about to start. Care to join me?'

He was still in his jeans and jacket, and could hardly wait to get into shorts and T-shirt. 'Give me twenty,' he called back. 'Time to change. I'll be back.'

Twenty minutes later he came aboard and stepped down into the cockpit. Gala handed him a glass, pointed to the bottle and indicated he should pour his own.

'You're just like old Philo. Never here more than a moment.'

'I have another life,' said Jacquot, sipping the wine, a sharp little *gris de gris* from the Ballon vineyards down the coast.

'Maybe he did too,' she said, lighting up a cigarette.

'Maybe,' said Jacquot. 'Did you ever wonder where he went? Did you ever ask?'

Gala shrugged. 'He'd spent his life at sea. Maybe that was enough. Maybe he just came back here every now and again to remind himself. By the way,' she said, changing direction, 'your friend came by last night.'

'My friend?'

'*Boufff*, you need to be told?' she teased. 'The one with the tight skirt and long legs. She was with you the other day.'

'Ah,' said Jacquot.

'Ah,' repeated Gala, giving him a look.

'She's a police inspector, Gala. She works for the *Judiciaire*.'

'I'm sure she is, and I'm sure she does,' Gala replied, but the look didn't shift from her face.

'She is an old friend,' replied Jacquot. 'There was a time . . . but those days are long past.'

'Still,' said Gala. 'Sometimes, with old friends, there's unfinished business, *n'est-ce pas*? That's all I'm saying.'

'I'm going to be a dad at Christmas, Gala.'

'That doesn't put you out of the frame – take it from an old hand at the game. All I'm saying, one sailor to another, is watch yourself.'

And then Gala paused, looked over Jacquot's shoulder and smiled. 'Well, what do you know?' she continued, tipping him a wink.

Behind him, he heard steps on the pontoon, the click, click of low heels.

He turned.

It was Isabelle.

73

'I DIDN'T MEAN TO BREAK up the party,' said Isabelle, as Jacquot ushered her aboard *Constance* and followed her down into the main cabin. 'Your friend looks like she throws a good one.'

'You're right. She does. But don't worry. You've saved me from a hangover. So, what can I get you? A beer? Some wine? Coffee?'

'A glass of wine would be perfect. Red, if you have it,' she said, slipping off her jacket and sliding on to the banquette, dumping her bag beside her and unclipping the holster and gun from her belt.

'So how's it been at the sharp end?' Jacquot asked.

'Non-stop. They're dropping out of the sky,' she replied, and as Jacquot pulled the cork on a half-finished bottle of wine, dished up some olives and bread, and reached for his cigarettes, Isabelle brought him up to date: Clara Garnolle, found dead in a street in Endoume, shot three times; her husband, Jean, the lead suspect in her murder until his own body was found two days later.

'Garnolle, that rings a bell.'

'Early sixties. An accountant, by profession, but long suspected of money-laundering for the families. Everything above board; a regular, respected practice in Toulon, and then here in Marseilles. But if anyone's money needed cleaning, if accounts needed to be fixed, Garnolle was the man they called in. As far as we can tell, the Famille Duclos in Toulon was his primary client before he was honourably discharged. Or rather, he made it to retirement without getting a bullet in the head. Maybe he's done a few odd jobs since then, on the side, a bit of consultancy, but nothing major.'

'So where did he turn up?'

'A crabbery in Saint-Cyprien. Caged in a lobster pot, and half-lowered into a tank of boiling water. It seems whoever did it had trouble with the lifting mechanism, or they left him like that deliberately. Half-boiled, and steamed.'

Jacquot winced.

'He'd been pretty badly beaten, too.'

'Like Dupont and his wife? Could it be the same team?'

Isabelle shook her head. 'I don't think so. First off, the Duponts were secured with wire, wrists and ankles. But Garnolle had rope burns, wrists only. And Garnolle definitely had the worst of it. Fingernails gone. Left eye popped. And he'd lost his teeth. Extracted, according to Clisson. Pulled out, not knocked out. Also, none of them were shot . . .'

'. . . in the knee and ankle, like Suchet. So you're telling me two different teams? Possibly more?'

'That's how it looks. Also, according to Clisson, Suchet wasn't the only one in that sinkhole with gunshot wounds to the knee and ankle. So far he's identified similar trauma on five of the bodies, like a trademark.'

'Punishment? Or did the killers want something?'

'I'd say they wanted something from Dupont. Remember the house? Properly turned over. But I can't be so sure with Garnolle and Suchet. Neither of their homes was touched. Their deaths may just have been payback for something they did. And there's another thing. Suchet was hidden, but Dupont and Garnolle were left to be found.'

Jacquot took a last pull of his cigarette and dropped it into the empty wine bottle, blowing the smoke towards an open porthole. He was quiet for a moment, thoughtful.

'In my experience, when it comes to the *Milieu*, there are usually two ways of getting rid of your enemies,' he began. 'You set an example, like Dupont and this fellow Garnolle. Or someone just disappears, like Suchet in his sinkhole. It's hard to say which is worse, for the families involved.'

Isabelle waved her hand dismissively. 'Daniel, you're going soft in your old age.'

'It's not soft, Issy, it's just . . . Even the bad boys have mothers and fathers. Wives, kids.'

'I know, I know. I do try not to forget it,' she replied, warmed by the 'Issy'; it was a long time since she had heard him use that name. 'But sometimes it's difficult, you know? You see so much . . . What's certain is that there'll be no shortage of weeping wives and mothers and kids after this is all over. It's like clearing up after a bar-room brawl, only bloodier. Oh . . . Did I mention Castel? You remember? The man Ranque transferred from solitary to the hospital wing?'

'He's dead?'

'Apparently he killed a prisoner, some kid they found in his cell. No one knew how the lad got in there – or if they do, they're keeping quiet about it – but some of his friends weren't too happy about it. A couple of days later Castel was let out in an exercise yard off "S" Wing and an access gate to the main prison yard was left unlocked. It was an invitation they couldn't resist.'

'That has to be deliberate, leaving a gate unlocked.'

Isabelle nodded. 'That's how it looks.'

'Ranque? Covering something up?' he asked, fetching another bottle of wine.

'Could have been. But now we'll never know. He's been hit too.'

'Ranque? Dead?'

'Shot, in the street. He was on his way to a restaurant for dinner with his wife. Their anniversary. A passer-by found him beside his car. A neighbour heard a motorbike stop, then speed off. Very professional. Again, the *Milieu*. Has to be.'

'Why on earth . . . ?' Jacquot started to shake his head, trying to fit a pattern to the various deaths but not succeeding. It all seemed so random, so . . . unconnected.

'If you ask me,' said Isabelle, holding out her glass, 'it looks like our friend Dupont was busier than we imagined. Otherwise, I just don't see how all this ties together.'

'Maybe it doesn't. Maybe it's not meant to. Just a settling of scores,' said Jacquot, pouring more wine into her glass and noting the sway of her hand; it looked like this wasn't the first drink she'd had that evening, a fact confirmed when she drew back her hand before he'd finished pouring and wine spilled over her wrist and sleeve and splashed on to her blouse.

'My fault, my fault,' said Jacquot, knowing it wasn't.

'It doesn't matter,' she said. 'Not a problem.' And then, getting to her feet, dabbing at the wetness, she asked, 'Do you mind if I change it? I've got a spare in my bag.'

'Help yourself,' said Jacquot, nodding to the for'ard cabin. 'And while you're at it, I'll get us something to eat. Hungry?'

'Ravenous,' she said, as she slid past him.

In the small galley kitchen, Jacquot set about unpacking the rucksack he had brought from home: plastic containers of cheese from the previous night's dinner, the remains of Claudine's blanquette, and a generous slice of the *tarte tatin* that Delphie had brought from Ladurée Royale in Paris.

He was bending down to slide the veal into the oven when a movement caught his eye. The door to the for'ard cabin was open, and Isabelle, with her back to him, was drawing the wine-stained blouse from her shoulders. Her skin was brown and smooth and he could see the narrow arch of ribs from her spine, the gentle swing of a breast as she reached forward for the dry blouse she had laid on the bed.

It was at that moment, straightening up, that she suddenly turned her head, caught him looking at her. She smiled, turned to face him, brought the blouse up to cover her breasts and then lowered it.

Jacquot's heart was in his mouth, and beating fast. Before he could say anything, she was coming towards him, the tight jut of her breasts utterly mesmerising. She dropped the blouse on the table and stood there, not a metre from him, the smile still on her lips.

'I wouldn't say anything,' she said, softly. 'No one need ever know.'

Jacquot knew she meant Claudine and saw for the first time the longing in her eyes, the hunger. She stepped closer and slid an arm round his waist, brought the tips of her breasts close to his chest, her mouth turning up towards his.

Jacquot was rooted to the spot, and astonished to find himself stirring at the closeness and heat of her body.

It would be so easy . . . so, so easy, he thought.

She was right, no one need know.

And they had been lovers before. It wouldn't be the first time.

But he knew that he wouldn't, couldn't go through with it, so he bent down and kissed her lightly, just to show he cared, just to show he didn't want to hurt her. They'd been lovers after all. There was still an affection there between them. An understanding.

But somehow, in the space of a few moments, that affection and that understanding changed, and his lips stayed on hers, and her tongue was at work, trying to part his lips, her breasts hot points pressing against his T-shirt.

'Isabelle . . .'

'It would be our little secret,' she said, and stepped even closer, taking his hand and leading it to her breast, holding it there, tightly, so that he could feel the hardness of her nipple and the beating of her heart, her other hand reaching behind him to press him against her.

'I want you, Daniel,' she whispered, the words just warm breath at his ear, 'and I think you want me. That's all. That's all I want.'

74

THE FOLLOWING MORNING JACQUOT WAITED till the rush hour had eased and then drove north out of Marseilles, up through Aubagne on the A52, stopping to fill up with petrol at the Baume de Marron service station. A few kilometres further on he crested that last ridge out of the city and saw the long, steely bulk of Mont Sainte-Victoire up ahead, its chalky flanks rising above the stream of mid-morning traffic on the Nice–Aix autoroute, and diminishing it. The sun was bright and sharp in a clear blue sky, the slipstream through his open windows warm and fresh and filled with a sharp sent of pine from the wooded slopes either side of him.

And as he drove, keeping to the slow lane, arm hanging from the window, he thought of Isabelle. Gala had been right, and he felt foolish that the old girl had spotted it, and he hadn't.

The whole thing had been so entirely unexpected, the evening before on *Constance*, him and Isabelle, the two of them in the main cabin, lights low, but no music, catching up on the Dupont case.

Unexpected for him, maybe.

But Isabelle? Not for her, he was certain. Isabelle knew exactly what was going to happen. Because she had decided to make it happen. Spilling the red wine on her blouse, the spare in her bag, changing in the for'ard cabin with the door open. She'd known all right. That bare back, the way she drew off the blouse, shoulder blades as sharp and straight as bookends. And then turning, catching his eye.

And he hadn't looked away. He should have done, of course, and been cool about it, waved it aside, joked, apologised perhaps. But he hadn't done any of those things. He had kept his eyes on her, straightening up from the oven and taking her in, standing in the doorway just a few metres from him, lowering the blouse from her breasts. And smiling, that soft, entrancing, wicked smile of hers as she came towards him, the sliding lick of her tongue between his lips when they kissed, taking his hand to her breast . . .

And he hadn't stopped the kiss, or taken his hand from her breast. He'd kept it there . . .

No, she'd kept it there. Hand, and lips too.

And he'd done nothing about it.

But it was the words that she'd whispered into his ear that really hit home.

'No one need ever know . . . Our little secret.'

Up ahead the traffic slowed for a *Péage* toll and Jacquot pulled into a lane, took his place in the queue, three cars back, taking the ticket. Light green, barrier up, and off.

Our little secret. Our little secret.

So easy, so easy. Right there, pressed against him. It had been four years but he could feel that warm body, moving against his, knew what she could do, would do. So familiar, all of it. The scent of her, the feel of her skin, the warm weight of that breast, the way she panted, urgently, when she made love, how she liked to push him back and rear up on him. All so familiar. Four years, and it was like yesterday, like coming home.

He didn't need to wonder what might have happened, then and there, on *Constance*, with Isabelle in his arms, if Salette hadn't stopped by with Philo's box of possessions, calling from the pontoon for permission to come aboard. In an instant, Isabelle was out of his arms, across the cabin and pulling on her blouse, tucking it in and sliding in behind the table, bag open, a file pulled out, all business by the time Salette swung down into the cabin.

Seeing Isabelle at the table had stopped the old man in his tracks; he hadn't expected Jacquot to have company. And a woman, too. He'd apologised for barging in. Introductions had been made. Chief Inspector Cassier, Jean-Paul Salette. Salette had offered to call by another time, but Isabelle had gathered her papers, her bag, her gun and holster and said she had to be going. A good-to-meet-you nod to Salette, a business-like shake of Jacquot's hand and thanks for his help, and with just the smallest smile and squeeze of his hand she was out through the wheelhouse, and off along the pontoon without a backward glance.

Unfinished business, thought Jacquot as he swung down the final slope of the auto route and the coast curved ahead of him, the blue waters of the Baie des Anges sparkling beyond the trees.

Business that was going to stay unfinished.

It wouldn't happen again.

He wouldn't let it happen again.

75

JACQUOT FOUND THE CINÉ LUXE Dorade with little difficulty, three blocks back from the Promenade des Anglais, in a quiet corner of the city where the apartment buildings had a dated charm – all rounded balconies, curling wrought-iron and Art Deco detailing. But the charm had been compromised by a faded salty decline: blistered stucco patched here and there with unpainted rendering, chips of mosaic missing from front steps, and window-panes dusty, cracked or boarded up.

The Ciné Luxe Dorade, in a line of these time-worn buildings, was different. Its cream stucco skin gleamed like icing on a wedding cake, its gutters and downpipes were a glowing copper, and the steps leading to its double glass doors were set with curving brass handrails. An art-house venue in the very best rig, a brand new face-lift courtesy of the law firm, Cluzot Fils in Avignon, and the bequest of a Marseilles fisherman called Niko Emanetti. What, wondered Jacquot, as he pushed open the etched and bevelled glass doors, would be the story here.

As he stepped into the unlit foyer he smelt the fresh paint and plaster, felt the thick pile of the scarlet carpet give beneath his feet, and smiled at the ornately caged box-office, its decorative brass filigree the colour of newly-minted gold. It was, he decided, a rare jewel of a cinema, everything faithfully and elegantly restored. No popcorn machine here, no hot-dog warmer, no pick'n'mix sweet counter to be seen. And, judging by the current programme – Jean Gabin in *La Grande Illusion* – a cinema that was unlikely to carry a Hollywood film any time soon. Delphie would have approved.

The foyer was empty but somewhere up ahead he could hear the humming sound of a Hoover. He followed the humming down a dimly-lit corridor, its dark crimson walls lined with black-and-white studio portraits of French film stars from the Thirties and Forties. On one side of the corridor the likes of Gabin, Fresnay, Rains and Dalio; on the other their leading ladies: Simone Simon, Michèle Morgan, Madeleine Renaud, Jany Holt and others.

At the end of the corridor, through a set of velvet-lined double doors, he stepped into a small theatre, its screen opulently draped in scarlet, and its plush-covered seats set in sloping, curving rows beneath the shadowy arc of a rising gallery. Light came from a square-cut chandelier hanging over the centre of the stalls, and in the middle aisle a woman pushed a vacuum cleaner to and fro.

'I'm looking for a Monsieur Dorade,' Jacquot called out, as he approached between the nearest row of seats.

The woman turned, cocked an ear, and he asked again for Monsieur Dorade. She could so easily have switched the cleaner off, but she kept it on, playing it back and forth as though her arm had a will of its own. With her free hand, the vacuum's cord coiled around it, she pointed behind him, 'Foyer. Stairs to the gallery. First landing, door on your left.'

Jacquot thanked her with a wave and a nod and retraced his steps, back down the corridor and into the front hall. Coming round the empty box-ofice he found the spreading, brass-runnered stairs, jogged up to the first landing, found the door on the left and knocked.

'*Oui, entrez*,' he heard from the other side of the door.

He opened it, looked round the edge.

Sitting at a desk in the window, with the back of the billboard rising behind him and cutting out the view, was a young man working his way through a pile of paperwork, fingers tapping away at a calculator. There was a coffee mug on the desk beside him, a half-eaten *pain au chocolat* on a plate, and a cigarette in the ashtray.

'I'm looking for a Monsieur Dorade?'

'Auguste or Louis?' asked the young man, glancing up, fingers poised above the keys. He was in his thirties and a little overweight, his ginger hair gelled into a Tintin quiff.

'The elder of the two,' said Jacquot, hazarding a guess.

'Then you'll be after my father, Auguste.' He looked at his watch. 'If you're lucky, you'll catch him at the café on the corner. If he's not there, he'll have gone home. Rue Bagnon, off Bordelaise. Number thirteen. Otherwise, come back in a couple of hours for the matinée. He never misses the first showing.'

'And if he's at the café . . . ?'

'You can't miss him.'

'Thank you, Monsieur. You have been most helpful.'

Dorade Junior was right. His father would have been hard to miss. The old man sat at a table in the window of the Café Bonne Claire and Jacquot spotted him from the street. A four button jacket, tightly done up, a paisley cravat settled into the collar of a vivid pink shirt and a shock of white hair at odds with a luxuriantly black moustache. He was reading a newspaper, held close to his face and turned to the light.

Jacquot ordered a coffee at the bar and took it over to his table.

'Monsieur Dorade? Your son said I might find you here. May I join you?'

'So long as you're not selling anything,' the old man replied, still reading his newspaper.

The voice was as crisp and sprightly as the pink shirt. A showman, thought Jacquot as he put down his cup and drew up a chair. Only then did Auguste Dorade lower his newspaper and settle curious eyes on him.

'You're a policeman,' he said at last.

Jacquot smiled. 'How did you know?'

He tapped his nose, but offered no explanation.

'And you would be correct. Chief Inspector Jacquot, from Marseilles.'

Auguste Dorade gave him another appraising look. 'You're a sportsman, as well. That's right, too, isn't it? Or rather, you were a sportsman, if you'll forgive the unpardonable suggestion that you are no longer as young as you once were.' There was a flowery extravagance to his speech, and Jacquot smiled again. 'You see, I have a memory for the moving image, Chief Inspector. And I have seen you before. Moving. On that terrible contraption, *la télévision*.'

'Once again, Monsieur, you would be correct.'

Old man Dorade nodded, narrowed his eyes, gave it some more thought. 'Rugby. You scored a try a long time ago. I'm right, aren't I?'

'A long time ago.'

'I saw it just a few days ago. You had a ponytail.'

Jacquot nodded. The forthcoming Rugby World Cup was doing him no favours. As far as he was concerned the past was the past, and it was foolish to linger there.

'So if you're not selling anything, what do you want from me?' asked Dorade, also moving on, as though he sensed that Jacquot had no interest in talking about his sporting past.

'Just a few questions. Someone you might know, something you might be able to help me with.'

'Film, or life?'

'Niko Emanetti.'

Dorade gave it some thought, then shook his head.

'*Rien*. Nothing. Not film, that's for sure.'

'What about Eddie? Or Edina?'

Dorade gave a start, and the next instant his eyes began to well with tears.

'She's dead. You've come to tell me she's dead, haven't you? Or maybe in trouble?' For a moment or two he looked hopeful.

'I'm afraid you were right the first time, Monsieur. She has passed away. A short illness. Two years ago.'

The old man nodded, tried to swallow back the tears.

Jacquot let a moment or two pass.

'So you did know her?'

'From when she was a child,' Dorade replied quietly, clearing his throat, gathering himself. 'Maybe twelve, thirteen. A real street urchin, she was.'

'Did you know her surname?'

'A street urchin with a surname? It was just Eddie. Always just Eddie. I never even knew it was Edina.'

'How did you meet?'

'In the street, where else?'

Jacquot spread his hands, to suggest he continue.

'She used to hang around my picture house, looking at the posters. I thought she was a pick-pocket, waiting to stitch my customers. First few times I chased her away. Her and her brother.'

'She had a brother?'

'Brother . . . stepbrother. I never knew. Chances are they weren't even related. But they were always together, this younger kid in tow as though she was teaching him the ropes. He was a little . . . slow. Always a frame or two behind the soundtrack, if you understand?' He pulled a handkerchief from an inside pocket, shook it open and wiped his eyes. Refolding it, he slipped it away.

'So what happened?'

Dorade chuckled. 'I gave her a job, that's what. In the end, when I couldn't budge her. Cleaning, first, with the boy. Going down the aisles between performances. She never missed a scrap of sweet-paper. Emptied the ashtrays, without being asked. As though she knew. When she was a little older, we put a tray on her, sent her down the aisles with the ice cream; the ones with the little light, remember?'

Jacquot nodded. He remembered.

'Never sold so many ice creams, before or since,' he continued, with a smile. 'She pretty much lived here, back then. Used to stand in the shadows, waiting with her tray, watching the films. Just entranced.'

'Were there parents? A home?'

'If there were, I didn't know about them. She just turned up, did her job, went off.'

'When did you last see her?'

Dorade fell silent. And then, regretfully: 'A long time ago. She must have been late twenties – thirty maybe? Just one of her visits.'

'She didn't work for you then?'

'No. She'd moved on long before. Worked down at the beach, the far end, below Colline du Château. A nightclub called . . . Studio . . . Studio something. But she always dropped by if she was passing, kept in touch. She was like that, Eddie.'

'And the boy?'

Dorade shook his head. 'I remember she said she'd got him a job as a driver, with a cab company. Couldn't do up his shoelaces without help, but he knew cars, engines. Drove pretty well and had a memory for street names and numbers. Could take you anywhere, she told me.'

Jacquot moved on, not really knowing where he was headed, but sensing a destination.

'What about boyfriends?'

'*Ooh là-là* . . . Many, many boyfriends. Of course. She was . . . gorgeous.'

'Anyone in particular?'

Dorade sighed. 'The man she married. The man she shouldn't have married. Not a good man. She should have known better. The one thing she did that I couldn't comprehend. In the end, of course, she ran out on him. That was the last time I saw her, when she came here to say goodbye. Driving the most beautiful old sports car. Red, it was. Like her lipstick. Open-top. English. A Jaguar, I think.'

'How was she?'

'Tearful, upset, but still . . . dazzling. And filled with hope. She told me she'd met someone else, someone she really did love. That she was running away with him, and that she'd be in touch.'

'Did she say where she was going?'

Dorade shook his head. 'If she did, I can't remember.'

'And that was the last time you saw her?'

'The very last time,' he replied, looking out of the window and down the street, as though she was actually there, outside his cinema in her red sports car. 'I never heard from her again.'

Jacquot sipped his coffee and waited. There was a fond, wistful smile on the old boy's face.

'Do you remember exactly when that was? The last time?'

'Of course I do. 1972. About this time of year. I remember we were showing . . . *Discreet Charm of the Bourgeoisie*. Luis Buñuel. A real sell-out. It had rained in the morning but when she called by the sky was blue again, the sun low but bright. I remember it flashing on the car's windscreen. And she had the roof down.'

'Did anyone come looking for her? After that visit?'

'No one. They probably didn't know about me.'

Putting down his coffee, Jacquot said: 'You had a . . . gift not so long ago. In the post, from a lawyer in Avignon.'

'That's correct,' said Dorade. 'A year ago. Eighteen months. The place was run down, times were hard. Hollywood! *Boufff*, the Ciné Luxe Dorade doesn't do Hollywood. *Alors*, not modern Hollywood, you understand. Just the classics. Black and white in the main. French preferably. Gabin, Renoir, those kinds of names. Someone wanted to redevelop the site, pull us down. There was a story in the newspaper about it. A campaign to keep us open. And suddenly, there was this money, everything we needed . . . And more.'

And then he stopped, abruptly, fixed his eyes on Jacquot.

'Are you saying . . . ?'

'You didn't know it was her?'

'My son, Louis, called the lawyer. He wouldn't give a name. Said his client wished to remain anonymous.'

Given the time frame it couldn't have been Eddie who had sent the money. But Niko would have. She must have told him about her days at Ciné Luxe Dorade, and how much the old boy had meant to her. And Niko had maybe read the story in the newpaper, and remembered, and done what he knew she would want him to

311

do. Just as he'd likely done with the refuge in Marseilles. On Edina's behalf.

'Do you remember the name of this boyfriend? The one she ran away with.'

Dorade pursed his lips. 'Filo. Something like that. Sounded Italian.'

'Did you ever meet him?'

'Just heard about him. That's all I needed to know. The way she looked when she talked of him . . . I got the impression that he was older than her. She seemed to like older men. But I never met him.'

'And the husband, the man she left?'

'Older too, and a *con*. Like I said, she should never have married him. And I told her so. It was madness. And running away from him? Like that? She'd never stop running, I told her. He'd never let her go. He'd search for her, and he'd find her. That's why, I suppose, I wasn't surprised I never heard from her again. Sometimes I feared that he'd done just that, found her and killed her.'

'Who?'

'I told you. That *salaud* she married. If you lived in Nice, you'd know the name. Polineaux. Patric Polineaux.'

76

ONCE A WEEK RENÉ DUCLOS dined at La Barque on a rocky outcrop above *plage* Briande a few kilometres west of Saint-Tropez. He always ordered the grilled sea bass, the cherry ice cream, and for a pleasant hour or two watched the boys on the beach as they worked out on the parallel bars and rings, played volleyball, or showered the salt off their lean brown bodies when they came out of the sea, his usual table on La Barque's terrace close enough to the showers to hear the water pelt and spatter over their skin.

But it wasn't just La Barque's proximity to the beach or its rewarding views that brought Duclos here every week. Nor was it the fact that he owned not just this restaurant but the six-restaurant franchise that his old friend, Garnolle, had set up for him along the coast. What brought him here on such a regular basis was the manager, a young Arab called Numar, whose job came with accommodation, a small *cabanon* in the woods above the restaurant.

On this particular visit though, there was altogether another kind of business to conduct, and Numar would have to wait. While Duclos sipped his Martini Mao Tai, mixed and served by Numar, and watched the boys on the beach, two black Range Rovers with tinted windows turned into La Barque's forecourt and drew to a stop. Before the dust had settled, Didier stepped out of the lead car, with Léo, Zach and Dhuc, in close attendance, the three heavies taking up position around the parking lot, all of them in black suits and wrap-around sunglasses.

By the time Didier reached the second Range Rover, Jarrive and Delon had started lowering the ramp with Patric Polineaux on it, wrapped up and strapped into his wheelchair.

'Is he here?' asked Polineaux, looking around suspiciously.

'There's a couple of his boys by the entrance,' replied Didier, nodding towards Beni and Jo-Jo, 'so I'd say yes.'

'Those two? In the leathers?' asked the old man, as Delon steered his wheelchair off the ramp.

Didier nodded. 'And there's a couple more over by the beach path.'

Polineaux glanced across the parking lot and grunted.

'Duclos' boys never had any style. For a *pédé*, you'd have thought he'd make more of an effort.'

If the short trip from the parking lot to La Barque was managed with the minimum of difficulty, it all changed once they were through the main restaurant and shown out on to the terrace. Duclos had made no arrangements for Polineaux's wheelchair and the old man was forced to wait while the five other chairs at the table were drawn aside and stacked and removed to make room for him. By the time Polineaux was wheeled into place, Duclos had turned away from the beach view and settled a cunning eye on his old adversary.

'*Mon cher ami*! How good to see you again. How long has it been?'

Both men knew that 'dear friend' was stretching the limits of their relationship, and that Duclos was grossly exaggerating his pleasure in sharing a table with Polineaux. But Polineaux let it slide, raising an eyebrow and giving the question due thought.

'Marseilles, a few months back. Arsène Cabrille's funeral.' He turned to Didier. 'That's fine, you can leave us now.'

'Of course. Of course it was. Though I don't know why we bothered. Such a nasty piece of work,' said Duclos, watching Didier join Jarrive and Delon at a table at the far end of the terrace. Not

314

a bad looking fellow, he thought to himself. A little weighty maybe, but lovely features.

'He had his good points,' said Polineaux.

'Name them.'

Polineaux spread his hands, smiled.

'Exactly. So, my old friend, let's not spoil our lunch any further by wasting time on the good Lord's little mistakes.'

Duclos looked over Polineaux's shoulder, lifted a finger, and Numar and his boys sprang into action. A bottle of Krug was popped, poured and laid in a bucket of ice, and a lobster salad presented, a pair of tails sliced paper-thin, and set in a fan on a nest of watercress.

'I don't eat fish,' said Polineaux, with a dismissive sniff at the lobster tails, knowing that Duclos owned the restaurant but pretending he didn't. 'An omelette will do me well enough. If they can manage it in a place like this.'

Duclos managed a smile. 'But of course . . .'

And so their lunch began, Polineaux playing with his *omelette nature* and *salade Niçoise*, Duclos tucking into his lobster and sea bass, their conversation limited to small talk, gossip and the old days. It was only after the cherry ice cream, when coffee and a very fine cognac made their appearance, that Duclos got down to business.

'It appears, *cher* Patric, that there is something else we have in common, apart from old friends and the pleasure of each other's company.'

Polineaux gave him a questioning look. He had had a fair idea what was on Duclos' mind when they'd spoken on the phone and arranged this meeting, but he'd decided to leave it to his lunch companion to make the running.

'And what might that be?' he asked.

'A mutual interest,' Duclos continued, certain that Polineaux would know what he was talking about. Why else would he have agreed to their lunch? 'And a small bone to pick,' he added.

'A bone?'

315

'Toulon, my patch. Nice, yours,' explained Duclos, probing gently.

'You've lost me already, *mon vieux*.'

'A certain action that I should have been involved with, Toulon being my neck of the woods and not yours.'

Polineaux frowned. 'And what action might that have been?' he asked, reaching for his cognac. A Courvoisier *Essence*, the tear-shaped Baccarat flask left promisingly on the table. And Delon at the other end of the terrace. Out of mischief, he asked, 'You don't suppose this place has cigars, do you?'

Duclos, his patience starting to fray, beckoned Numar over and asked for the humidor.

'Don't bother with the box, sonny,' said Polineaux. 'A Cohiba Robusto, if you have such a thing.'

'As I was saying,' Duclos began again. 'Twenty or more years ago now, a certain action on my patch . . .'

'An action, you say?' Polineaux's eyes narrowed.

'An action, yes. A job. Well, it now appears that one of my operatives was involved in this action . . . one he subsequently assured me that you had organised.'

'Astonishing,' said Polineaux, determined to give nothing away. He knew, of course, which operative Duclos was referring to, and was anxious to learn just how much information his lunch companion had managed to squeeze out of the man before consigning him to that crab cage in Saint-Cyprien. The newspaper reports that he had read had failed to provide these details.

'Astonishing indeed,' said Duclos. 'I could hardly credit such a thing.'

At that moment Numar returned with the Cohiba. He offered it to Polineaux who pulled out his cutter and snipped off the end. A match was lit and applied to the cigar.

'And what exactly was this "action" I'm supposed to have organised?' asked Polineaux, drawing happily on his cigar. 'And on your patch, to boot.'

'A ton of gold,' said Duclos, leaning forward. 'The missing gold from the Gineste heist. I have reason to believe it is still out there, somewhere. And together, Patric, if we pool our resources as we should have done back then, we might still be able to locate it . . . or what is left of it.'

Polineaux started nodding, as though his memory had been stirred.

'*Mais oui*, I remember that action,' he said, finishing his cognac and nodding at the flask.

Duclos obliged.

'It was an extraordinary affair,' Polineaux continued, watching the liquor swirl into his glass. 'Beautifully planned, perfectly executed. But nothing to do with me, I assure you. *Alors*, I always thought that Ballantine or Rachette were behind it. Perhaps you would be better served talking to them. Though, of course, if I can be of any assistance, I'd be only too happy to . . .'

Duclos pursed his lips. 'Patric, Patric. Please . . . It is of no concern to me now who was or was not involved. All I am saying is that my information is solid, and that after considerable efforts my associates are already closing in on a certain individual who may hold the key to the whereabouts of the gold.'

'*Alors*, so you are there already. In which case, what possible help could I provide?'

'As I said, if we were to pool resources . . .' Duclos took a deep breath, sighed, unable to decide whether Polineaux was playing him or really didn't know anything. And Garnolle had been so certain, so convincing. 'I believe that you may know something of the individual in question,' he continued. 'That you may be able to help us find him. In which case, of course . . .'

'And this individual is who, exactly?'

'His name is Emanetti. Niko Emanetti. We traced him to Madrague, but according to a neighbour he moved to Aubagne a few months back.' Duclos paused, reached for his glass, tipped back the cognac. What he was about to say next needed all his nerve. 'I understand from my sources that this Niko might have . . . might have been . . . acquainted with Edina. That the two of them . . .'

317

The mention of Edina's name had an immediate effect.

'Emanetti? Emanetti? I know of no man called Emanetti,' declared Polineaux, throwing down his napkin and flicking his fingers over his shoulder. At the end of the terrace Didier, Jarrive and Delon leaped to their feet. 'And your . . . your . . . snide little insinuation that my Eddie might in some way be involved,' he continued, his face starting to redden and bulge, 'does you very little credit, René.' He took a final pull on his Cohiba and dropped it into the cognac. 'So. There we are. *C'est fini.* And my thanks for the *omelette.*'

Ten minutes later, as the Range Rovers sped away from La Barque, old man Polineaux turned to Didier and smiled.

'I was right. It's that *con*, Emanetti. Have Léo and the boys check it out, and let's keep an eye on Duclos.'

And if we're lucky, thought Polineaux, we might just find Eddie too.

77

BY THE TIME JACQUOT STEPPED aboard *Constance* that evening, he had a pretty shrewd idea what had happened. Where old Philo had found his fortune, what it was, and how he'd come by it. Piecing it all together over a late lunch at Bistro Pierre, and on the drive back from Nice, settled behind the wheel, the slipstream rush of warm air through his window, going over what he knew, what he'd learned.

It was one of the reasons Jacquot loved cars, loved driving. Night time was best, of course: the isolation, the darkness, chasing his headlights' beam, following something through in his head. But evening was just as good, even if it meant driving into the sun, visor down. It was still speculation, he would have been the first to admit, but it was getting good enough for Jacquot. Suddenly there was a trail ahead of him, and he was following it.

It all started with that name Polineaux.

Monsieur Patric Polineaux.

Jacquot didn't need to live in Nice, as old Monsieur Dorade had suggested, to know that name. 'Old Legless', they called him at police headquarters on rue de l'Évêché, suspected of involvement in dozens of major crimes going back forty years or more, but never once brought to book. Not a minute spent in police custody.

Always alibi-ed up, and protected by an army of lawyers. And even without legs he was still a deadly bastard.

Dorade was right. Polineaux wasn't the kind of man to forgive or forget. If his wife did a runner, he'd have been after her. No one crossed Polineaux and lived to tell the tale.

Which was why she and Niko had come to Marseilles, battened down, kept a low profile.

Had she had plastic surgery? he wondered. There'd certainly have been enough money, but he didn't think so. There were so many other ways a woman could change her appearance without resorting to a surgeon's knife.

As for Niko, hanging on to the apartment in Madrague had to be a given – no obvious disappearance to draw attention to himself; staying a few nights now and then, to maintain a presence, a cover; meeting up with Salette and the Brotherhood; taking the odd job. Living two lives, because he had to, but never saying a word.

About Edina.

About the gold.

The gold . . . Twenty-seven years ago. It all fitted. They had to be mixed up with the gold. The Col de la Gineste heist. Three security trucks hijacked, two recovered with crew and gold on board, the third missing until Barsin called it in. Just the truck and the empty pallet and a body. Down on the Madrague quay.

Lombard territory. Like anywhere along the Marseilles coastline.

And now Lombard was dead, after possibly stirring up old memories.

And his lawyer, too, for helping him do it.

And Suchet, who hadn't always been a chief executive.

And this Jean Garnolle, a gangland money man. His wife, too, Isabelle had said.

And Ranque, for whatever reason.

And the prison killer, Castel.

And how many others? Jacquot wondered.

More bodies still to find probably, like the ones pulled from that sinkhole in the Esterel Hills.

It was all starting to fit together. Just a few important pieces left to find to finish the jigsaw.

Like where was the gold?

Where had Niko and Eddie hidden it?

And was there any left?

They surely couldn't have got through it all. A ton of gold? Say . . . what? . . . twelve million francs. A lot of money back then. A lot of money still. Even with the house and the books and the travel they'd have been hard pressed to work their way through a fortune like that.

Jacquot remembered the drama down on rue de l'Évêché the day after the Gineste heist. The whole place in uproar. Everyone hauled in from other duties to track down that missing gold, and find out who was behind it all. The crews they'd pulled in from the two trucks weren't saying a word, so it had to be someone big.

Someone dangerous.

Someone the crew members feared more than the cops.

Someone like Polineaux.

They'd never been able to prove a thing, of course, but the *Judiciaire* had always been convinced that 'Old Legless' was behind it. Maybe some of the other families, too: Ballantine and old Bouri had been mentioned; Duclos in Toulon, his patch, where the gold had come ashore. But there'd been nothing to stick on the man, or on any of the others.

Jacquot remembered, too, how Barsin had got himself in charge of the investigating squad, sniffing out all the leads himself, making everyone else work back-up. Knowing Barsin like he did, Jacquot wouldn't have been surprised to learn that his boss had been playing off-side, had his finger in the pie. Which, come to think of it, was maybe how he'd come to collect those four 9mm bullets in that underground car park.

As for Niko, well, Edina was surely the key here. She was certain to have known what was going on, sure to have overheard Polineaux planning things, or learned of it through her 'brother'. And with Niko, she'd hatched a plan, not just to get away from her husband, but to take enough money with her to disappear for good, for the two of them to be safe for ever. Somehow she and Niko – and that 'brother' of hers, maybe – had got their hands on that missing truck, and the gold it carried.

And now, by the look of things, Jacquot wasn't the only one on their trail. There were those two hoods he'd followed from Madrague to Toulon. Duclos territory. And everything that Isabelle was investigating following the Duponts' murder tied in neatly with what he'd found out by himself, after taking possession of *Constance*.

As he parked in the underground lot below Cours d'Estienne d'Orves and set off along the quay, he thought about the roadster that Dorade had mentioned and wondered how much such a car would have been worth back then. Because she'd certainly have sold it. If you wanted, or needed, to keep a low profile, buzzing around town in a lipstick red Jaguar was hardly the way to go about it. No, she'd have sold it. Probably enough, with change, to buy the boat they'd have needed to carry away the gold, the boat that Niko had bought at auction, the boat he, Jacquot, now owned.

And as he stepped aboard, unlocked the wheelhouse hatch, he wondered how long it would take before someone found out about *Constance* and came calling.

322

78

THERE WAS A SPRING IN Isabelle Cassier's step as she arrived at police headquarters on rue de l'Évêché, and a lightness in her head and in her heart that she hadn't felt for months, years even. Since she and Jacquot had first spent a night together, she decided, up in Le Panier, in his top-floor apartment. A few months later she might have ended it, but four years on she was in no doubt that he still had feelings for her. And two nights earlier, on *Constance* he had shown those feelings, had responded to her. Of course, he was a man, she thought to herself, jogging up the stairs to the third floor rather than waiting for the lift. Maybe it was just the thought of sex that had held him there. But sex was as good a place to start, or restart, as any other. Just one step on to making love.

And maybe, back then, she'd been a little too demanding, wanting too much, too soon. Four years ago a long-term girlfriend had just left him (she must have been mad, thought Isabelle), he'd lost his job on the squad and been transferred to some outpost in Provence. Jacquot, of all people. He must have been reeling. She realised now that she'd made her move too soon, should have given him more time, more space. Well, there was plenty of that now, with Jacquot down on that darling little boat just a few minutes' walk from her office. How much better did it get?

And if it hadn't been for that old man, Salette, turning up when he did, who knows what would have happened? She knew; he'd have taken her to bed, in that cosy little for'ard cabin, or pushed her up against the chart table, or lowered her on to the banquette. He was seconds from it. From taking her. Just as he'd done before. The two of them back together again; a new start. As for his current girlfriend, and the baby . . . Well, they'd deal with that when the time came. For now . . .

'You just missed a call,' said Laganne as Isabelle worked her way between the desks to her corner spot, giving her hips an extra swivel for the hell of it. Let him look as much as he liked, she thought. That's all Laganne was ever going to get. But Daniel was a different matter.

'Anyone interesting?' She dumped her bag on her desk and leafed through a pile of phone messages.

'It's about Jacquot,' said Laganne, sitting at his desk, fashioning a dart out of a piece of paper. His phone started ringing. He ignored it. 'Some old biddy down in Madrague wants him to call her. Those old girls just fall over themselves for that dude.'

Not just the old ones, thought Isabelle.

'Did she leave a number?'

Laganne tipped back his arm and let the dart fly across the room, swooping over to make a perfect landing on her desk. He gave her a wink then leaned over to answer his phone.

She looked at the dart, a number pencilled across its wings, then reached for her phone.

The woman who answered had a voice as broad and as sharp as a Vieux Port fish-wife.

'I'm not saying what it's about,' she told Isabelle. 'Like I said to the other man, I just want to speak to that Jacquot.'

'Maybe I can help . . . ?'

'And that's women, too, *chérie*. Just that Jacquot. It's important.'

'I'll give him your number, and make sure he calls.'

'You do that, dearie. Just Jacquot, remember.'

Isabelle put down the phone, gathered up her bag and headed

324

for the door. This time she didn't bother with the hips. Tough luck, Laganne.

Down in the car park she signed out an unmarked squad car and headed up the ramp, took a left at the barrier, and another left on to avenue Schuman, heading for the harbour. It might be a wasted journey, she thought, but it was worth a try. The call from Madrague gave her an excuse for the visit. But she'd play it cool, everything above board, professional and friendly.

She knew that the next move had to be decisive.

And it had to be his.

Parking the unmarked squad car at the security gate on Quai Rive Neuve – the P sticker in the top left corner of the windscreen would see off any tickets – she tapped in the code that Jacquot had given her and headed down the pontoon towards *Constance*. As she passed Gala's boat she waved to the old girl and smiled. Another old biddy after Jacquot, she thought. What was it about him? Young or old, the girls all loved him.

And there he was, in paint-stained shorts and espadrilles, leaning back in his skipper's chair with his feet on the console, a coffee mug in one hand, a cigarette in the other, just watching the traffic out in the harbour.

Not a care in the world.

A man worth having, she thought.

A man she was going to get. One way or another.

'Someone wants to talk to you,' she called out from the pontoon.

Jacquot spun his head round, green eyes settling on her.

'And who might that be?' he asked, levering himself off the skipper's chair and coming over to her. Nice, easy, friendly and, she was pleased to note, no sign of embarrassment or discomfort at her surprise visit.

'She sounded very glamorous,' said Isabelle, keeping her tone light. 'I thought it might be important.' It was the first time she had seen him bare-chested in four years, and she found it hard to keep her eyes off his body, tight and tanned, bulky and strong in the shoulders. For his age he was still in very good trim.

'And who . . . ?'

'She said her name was Clémentine.'

Jacquot frowned. Either he didn't know the name, or it meant something.

Isabelle took her mobile from her bag, reached over and passed it to him.

He dropped the cigarette into his coffee mug, took her phone, examined it.

'You use one of these?'

'It's the next big thing. Already, and for ever. You had better get used to it, Jacquot. Things change.' She gave him a smile, nothing more.

He put down his coffee mug on a seat locker and flipped open the phone.

'Aerial too,' she said, relieved that her voice was steady. Her mouth was suddenly dry and she could feel the beat of her heart.

He did as he was told, pulling out the tiny black stalk from the top of the phone.

'And the number?'

'It's already primed. Just press "Call". The green telephone on the top row.'

'Okay, okay,' he laughed. 'I have done this before, you know? But mine's an older model, still a bit Stone Age.'

She watched him press the button and put the phone to his ear. While he waited for the call to be answered he held out his hand, as though to help her aboard.

She waved the hand away, and stayed where she was. A good move, she thought. Suitably distant.

The call was swift.

'*Bonjour*, Clem, *c'est Jacquot ici.*'

He paused. '*Maintenant*? *Oui, s'il te plaît.*'

He cut the connection, pushed the aerial into its socket and handed the mobile back to Isabelle. He gave her a long look, as though working something out. It made her feel warm, that look.

'You got a car?'

She nodded.

'I've got to go to Madrague. You want to give me a lift?'

'Is it important?'

As far as Isabelle was concerned it didn't matter one hoot if it was important or not. Any excuse. Just the chance to be with Jacquot was enough for her.

'Could be,' he replied. 'Just give me time to put on a shirt, some jeans, and I'll be with you.'

'I'll be out on the quay,' she said, turning back along the pontoon. 'Red Citroën, unmarked.'

79

FOR THE FIRST FIVE MINUTES the two of them drove in silence, Jacquot wondering what could have possessed him to invite Isabelle along, and Isabelle concentrating on the road, negotiating the traffic up through Catalan and on to Fausse Monnaie before accelerating away on to the Corniche. The sea on their right glittered in the sunshine, a vast bowl of blue flecked with rearing white horses that reached to the chalky headlands of Montredon and Cap Croisette across the bay.

'So what's it all about? This Clem lady?' asked Isabelle, wanting to fill what was beginning to feel like an uncomfortable silence but determined to keep it professional. So far Jacquot had made no mention of their last encounter; indeed, had offered no excuses, or second thoughts, or in any other way dismissed what had happened two nights earlier in *Constance*'s main cabin.

'It's a long story,' he said, pleased to note that Isabelle had so far failed to bring up that awkward, if arousing confrontation aboard *Constance*, behaving as though it had never happened. Maybe there'd be no need for him to say anything, he thought, which would be a relief. Maybe she'd had too much to drink, let herself go, and was now embarrassed, even mortified, by her flagrant behaviour. But those were two very big 'maybes', he decided. He'd have to see how things panned out.

'It's another twelve minutes to Madrague,' she suggested. 'Try the shortened version.'

'It started with my boat, *Constance*,' he said.

'Left to you by an old fisherman.'

'An old, wealthy fisherman,' Jacquot continued.

'I didn't know fishermen got to be wealthy.'

'Normally they don't, but this one did.'

And as Isabelle followed the curve of the Corniche flyover, Jacquot told her how his curiosity had been aroused by this extraordinary bequest, his desire to find out a little bit more about his fairy godfather, and how he had followed the trail from a bookshop near the Opéra, to a mansion in Roucas Blanc and a museum in Aix, from a prestigious legal practice in Avignon to a women's refuge in Belsunce and an Art Deco cinema in Nice.

What he'd found out along the way and pieced together.

And what he'd come up with.

His . . . theory.

'Back in the early-seventies,' Jacquot continued, 'my old fisherman fell in love with another man's wife . . .'

'Not this Clem?'

Jacquot chuckled. 'Not Clem, no.'

'A rich man's wife?'

'A rich man's wife.'

'And they ran away together?'

'Correct.'

'And the lady's name?'

'Eddie. Edina Polineaux.'

Isabelle was silent for a moment.

'*The* Polineaux? "Old Legless"?'

'The same.'

'And that's who the money came from?'

'Yes. And no. Some of it. To start them off. But not all of it. You see, we're talking about a very, very large amount of money here. What they took. Far more than they could ever have spent. Far more than you or I . . .'

329

'Come on, Jacquot, spit it out. What are you talking about?'

'I think my old fisherman and Polineaux's wife might have had something to do with the Col de la Gineste heist. Before your time, I know, but . . .'

'1972. Three security trucks hijacked, a ton of gold in each. Two of the loads recovered, but one missing. Have I got the right heist?' She shot him a look, eyebrow arched, then changed down gears to pull out past a lumbering tourist coach.

Jacquot chuckled. 'You have the right heist.'

'And you think your fisherman and his girlfriend were involved. That they took this missing gold?'

'That's what I think. It's the only possible explanation.'

'So where does Madrague come into it?'

'That's where the third security truck was found, four or five hours after the heist. Short of its cargo. Seventy-five bars. With a body on the quayside. And Madrague's where Philo lived until he died a couple of months back.'

'And Edina? What's happened to her?'

'She was the first to go. Two years ago. Shortly after she died, Philo sold the house and contents in Roucas Blanc and came back to Madrague full-time. As far as I can establish, the proceeds of the house sale and the contents were distributed among a number of beneficiaries; deserving causes, that sort of thing.'

'And the gold? What happened to the gold? They couldn't have got through it all.'

'Maybe they did. Who knows?'

'Or maybe they had to split it. Share it out with accomplices.'

Jacquot shook his head. 'I don't think so. It was just the two of them.'

'And you reckon there's still some left?'

'Possibly.'

'Buried somewhere?'

'Or stored somewhere safe. Somewhere no one can find it.'

Isabelle was silent for a moment, then glanced across at him. 'Jacquot, you really do know how to show a girl a good time.'

'Just the average kind of boat-owner's day. Life afloat.'

Up ahead the road curved past a red-clay football field and dropped down into Madrague.

'So, where do you want me to go?' asked Isabelle.

'Second turning on the right. Rue Tibido. Down at the end, wherever you can park.'

80

SITTING AT THE SAME CAFÉ table that Jacquot had used for his own surveillance, a young man in a zippered nylon blouson and jeans put down his newspaper and watched a red Citroën cruise down rue Tibido. He was tired and he was bored and his back-up was late. For the last few days, he and three other colleagues had kept a twenty-four-hour watch on the wooden gate a few steps down from rue Pélanne. Most of the time they spent in their cars, always parked on the shaded side of the street during the day, and far away from any streetlight at night. Since sitting too long at the café might have aroused suspicions, the watchers had limited them-selves to just a couple of hours per shift. The rest of the time it was the car, or a stroll up and down the street. Just so long as the gate was always in sight.

At first there'd been little activity beyond visits from *La Poste* and a couple of trips out and back for the old lady, to the local shop on the quay judging by the carrier bags she struggled back with. But the night before three heavies had paid a call, stayed an hour and then come back out. His friend, who'd been on watch, had called it in, and they'd all been told that if the boys came back – or if anyone of interest happened to drop by – then they should report it pronto and follow up. But the heavies hadn't returned – and nor had anyone else – and the young man in the blouson didn't really expect them to.

Idly, not expecting anything of interest, he watched the Citroën reverse into a parking space on the opposite side of the street, no different from the other four cars that had come down this street in the last two hours, no reason at all to suggest its occupants might be about to push through that old gate.

And they didn't. Instead they set off down Tibido towards the harbour. The woman in black trousers – a looker; the man in jeans – older and rougher looking. Maybe going for lunch at Chez Aldo or Au Bord de L'Eau, the young man guessed. But he was wrong. They kept straight on and disappeared round the corner and on to the quay.

Out of sight, out of mind, he decided, and settled back to his newspaper.

81

'THIS IS WHERE IT HAPPENED,' said Jacquot, coming out on to the quayside at the end of rue Tibido. Without any buildings to protect them, a gusty breeze tugged and snatched at their hair and clothes and fretted the sea into dashing white caps that crashed and slapped against the breakwater. The waves were not large enough to breach the wall but the glittering white wash they threw up filled the air with a warm, salty breath. Across the bay, through a dusty blue haze, lay the city they had just left and, beyond it, the low, grey bulk of the Sausset highlands.

'This is where they found the truck?' asked Isabelle, pushing the licks of black hair from her face.

'Reversed up to those bollards,' said Jacquot, gesturing to their left, his white T-shirt, she noticed, pressed tight by the breeze against his body. 'As close as they could get to the quay. Doors open, gold gone. I arrived about ten in the morning. Barsin was already here, the first on the scene following reports of gunshots. They'd moved the body by the time I got here, but the blood hadn't been hosed off.' He pointed to a patch of ground midway between the bollards and the quay. 'All that was left was the empty truck and the waistcoats they'd used to carry the gold. Three waistcoats in all, counting the one on the body. Three pouches in each. For three bars. Say, twenty or so trips between them. They'd planned it well, with time to get those waistcoats made.'

'And they got away in a boat?'

Jacquot nodded. 'That's how it looked. You could see the path their feet had made, weighed down, back and forth from truck to slipway, and over there we found a mooring rope still tied to one of the quay rings. A clean cut to one end. When they left, they left in a hurry.'

'On *Constance*?'

'That's what I think.'

'Quite a history, your little boat.'

'If that's how it happened. If it was *Constance*.'

With the wind whipping about them, Jacquot and Isabelle walked along the quay, past the line of fishing skiffs, to the low wall at its end.

'From here, they could have gone anywhere,' said Jacquot. 'Out to the islands, to Cassis, back to Marseilles, L'Estaque. Anywhere. On *Constance* a full tank'll get you four hundred kilometres, maybe a little less with the load they were carrying. But still a good, safe distance. And at night, no moon, you wouldn't have seen a thing by the time they got past the breakwater. Impossible to follow. Free and clear.'

They turned and walked back to Tibido in silence, both of them in the blustery, late summer sunshine thinking of that distant chill November night twenty-seven years before, the sound of whispers and running feet and panting breath.

'They had some nerve,' said Isabelle.

'Oh yes,' said Jacquot. 'Nerve, and luck.'

And each other, he thought. The pair of them watching the harbour lights diminish as they lumbered out to sea, heavy in the water, starting out on a new life together.

Half-way up Tibido Jacquot pulled the key from his pocket and stooped to unlock the wooden gate.

Had it been worth it? he wondered, pushing the gate open and stepping aside for Isabelle to pass through.

The risk. The danger.

Capture by the cops.

Or a bullet in the back of the head from a vengeful Polineaux.

Or, best case, the rest of their lives looking over their shoulders.

Twenty-seven years on the run.

Probably, he thought, following Isabelle through the gate and closing it behind him.

But only because they got away with it.

To live rich and happy, for the rest of their lives, each with the person they loved.

As pay-offs go, not a bad return.

82

THE WATCHER WAS THINKING ABOUT ordering another coffee, or maybe a beer, when he spotted the same man and woman coming back up the street, heading for their car. But they passed it without stopping, walked on until they reached the gate where the man bent down to unlock it and then pushed it open, the two of them stepping through and closing it after them.

The watcher felt a tightness in his gut, an involuntary straightening of the back. After the long wait, something was happening.

In no apparent hurry, he left some coins on the table and strolled across the street, pausing at the Citroën to light a cigarette. As he cupped his hands and flicked the wheel on his lighter, he checked it out. Bodywork a little dented round the wheel arches, a few scrapes and scratches, and a fine dust over the red paintwork. The back seat was empty, but its footwells were littered with fast-food packaging and discarded Styrofoam coffee cups. In the front there were some maps in the driver's door pocket, and a coiled wire plugged into the cigarette lighter. The wire disappeared under the front passenger seat. The watcher knew what would be on the end of it. A domed flashing light with a sucker or a magnet to clamp on to the roof. To confirm it, he checked the windscreen, top left corner. No doubt about it.

Five minutes later he was back in the café and making a call from the pay-phone just inside the door, with the wooden gate still in view.

'Beni, it's me. There's a couple of people just gone in. Man and a woman. Cops.' He listened for a moment. 'Of course, I'm sure. Unmarked car . . . Got a "P". Top left windscreen, that's right . . . Okay, I got that. Yeah, I'll get back to you soon as I know.'

Having completed the call, the watcher went to the bar, ordered himself a salami baguette to go and returned to his car.

83

CLÉMENTINE HAD MADE EVERY EFFORT to clean up her cramped, ground-floor apartment in Madrague: two broken kitchen chairs dumped outside her front door, the smashed doorstep flower pots swept into tidy piles, the surviving furniture put back in place, rugs straightened, and the rope of tied herbs and *saucissons* restrung above the range. But if she'd managed to get her home back in order, there wasn't much that she could do about the cut across the bridge of her nose, and two swollen, yellowing black eyes.

'They hit me just the once. Here,' she said, pointing to her nose, as though she needed to. 'If I'd been wearing my teeth, I swear I'd have swallowed them. Choked to death. As it was, that's what I did. Played dead, with blood spouting out of my face while they turned the place over. If I'd had floorboards down here, they'd have ripped those up too.'

Jacquot and Isabelle took the seats she indicated at the kitchen table.

'When was this?' asked Jacquot.

'Last night. After dark,' she replied.

'Did you report this to the Police?' asked Isabelle, and immediately felt foolish, cheeks flushing, as both Clem and Jacquot turned to look at her.

'I called Jacquot, didn't I?'

'I mean . . .'

'The same two men?' said Jacquot, sparing Isabelle any further blushes.

'Different,' replied Clem, going to a cupboard and pulling out a label-less bottle, fingering up three small glasses from the sink. 'And three of them this time, one of them *un petit Chinois*. Real toughs. Worse than the first lot. And they were bad enough.'

Isabelle gave Jacquot a look as the old lady put the glasses on the table and with an oily plop pulled the cork from the bottle.

'Calva. A gift from Philo. 1927, he told me. Nearly as old as me,' she added with a cackle as she poured three good shots.

My kind of girl, thought Jacquot fondly, toasting her and tasting the spirit, the scent and flavour of apples that had grown in Normandy more than two decades before he was born hitting with a warm, autumnal intensity.

'They thought I was dead, you know? "You killed her, Léo," one of them said. Even bent down to feel for a pulse but couldn't find one, not with all my fat, and *grâce à Dieu* for that,' she said, crossing herself.

'Léo?' asked Isabelle.

'That's the name I heard,' Clem replied. 'Léo, loud and clear. But I don't know which one it was. Not the chink, *c'est certain*,' she said with a grim chuckle.

Jacquot put down his glass and looked across the table at Clem. He sensed a certain discomfort in her, just as he had on his previous visit. He wondered if it was Isabelle being there, or some after-effect from the blow to her face, but he discounted both. There was something else, something quiet and hesistant about her as though she still hadn't told them everything she knew.

'Could you identify them?' asked Isabelle.

Clem gave her a patient look. 'They weren't wearing masks, you know? Didn't need to. That sort, they don't care. No one's going to stand up and say "that's him", "that's him". Me included. And they know it.'

'So tell me, Clem, what were they looking for?' Jacquot asked quietly.

'Whatever it was, they didn't find it,' she said, refilling their glasses, pushing home the Calva cork with a defiant roll of her shoulders.

'What were they looking for, Clem?' Jacquot persisted. He knew now, for sure, that there was something she was holding back, felt it deep inside, with a sharp and thrilling certainty, warm like the Calva.

Clem said nothing, chewed her toothless gums. She stared into her glass and then tipped the Calva back, making her chins wobble.

Jacquot knew with that swallow that she'd made up her mind about something. He was right.

'It was always a joke between Philo and me. He gave it to me a few weeks before he died. He was old then, and ill. He was on the way out, no question.' She gave a sigh, played with her empty glass. 'One time I used it as a doorstop and no one noticed. Out there, in the yard. That made him laugh. And back then, towards the end, he didn't laugh much, *le pauvre*.'

'So you hid something?' asked Isabelle.

The old lady didn't turn to her, kept her eyes on Jacquot.

'In the stockpot,' she said, at last. 'That's where I put it when I heard them at the door. And they didn't find it.'

Jacquot got up from the table and went to the stove, lifted the high-sided saucepan from its ring and lowered it to the floor. It was heavier than it should have been, much heavier. He lifted the lid and looked inside. The fish soup had been replaced by a creamy tripe stew. Rolling up a shirtsleeve he dipped his hand between the cold, puckered folds, parting them, pushing down. And then his fingers brushed against something that shouldn't have been there. Something heavy and solid, something difficult to get a proper grip on, something that slid from his grasp, slippery from the covering liquid. But finally he drew it, dripping, from the pot and carried it to the sink, turned on the tap and as the water flushed over it, the gold gleamed.

'*Voilà*,' said Clémentine. 'Now you have it.'

341

84

'HOW DID YOU KNOW? ABOUT the gold?' asked Isabelle, as they drove back into town, Clémentine's one-time doorstop wrapped in a Carrefour carrier bag between Jacquot's espadrilles. The sun was slanting between the buildings as it started its afternoon dip over Marseilles. Columns of light and shade flashed across the Citroën's windscreen.

'I didn't. I was as surprised as you. I just knew she wasn't telling us everything. That she was holding something back.'

'She didn't seem to mind when we took it with us,' said Isabelle, turning due west out of Fausse Monnaie, the light and shade now replaced by the sun full on, showing up the dust and insect smears and wiper tracks on the windscreen. She eased off the accelerator and snapped down the sun visor.

'I think she was relieved,' replied Jacquot, pulling down his own.

'I'm not so sure I'd be relieved if someone took a gold bar off me. But I'd say it confirms your suspicions about Philo,' said Isabelle. 'What I'd like to know is just how much of the gold they got through. Some of it? All of it?'

'Enough to live a very pleasant life,' replied Jacquot. 'And still have a bar to spare nearly thirty years later.'

'Just the one bar?'

Jacquot chuckled. 'I don't think so. Do you?'

'So where is it?'

'Well, the place to start looking is probably Roucas Blanc. Les Étagères. Where he and Eddie lived. Maybe he buried it there.'

He thought of Madame Jeanne Vaillant and her fears that her terraces might have to be dug up. She would not be pleased.

And nor would he if the *Judiciaire* decided to take a closer look at *Constance*. For *Constance* had clearly been used for the get-away, transporting the gold to wherever Philo had stashed it. He knew that nothing was hidden on board, but it might prove difficult persuading the authorities of that.

'I hope you're not going to send anyone down to rip up my decking,' said Jacquot as they passed *plage* Catalan and made their way down to the Vieux Port. Without letting Isabelle know it, he glanced at the dashboard clock. In two hours Claudine and Delphie would be coming aboard.

'I'll take your word she's clean,' Isabelle replied, pulling into the kerb at the same spot where she'd parked a couple of hours earlier. She kept the engine running. Jacquot realised it was a drop-off. Finding the bar of gold meant an immediate return to police headquarters on rue de l'Évêché for Isabelle, to make her report and get the ball rolling. It was, Jacquot judged, the perfect moment to say what needed to be said.

He pitched his voice low, a caring sort of tone, not wishing to hurt her.

'Listen. About the other night . . .'

'What about it?' she asked, one hand on the wheel, the other on the gear-stick, a smile playing across her lips. Her look was level, in control. There was nothing he could say that could hurt or disappoint her. She knew where this was going. She'd known it since that moment on *Constance*, pressed up against him, his hand on her breast, his lips on hers.

'I'm not the one for you,' he said, trying to construct the right words to explain his situation. 'It's not going to happen, Isabelle. Things have changed.'

'You're right. They have. But right now I've got work to do, so get out of here,' she said, and leaned across to give him a peck on the cheek, touching her foot to the accelerator at the same time to let him know she was anxious to be gone.

'I'll be in touch,' she said, as he unbuckled his seat belt and climbed from the car, wincing at an unexpected jab in his buttock. 'When I know what's happening. You might have to come in if you want to keep your decking.' And by the time he'd closed the door and bent down to say goodbye she was already checking traffic behind her, edging out into the flow with a wave and a toot of the horn.

Neither of them had noticed the dusty blue Renault that had followed them from Madrague and parked across the road, the driver's window down, a long-lens camera clicking away.

Part Four

Part Four

85

CLAUDINE AND DELPHIE ARRIVED AN hour earlier than
planned, but Jacquot had had enough time to get things organised
for their arrival. When Isabelle drove away in the unmarked car,
he'd checked his wallet and gone straight to the shops. An hour later,
he'd struggled back to *Constance* with a sealed jar of *foie gras* from
Charcuterie Brignolards on rue Cevennes, two bottles of Château
Plaisance Meursault and two carrier bags bulging with other essentials
– the wrinkled Lucques olives that Delphie loved, a tin of oiled
soupions, cold meats, bread, fruit and salad. By the time he'd stored
any perishables in the fridge and cool box, tidied up the main cabin
and made up the bed in the for'ard cabin for Delphie, the top of his
thigh and left buttock had started to ache. It had been a long day,
and it still wasn't over. Swallowing a couple of his prescription
painkillers, he'd cracked open a bottle of beer, found his cigarettes
and retreated to the wheelhouse where he perched on the skipper's
chair and stretched out his left leg, going through a few of the exercises that the physio had recommended for times such as these.

Jacquot had finished his exercises and his beer and was reaching
for his cigarettes when he sensed the sisters' approach – the hollow
thump of their footfalls on the wooden-decking of the pontoon,
and the squeaking rise and fall of the hoops on the pilings. When
he looked up, the sun, hovering above the rooftops of Le Panier,

splashed gold across their faces as they came towards him, rucksacks over their shoulders. Claudine, a few centimetres taller than her sister, raising an arm to wave; Delphie, a few centimetres rounder, pushing back her hairband and holding it down to keep more of her flyaway hair in place. He was pleased to note that both women had dressed sensibly in cotton trousers, plimsolls, one good woollen jumper apiece and whatever they had stowed in their rucksacks. The breeze had increased since he'd stood on the quay at Madrague and his plan for supper and an overnight stay in one of the calanques between Marseilles and Cassis had been shelved. According to the forecast the wind would be gone by the following day. They could go then, for lunch. Something to look forward to.

One by one, the two women came aboard, Claudine first, stepping down to be taken in his arms, Delphie next, giving him a quick hug then turning to take in her accommodation.

'You never said.' Her eyes were wide. This was clearly not what she'd been expecting.

'Never said what?' asked Jacquot, taking Claudine's bag, picking up Delphie's and turning for the wheelhouse and the cabins below.

'Never said how beautiful she was. I had no idea.' Delphie was shaking her head, hands on her hips, taking it all in like a trainer sizing up a thoroughbred: the boat, the mooring, the Vieux Port all around them, the seagulls arcing above as the breeze tugged at her hair and snatched at the sleeve of the sweatshirt slung over her shoulder. 'Forget Paris,' she continued, breathing it all in. 'I want to move in. I want to live here. On this boat. For ever.'

Claudine reached for Jacquot's free hand and pulled herself close to him. 'Sorry, sister. It's taken. And so's the man.'

Below decks, Jacquot showed Delphie to the for'ard cabin. Clean white sheet, sea-blue pillowslips and matching duvet cover neatly tucked into the curving, planked bow space, the hatch propped open to catch the breeze, Isabelle's wine-stained blouse, which he'd found between mattress and bulkhead, spirited away.

'Daniel, it's adorable. Just adorable. I love it. I want it.'

Her smile, her delight, were infectious and Jacquot beamed with pleasure.

'And all these books,' Delphie continued. 'I didn't realise you were so well-read.'

'They came with the boat. But I'm making headway. Talking of headway, there's the head,' he said, opening the narrow door between the main and for'ard cabins. 'And a small shower, too, on the other side. Water's hot if you need it. Come and join us when you're ready.'

'Hey, I'm ready now. Open a bottle. Let's get started.'

Ten minutes later, bags stowed, the first bottle opened, the three of them sat out on the aft deck, chinked glasses, and toasted the setting sun, the two women drawing their jumpers around them as the temperature started to fall and the evening began. Around the harbour the city turned on its lights, the sky darkening through bands of rose and mauve and purple, latticed by the masts and rigging all around them, the earliest stars starting to wink, the façade of the Hôtel de Ville and Fort Saint-Jean across the harbour both floodlit, the neon lights of bars and restaurants turning to a warm night-time glow.

But protected from the breeze by the wheelhouse, they stayed on deck, setting up the trestle table for the *foie gras* and toast and Meursault. In place of candles, the one thing Jacquot had left off his shopping list, he brought out the two hurricane lamps from the seat locker and hung one from the wheelhouse roof and put the other on the table so that they could see what they were eating. And when every last smear of the *foie gras* was gone, he served a dish of figs and peaches to sluice away the richness of the liver, followed by a platter of Picodon and Banon goats' cheeses, aged and hardened into ball-sized discs, but softened by a mellow red from the Bellet vineyards down the coast. And when their supper was finished, Jacquot uncorked the Calva, nowhere near as good as Clémentine's but up to the job, and poured two tumblers, Claudine happy with the water she'd been drinking since the last of the Meursault was finished.

Delphie took a sip and leaned back in her seat.

'Now that is what I call a meal,' she said, as her younger sister got up to clear the table, bent down to kiss Jacquot's head and left them on deck. 'What a wonderful gift,' she continued. 'And from someone you hardly knew. Claudine told me on the way down. You must have been astonished.'

Jacquot admitted that he had been, but did not tell her how astonishment had turned to a cop's curiosity and what his enquiries had uncovered, the secrets he had learned about his benefactor.

'Looks like she's been in the wars, though,' said Delphie, letting her eyes settle on the woodwork above the wheel house.

'How do you mean?' said Jacquot, turning to look where she was looking.

'Well, if I didn't know better, I'd say those were bullet holes.' She pointed at the curve of the wheelhouse roof where the hurricane lamp was hooked up. 'A couple of holes there, on the left, near the corner, one in the middle and a bigger tear on the right, half-way down. But then I guess a Customs boat tends to get itself into bad company. Goes with the job, I suppose.'

Putting down his glass, Jacquot got to his feet and went to the edging of the roof.

Saw the marks that Delphie had spotted.

Ran his fingers over them.

Small, yellowing holes that years before had been filled with plastic wood and varnished over, a new coat every season. For twenty years or more. He'd covered them himself, just a few weeks earlier and never noticed. Never thought to notice. Maybe it was the play of the light, but now they seemed to scream at him and he was astonished that he'd missed them. Of course, they could have been caused by any number of other things, but Jacquot knew, with a kind of warm satisfied certainty, that Delphie was right. These were bullet holes.

For a moment, standing there on the aft deck, he could hear the crack of gunshots, the zip and whine of bullets, the splintering thunk as they gouged into the woodwork, Philo at the wheel, right here, where he was standing now, Eddie taking cover in the cabin or flat out on the deck, returning fire maybe, the pair of them – and the gold – lumbering out of Madrague on to an inky black sea.

350

86

RENÉ DUCLOS PUT DOWN THE phone and felt his pulse quicken. He'd been asleep when the call came, but answered '*Oui, c'est moi*' softly, keeping his temper in check, even as he came awake. He knew that no one would dare call him at this time of night unless it was important. Very important. Something he needed to know.

He'd tried to prop himself on an elbow, as he might have done in the old days, but had felt a stab of pain in his shoulder and laid himself back on his pillows, the phone held to his ear. When the call was over, he'd replaced the phone in its cradle, and continued lying there in the darkness, watching the moonlight fall like silver bars through the shutters. The windows in his bedroom were open and from the boundary of his estate he heard the quick bark of a dog, one of the dobermans that patrolled the property. Salome was always flirting with them, brushing past them, pushing her eager snout between their taut back legs. But the dobermans paid no notice, just the cock of an ear and a supercilious look. The performance always amused Duclos.

But now there were more important things to consider than Salome's lustful advances and the dobermans' cool disdain. According to Aris, his senior lieutenant, a man and a woman had visited the fisherman's apartment in Madrague. One of Beni's boys

351

had called it in. They were driving an unmarked police car, but the watcher couldn't be certain that they were both cops. The woman had looked the part but her companion was just a little too scruffy. This had been borne out when he'd followed them back to Marseilles. The man had been dropped at the old port and the woman had driven on, more than likely returning to police headquarters.

Apparently the watcher had taken some photographs which were currently being developed, and had reported back to Beni that the man had gone shopping and returned to the quay an hour later. He'd let himself through the security gate and gone to a boat moored out of sight at the very end of a pontoon. Without the security code Beni's boy had been unable to access the jetty, but when two women went through the gate an hour or so later he'd slipped in after them. He'd let them get ahead of him and then followed them down the pontoon, far enough away not to be noticed, but close enough to see the same man he'd been following come out on deck and greet them.

'And the name of the boat?' Duclos had asked.

'*Constance*,' Aris had told him.

Constance, Constance, Constance, he whispered, lying in the darkness.

He wondered if Polineaux knew about *Constance*. He certainly hadn't mentioned it when they'd met for their lunch on *plage* Briande. But then he hadn't mentioned anything, hadn't so much as hinted he might know what was going on.

Bastard, thought Duclos, and closed his eyes.

87

THE WEATHER FORECAST HAD BEEN right. When Jacquot came out on deck the following morning, the sky was a deep cloudless blue, the harbour waters barely rippled by a breeze, and the *tricolores* above the entrance to the Hôtel de Ville and on every mast in the old port were still. But without the breeze, Jacquot knew that even this late in the summer it would be hot by midday, so he set about preparing *Constance* for their trip to the calanques while Claudine and Delphie slept on below.

Sliding the companionway hatch closed, he slipped the mooring lines and hauled up the fenders. Then, treading carefully so as not to disturb the sisters, he went for'ard to raise the anchor, hand over hand, coiling the dripping rope and chain and stowing it all in the anchor locker. Back in the wheelhouse, floating free now, Jacquot started up the engine and felt the soft rumble as the twin Volvo diesels caught. Opening the throttles, he steered *Constance* into the fairway between the pontoons, put the helm hard to starboard and edged her into the main harbour.

It was the first time that Jacquot had taken her out since his trip with Claudine, and as he stood at the wheel, checking for traffic passing to and fro in the harbour, he felt a great lift of exhilaration. A skipper at the wheel of his boat, preparing for the open sea. The feel of the deck, smooth and warm beneath his feet, the slight judder in the wheel as he passed it through his hands, the comforting bass throb and throaty gargle of the engines beneath and behind him, and the first gentle rock as he steered out over a passing wake and pointed *Constance* between the forts of Saint-Jean and Saint-Nicholas.

Ten minutes later he was past the breakwater and heading east, cutting smoothly through a low chop, past *plage* Catalan and the Malmousque boatyards, the sea a dark, glittering blue. Looking to starboard he could see rougher water out past the Frioul islands and Château d'If, silent white-caps riding in from the open ocean, prancing along like snowy dolphins beside a ferry from Tunis coming in to La Joliette and a low-slung container ship, further off, heading out in to Golfe du Lion.

Jacquot took a deep breath and felt it course down to his toes, firing up every nerve ending, filling him with a bubbling joie de vivre.

God, this is the life, he thought. This is the life . . .

88

NIKO EMANETTI WAS DEAD.

Buried at sea.

While Duclos' boys were chasing their tails up in Aubagne, Léo, Dhuc and Milagro had found an old netmaker in Madrague who had known him, been one of the funeral party that had pitched him overboard. Dead and gone, the netmaker told them, all that's left an empty apartment on Tibido up for rent and his old boat down in Marseilles' Vieux Port.

But Didier Lacombe was not a happy man. Not only had Polineaux vetoed his plan to bring in the boat's owner after they'd finally tracked *Constance* down, he'd insisted that Didier take charge of the watching brief.

On Polineaux's motor cruiser, *Corsaire*, now berthed in Marseilles' Vieux Port.

And Didier liked neither the sea, nor Marseilles.

As far as he was concerned the ocean was a lovely thing to look at, but that was as far as it went, an altogether alien environment that hid below its surface all manner of lurking dangers. Didier preferred his size twelve Berluti loafers planted on firm ground, and if he wanted to swim he'd jump in a pool, *merci beaucoup*.

As for Marseilles . . . well, it was a pit. Nothing to recommend it. Where Nice was sleek and glamorous, Marseilles was dowdy and dismal, as far from the picture-postcard charms of the Côte d'Azur as it was possible to get. Their mooring on Quai des Belges stank of fish from the daily market, the seagulls never seemed to cease their screeching and there was absolutely no privacy. Whenever he went out on deck, there were always people walking by, just a few metres from the boat, looking in, pointing, admiring. Hardly surprising, he supposed. It was old now, but *Corsaire* was still a fine ship, handsome more than elegant, solid more than sleek, a thirty-metre cruiser from one of the finest Italian yards. Just the kind of thing the old man loved but which he, Didier, loathed.

And it moved, constantly. Didier could sense it in every step he took. A shift, a sway, sometimes so gentle he wondered afterwards if he'd imagined it. He'd have checked in to one of the hotels along the harbour if there had been one worth staying in. But this was Marseilles, and Sofitels and Novotels and Mercures didn't do it for Didier. And the Nice Passédat was just too far away from the port to be a viable proposition in terms of surveillance.

Not that he'd done much of that. Since leaving Antibes the previous afternoon and berthing in Marseilles he'd spent most of his time aboard *Corsaire* in his cabin, watching movies and flicking through the sports channels while his boys kept an eye on *Constance*. The night before he'd drunk too much of Polineaux's cognac and had woken with a dry mouth and squinting eyes to the screeching call of gulls. He was lying in his bed, wondering if he was strong enough to handle breakfast, when the phone beside his bed trilled lightly.

It was Cassel, *Corsaire*'s skipper, up on the bridge.

'She's moving out. You want us to follow?'

Didier pushed himself up with a low groan. 'Who's aboard?'

'Same as last night. The man and the two women.'

He licked his lips. 'Follow them.'

89

LIKE JACQUOT, GALA DESFORNADO HAD woken early, taking her breakfast beneath the sunshade stretched above the cockpit of her yacht, delighted that at last the breeze was gone. It seemed the *Metéo* boys had got it right for a change. The last three days she'd had to paint below decks, where the sand and dust and grit snatched up by the wind could not reach her palette and canvas, always having to compensate for the occasional tilt and roll before touching brushtip to canvas. Passing wakes were bad enough but the continual shift of a harbour chop was the very devil for the detail strokes.

But while painting in the main cabin was the safe option, there were significant problems attached to working on a canvas below decks. First of these was the size of the main cabin – too cramped to properly accommodate her easel and canvas – and by mid-morning, too hot to paint comfortably. And when she painted she liked to see what she was painting, in this case the rising, clustered roofs of Le Panier across the harbour. But below decks, hemmed in by boats to either side of her, there was no view to speak of, and she had to keep clambering up into the cockpit to remind herself of the shades of colour, the play of light and the angles. Sometimes she wondered why she bothered. And then she remembered. It was cheaper painting here than hiring a studio in town.

But today would be different. She could set up her easel right here, in the stern, and paint without interruption from the breeze.

She was finishing her second mug of coffee and lighting up her third Gitane when she heard an engine fire up at the end of the pontoon, spotted a curl of blue exhaust smoke from *Constance* and saw Jacquot at the wheel, manoeuvring Philo's old Customs cutter out of its berth. She watched him nose into the fairway between the pontoons and negotiate the turn out towards the harbour, pausing a moment before pulling out into the main channel. He stood tall at the wheel, feet apart, checking to left and right, confident in command. Not bad for just a few short weeks, she thought to herself. He looked as if he was born to it. And as far as she could see, no sign of the two women who had come aboard the previous afternoon. If he hadn't told her that his wife and sister-in-law were visiting she didn't know what she might have thought. That Jacquot. Every woman after him, like as not. And she could see why. Twenty years younger, and a few kilos lighter, and she'd have given him a try herself.

Thirty minutes later, a paint-stained smock over her one-piece swimming costume, her hair tidied away under a scarf, and her easel set up in the cockpit, Gala was mixing a dab of blue and yellow on her palette for the treetops above Le Panier when she saw three men coming down the pontoon, looking from side to side, checking the names of the boats. Her first thought was, They're hoodlums. Just from the look of them. Two in jeans, sneakers and black tees under black leather jackets, the leader, in front, taller than his companions, with a blue shirt under a cream linen jacket, pleated cotton trousers and tasselled loafers. They passed her with just a brief glance at the name of her boat and headed on down the pontoon until they came to the empty berth where *Constance* had been moored. She watched them shade their eyes and look out into the harbour, confer in a huddle and then come back down the pontoon.

They stopped at her mooring and the boss man called out to her, wished her *Bonjour* and asked if there was a boat called *Constance* on the pontoon. His hair was black, rippled with curls, oiled back, curling behind the ears and over his shirt collar. In need of a trim. He also had a goatee, black and pointed, the rest of his jaw cleanly shaved.

For a second Gala was tempted to say 'no', pretend she'd never heard such a name. But there was just something about them. The kind of men you didn't lie to. She felt a quiver of guilt as she said, '*Mais oui*, the empty mooring at the end.'

'You know where it's gone?'

This time she was quite happy to answer, because she really didn't know where. When Jacquot had told her about his wife and her sister visiting, he hadn't said anything about a trip.

'*Je sais pas*,' she replied, with a shrug, a paintbrush in one hand, the other pressing down on the hem of her smock so it wouldn't blow up and show anything. 'Cassis? L'Estaque, maybe?'

'The owner. You got a name?' He asked the question like a cop might ask it, or like a true-blood, no-good bastard gangster – which he clearly was; the kind of bruiser who was used to getting answers to his questions. The right answers. Without too much delay.

She frowned, tried to look confused, as though she didn't know or couldn't remember the name. Goatee man's eyes bored into her.

'Jacquot,' she said. 'Daniel Jacquot.' And felt the wince of betrayal. Whatever trouble Jacquot had got himself into, she wasn't making it any easier for him.

'He's a cop, right?' Goatee called up to her.

Gala nodded. 'Yes. That's right. He is.'

'In town?'

'*À l'intérieur*,' she replied. 'Up-country.'

Goatee took this in, looked around, left and right, then straight back at her. Laser eyes. Black. Cold as ice.

'When he gets back, no need to say we called by, you understand?'

It wasn't a suggestion.

'Hey, I'm an old girl. Blind as a bat, me.'

She felt ashamed of herself, but she couldn't do anything about it. She was suddenly very frightened, skin chilled and puckering even as the sun bore down on her. Exposed. Vulnerable. With Michel still away in Corsica there was no one within fifty metres of her. Except these three *gorilles*. At the end of her gangplank. From now on, she swore to herself, she'd keep her gangplank up. Just in case. Not that they'd dare do anything in broad daylight. Then again . . .

'You got a radio on board? VHF?' Goatee asked, as though he'd just thought of it.

'Yes, I do. But it's broken.'

'Don't you need it when you take the boat out?'

Gala managed a smile. 'This boat hasn't left its berth in five years or more. All I've got down there is a cassette player.'

'Okay, then. Good,' said Goatee. 'See you around.'

And with that the three men turned and headed back to the quay and Gala Desfornado hoped, and prayed, that none of them would ever see her around again.

90

JACQUOT WAS CLOSING ON CAP Croisette, with the ports of Pointe Rouge and Madrague just a couple of kilometres off his port side, when the companionway hatch slid open and Claudine climbed up on deck. She was wrapping a silk gown around herself, pushing a hand through tousled hair, and when she caught his eye she gave him the kind of smile that would fill any man's heart. Two hours earlier he had woken her softly with warm exploring fingers, their love-making silent. Not a whisper, hardly a movement, with Delphie so close. Cupped like spoons. Just a final sigh, like someone falling asleep. Which was what Claudine had done. Now she was beside him, sliding an arm round his waist, resting her head on his shoulder.

'*Bonjour, mon Capitaine.* And how are you?'

'Pleased to have my crew reporting for duty,' he replied.

'You seem to have managed quite well all by yourself,' she said. 'I thought I'd leave it to you.'

'Is that so?' said Jacquot taking a hand off the wheel and wrapping his arm around her, bringing her closer.

'Mornings like this,' she sighed, 'does it get any better? It's just so beautiful, isn't it? Out here, at sea. Just us and the ocean.'

'And Delphie.'

'And Delphie. She's up by the way, and taking a shower.'

'Tell her the skipper says not to use too much water. She's not in Paris now.'

Claudine gave him a pinch, nuzzled closer.

'So is *Constance* really ours? Does she really belong to us? All this?'

'She's ours for as long as we want her.'

Claudine nodded. 'That's good. Because I want her to be mine, too. You're going to have to share. And teach me how to drive her.'

'Then I'll need more insurance,' he said, and gave her a squeeze, kissed the top of her head, smelled the warmth of their makeshift cabin bed on her, the sweet remnants of her scent, and sex.

'So get it. And be quick about it,' she said, pulling free of him and turning back to the cabin door. 'I'm making coffee. You want some?'

Twenty minutes later both sisters were out on deck watching the coastline and the islands of Jarre, Calseraigne and Riou pass them by as they sipped their coffee and shared a basket of flaking croissants, their hair flicking in the breeze, the sleeves of their silk wraps billowing and then filling like tiny sails. Standing at the wheel, Jacquot decided he had never been happier. The two Eddé sisters and him, and hidden away two tiny people who by Christmas would make his world complete.

'So where are you taking us?' called Delphie, as a Cassis Sunseeker powered past them, its prow high, heading for Marseilles.

Jacquot eased off the throttle and turned into the approaching wake, cursing the inconsiderate skipper, whoever he was.

'A little place I know,' he said, riding the first crest, then straightening up and applying some revs.

'Where we went last time?' asked Claudine.

Jacquot shook his head, smiled. 'That's ours. Just you and me. No strangers,' he said, nodding at Delphie.

'Stranger? I'm family, for fuck's sake.'

The retort was ripe and fruity, just as Jacquot had expected. And friendly. No offence meant, and none taken.

'Where we're going now is for threesomes,' he said.

'You should be so lucky, mister,' said the two sisters, almost together, and burst out laughing.

'It's called Calanque des Sirènes. It's smaller than the others and too narrow for the tourist boats,' he told them, nodding at a thirty-metre monster overtaking them on their port side, heading for Morgiou or Sormiou, its rails crowded with passengers. 'You'll love it. We can have lunch on board, or there's this little *cabanon* where they have an outside grill and their own vineyard. It's Marseilles' best-kept secret.'

91

ISABELLE CASSIER WAS HALF-WAY ACROSS the squad room when the phone on her desk started ringing. She dumped her bag on the floor, dropped into her chair and reached for the handset.

'*Oui*? Cassier.'

'Chief Inspector Cassier, this is Gala Desfornado.'

Isabelle frowned, tried to place the name but couldn't.

'I am a neighbour of your friend, Daniel Jacquot,' the voice on the other end of the line continued. 'Down in Le Vieux Port. He was with me the other evening when you came calling.'

Isabelle sat up at the mention of Jacquot's name, remembered the lady on the yacht, an artist. Every time she'd seen the woman, she'd had a glass in her hand. 'Yes, Madame. I remember. You're the artist. What can I do for you?'

'I wasn't sure what to do, but I thought I should do something.'

'Is there a problem?'

'About twenty minutes ago, three men came looking for Jacquot. Nasty-looking men. Real toughs, if you know what I mean.'

'Okay . . . So what happened?'

'Nothing. Jacquot wasn't there. Took off earlier this morning with his wife and sister-in-law. They're staying with him.'

Isabelle wanted to correct her, then and there. Claudine was not

Jacquot's wife. Instead, she thought of the gold bar, and Clem, and said, 'These men, have you seen them before?'

'No. And I hope I never do again.'

'Did they speak to you?' asked Isabelle.

'When they discovered he wasn't there, they came back down the pontoon, asked me if I knew where he was.'

'Did you tell them?'

'I said I didn't know. Just that he'd set off an hour earlier.'

'A day trip? Back tonight?'

'Possibly, but they had supplies. Yesterday I saw him with a stack of shopping bags. Maybe an overnight somewhere? The calanques . . . the islands?'

'And that's it?'

'I think he might be in trouble, that's all. You don't have *gorilles* like that come calling just to wish you a *Bonjour, ça va*. Jacquot said you worked for the *Judiciaire*. I thought I should call you, let you know.'

'That's very good of you, Madame. Thank you.' And then, '*Dites-moi,* could you describe the men?' asked Isabelle, wondering if they might be the same ones who'd called on Clémentine.

'*Gorilles*, like I said. All three of them dark, swarthy. One had a scar on his eyebrow, and the one asking the questions had a goatee . . . you know, where the moustache comes around the mouth and down into a little pointy beard. The muscle wore jeans, sneakers, leather jackets and T-shirts; but Monsieur Goatee was smarter: blue cotton shirt, cream linen jacket, taupe trousers pleated at the top.'

A very good description, thought Isabelle. Most people wouldn't have been so precise or confident in their recall. But then Madame Desfornado was an artist. She would have an eye for form and colour and detail.

'Was one of them Chinese?' Isabelle asked.

'No. No Chinese. More Arab-looking.'

Which meant they probably weren't the same boys who'd paid a call on Clem.

'And what did they do after you told them that Jacquot had gone?' she asked.

'Goatee told me not to say anything if I saw him. And not to call him. They wanted to surprise him, he said. Then they headed back the way they'd come.'

'You've been very helpful, Madame. Thank you. And if Jacquot hasn't returned by tomorrow morning, please call me again to let me know.'

92

WITH LITTLE MORE THAN TEN metres leeway between the
two scrubby bluffs that guarded and partly concealed it Jacquot
brought *Constance* into Calanque des Sirènes, a splinter of deep
blue water set between towering limestone cliffs. Keeping the revs
low, the sound of her rumbling engine bouncing back from the
sheer sides of this secret inlet, he glanced down at the water,
watching the fathomless blue lighten and clear as a pearl-coloured
seabed rose up out of the depths to meet them.

A hundred metres in, around a gentle curve, the calanque began
to widen, and a narrow arc of beach appeared ahead of them, its
creamy shingle glaring in the midday sun, not another vessel to be
seen save for a small fishing skiff tied to a mooring post on the
right side of the cove. A few metres beyond it a path wound up
through the scrub, and between a stunted curtain of pine and tamarisk he spotted the old *cabanon*.

With *Constance* safely anchored, Jacquot killed the engine and
for the first time since entering Sirènes, he heard the busy electric
clatter of crickets rising in volume to fill the silence, ringing off
the steep scrubby sides of the inlet with a steady pulsing buzz.

Delphie was first up out of the cabin, where she and Claudine
had gone to change into swimsuits the moment *Constance* nosed
in through the entrance and they saw the calanque. Throwing down

her towel, she clambered up on to the transom and dived down into the clear water, her progress beneath the surface marked by a bubbling white sheath. Claudine was next, passing Jacquot with a kiss, the angry red wounds on her leg now just a shiny puckering of pale pink. Handing him her towel, she stepped up on to a seat locker and followed Delphie's example. A moment later, after lowering the transom steps and pulling off his T-shirt, Jacquot joined them.

After their swim they climbed the path to the *cabanon* and settled themselves at one of three empty tables set out under a split-cane roof. Twelve customers maximum when the place was full on a summer weekend, Jacquot told them. Lunch only, and no one ever in a hurry to leave. Fresh vegetables and salad leaves from the family smallholding out back, whatever fish they'd brought in that day, and the patron's own wine, white only, sometimes a little cloudy but fresh and strong and always ice cold. And the bill, when it came, would be scribbled down on a scrap of paper torn from a school exercise book. No service charge. Everything included. Eighty francs a head. The best deal in town.

As they made themselves comfortable the patron's wife appeared, a plump, cheery woman in a housecoat and plimsolls who proceeded to spread out a paper tablecloth between them, secure it with metal clips, then nudge the table to stand level and steady on the uneven ground. '*Voilà*,' she declared, heading back inside to bring out a pitcher of spring water, chinking with ice, another filled with wine, and six sturdy Duralex tumblers clamped under her arm. By the time Delphie and Jacquot had finished their first cigarettes, Claudine taking a sly puff from each, a basket of bread had been put on the table with a bowl of tapenade, a saucer of wrinkled black olives, strips of sweet orange peppers and a dish of sun-warm tomatoes drizzled with home-pressed olive oil and flecked with wild thyme from the slopes. There was no menu and only one main course available, the patron's wife explained, showing them a bucket of glistening *rougets* that her husband had caught that morning in a lucky drag of the net off Sormiou, which he would happily grill for them if they so wished.

It was one of those lunches, Delphie declared afterwards, that it would be impossible to forget, or to beat. Not a label, not a brand-name to be seen. Perfect in every respect: from the shifting shadows cast by the stand of tamarisk around the *cabanon*, to the static drill of insects and the dry scuttle of lizards; from the sharp richness of the tapenade to the crackle of the charred pink skin of the mullet, their firm, pearly fillets peeling off the bone in two succulent mouthfuls. The potatoes that came with them had been baked in a fish stock and were waxy and yellow, their salad was crisp and dewy, the goat's cheese round and hard, and a bunch of fat purple grapes served in a plastic colander bursting with sweetness. Above them, through the trees, the rocky tops of the inlet cut a jagged line against the blue of the sky, and forty metres below them *Constance* lay anchored to her shadow on the sea-bed.

When the meal was finished and the plates cleared, the patron brought out a chipped enamel coffee percolator from the kitchen, still bubbling and hissing and spitting, and three tiny saucerless cups. He wore a white singlet and blue shorts, a flowery apron that looked as though it belonged to his wife, and a pair of laceless plimsolls. His hands were large and calloused from a lifetime hauling nets and the hair on his shoulders had started to grey.

'It's a long time since I've seen *Constance*,' he said, standing back, wiping his hands on the apron and nodding his head at the creek.

Jacquot's ears pricked up. 'You know the boat?'

'She's been here a few times. Way back now. Four, five years at least. Old fellow and his wife. Just the two of them. They'd moor here for a couple of days, come up for lunch, swim, snorkel, then they'd be off. Till the next time. Said he'd been born here,' the patron continued, thumbing back to the *cabanon*. 'Right here, would you believe? Small world, eh? So they sell her to you, did they?'

'The old man left her to me.'

The patron considered this. 'Passed on, then?'

Jacquot nodded.

'Sorry to hear that. Comes to all of us, but it's never nice.' The man rubbed his chin, looked down again at the boat. 'And too much for the wife to handle, eh? The boat. Needed the cash, I suppose.'

'The lady died, too.'

'Now that's a surprise. She was a lot younger than him, I recall. You meet her?'

Jacquot shook his head. 'Just photos,' he lied.

'Then you'll know. A beauty. Always playing with her hair, she was. Always different, every time she came here. Blonde one time, brunette the next, grown long, or cut short. She was better a blonde, you ask me. Wavy, like Marilyn Monroe. A bit curlier maybe. Like a halo in the sunshine. *Oui, formidable, c'est sûr.*'

And with that, he pulled out a scrap of paper torn from a school exercise book and slipped it under the ashtray.

'I hope you enjoyed your lunch, Mesdames, Monsieur.'

93

LÉO AND ZACH HAD WORKED up a good sweat by the time they reached the ridge above Calanque des Sirènes. It was a little over an hour since their skipper, Cassel, had taken them ashore and pointed out the path, two hours since he'd brought them to the next inlet along from Sirènes – too difficult to access for a vessel their size, he'd told Didier.

The climb had been a brute, steep and twisting, the two men panting in the midday sun, the dust they kicked up rasping in their throats. Twice Léo had to stop to let Zach pull off one of his trainers and shake it out before clambering on. But now they were in place, the climb over, and far below them *Constance* lay at anchor ten metres out from a small curve of beach. Dropping on to their stomachs, elbows in the dirt, they trained their binoculars on the boat, couldn't see anyone aboard and then cut to the slope above the beach as the man and his two women came down a pathway through the trees.

'Looks like some kind of restaurant up there,' said Zach. 'They must have gone there for lunch.' He sniffed. 'You can smell the cooking.'

Léo watched the three of them come out of the trees, cross the beach and wade out to *Constance*. The man was carrying a small grab-bag. Cigarettes, lighter, wallets, purses, Léo decided. Nothing

371

more. Certainly not a gold bar. He shifted the glasses on to the two women. One was a bit short and on the tubby side, but the other one was tall and tanned, dark hair in a ponytail, black one-piece swimsuit, a light blue sarong knotted around her waist. And pregnant by the look of her – a deep, shadowy cleavage and a certain swell around the belly when the angle was right – but still a scorcher. The three of them were chatting, laughing, but he couldn't hear a sound.

Léo lowered the glasses and checked his watch. He picked up the walkie-talkie he'd brought with him and buzzed through to Didier down on *Corsaire*, told him what they'd seen.

'Stay on site a few more hours and I'll send up Dhuc and Milagro to take over from you. If our friends look like they're going to head off somewhere, let me know immediately. If we're not here when you get back down, wait for us and we'll come back for you.'

Over and out, thought Léo, and passed on the news to Zach.

'There's harder ways I can think to earn money,' said the younger man and pulled off his T-shirt for the last of the sun. 'You bring any water with you?'

'In the bag,' said Léo. 'But don't drink it all, hear? It's got to last.'

He looked through the glasses again, and adjusted the focus. Down on *Constance* it was clearly siesta time. The man was settling himself on the cabin roof, and the two women were heading below deck.

Must be a gay boy, thought Léo. If it had been him down there, he'd have gone below with the girls for some two-on-one, not out on deck for a snooze. He'd have jumped the both of them, no question, even the tubby one.

372

94

IT WAS LATE-AFTERNOON WHEN ARIS Moussa, sitting with Beni and Jo-Jo at a café on the quayside at Cassis, spotted Duclos' motor cruiser, *Désiré*, come past the rocky outcrop of Cap Canaille and turn into Cassis bay. The gleaming white Adagio 60, built in Genoa and delivered just a month earlier to the family berth in Sanary-sur-Mer, was Duclos' latest toy, and the old man had clearly decided to give her a spin. Aris watched for a moment longer, to make sure, then nudged Beni and pointed as *Désiré*'s skipper throttled back and the long curved stem settled into its bow wave, coasting in towards the harbour's breakwater jetty where the tourist ferries from Marseilles moored up. Beni turned to Jo-Jo on his other side, legs out, chin on chest, snoozing, and prodded his shoulder.

'Hey, wake up. They're here.'

Tucking some notes under his coffee cup, Aris got to his feet and started off at a brisk clip along the quay, his two companions close behind him. It wouldn't do for Duclos to see them sitting in a café, even if they had been working their butts off since early morning. And apart from this brief but welcome breather in Cassis, that's exactly what they'd been doing.

After leaving that pontoon in Marseilles' Vieux Port, Aris had put a call through to Duclos and passed on the news that *Constance* was not at her berth. According to a neighbour, he told Duclos, the owner, a man called Jacquot, had taken off earlier that morning with two women aboard. They'd had supplies with them and as of now could be anywhere along the coast.

There'd been a moment's silence at the end of the line, and then Duclos had told him in no uncertain terms what he wanted. Check every port and every beach and every possible berth or mooring between L'Estaque and Madrague, then head down to Cassis where he, Duclos, would pick them up, having checked every port and mooring and beach and berth between Sanary-sur-Mer and Cassis.

It had been a long, hot day, driving first to the harbour at L'Estaque, then doubling back via Pointe Rouge, Madrague and Samena, past the beaches of Catalan, Prophète and the wide ivory sweep of Prado, on the look-out for one solitary vessel called *Constance*, a twelve-metre motor launch, according to Beni's man, with an open wheelhouse on a black hull. And that was all they had to go on. A single boat along a coastline swarming with other similar craft. It was like looking for a stick of chalk in a snowstorm. But Aris knew that when Duclos said do something, you did it, or else.

And now he was here, the old man himself, up on *Désiré*'s flying bridge beside Hamid, the skipper. Aris spotted him and waved.

Duclos did not wave back.

Five minutes later they were safely aboard and Aris was climbing up to the bridge to report. Duclos was not a man who liked receiving bad news and Aris felt a nervous knot in his stomach as he came out on to the bridge.

'Well?' said the old man, reaching for the hand-rail as his skipper opened the throttles and *Désiré* powered away from the jetty. Duclos was wearing white plimsolls, a pair of baggy Chinos, with a blue pashmina scarf wrapped round his neck and tucked into a cream-coloured quilted parka. On his head he wore a jaunty little sailor's cap, its peak decorated with two stripes of gold braid and a small gold anchor. He also wore a pair of large, round-framed sunglasses. With his puffed-up quilted chest, he looked like a black-eyed owl.

Aris shook his head. 'Nothing boss. Not a sign. We looked everywhere.'

Duclos sighed and Aris held his breath, waiting for the explosion.

But none came.

'Nothing for us, either,' said Duclos, in a tight little voice. 'But she's out here somewhere. And we're going to find her. And then we're going to make this Jacquot sing.'

If Aris had imagined that the old man was going back to Sanary-sur-Mer, the day's work over, he was badly mistaken. As they headed out into the bay and left Cassis in their wake, he saw Hamid ease his wheel to starboard and take a bearing on the setting sun. Ten minutes later, he throttled back and slid into the Calanque d'En Vau, a dozen craft already moored there.

'We're going to spend the night here,' said Duclos, over the rumbling engines, 'and start up again tomorrow morning. There's a cabin for you and one of your men, but the other's going to have to make do in the salon.'

And then Aris saw Duclos freeze, peer ahead as though he couldn't believe his eyes, and duck away from the windshield.

'Well, well, well,' he said with a smile, staying low. 'It seems like someone else has had the same idea.'

'I'm not with you, boss,' said Aris.

'You see that rather vulgar-looking craft up ahead?'

Aris looked through the smoked-glass windshield and nodded.

'It's the *Corsaire*,' said Duclos. 'And it belongs to my very good friend, Patric Polineaux.'

95

AT ABOUT THE SAME TIME that *Désiré* moored in Calanque d'En Vau, Jacquot woke to a sudden chill. The sky above him was still a deep sapphire blue but the sun had slipped behind Sirènes' western ridge, marking out a shadow on the opposite slope already a good ten metres above the water. The heat had dwindled too, maybe four or five degrees cooler, and the buzz of crickets had softened to an occasional soft bleating, like a shorting electrical appliance.

Jacquot raised his head and looked towards the wheelhouse. Delphie was reading a book in the skipper's chair, but there was no sign of Claudine. He rolled over onto an elbow and looked down through the hatch. She was asleep on their bed, dead to the world, curled up under the sheet, one long brown arm flung across a pillow. Six months pregnant, a few glasses of wine at lunch, the heat . . . he wasn't surprised. The rest would do her good.

Not wanting to wake her, Jacquot got quietly to his feet and made his way to the wheelhouse, pleased to note that he felt not the slightest twinge from his thigh or buttock, just a very subtle tightness.

'I helped myself to some wine,' said Delphie softly, putting down her book as he swung round the wheelhouse. 'On my way through the cabin. I was quiet as a mouse. Do you want some?'

'A swim first, just to freshen up, and then I'll be back,' he replied, and he stepped over the transom and down into the water, feeling it rise over his legs and belly and spill around his shoulders, cool and clean and clear. Letting go of the steps he stroked away from the boat, feeling the water sluice through his fingers, the warm saltiness of it play through his hair, duck-diving into the depths, pulling himself towards the sea-bed, then turning back for the surface.

By the time he got back to *Constance* and hauled himself out of the water, Claudine was helping Delphie set up the trestle table on the rear deck. He stood on the top step, dripping wet, watching them.

'I'm sorry, skipper,' said Delphie. 'It's been decided. We're staying here another night. And there's nothing you can do or say to dissuade us.'

Claudine glanced at Jacquot, smiled.

Swinging himself aboard and reaching for a towel, he shot them both a stern look, a skipper facing down a mutinous crew, then softened it into a smile.

'*Si vous voulez.* Why not?' he said, rubbing himself dry. 'There's enough food for our supper and breakfast. Wine and beer if Delphie hasn't finished it all, and for lunch tomorrow there's another little place I know, not far from here . . .'

96

THE SUN WAS LOW IN the west when Dhuc and Milagro arrived at the ridge, panting from the steep climb. Léo and Zach, who'd taken turns on watch, were relieved to see them, to know that their own stint was over. Zach had taken a little too much sun and burned the bridge of his flattened nose, and Léo had spent the last hour wishing he'd brought a beer as well as the water.

'They haven't moved,' said Léo. 'Either they'll leave in the next hour or so, or they'll stay overnight.'

Dhuc, a wiry Vietnamese, tipped the rucksack he was carrying off his shoulders and opened it up. He'd come prepared, Léo could see. A flask of coffee, a bed roll, and one of the deck cushions from *Corsaire*. He took the binoculars from Léo and laid out the roll, threw the cushion at its head and settled down on his belly, resting his chest on the cushion and taking a bead on the boat far below.

Milagro pulled a pack of cigarettes from his pocket, offered them around and the three of them lit up.

'What's for dinner?' asked Zach.

'Steak. It's good,' Milagro replied. He was Mexican, built like a metrobus, and an ex-Legionnaire sniper who could hit a playing card from five hundred metres.

'How long have we got?' asked Léo.

'The boss told us three o'clock.'

Léo took an angry swipe at his cigarette, spat out a shred of loose tobacco. Say thirty minutes down to the boat, an hour for something to eat and drink, and just a few hours' sleep before they had to climb back up here. He was tempted to stay where he was, but the thought of steak and a couple of beers decided him.

'See you later then. Have fun.'

'*Et toi*,' said Milagro with a grin. He reached into the rucksack and pulled out a sweater, balled it up into a back-rest and settled himself against a tree. From his pocket he took out a switchblade and started work on his nails. 'Six hours, remember. And don't be late.'

97

'ALL I CAN SAY,' SAID Delphie, 'is that I wish your old fisherman had left *Constance* to me. This hard-working, dedicated Parisian journalist would have made a much more deserving case than some beat-up old Marseilles cop.'

After their long lunch, the three of them had been happy with just a light supper: a few cuts of cold meat, some bread, some cheese, and wine.

Delphie reached for the bottle and topped up her glass, passed it to Jacquot.

'So tell me,' she continued. 'How well did you know the old guy? What did you have to do to get your hands on *Constance*?'

And there, in the light from the hurricane lamps, warmed by the wine and the company, Jacquot told them what he knew of Philo, and what he had found out since he'd taken possession of the old cutter. Everything he'd told Isabelle, he now ran the two sisters through: the bookshop, the house on Roucas Blanc, the double life.

And the gold.

'You are kidding me?' said Delphie, when he got to the end of his story. 'The Gineste heist?'

'You know about it?'

'Doesn't everyone? Just about the biggest goddamned haul in

French criminal history. Three tons of gold, wasn't it? It was the first big story I remember. Every newspaper was full of it. TV . . . everything. And you're saying that this Niko-Philo character was involved?'

'Everything points to that. And he got away on a boat.'

'On *this* boat? On *Constance*?'

'On *Constance.*'

'With the gold? The gold that was never found?'

Jacquot picked at a crumb of the Banon, chewed thougthfully.

'Until recently,' he said at last, quietly, unable to resist, chuckling at the sisters' reaction. Their eyes widening. All ears.

'What do you mean . . . "until recently"?' asked Delphie, voice suddenly sharp and demanding. He glanced at her, a woolly cardigan drawn over her swimsuit and sarong. She was sitting sideways to the table with her legs crossed, an espadrille swinging on the tips of her toes. The swinging had stopped abruptly. This was no longer Claudine's sister, a guest on board his boat, engaging in idle after-dinner chatter in Calanque des Sirènes. In a matter of moments, she had turned into Delphine Baron, a by-lined columnist with *Le Monde*. If she'd had a notebook in her hand, Jacquot was certain she'd be scribbling away.

For a moment he wondered if he should continue. But what was the harm? It would all come out sooner or later, after Isabelle had dug up Madame Jeanne Vaillant's terraces in Roucas Blanc and found what remained of the hoard. As he was certain she would. Where else would Philo have hidden it? Close enough to be safe. Close enough to draw on when funds were needed. Taking only what he needed when the house was sold, leaving whatever remained to history or maybe a lucky gardener who dug too deep. And what was wrong with giving Claudine's sister a head start, if she wanted to run with it?

And so, as the stars twinkled above them, and the lights from the distant *cabanon* were extinguished, he told them both how he'd spent his last few days: visiting Clem in Madrague, finding the gold bar in the stockpot, establishing once and for all, with an absolute certainty, that Niko and Edina had been involved in the Gineste heist. And got away with the missing gold. How much of it, he couldn't say.

'Niko and Edina. Was that her name — Edina?' asked Delphie.

'Apparently she was known as Eddie.'

'The Edina in the books? Her name's in the Simenon I'm reading.'

'That's right. The same.'

'And what's with all the bookmarks?' she asked, leaning across for her book, finding the bookmark and fluttering it between her fingers.

'Bookmarks for books,' replied Jacquot.

'Surely you only need one bookmark,' said Claudine, tugging the sleeves of her sweat-shirt around her.

'Unless you're reading more than one book,' suggested Jacquot.

'Maybe so,' said Delphie, 'but pretty nearly every book's got a bookmark. Was he reading them all at the same time? And that box of yours in my cabin has a stack of them. Why so many? And what's with the initials and numbers?'

'Niko Emanetti. N. E. That was his name.'

'Or Niko and Edina,' said Claudine.

'I hadn't thought of that,' said Jacquot, surprised. 'Why not? Makes sense.'

There was a silence then, save for the lap of water against the hull and the gentle splash of wine as Jacquot shared out the last of the bottle. He lit a cigarette, passed the pack to Delphie, but she shook her head. Her eyes were narrowed, the bookmark flicking between her fingers.

'Or,' she began. 'Or . . . What about . . . ?'

She waited until Jacquot and her sister turned to look at her.

'What about . . . North and East?'

Claudine frowned. 'I don't understand. Why North and East?'

'Because, my darling sister, if it's North and East, and not Nico and Edina, then all these numbers here . . .' she waved the bookmark like a fan.

'. . . would be co-ordinates,' whispered Jacquot.

'We're north of the Equator,' explained Delphie, warming to her theme, 'and east of the Greenwich . . . what do you call it? The Greenwich Meridian. It makes sense, doesn't it?'

'If you say so,' said Claudine uncertainly.

'Look,' continued Delphie, turning the laminated strip to the light from the hurricane lamp. 'Four numbers, one above the other: 4305, 1022, 4023, 2836. One half of the numbers under the "N", and the other numbers above the "E". Now, if you look closely, there's the tiniest space, here, making two columns of figures . . . see? 43, 10, 40, 28 under the "N" – North. And under the "E" – East: 05, 22, 23, 36. It's obvious, isn't it? Degrees, minutes, seconds . . . all that nautical stuff. Or have I drunk too much wine?'

'I don't think you have,' replied Jacquot. 'Or maybe just the right amount.' And he was up and out of his chair, heart hammering, and clambering down into the main cabin.

He couldn't believe it. It couldn't be. And not once had he . . .

He came back out on deck with the hand-held GPS receiver that Philo had left in a drawer, prayed the battery was working, and switched it on.

Nothing happened immediately. No response.

And then, with a tiny whine and beep, the face of the machine lightened, the manufacturer's name appeared on the circular screen, to be replaced by a compass heading.

Jacquot pressed a button and the compass changed to a digital clock. Time and date. He pressed again and a wavering line of green digital figures appeared on the screen.

He counted them out.

'What have you got?' asked Delphie.

'Sixteen figures. Two sets of eight.'

Delphie looked at the bookmark. 'Sixteen. Two sets of eight. It's the same. I'm right, aren't I? They're co-ordinates.'

'You're right,' said Jacquot. 'They're co-ordinates.'

'For here?' asked Claudine, not daring to believe it. 'Is that why Niko and Eddie came here so often? They stashed the gold here, in the calanque?'

'Well, let's find out,' said Delphie. 'What are the numbers you've got for where we are now?' she asked Jacquot.

'North 43°, 11', 52, 77",' he read out. 'East 05°, 29', 54, 47". What have you got?'

Tilting the bookmark to the hurricane lamp so that she could see the figures more clearly, she said: 'North 43°, 10', 40, 28"; East 05°, 22', 23, 36".'

The two sisters looked at Jacquot.

'What do you think?' asked Delphie.

'Well, they're not the co-ordinates for here. But they're pretty much the same latitude and longitude, give or take . . . I'd say we're close. But exactly where or how far,' he shook his head, 'I wouldn't like to say.'

'So all we've got to do is follow the numbers?' asked Claudine, eyes bright with excitement. 'Is that all we've got to do?'

Delphie beamed. 'That's what it looks like, sis. And find the buried treasure.'

98

'THERE'S SOMETHING GOING ON,' said Beni, turning to Aris and passing him the binoculars. 'Torches. Up in the trees.'

The two men were up on *Désiré*'s flying bridge, its lights switched off, keeping watch on *Corsaire*. When they'd dropped anchor in Calanque d'En Vau, there'd been more than a dozen boats moored in the inlet. By the time the sun had sunk below the ridge, more than half of them had weighed anchor and sailed home, back to Marseilles or Cassis or wherever they had come from, their day trip to the calanques at an end. Now just five boats – three smaller cruisers and two yachts – separated *Désiré* from *Corsaire*. For the time being they had the pip on *Corsaire*, and Aris knew that the last thing Duclos would want was for Polineaux's boys to spot them. They had to play their advantage, and play it sweet, or the game was up.

Aris took the glasses and looked where Beni was pointing. At first, in the darkness, he could see nothing, just the glitter of cabin lights on the anchored vessels, a wash of bright, pinprick stars high above the ridge, and between them just varying shades of black. And then two yellow beams of light flashed across his field of vision, jerking and skittering through the trees, heading down the slope for the beach, two shadowy figures briefly visible.

'They're sending out a launch,' said Beni, and Aris swung his glasses back to *Corsaire*. There was activity on the aft deck and they both heard the distant firing of an outboard motor. A moment later the two torch beams reached level ground and a pale wash of phosphorescence marked the passage of the launch heading to the beach to pick them up.

'What's happening?' It was Duclos, accompanied by the skipper. Hamid, a slim Arab in his thirties with black curling hair and luxuriant beard. He helped the old man to one of the bridge seats and settled him down.

'Looks like two of Polineaux's people coming down the slope,' said Aris. 'They've sent a launch to pick them up.'

'What's up there, Hamid?' asked Duclos, turning to his skipper.

'It's a path up to the ridge. The other side it leads down to a small creek called Calanque des Sirènes. Too small for us to get into,' he added, as though to cover himself.

'And therefore too small for *Corsaire*,' said Duclos, almost to himself. 'But clearly there's something of interest up there, or down in the calanque.' He fell silent for a moment, then made a clicking sound with his tongue. 'Hamid, get one of the jet-skis out, and Aris, get your boys ready. They're going for a swim.'

Thirty minutes later, dressed in black neoprene wetsuits, Beni and Jo-Jo pushed away from *Désiré*'s stern platform and, holding the revs as low as they could, they headed for the entrance to Calanque d'En Vau, keeping *Désiré* and the other yachts and launches between them and *Corsaire*.

It was a quiet, calm night and the sea was flat to begin with, only turning to a small chop as they curved around the headland and came into open water. Keeping the cliffs a good twenty metres to their right and riding a low broadside swell that rocked the jet-ski like a baby's cradle, they followed the line of the coast until Beni, standing over the saddle of the jet-ski, gripping the handlebars, spotted the narrow entrance to the next calanque and turned with the swell, dropping the revs to a whisper and steering between the bluffs.

For the first twenty metres, there was complete darkness, just

386

oft starlight to see by, the inlet's rocky slopes rising up like two
black walls either side of them. Slowly, as silently as possible, just
a watery burbling from the engine, they motored forward, keeping
close to the left-hand wall of the calanque, Beni leaning over the
handlebars to peer ahead.

It was dark enough for Sirène's dog-leg corner to catch him by
surprise, the inlet suddenly swinging left and opening up. And
here, no more than fifty metres ahead of them, they could see a
box-like glow of lights from the single vessel moored in the
calanque.

Beni swung the jet-ski into a tight turn and brought it perilously
close to the rocky side of the inlet, close enough for them to smell
the pine and scrub and sun-warmed dusty stone only now beginning to cool. For a moment he didn't think he'd make it, coming
in too close, but he managed to reach out and push the craft away
from any direct contact, hand against the stone, his fingers scrabbling across it.

'Watch out,' whispered Jo-Jo, as a gnarled branch jutting from
the slope came out of the darkness, low enough to sweep him off
the saddle.

Beni ducked, with just centimetres to spare, but as he passed
beneath the branch, he reached up, caught hold of it and swung
the jet-ski to a stop. Both men held their breath. If the limb snapped
off, they knew that the sound would echo round the inlet, an unforgiving crack and wrench, maybe a skitter of loose stones splashing
into the still water. But it held, creaking just a little.

'I'll wait for you here,' said Beni, as Jo-Jo sat side-saddle to pull
on his fins and brought the wetsuit's rubber hood over his head.
'The boat's about thirty metres ahead, centre of the inlet. Keep to
the side and you should be okay.'

With a thumbs up, Jo-Jo pulled on his mask, clamped a snorkel
between his teeth and lowered himself into the water. With the
briefest slap of a fin, he set off into the darkness until Beni lost
sight of him, the back of his black wet-suit just another patch of
shifting starlit water.

For the next ten minutes Beni held on to the branch, steadying the jet-ski between his legs, waiting for Jo-Jo to return. Every few minutes he swapped hands on the branch, careful not to lose his hold. And then, sooner than Beni had anticipated and with no warning, Jo-Jo was back, tipping the jet-ski as he hauled himself up. He pulled the mask off his face and the snorkel from his mouth, the fins from his feet.

'It's her,' he whispered, swinging a leg over the saddle, his voice low and hoarse from the salt water.

'Her who?' asked Beni, pushing away from the branch and setting the revs just high enough to turn and head back out to sea.

'*Constance.*'

99

'CHARTS,' CRIED DELPHIE. 'YOU MUST have charts. Every boat has charts.'

Jacquot knew that he did have charts, Philo's charts, stacked below his chart table in the main cabin. He'd gone through them when he'd first taken possession of *Constance*, a dozen table-sized maps of the Mediterranean coast from Gibraltar to Genoa and Livorno, both large- and small-scale. But having the charts didn't necessarily mean that he understood them, beyond the most basic information they provided, the most important of which, for Jacquot, was depths. He might know enough of the coast between Marseilles and Cassis to take the right direction when leaving port, and where to head when he wanted to come home – like the time he had sailed with Salette on his practice run to the calanques, and when he had taken Claudine to Île de Riou – but that was as far as it went. He had never once tried to plot a course according to a set of co-ordinates, never once opened a chart and set to it with ruler and dividers.

Not bothering to sort through the charts, Jacquot brought them all up on deck, a dozen or more, which he and Claudine and Delphie opened up, one after another. The best they could find were Imray Pilot guides to the approaches to Marseilles, and from Marseilles to Genoa and Calvi. Flattening this last one out and trapping its corners under the hurricane lamp, an ashtray and their wine glasses the three of them pored over it.

'So how do we do it?' asked Claudine, puzzled by the lean, spare tattooing of numbers, symbols, lines and angles. So different from any kind of map she was used to.

'Well, let's start with latitude and longitude,' said Delphie, taking control, which was a relief to Jacquot. 'That's us here,' she continued, running her finger along the 43° line north to south, and then doing the same east to west along the 05° line. She tapped the spot, on the very edge of the coastline. 'I'm right, aren't I, Daniel?'

'Looks good,' he agreed.

'You don't know?'

'Hey, I'm a cop not a yachtsman. All I'm saying is it sounds right. Looks right.'

'So you don't know how to chart a course?'

Jacquot gave her a grim, apologetic look. There was no point pretending.

'I know where the sun comes up,' he said, 'and I know where it sets. Anything else – something like this – it's never going to be much better than guesswork. Until I do some homework, or take a course.'

Out on the water there was a sudden, loud splash and the two sisters jumped.

'What the hell was that?' asked Delphie, gathering her shawl around her and looking nervously into the darkness.

'A fish. The sea's full of them,' said Jacquot with a smile. 'And night-time they like to feed.'

'Sounded like a big one to me,' said Claudine with a shiver.

'They come in all sizes, *ma chérie*.'

'Like men,' said Delphie. 'Big and small and always thinking of their bellies.'

Jacquot grunted and turned back to the chart.

'So, okay, I'm no expert, but if I had to guess, I reckon we need to head south-west,' he said, tracing a line with his fingertip. 'In that general direction, out towards the islands, and keep checking the co-ordinates as we go. It can't be that difficult, can it?'

100

THERE WAS A FINE DEW on the deck and the roof of the wheel-house when Jacquot came up from the main cabin the following morning, leaving footprints in its wet silvery skin as he set about tidying up from the night before. It was chill, too, the sun already a few hours old but yet to reach Calanque des Sirènes, just the very top of its western ridge bathed in early morning light. Jacquot knew it would be a couple of hours, at least, before that line of sunshine reached the inlet where they were moored. But by then they would be at sea, searching for the spot marked 'X' and a pot of gold.

If, indeed, there was any gold.

And if, indeed, they could even find it.

Last night he might have shared the sisters' enthusiasm, been caught up in the marvel of it all. But in the cold light of day, it all seemed very improbable.

But they'd give it a go. They'd take a look. At the very worst it meant a pleasant day cruising along the coast. Which wasn't too bad a return.

Jacquot had weighed anchor and *Constance* was drifting free when he smelled coffee from the main cabin. As he started up the twin Volvo diesels, Claudine came up from below deck with a mug of coffee.

'There's a splash of your favourite flavouring in it,' she said with a grin, and he smelled the Calva as he raised the mug to his lips. 'To warm you up,' she continued. 'We girls need to keep our skipper happy, you know?'

'There're other ways to warm up a sailor, and keep him happy,' he said, and leaned forward to snatch a kiss.

But she pulled back, waved a finger at him.

'Coffee, Calva, croissants – that's all you're getting for now, *Capitaine*. We need to have you in prime order for the task ahead. Think of yourself as a footballer, *chéri*, holding back for the big game.' And with a sweet, coy smile she climbed back down into the main cabin.

Racking the wheel to port and opening the throttles, Jacquot turned *Constance* and headed for the inlet's entrance.

101

LÉO AND ZACH WERE ASLEEP, the pair of them. Zach was curled up under his tree, head cradled on an exposed root softened with a sweat-shirt, and Léo was stretched out on the bedroll and cushion that he'd persuaded Dhuc to leave when they'd come back up to take over the watch.

It was the turning of *Constance*'s engine, a dull chortling rumble climbing the sides of Calanque des Sirènes, that woke Léo. For a moment he wondered where he was, opening his eyes and taking in the spread of soft tamarisk branches above his head. The next thing that dawned on him was that he was damp – a fine dew beading his clothes. And then, only then, did he remember where he was and what he was doing – or rather, what he was supposed to be doing.

Without thinking he scrambled to his feet and then ducked down, scurried forward and peered over the ridge. Sixty metres below him *Constance* was making a tight turn, a wash of white water bubbling up from her screws and forming a u-shaped hook. They were on the move.

'Zach, wake your arse! They're off,' said Léo, snatching up the bedroll and cushion, binoculars and thermos flask, and stuffing them into Dhuc's rucksack. The only thing he didn't pack away was the walkie-talkie. It was going to take them a good twenty minutes to scramble back down the path to the beach, in which time *Corsaire* could have upped anchor and set out after *Constance*. If he held back for a few more minutes before calling, and put on some speed down the path, then they wouldn't get left behind.

Five minutes later, legs aching from the scrabbling descent, Léo paused and flicked the transmit button.

'Didier? Cassel? You there?'

He waited a few seconds for a reply, and then repeated the call. This time there was an answering click and Cassel, *Corsaire*'s skipper, came on line.

'Cassel, this is Léo. They just pulled up anchor. We're on our way down. We'll be on the beach in ten.'

'Got it. I'll send the launch. And ten minutes max, okay?'

102

DUCLOS WAS HAVING BREAKFAST IN his stateroom when Aris knocked and entered.

'*Corsaire*'s on the move, boss. Engines have started up and they've sent a launch to the beach. Which means that *Constance* is probably on the move too. Problem is, I can't find Hamid.'

Duclos smiled. 'I asked him to sort out the coffee. It's disgusting. He's probably down in the galley.'

Aris nodded, was about to close the door.

'And when you find him,' continued Duclos, 'tell him to prepare for departure. As soon as *Corsaire* is past, we'll follow her at a safe distance. And don't let anyone see you or the boys on deck. Just in case they recognise you.'

When Aris had gone, the bathroom door opened and Hamid came out. A towel was wrapped round his waist, his body brown and smooth.

'I better get moving,' he said, going to the far side of the bed and picking up his whites. He pulled off his towel and began to dress.

Duclos sipped his coffee and watched with an appreciative eye. The tight white underpants, the white shorts, the white polo shirt, his lover sitting on the edge of the bed to pull on his long socks and tie his plimsolls. With every movement, the young man's body flexed and rippled, the room filled with the musky warmth of him.

'One more kiss,' said Duclos, as Hamid stood up from the bed. Hamid did as he was told.

103

ISABELLE CASSIER PUT DOWN THE phone, her ear ringing from the tirade she had just endured from Monsieur Jean-Claude Vaillant, the chief executive of Basle et Cie. A court order had been secured by the *Judiciaire* the previous afternoon and served on his ex-wife, Madame Jeanne Vaillant, authorising a search of her home on rue Savry in the Roucas Blanc district. Isabelle checked her watch. At some stage in the next few hours a forensics team from Avignon would be entering the property to start a series of shallow excavations in the basement of her home and in its terraced gardens.

And her ex-husband wasn't happy about it – not at all – as he had made abundantly clear.

Tant pis, thought Isabelle as her phone began to ring again. With a sigh she reached forward and picked it up. Who was it going to be now?

'*Oui*? *Allo*? Chief Inspector Cassier.'

It was Gala Desfornado, her voice low and urgent.

'You told me to call if he didn't return. Monsieur Jacquot. There's still no sign of him. The berth is empty.'

'As you said, maybe he decided to moor somewhere overnight,' said Isabelle. 'The weather is good, he is still on sick leave, he has company . . .' For a moment she felt a twist of envy. An overnight stay on *Constance*, with Jacquot, moored somewhere remote, romantic. It was almost too much to bear.

'It's just that I'm worried,' Madame Desfornado continued. 'I had a friend at the Vieux Port *Capitainerie* call him up on the radio, but there was no response.'

'Maybe his radio is switched off. Or not working properly. Or maybe he was ashore, or swimming,' replied Isabelle, which made her think of his body in the water, what it would be like to hold on to him, his arms around her, pulling her tight, the warm, salty taste of him . . .

She looked up, saw Laganne heading for her desk. There was a sly smile on his face. One of these days, she thought, he was going to pluck up the nerve to ask her out. And she was going to have to let him know in no uncertain terms that such a thing would never happen. She was spoken for.

'You're right, you're right. I'm being silly,' said Madame Desfornado on the end of the line. 'I shouldn't worry so, but I do. I just have a feeling . . .'

'Why don't we leave it another twenty-four hours? See what happens,' said Isabelle, as Laganne dropped a print-out on her desk and tapped it with his finger, then tapped his nose with the same finger. Something was up. 'I'm sure there's absolutely nothing to worry about, Madame, but thank you again for calling, for letting me know.' And before Madame Desfornado could say anything else, Isabelle replaced the phone in its cradle and reached for the print-out. She turned it towards her: harbour movements along the coast from Nice to Marseilles.

'And?' she asked, shooting Laganne a what-about-it look.

'Just a hunch,' said Laganne. 'About the gold. Seems things have suddenly got very active all of a sudden. *Corsaire* out of Antibes, then here in Marseilles, moored across the harbour from Jacquot. Then *Désiré* out of Sanary yesterday morning. And both boats still out. Like Jacquot, so I hear.'

'*Corsaire*? *Désiré*? You've lost me.'

Her phone started ringing again. Probably the Mayor, or the *Préfet*, calling to give her grief about the Vaillant order. She let it ring.

Laganne slid her a smile.

'Monsieur Polineaux. And Monsieur Duclos. *Corsaire* and *Désiré* are theirs.'

104

WHEN JACQUOT TOOK *CONSTANCE* BETWEEN the bluffs of Calanque des Sirènes and out into open water, they crossed the line from shade to light, from early morning chill to a glorious, embracing warmth, the sun over Cap Canaille now flooding down on them, splashing through the wheelhouse windows on his port side, flashing off the glass dials on his instrument panel and warming his skin.

There was another good thing about open water. Radio reception.

Jacquot had thought about it the previous night but knew he'd have to wait until morning before he could do anything about it. He might not know how to accurately read a chart in relation to a set of co-ordinates, but he knew someone who did. He reached up to the radio extension screwed into the wheelhouse roof, switched it on and, unhooking the mic, put a call through to Salette's sloop in L'Estaque. The old harbour master was aboard and a few seconds later he came on air.

'I have a favour to ask, old man,' said Jacquot.

'There's no old man here, *salaud*,' replied Salette.

'Well, he's the one I'm after. The good-looking one. The one all the girls tell me about. The one who knows everything.'

'Ahhh,' came the reply. 'That one.'

'You have a chart handy? Marseilles to Genoa?'

'Don't you?'

'*Alors*, I've got some co-ordinates here,' said Jacquot, ignoring the jibe. 'Can you give me a rough idea where they point to?'

'You can't do it yourself?'

'Just double-checking,' he replied.

'Of course you are. So give them to me. See if I come up with the same answer as you, Monsieur Magellan.'

Pressing himself against the wheel to keep a steady course, Jacquot reached into the pocket of his shorts and brought out Philo's bookmark, read out the co-ordinates.

Five minutes later, as Claudine and Delphie settled on the aft deck with their mugs of coffee, turning their faces to the sun, Salette called back.

'Did your calculations put you anywhere near Île des Pénitents?' he asked.

'Pretty close,' replied Jacquot, with a pulse of excitement. The scrubby slopes of Pénitents were in sight, on his starboard side, rising out of the chop just a few kilometres to the south west.

'It's difficult to be precise without a proper GPS fix, but I'd say north side, somewhere around *plage* des Solitaires or the old prison ruins.'

'Onshore, or offshore?' asked Jacquot.

'Landside, that's my guess,' the old harbour master told him. 'So what's it all about? Why the interest?'

'I'll tell you later,' replied Jacquot, not wanting to say too much on an open channel. Signing off he hooked the mic back in its cradle and switched off the radio. Then he turned the wheel and watched the bow pull round on to the sun-bleached limestone slopes of Île des Pénitents.

401

105

CORSAIRE'S SKIPPER, HENRI CASSEL, MIGHT have missed the co-ordinates Jacquot had passed on to Salette, but he'd caught the end of their exchange. As he came out of Calanque d'En Vau and passed the headland into open water he could see *Constance* ahead by two or three kilometres and, beyond, the looming crags of Île des Pénitents.

After keeping watch on her in Marseilles' Vieux Port, *Constance* wasn't difficult to spot, but even that early in the morning they weren't the only vessels around: a tourist ferry bearing down on his starboard side, a couple of speedboats heading for Callelongue, a fishing skiff idling along close to the limestone slopes, and, far enough away to seem stationary, a flock of white-sailed yachts heeling to the off-shore breeze. Reaching for his Leica binoculars Cassel took a bead on her just to make sure. And there she was: the black hull, the white wheelhouse roof, rearing through some chop by the look of it, an occasional spray lifting off her bow.

Up on *Corsaire's* bridge, Cassel was hardly aware of any swell, but the smaller craft ahead of him was starting to roll as she took on some looming broadside peaks and deepening troughs. The previous day, it had been flat calm out here, but this morning, the sea had a sharper, edgier character.

Cassel put down the glasses. Whoever this Jacquot was, he wasn't the most experienced skipper. In conditions like these he'd have been better off keeping close to shore until he hit the wind shadow of the islands. In the calmer water he could have turned into the lower swells head on and made his life a great deal more comfortable. Instead he was taking a direct course to the islands, diagonally across the chop, and giving himself no end of trouble.

He sure was in a hurry, thought Cassel.

106

THE MOMENT *CORSAIRE* WAS OUT of sight behind the headland, Hamid started up the engines and swung *Désiré* in a wide circle. By the time he reached the point of the headland and passed out of Calanque d'En Vau, *Corsaire* was heading due south into the swells, ploughing a steady course out to sea. And there, a few kilometres ahead on its starboard side, was a small launch making heavy weather of the incoming conditions.

'They're pretending not to follow,' said Aris.

'Not an easy trick to pull off when you're our size,' replied Hamid, turning the wheel and heading away from both boats. 'My guess is that they'll keep south and then circle.'

'And *Désiré*?'

'We'll keep close to shore, hold them on our port side. *Corsaire* has just the one boat to worry about. We have the pair of them. The boss wants us to hold back until *Constance* and *Corsaire* engage, if indeed they do. If *Constance* had headed back to Marseilles, we'd have been wasting our time, but it looks like she's up to something. After something.'

'The gold?'

Hamid turned and smiled. 'Maybe. If we're lucky.'

'You think it's out here? After all this time?'

'The boss thinks so. And that's all that counts, *n'est-ce pas*?'

'What I can't understand,' Aris continued, 'is why this fellow, Jacquot, hasn't called it in. He's a cop, after all. The place should be swarming with patrol boats.'

'Maybe he's making sure it's there before he does anything.'

'Or maybe he wants to keep it for himself. Fatten his pension.'

'That too. Some pension.'

107

'IS IT SUPPOSED TO BE like this?' Claudine called out. She was down in the main cabin with Delphie, the two of them wedged between table and banquette in an effort to counter the roll and plunge as *Constance* rode the swells.

'Not far now,' Jacquot called back, closing on Pénitents and seeing up ahead that the swells appeared to be lessening in the lee of the island. Too late now, he remembered what Salette had told him on that first voyage they had taken together in *Constance*. And here he was taking some of the rollers close to beam on, doubling their power and menace – exactly what Salette had told him not to do. He wondered what his old friend would have to say about his seamanship. And Philo, too. Would Philo have made the crossing in conditions like these? Or would he have stayed in Sirènes with Eddie and waited it out?

Jacquot looked around, back to the sloping limestone cliffs they had come from, behind him towards Cassis, and ahead to Callelongue and Marseilles. The only vessels out here in open water were large cruisers and the tourist ferries, while smaller craft hugged the coast or holed up in more sheltered moorings.

Not that Jacquot had any doubts about *Constance*'s seaworthiness. If he had been by himself he would have loved the rough and tumble, the nervy exhilaration of bucketing through the waves, the feel of his bare feet planted on deck, white bubbling spray stripping off the bow in snowy wings and smacking like silvery bullets against the windscreen, safe in the knowledge that the cutter was a tough little operator and up to the task. But with two women below, one of them pregnant, he was keen to get out of the battering seas, bracing himself whenever he saw one of the incoming swells crest and break.

The change happened sooner than he expected. As Île des Pénitents drew closer, its chalky crags rising up on his port side, the breeze slackened, the swell began to subside and the rolling and bucketing settled into a more gentle progress, enough for him to push forward the throttles and take a bead on *plage* des Solitaires, a small shingle beach about midway along Pénitents' otherwise inhospitable northern shore.

Ten minutes later he cut the engines and cruised in to the rocky cove, dropping anchor as *Constance* slowed to a halt. There were three other boats ahead of him, two yachts and another small cruiser. The skipper of the cruiser waved a greeting.

'You had yourself quite a ride,' the man called out. He was about twenty metres away, but his voice carried over the water.

'She's a tough old girl,' replied Jacquot, noting a woman and a young boy on the aft deck. A family outing, he decided.

'Forecast says there's more coming in,' the man continued. 'Time for port, you ask me.'

Jacquot had forgotten to check the weather forecast but didn't admit it.

'That's right,' he said. 'Good time to head back, I reckon.'

'No point taking chances.'

Jacquot gave the man a wave and swung back to the wheelhouse where Delphie was waiting for him.

'It's looking good,' she said, and handed Jacquot the GPS handset. 'I'd say we're close. Closer than we were last night, at any rate.'

He checked the figures. 'Let's hope the batteries last.'

108

CASSEL CRUISED PAST *PLAGE* DES Solitaires, keeping *Corsaire* a discreet three hundred metres off-shore, Léo and Zach in the cabin below monitoring *Constance* through binoculars.

'They could be just out here for a picnic,' said Zach, as he watched the man check his anchor with a few hefty tugs before stepping along the narrow side deck back to the wheelhouse. 'Him and the two girls. A little bit of action, that's all.'

'Then they might as well have stayed in that calanque of theirs,' said Léo. 'Why bother hauling their arses out here, through that kind of water? They're up to something, if you ask me. And if they're going for the gold, then we'll have them. If not . . . hey, we just keep watching.' He laid down his glasses and spread out across the leather sofa on which they were kneeling. 'And living on the high seas like this sure beats the crap out of my one-bedroom shack in Coldanne. I could really get used to this,' he said, running his fingers over the soft cream hide.

'Pity the boss can't.'

'You ever been sea-sick?' asked Léo, not bothered whether he got an answer or not. 'It's the shits, I'm telling you.'

'You know that for a fact?' asked Zach with a grin.

'You just need to look at the colour of him. If it wasn't for the old man, he'd be landside and happy to be there.'

Somewhere below them, the soft rumble of the turbines died and *Corsaire* settled in the water, a distant clanking sound as the anchor dropped. The boat swung round and squares of sunshine slid across the carpet – as though the sun was moving faster through the sky than it should – settling finally at Léo's feet.

'You take the first watch,' he said. 'Then tell Dhuc to take over. Me? I'm going for a swim. Make it look all natural. Like that's why we're here. For the swimming.'

109

'DO YOU MIND IF I STAY?' asked Claudine, from the shade of the wheelhouse. Out on deck Jacquot and Delphie were packing the watertight grab-bag for their trip ashore: sun cream for Delphie, sandals and espadrilles, a towel, bottled water, a torch, Jacquot's cigarettes, a camera and the GPS handset. 'I'll look after the boat,' she said.

'Are you all right?' asked Jacquot, suddenly anxious. They had all been looking forward to the hunt for the gold, if there was any, and this unexpected request to be left behind came as a surprise. He could have kicked himself for causing the two sisters such discomfort. Delphie seemed to have managed but for Claudine it must have been a trial. But she hadn't been sick, she hadn't asked him to head back to their Sirènes mooring and wait for the weather to change, and there was bright colour in her cheeks.

'It's okay. Just a rest, is all,' she told them, and swept a hand through her hair. 'I'll be fine, really. Maybe I'll read a book, if I can find one.' The attempt at humour didn't altogether cover the note of disappointment in her voice, regret at missing out on all the fun now that they were here, so close. They'd all been excited by the prospect of hunting for the gold, the three of them together. Now it was just two of them going.

While Delphie finished packing the bag, Jacquot went over to Claudine and gave her a kiss.

'If you're sure you're all right?'

'I'm fine, don't worry. It's just, you know . . .' She patted her stomach. 'Sometimes it's like a little voice telling you to take it easy. And now is one of those times. That's all.'

'I'll bring you back a present.'

Claudine gave him a smile, reached out a hand to smooth his cheek, then gripped his nose hard between thumb and forefinger. 'You had better. And shells and pretty stones just won't cut it. What I want comes yellow and heavy and shaped like a brick. *C'est clair*?' She gave his nose a final twist and then released him.

'*Oui, c'est clair*,' he said, rubbing his nose and leaning forward to give her a peck on the cheek. 'We won't be long.'

'Take as long as you need. And don't worry about me,' she told him. 'I'll be fine.'

Because of the other boats moored in the cove, *Constance* was anchored too deep for Jacquot and Delphie to wade in to the beach. So, with Claudine watching, they lowered themselves off the transom ladder, slid into the warm, salty water, and they swam towards the beach, until the stony sea-bed was visible and they felt the ground beneath their feet.

Up on the beach, the first thing Delphie did was pull the GPS handset from the grab-bag. She switched it on, shielded its face with her hand, and stepped towards the water's edge, looked again, then took a few more paces up the beach.

'Still close, but no cigar,' she said. 'But at least we won't be diving for it.'

Jacquot slipped on his espadrilles, pulled on a T-shirt from the bag – the salt already drying on his skin scratchy against the cotton – and glanced around. To their left a shoulder-high shelf of slanting rock rose up from the water and the beach and ran at least fifty metres inshore, effectively cutting off any easy access to the east. On the other side of the beach, just a few steps away, was a narrow jetty built into the other shelf of rock that enclosed the cove, its concrete cracked and tilted into broken jigsaw pieces, worn down by years of weather and disuse. From before the Revolution, prisoners had been brought here by ship's tender, rowed ashore and unloaded on this jetty to begin their sentences in the prison barracks a few hundred metres west, where the slopes from Pénitents' rising crags flattened out before dropping into the sea.

Standing there on the beach, Jacquot was stunned to realise how long it was since he had been there, on *plage* des Solitaires, one of a dozen or so youngsters who'd come out here on summer weekends for overnight parties – a fire on the beach, beers, wine, some dope, one of the girls quite handy with a guitar . . . Suddenly it seemed like a different life.

'Hey, dreamer. So which way do we go?' asked Delphie, putting down the handset to squirt cream on to her shoulders and arms. The sun was high now, with no real shade to soften its burn.

Jacquot shook away the memories. 'If you had to carry a ton of gold, which way would you go?'

'If it was me,' she said, pulling on a straw hat, 'I'd have dropped it over the side. In Sirènes. In one of those wire cage lobster pots disguised to look like a rock.'

'Too many divers, snorkellers. Someone would have been sure to find it.'

'An underwater cave?'

'You've been reading too many thrillers.'

'So what do you reckon?'

Jacquot nodded to the jetty and a narrow path leading away from it up into the low stony scrub.

'They could have brought *Constance* in close, driven her right up on shore maybe, and then unloaded. Hard work but they could have done it. And late November, there aren't too many people come out here. Also they're far enough away not to be seen, they wouldn't have had to worry about someone spotting them. No roads along that stretch of the coast,' he said, nodding back to the mainland cliffs. 'I'd say they went for the path, a couple of bars apiece unless they had some more of those waistcoats. And they wouldn't

412

have gone too far, even if they'd had them.'

'So what are we waiting for?' asked Delphie, leaving the grab-bag for Jacquot and heading for the path, looping the GPS's cord around her neck.

Jacquot watched her stride off, then picked up the bag, slung it over his shoulder and looked back at *Constance*.

He could see Claudine standing on the rear deck. She waved, Jacquot waved back, and then he turned to follow Delphie.

110

'WHAT ARE THEY DOING?'

Zach lowered the binoculars, and turned away from the cabin window where he and Dhuc were keeping watch.

It was Didier, looking a little peaky but putting on a show in a pair of crisply-ironed white shorts, a pale blue polo-shirt with the collar up, tennis socks and plimsolls.

'Two of them have gone ashore – the man and one of the women. The other one's stayed on board.'

'And?' Didier took the binoculars from Zach and peered through them, swinging the glasses left and right until he caught the pair of them walking along a path, the woman first, the man a few steps behind her, with a bag over his shoulder.

'That's it. Except they look like they know where they're going.'

'What's she got there?' asked Didier, squinting through the glasses. Every few steps the woman would pause, check something in her hand, and then move on.

'Looks like a compass,' replied Dhuc, still watching through his glasses.

'More like a GPS handset,' said *Corsaire*'s skipper, Cassel. 'She had it on the beach, walked around a bit, checking it, then set off along the path. If you ask me, I'd say they're trying to match a set of co-ordinates.'

Outside, from the aft deck, came the sound of a splash, something hitting the water. Didier frowned.

'It's Léo,' said Zach, seeing the frown. 'He said he was going for a swim, to make it all look natural.'

Didier considered this, then turned back to Cassel. 'Where does that path lead?'

'Not far. Maybe three, four hundred metres,' the skipper replied. 'There's an old prison camp at the end of it. Not much left of it now. Just the foundations, really. A couple of walls, maybe. But nothing more than a metre high.'

'What happens if they go off the path?'

'They'll have to start climbing. It gets steep quickly.'

Didier narrowed his eyes. 'Are there caves up there?'

Cassel shook his head. 'Nothing you could hide anything in, if that's what you mean. And hauling up a ton of gold would have been a hell of a job.'

'If those two went off the path, would they be out of sight?'

'A few minutes, maybe; nothing more.'

'What about the other side of the island? Maybe they landed here because it's too rough to moor round the other side?'

'They couldn't get far, not from this side. Round the end there,' Cassel said, pointing, 'the slope just drops straight down into deep water. If they're looking for something, like I said they'll be looking for it near the old prison. That's my bet.'

Didier nodded. It made sense. And while there were other boats moored in the cove, they wouldn't be coming back loaded down with gold bars. They'd wait till the other boats had moved off. As if on cue, he noticed activity on the two yachts. One of them was already turning and a sail going up. On the other, a man was hauling up an anchor.

Just the two launches left.

He swung the glasses on to the second craft. A man and a woman sitting on the cramped aft deck, and a young boy, sitting on the bow, casting out a fishing line.

Easy to get rid of, thought Didier. If they decided to stay.

111

'HOW INFURIATING!'

Delphie was fuming. She was stalking around the ruins of the old prison, one hand holding down her straw hat, the other cradling the GPS. It was a bleak, desolate, sun-blasted place, the buildings that had once stood there reduced now to bare footings. Not a single wall remained, no roof, no doorway, no windows, just an occasional ledge of brick or stone to indicate where a door might have been, none of them more than three or four courses high, low enough to step over, the larger sections sprayed with ground-level graffiti: *Vive La Fédération*, *P et D '92*, *Nautilus, Club25* and other less decipherable squiggles and shapes in lurid shades of blue and black and pink.

For the hundredth time, Delphie paused, shook the handset, peered again at the figures.

'I just can't get the damned thing to do what I want.'

'That's the whole point,' said Jacquot, making himself comfortable on a makeshift bench at the edge of what had once clearly been the largest room in the prison – a mess hall or sanatorium, he guessed, or maybe an enclosed exercise yard. He opened the top of the grab-bag and dug around for his cigarettes. 'You do what it tells you to do. Probably a concept not altogether familiar to you and your sister.'

416

It was a poor attempt at humour, trying to lift her mood, but Jacquot knew that he had to do something. He was the one who'd put them up to it, the one who'd told them about the gold and raised their hopes, and it was for him to ease the disappointment. For the last hour the pair of them had trudged around these ruins, stopping to check the co-ordinates then moving on again, the GPS nowhere near as accurate as they had hoped. So far they'd stepped out an area some thirty square metres which matched the bookmark co-ordinates, but the digital read-outs continued to flicker indecisively, never properly settling.

Cupping his hands, Jacquot lit up two cigarettes.

'Here,' he said, waving Delphie over. 'Time for a smoke.'

Ten metres away, she stamped her foot, looked round one last time and then came over to the bench, sat down beside him and almost snatched the cigarette from his fingers. She took a deep pull and blew out a plume of smoke, whipped away by the breeze.

'It's just so frustrating. So . . . I don't know. *Maddening*. In the movies they'd have found it by now. In real life . . . well, it just doesn't seem to work like that.'

Jacquot chuckled.

'*Calme, calme,*' he told her. 'Just relax. We're here. It's close, if it's here at all.'

'But where, Daniel? Just where exactly?' she snapped back, waving her cigarette at the ruins. 'I mean, look around. There's just . . . nothing. Nowhere they could have hidden it.'

She was right, and Jacquot knew it. Apart from three grated wells which Delphie had got very excited about – until they'd established the metal gratings had rusted into the stone, and the bottom of each was filled with rubbish – there appeared to be nowhere that the gold could have been concealed. Which was why he had stopped for a smoke, to take in the view and think it all through. Across the weed-strewn foundations where they now sat he could see all the way to the rising hump of Cap Canaille in the east, to the mainland directly across the channel, and to Callelongue and Cap Croisette to the west, a marvellous panorama, wide and open, just the perfect spot for a tourist viewing bench. Below them, at anchor a hundred or so metres offshore, lay a glistening white cruiser and Jacquot spotted the two yachts that had been moored in the cove come into view, their sails filling and heeling to the breeze. The man in the launch had been right. The weather was changing.

'We just have to think positive,' he began. 'If this is the place the co-ordinates have brought us to, then all we have to do is try and work out where the gold could be. And there would have been a lot of it, remember. Which should limit the options. So . . . if we were Philo and Eddie, where would we have stashed it? Say, within twenty metres of where we are now.'

'You're joking, aren't you? Please tell me you're joking.' Delphie unscrewed the cap on the water bottle and took a gulp. She looked done in, as though the lure of finding the gold had worn off, the whole escapade reduced to a tiresome wild goose chase which she was now keen to put behind her. He couldn't blame her. The sun was high above them, hard and strong, and searing down over Pénitents' stony slopes, the occasional gust of breeze across their faces and shoulders as hot as the draft from the opened door of a baker's oven. This was not what they had planned.

As they sat there together, smoking their cigarettes, Jacquot wondered what it must have been like to have been a prisoner here, held in one of those tiny cells, roasting in summer, shivering in winter. And maybe just to make the punishment sweeter, the cells' barred windows looking out across the channel to the mainland. Home for most of the people kept here, none of whom would ever likely set foot on the mainland again. *Les Oubliés*. The forgotten.

And then Jacquot frowned. Some thought. Some image. Something that flashed through his mind so quickly it barely registered. It was a familiar feeling. Often, investigating a crime, something 'clicked' – some memory, some association.

And he had it now.

But what? What was it?

Delphie took a breath, was about to say something.

He held up his hand to stop her. He needed to think. To think. He narrowed his eyes and looked across the channel, the white slopes of the coast freckled with the green stubs of trees and shrubs tortured by the weather.

And then it started to trickle back, to take shape.

A view.

Everything in plain view.

And a taunt.

Here it is. Right in front of you.

Like Clem's doorstop.

Like the bookmarks.

Everything there if you knew how to look, where to look, what to look for.

Everything in plain view, he thought again.

In plain view.

Right in front of you.

But there was nothing: just a wide stretch of bare ground made up of hard-packed, sun-baked earth and the polished rumps of stones set deeply into it. And all around them nothing but the stone footings of four walls, just a few low segments of plastered brick no more than two or three courses high to mark out the shape of four long-gone doorways – the ones to his left and right leading to the cells, the one behind him leading to the wells, and the one in front of him with the channel and mainland beyond. High walls once, but now just low bookend stumps of worn brick and plaster.

In plain view. In plain view.

He'd been looking right at it since he'd sat down.

Now he flung his cigarette aside, jumped up and snatched the GPS handset from Delphie.

'What are you doing? What on earth . . . ?' she called after him.

But he didn't reply. Instead he hurried over to the gap in the wall footings in front of them and checked the GPS reading. The co-ordinates flickered but they still matched. Then he took a few steps through the doorway and checked the numbers again. The same erratic flickering, and still the same co-ordinates. Then he went back to the footings and straddled what was left of the wall, one foot either side of the ledge, and took a third reading.

For the first time, the numbers glowed bright and steady.

'This is the place,' he said, and pocketing the handset he dropped down on his knees to look more closely at the rough brickwork, some of it still covered in a brown *crépi* plaster.

Then he sat back on his haunches, looked at Delphie, and pointed at it.

And started to laugh.

Like a lot of the walls they'd seen – what was left of them – graffiti had been sprayed on to every spare centimetre of stone: names of pop groups, people, initials, declarations of love. The usual things . . .

And there, on that small patch of plaster, no more than a dozen centimetres high and twice as long, in a light blue spray, no attempt at artistry, a single word.

Just five letters.

VOILÀ.

Philo's little joke.

'Bring me the torch,' said Jacquot, as he leaned forward to examine what remained of the wall, brushing his fingers over it, then getting up to step across it, looking at it from the other side, then pushing at it with his foot. Rock hard. No give. By the time he'd walked around it a couple of times, Delphie was there with the torch.

Jacquot took it – a solid, metal-cased Maglite – and squatted down again, tapping the torch's back-end against the stone, little bits of plaster and brick dust settling on his wrist as he did so.

How would Philo have done it, Jacquot wondered?

How would he have hidden the gold?

There was only one possibility.

Take down what was left of the wall, dig up the foundation stones, then throw them away to make room for the gold bars. Once set in the footings, Philo could rebuild the wall above them, mortar it all up and plaster it over. All he'd need was some mixing cement, a bag of *crépi* plaster powder and a wash of terracotta thin enough to dry in minutes, weathering back to the original colour in a matter of days. Out here on Pénitents, in the ruins of an old prison, no one would ever have noticed.

And all he and Eddie had to do when they wanted to make a withdrawal was to stay on after other visitors had headed back to their boats.

Until they were alone, and the island was theirs.

And to bring a hammer and chisel.

To help themselves to another brick.

Or two. Or three.

Whatever they needed.

Like a kind of bank.

That's what they'd done with the gold, Jacquot was sure of it.

And he was going to find it.

Gripping the torch as firmly as he could, he started hammering away at the plastered brickwork.

Again and again and again, blow after blow, harder and harder, spraying dust and plaster chips with every hit.

Until, at last, a slab of brick and plaster broke away, clean down to the footings.

Jacquot stopped hammering, threw down the torch, and started sweeping away the chips of brick and stone and mortar. Then he sat back on his haunches, as though he'd been pushed over, and Delphie gasped.

'I don't believe it,' she whispered, hands going to her mouth, then getting down beside him.

She started laughing. 'I – don't – fucking – be*lieve* – it.'

112

'WHAT WAS THAT?' ASKED DIDIER, looking through the salon window towards the old prison.

'Looked like a flash,' said Léo, his hair slicked back, still wet from his swim. 'Like they're taking a photo.'

There was another flash, and another.

'*C'est certain.* A camera flash,' said Zach.

'They've found it,' whispered Didier. 'They've got it.'

Kneeling between them on the sofa, the binoculars squeezed into his eyes, Zach worked the focus wheel, leaning his elbows on the back of the sofa to steady his grip.

'It looks . . . it looks like she's jumping,' he told them. 'Up and down. Or dancing, or something. And clapping her hands.'

'They've definitely found it,' said Didier, and started to chuckle.

Cassel came down from the bridge. 'You see that?' he asked. 'The camera flash?'

'We saw it,' said Léo.

'So what do you want to do, boss?' asked Cassel, turning to Didier.

'Exactly what we planned. And right now, before they start back for the beach. You all know what to do. Let's do it.'

'I'll go tell Dhuc,' said Léo, pushing away from the sofa and heading for the door that led forward to the cabins. 'Zach, get the launch ready.'

Suddenly, after hours of silent observation, *Corsaire* came to life.

113

DEEP INSIDE HER, CLAUDINE FELT a movement. A fluttering, as fragile as the wings of a butterfly caught in cupped hands. The same gentle fluttering she'd felt that morning as they surged through the swell, she and Delphie down in the main cabin, hanging on for dear life. It hadn't worried her then, that soft shifting sensation, as they laughed together at Captain Crazy leading them into a storm, just his legs visible, planted firm on the deck, bending and flexing to counter the swell. And it didn't bother her now. It just made her smile. Because she knew what it was, remembered it from the time she was pregnant with Midou. One or both of her babies rearranging themselves. Making themselves more comfortable.

Claudine was in the for'ard cabin, lying on Delphie's bed, both hatches and all six portholes open to catch the breeze and cool *Constance*'s interior, the cabin door and wheelhouse hatch similarly left open. She'd been sleeping when the movement came, but it was strong enough to wake her. Not so much a kick as a strange prodding sensation, from the inside. She imagined a little fist pushing against the walls of her womb, down there in the warm, watery, absolute darkness. And she smiled again, laid a soothing hand over her belly. She waited for another movement, wishing for it, but nothing came. She breathed deeply – long, steady even breaths to comfort them – then slowly, carefully, she sat up and swung her legs off the bed.

She wondered what time it was, how long she had slept. Long enough for a thin film of sweat to form on the back of her neck, for the pillow to feel damp. Bending forward she looked through into the main cabin until she could see the brass clock above the chart table. A few minutes after two in the afternoon. So they'd been gone a little over two hours . . . two hours since she'd waved at them on the beach and watched them follow the path up from the jetty, passing out of sight below the stony bluff that marked out the edge of the cove.

Getting to her feet, Claudine moved through into the main cabin. They'd be back soon, and whether or not they'd found the gold, she knew they'd be hungry and thirsty. She should start preparing a late lunch. And as she reached into the small fridge to see what she could knock together, she wondered if they had managed to find anything. If, indeed, there was any gold. Or had it all been wild speculation the night before? Just the three of them wanting it to be true, wanting to find gold. Only to be let down, disappointed. It really was too extraordinary to be possible. Fool's gold, she thought to herself, and as she thought it she felt something bump against the hull, beyond the aft deck, and realised they must have come back. Winding the sarong around her waist, pushing back her hair, she turned to the companionway leading to the wheelhouse and started up.

She was about to call out, welcome them back, wondering if they came with good or bad news, when a head appeared over the transom and brought her up short. A man she had never seen before, climbing aboard, with a dark face, spiky black hair and slanting eyes. He wore a white sleeveless vest and blue shorts, his skin smooth and shiny and brown, the muscles of his legs and shoulders bunching as he hauled himself over the transom and hopped down on to the rear deck. He looked like a pirate boarding a ship with intent to do harm, the only thing missing a long silvery cutlass clenched between his teeth.

425

But if he didn't have the cutlass, Claudine now saw that he carried a gun and when their eyes met and he saw her there, framed in the shadow of the wheelhouse hatch, he raised the gun, aimed it at her and put a finger to his smiling lips.

114

THERE WAS A JAUNTY SPRING in their steps as Jacquot and
Delphie made their way back to the cove.

'How many bars do you suppose there are?' asked Delphie.

'Apart from the ones we uncovered? You want there to be more?'

'Of course I want more. Don't you? So how many? Take a guess.'

Jacquot gave it some thought, saw again the second line of gold
set down into the foundations of the wall.

'Maybe another dozen or so,' he said.

'So what . . . ? Twenty?'

'Around there,' replied Jacquot, and felt the swinging weight of
just that one bar he'd brought with him for Claudine, swaddled in
the grab-bag with the sun cream and the GPS handset and the rest
of their stuff, jolting against his shoulder. A good twelve kilos.
What must it have been like to shift so many of them? How had
they managed it that long-ago night?

Delphie was silent for a moment. And then, 'Do you think they'd
miss a couple? I mean, one for you and Claudine, one for me and
the old man? They'd never know. How could they? I mean, if we
wanted to we could keep the lot.'

Jacquot smiled. He'd had the same thought, of course. It was
only natural. They'd found the gold. Maybe twenty bars. Two
hundred and fifty kilos, give or take. Somewhere over twelve

million francs, he estimated. And no one knew about it. Gold that had been lost, written off, more than twenty years ago. The temptation was enormous, and mesmerising.

'It's funny you should say that. I was thinking just the same thing,' he admitted.

'You were?' Delphie glanced up at him. 'Really? A couple of bars? Or, I don't know . . . Maybe a few more? You think we should? I mean, could we get away with it?'

'Ah,' said Jacquot as they dropped down past the shelf of stone and the cove revealed itself, the two yachts and the launch long gone, just *Constance* moored quietly in the bay. 'Now there's a question. Would we get away with it?'

'Your friend, Philo, did. And Eddie.'

'Yes, they did,' said Jacquot, coming off the path and feeling the shingle of the beach give beneath his feet. 'They took a gamble and it paid off. More than twenty years living off the proceeds. And living well. The big house, the travel. But could you take a gamble like that? Could you risk everything? Your family? Your job? Your freedom?'

Delphie fell silent. 'It's just a dream, isn't it?'

'I think that's exactly what it is,' said Jacquot, as they waded out into the water. 'For people like us.'

'If I just had the nerve,' said Delphie, getting out of her depth and starting to swim. 'But inside, in my heart of hearts, I know I couldn't do it. It's just . . . thinking about it, you know? The possibility. The gold, there for the taking. And no one would know.'

Her words rang a little bell in Jacquot's head.

He'd heard them before, but he shook away the memory.

'It'll make a great story,' he said.

'Front page. No doubt about that,' said Delphie, with a whoop of glee. 'So what do we do now?'

'Call it in,' said Jacquot. 'Report the find.'

'Spoilsport,' she said, swimming on ahead.

Beneath his feet the shingle fell away and Jacquot lunged after her, kicking out with his legs, reaching through the water with his arms, long, powerful strokes, feeling the weight of the grab-bag on his back and shoulders. He was glad he didn't have too far to swim.

Delphie was first to reach *Constance*, pulling herself up the steps, then leaning back down to take the bag from him, heaving it aboard and dropping it with a heavy clunk on to the aft deck.

'We're back, Claudie,' Jacquot heard her call out. 'And we've brought you a little present.'

With the weight off his shoulders, Jacquot hoisted himself aboard, water streaming off him.

And there was Delphie, standing just in front of him.

And there, coming up out of the main cabin, stepping into the wheelhouse, was Claudine.

But there was something wrong.

Her face was ashen, her eyes wide, and she had no words to greet them with.

And then he saw why.

There was someone coming up behind her.

A man. Tall, dark, in a crisp pale blue polo-shirt and perfectly-creased shorts.

'Welcome aboard,' the stranger said.

And with a dangerous smile he levelled a gun at them.

115

IF THIS JACQUOT WAS A cop, wondered René Duclos, was he straight or bent? If he was straight and he knew the gold was there, the place should've been crawling with *flics*. But it wasn't.

So, the obvious conclusion? He was bent. As bent as any other *flic* that Duclos had ever dealt with. Out for himself. Hand in the till. No surprises there, then.

Duclos was sitting at a glass-topped wicker-framed dining table on *Désiré*'s aft deck, sheltered from the sun by the flying bridge. He had taken a light lunch – a selection of cold meats, buttered new potatoes, a baby leaf salad, a bottle of *gris de gris* Provençal rosé – and was busy scraping the last of a peach *crème brûlée* from its copper dish. For the last two hours Hamid had taken *Désiré* back and forth along the coast, no more than a hundred metres from the mainland cliffs, and in the main salon Duclos could see Aris, Beni and Jo-Jo keeping watch on *Corsaire*, switching sides every time *Désiré* turned about, at least one pair of binoculars focussed on Île des Pénitents at any one time.

As Duclos pushed aside the cleaned copper dish, Aris opened the sliding salon doors and stepped out on to the deck. He came to the table but he did not take a seat.

'They're back aboard *Constance*. The cop and the woman.'

'And Didier's introduced himself?' asked Duclos, taking his napkin from his lap.

'They're all there. Didier, a couple of his boys, the cop and the two women.'

Duclos put down the napkin and turned towards Pénitents, shading his eyes. They were too far away for him to make out any detail, but he sensed the time had come. Things were starting to move.

'Have Hamid bring us in. From the east. Like we're coming in to moor. Just visitors. Oh, and have Beni tool up the crew. Just in case we need them.'

116

'SO WHAT HAVE WE HERE?' asked Didier, settling into the skipper's chair and pointing his gun at the grab-bag. He looked at Delphie, and then at Jacquot, both of them still standing where they'd clambered aboard, both too stunned to speak. 'Well? Lost our tongues, have we?'

Jacquot might not have been speaking, but his mind was racing. He knew a bad boy when he saw one, and this one looked the part down to his neatly laced tennis shoes and long socks. The complacency, the confidence, the polished turn-out, a gun in his hand, a neat little walkie-talkie holstered on his pleated Gucci belt. But who was he? And where had he come from? And how did he know about the gold? About Île des Pénitents? The questions rattled through his head like machine gun fire. But none of them settled.

Jacquot looked around for a boat tied up alongside, but there was nothing, only the wedding-cake cruiser a few hundred metres away. He must have been brought over by launch and just come aboard. On to his boat. *Constance*. Without so much as a by-your-leave. Jacquot bristled, but there was nothing he could do about it. Right then, his overriding concern was Claudine, whose arm the stranger held so lightly, almost affectionately. How exactly was he going to get that gun out of the man's hand?

Then the man turned his head and called out: 'Dhuc, Léo. Come on up and meet my new friends.'

If Jacquot had had any doubts about the stranger's gangland bona fides, just a glance at the two men coming up from below would have dispelled them. The first was Asian – Chinese? Vietnamese? Cambodian? Jacquot couldn't tell which. All he could say with any certainty was that the man was dangerous. Lithe and tough-looking. Nothing he wouldn't do, if his boss wanted something. And Polo-Shirt was clearly the boss. The second man up, Léo, was no different. Taller than the one called Dhuc, but just as deadly. Cold black eyes. Lean and mean. The man who'd hit Clem, who'd put her down and left her for dead. And both men carried guns. Automatics. Berettas by the look of them. Hammers cocked. And in that instant Jacquot knew that the odds had trebled against him. One man was possible. Three was another matter. Jacquot just hoped they kept their fingers off the triggers.

'You,' said Didier, waving his gun at Jacquot, and then pointing it at the grab-bag. 'If you wouldn't mind.'

'Who are you? And what are you doing on my boat?' asked Jacquot, stepping past Delphie and heading for the stranger. But three guns turned in his direction and he stopped in his tracks.

'Do as I say, *copain*. Or the ladies'll go first,' said Didier, turning his gun on Claudine and letting its muzzle slide up and down her arm. 'And do it now.'

Without further argument, Jacquot kneeled down and opened the bag, tipped it up and spilled the contents on to the deck. Sun tan cream, Delphie's camera, his cigarettes, lighter, the GPS handset, sandals, espadrilles. Wrapped in a towel and caught in a fold at the bottom of the bag, the gold bar was the last item out. It hit the deck with a muffled but solid thunk.

With a nod from Didier, Dhuc sprang forward, waving Jacquot back with his gun. He picked up a corner of the towel, snapped it out and the gold bar tumbled into the sunshine.

There was a moment's silence. No one spoke. No one moved.

433

And then, '*Ooh là là*,' said Didier. 'What a catch, Monsieur. You have been busy.'

Jacquot could see that the man was not surprised. So he'd known about the gold. He'd known what was in the bag. He'd been expecting it.

'Dhuc, *s'il te plaît* . . .' he said, releasing Claudine's arm and holding out his hand.

Dhuc picked up the bar and carried it over to his boss.

Didier took it and his arm sagged with the weight.

'My, my,' he chuckled, his eyes licking over the golden brick. 'So, tell me, Monsieur . . . Monsieur?'

'Jacquot. Daniel Jacquot.'

'Jacquot, Jacquot, Jacquot,' said Didier quietly, repeating the name, as though to see if it registered. It clearly didn't. 'So Monsieur Jacquot. Tell me about the gold.'

'It was buried on the island,' he replied, matter of factly.

'And how did you know about it?' asked Didier, handing the gold bar back to Dhuc who laid it on top of the instrument panel.

'I might ask you the same.'

'You can ask all you like, Monsieur Jacquot, but I'm the one with the gun,' replied Didier, an easy smile playing over his lips.

'The man who owned this boat. He hid it here,' said Jacquot. There seemed little to gain from being obstructive.

'And he told you that?'

'Not really. But he left some clues.'

'His name?'

'Philo.'

'Philo? Not Niko? Niko Emanetti?'

'One and the same,' replied Jacquot. 'Philo was a nickname.'

'And clues, you say?'

'Co-ordinates. How to get here. Disguised as a bookmark.'

'A bookmark?' Didier nodded, giving this information due consideration.

Jacquot pointed to the wheelhouse windshield. 'There's one there, just behind you.'

Didier turned, saw the bookmark and picked it up, examined it.

'Ingenious,' he said. 'Just numbers to me. What a clever fellow you must be.'

Jacquot made no reply.

'Was there a woman? Edina?'

'She died, too. A couple of years ago.'

Didier nodded, as though it all made perfect sense.

'And your friends here? These two lovely ladies.' He waved his gun at Claudine and Delphie.

'My wife and her sister.'

Didier frowned. 'Your wife? Really? I see no ring.'

'We haven't got round to the formalities quite yet.'

'Although it's clear you've got around to other things,' said Didier with a chuckle. His two companions grinned at their boss's joke. 'But let's get back to business, shall we? The gold. I'm assuming there's more where this came from?'

Jacquot didn't reply.

Didier lifted his gun and rested the barrel against Claudine's belly. 'I said . . .'

'Yes. There's more.' Jacquot glanced at Claudine, smiled encouragement. She managed a smile back.

'Good. That's more like it. And just how many bars have you found?'

'Hard to say. Maybe twenty.'

'Along that path?' asked Didier, nodding towards the shore.

'That's right. About half a kilometre.'

'Good, good. So, here's what you're going to do. First of all, you're going to get this little tub of yours a little closer to the beach, then you're going to show my boys where the gold is, and help them bring it back here. Do I make myself absolutely clear, Monsieur Jacquot?'

Jacquot nodded.

'Because if you do anything to upset me, if you try anything stupid, these two ladies will suffer. Please assure me you understand completely?'

'I understand,' replied Jacquot. 'But you'll need some tools to dig up the bars.'

'Tools?'

'A good hammer, some kind of chisel to lever them out.'

'You have these tools? Here on the boat?'

Jacquot saw no reason to lie, to play for time, for Didier to have someone on his cruiser come over with what was needed when he had them in a drawer below deck. He knew this man, whoever he was, was a serious player. If Jacquot did something stupid, it had been made abundantly clear that either Claudine or Delphie would suffer for it. Possibly the pair of them.

'Yes, I do,' he said. 'In a drawer in the main cabin. Below the chart table.'

Didier considered this then smiled, teeth gleaming in his tanned face. 'So, *mes amis*. Let's get to work.'

117

WHILE DIDIER STAYED ON BOARD *Constance* with Claudine and Delphie, the two sisters locked in the for'ard cabin, Jacquot, Dhuc and Léo set off along the path. By now the sun was dropping towards Marseilles and the Golfe du Lion, the air warm and dusty rather than searing, their shadows longer now. Earlier that day he had come along this same path with Delphie, excited at the prospect of finding gold. Now he made the same journey knowing it was here, with Dhuc and Léo, guns drawn, following just a few paces behind him.

Jacquot carried everything – three rucksacks for the gold, and the tools they'd need to dig it up – vividly aware that time was running out. He prayed that the two men behind him wouldn't shoot him, here on the island; prayed they'd keep him alive at least until he'd helped them carry the gold back to the boat. Or until he found some way to put them down, and remove the threat.

Without any attempt at delay, Jacquot led them straight to the courtyard where, for centuries, the men imprisoned there had exercised, or lain sick in their beds, or come to eat, and pointed to the low wall.

'It's there,' he said, dumping the rucksacks on the ground. 'You going to help, or just watch me?'

'We'll just watch,' said Léo, and the two of them squatted down

437

a few safe metres away. Léo laid his gun in the dirt and pulled a pack of cigarettes from his shirt pocket, lit up. Dhuc kept his gun trained on Jacquot.

'What are you waiting for?' Léo called out, taking a drag, letting the smoke whistle through his lips. 'Get a move on.'

Setting to work, Jacquot hammered away at the low wall knocking the bricks aside. And there, just as he and Delphie had left it, set down in the footings, was the gold.

As soon as they saw the sun glint off the bars, Léo and Dhuc came forward.

'Jésu. Will you look,' whispered Léo, pushing his gun into the band of his trousers and leaning forward to pull one of the bars free.

For a moment Jacquot was tempted to swing the hammer he was holding, take at least one of them out, then try to wrestle the gun from the second. It was a risk, but a fair one, the two men clearly distracted by the gold. But as he clenched his fingers round the handle of the hammer, he felt Dhuc poke him in the shoulder with his gun.

'Keep digging,' the man said.

It took Jacquot another twenty minutes to loosen and dig up all the bars, handing them back to Léo one by one until his shoulders ached and his hands and fingers were almost numb. He was also aware of shooting pains in the top of his thigh, like a kind of cramp, kneeling there in the dirt. Twice he'd had to stand up, stretch, before starting back on the dig.

When the last brick came up, it was clear that Jacquot's estimate hadn't been too far off. Stacked on the ground in front of Léo and Dhuc were twenty-four gold bars.

The three men looked at the haul for a moment or two.

'You thinking what I'm thinking?' Léo asked Dhuc.

Dhuc smiled. 'I think I think what you think,' he replied, with a squeaky little laugh.

Léo turned to Jacquot. 'How many did you tell the boss?'

'Twenty. Thereabouts.'

'And we've got twenty-four.'

'Don't tell me.' said Jacquot, giving them both an amused look. 'You want me to put a couple back. For later.'

Just what he and Delphie had considered.

Only these boys were going to do it.

'Exactly right, my friend.' said Léo, and gave him a sly smile. 'But make it the four.'

Jacquot knew what that smile meant.

It meant that he was a dead man.

118

IF LÉO AND DHUC HAD had any intention of killing Jacquot and leaving his body in the prison ruins, they thought better of it when they'd finished loading up the three rucksacks. Six bars to a rucksack. Almost impossible to lift. Dhuc, who was clearly the fittest and strongest, and the shortest, had to have it hefted onto his back by Jacquot and Léo, and he staggered under the weight.

'Too, too heavy,' he said, trying to work the padded straps into a more comfortable position on his shoulders. He could hardly budge them. 'We need take some out,' he said in his whining, sing-song voice. 'Make two trip. Come back for rest.'

And as though to support this suggestion, there was a ripping sound as one of the straps tore loose, the rucksack swinging to one side and almost throwing Dhuc to the ground.

For the second time Jacquot spotted an opportunity to take the two men out, to make his move, and once again he felt his muscles tighten. The hammer he'd used on the wall was now just a metre away from his left foot, but close enough, he reckoned, to make a quick snatch, aim a lucky swing and even the odds. But actions are slower than thoughts, and a hammer against two guns, he now realised, was always going to be a risky move. Once again the moment passed, and he gritted his teeth with irritation,

determined not to miss the next chance that came his way, whatever the odds.

But it wasn't just the strap of Dhuc's rucksack that had gone.
With a sudden tearing sound the thin, nylon ripped along a seam
and the six gold bars tumbled to the ground.

'Holy Mother,' said Léo, shaking his head in exasperation.

And then, without any warning, he started to giggle. At Dhuc's
stunned expression. At the ripped, useless bag hanging from his
shoulder. And at the tumble of gold in the dirt.

Then Dhuc started up, too, a high-pitched whinny that showed
his flashing white teeth.

It was the gold, Jacquot knew. Just looking at it brought on a
kind of madness, a lightheadedness. The same thing had happened
when he and Delphie had finally found it. The sheer, stunning
improbability of it. So much of it. So much money. Yet so heavy
to move, so cumbersome to handle.

'Okay, okay, so let's think about this,' said Léo, swallowing back
the laughter, grabbing the torn bag from Dhuc and tossing it away.
'Four bars in each, and we'll come back for the rest. And you,' he
said, pointing at Jacquot, 'you carry as many as you can.'

With the two remaining rucksacks suitably lightened, Dhuc
knelt down and Jacquot heaved the first of them onto his shoulders, with Léo's gun following every move. Then, with Dhuc
holding a gun on him, he did the same with Léo. With the two
men loaded up, he stooped down to pick up a bar, cradling it in
his arms.

'And another,' said Léo, giving him a humourless look. 'You
look like you can manage it.'

Jacquot did as he was told and rose unsteadily to his feet.

Just two bars. More than twenty kilos. Hell, it was a heavy,
awkward load.

'So let's go. You first,' said Léo, digging the muzzle of his gun
into Jacquot's shoulder.

Just as they had done on the way to the prison ruins, Jacquot
walked ahead with Léo and Dhuc behind him. He couldn't

441

see them, didn't know how far back they were, but he could hear them: the scuff of their shoes on the path, their panting breath. And as he walked, his arms soon burning with the weight of the gold, he tried to think which man he should go for first, when the next opportunity presented itself. The one called Léo was taller and heavier than his accomplice and looked like he'd be difficult to put down. But Dhuc seemed to Jacquot the more dangerous of the two – slim, lithe and fast on his feet. And being Asian, Jacquot was pretty certain he would know how to look after himself, in ways that Jacquot couldn't imagine. The springy, wiry little Asian would have to be the one to neutralise first – and on their way back for the second load seemed the most likely time to plan for.

Ten minutes later they came off the path and down onto the beach where Jacquot let the bars drop from his arms, the two of them sinking into the shingle with a soft crunching sound.

'Hey, pick them up,' said Léo, coming up alongside him and poking him again with the gun. 'No one said you could drop them.'

Jacquot flexed his arms, rubbed the red marks where the bars had pressed into his skin, and felt the ache in his shoulders. But he did as he was told. Leg muscles burning, the wound in his thigh beginning to scream, he staggered to his feet and waded out to *Constance* where Didier was waiting for them, his eyes bright with anticipation.

'How many?' he asked, taking the two bars from Jacquot, one by one, laying them on a seat locker, so Jacquot could help Léo and Dhuc with their rucksacks, levering them off their shoulders and manhandling them aboard *Constance*.

'Twenty,' Léo replied. 'Like the man said. But it'll take another trip to bring them all in.'

Didier tore open the two rucksacks, peered inside.

'So there's what? Another ten left?'

'That's right, boss. Too much for one man.'

'So go fetch them,' said Didier, tossing the two empty rucksacks at Léo after he'd spilled out their contents onto the aft deck. 'Five each. Shouldn't be a problem. And make it quick. You,' he continued, pointing to Jacquot, 'get your arse up here.'

Léo's face fell. 'I thought . . .' he began, 'I thought he could help . . .'

'Don't think,' snapped Didier, as Jacquot clambered aboard. 'Just do what you're told.'

119

BY THE TIME LÉO AND Dhuc had waded ashore, crunched over the shingle and reached the path, Didier was back in the shade of the wheelhouse, in the skipper's chair, blowing down the barrel of his Beretta like a kid might blow in the neck of a bottle.

'I'd like to see my wife,' said Jacquot, feet planted among the spilled gold bars. He didn't know why the man had kept him back, but he felt a rise of confidence. There was still a gun to take into account, but now it was just one on one.

'My little friend here says you're in no position to ask anything,' Didier replied, pulling back the hammer and moving the barrel back and forth between Jacquot's head and belly as though trying to decide which target to settle on.

'Still,' said Jacquot. 'I'd like to see her. And her sister. If it's okay with your little friend.'

Didier looked at him carefully. 'You're either a brave man,' he said at last. 'Or a stupid *con*. Which do you suppose it is?'

Jacquot shrugged, but held the man's eye.

'They're fine. Shout down to them if you want. They'll answer.'

'I told you I want to see them.'

'And I'm telling you it's not going to happen,' Didier replied. And tilting his head, eyes still fixed on Jacquot, he called out,

'Hey, you two. You okay down there? Your man's back and he's worried about you.'

'Daniel? Are you there, Daniel? Are you okay?' It was Claudine.

'I'm fine,' he called back. 'And you, and Delphie?'

This time both women answered. Yes, they were fine. And what was happening?

'Okay, Okay. That'll do. Quieten down now.' Didier turned back to Jacquot. 'You happy now? Good. So start stacking the gold, there's a good boy.'

With a nod, Jacquot did as he was told, kneeling on the deck and reaching for the bars, wondering whether he dared throw one, or if he could somehow get past the gun and put the man down. But the gun never left him, its single black eye following every move he made.

'You a sailor then?' asked Didier, when Jacquot had the deck tidied and the gold stacked. 'You look like a sailor.'

Jacquot wiped his hands on his shorts and pointed to one of the seat lockers. Didier nodded, and Jacquot sat down.

'I asked if you were a sailor? I won't ask again.'

'Yes . . . day charters, that kind of thing.'

'So you know the coast around here? Know how to get places?'

'Yes, I know the coast.'

'That's good. That's good,' said Didier.

'You got anywhere in mind?'

Didier gave it some thought. 'I'll leave that to you.'

Jacquot frowned. 'I don't understand . . .'

'I don't expect you to. What I expect is for you to find me somewhere nice and quiet, where we can moor up and shift the gold without anyone else around.'

'There're places like that,' said Jacquot, wondering why the man would want to use *Constance* when he had his very own gin palace moored just a few hundred metres away. That's when it suddenly struck him that maybe, just maybe, this wasn't the main man. That there was someone bigger, someone further up the chain than him, someone he now planned to screw just like Léo and Dhuc were

445

planning to screw him. For a moment he wondered whether he should say anything about the four gold bars they'd had him re-bury, but he decided against it. Maybe later.

'That's good, that's good,' said Didier. And then, 'You got any food on board?'

Forty minutes later, after providing Didier with a chicken baguette, some cheese and a bottle of beer – watching him chomp and swig his way through it from the far end of the aft deck – Jacquot spotted Dhuc and Léo returning to the cove. Bent under their rucksacks, they tottered down the path and onto the beach.

'Your friends are back,' said Jacquot.

'Perfect timing,' said Didier, and with a hefty belch he slid off the skipper's chair and gestured Jacquot ahead of him.

'You get it?' he called out, as Dhuc and Léo waded out to them.

'All here, boss,' replied Léo, breathless, and drenched in sweat.

'So what are you waiting for?' said Didier, waving his gun at Jacquot. 'Help them get it up here. *Et vite.*'

Once again the two loose bars that Dhuc and Léo had carried in their arms were handed up first, then the rucksacks, shrugged painfully off shoulders and heaved aboard.

When the second rucksack hit the deck, Didier leaned over the side, raised his gun and shot both men in the head.

He turned to Jacquot.

'Gold,' he said, with a twisted, satisfied little smile, his eyes glittering with a kind of madness. 'Who'd have thought it . . . ?'

120

THE TWO GUNSHOTS FROM *CONSTANCE*, ringing back from the slopes of Pénitents, had Zach reaching for his glasses and fixing them on the launch.

'Someone's shooting,' he said. He was up on *Corsaire's* bridge with Cassel. 'Looks like the boss. Can't see Léo or Dhuc, but he's still got that skipper there.'

There was a crackle of static from the walkie-talkie on the instrument panel. 'Cassel. You there?'

Cassel snatched it up.

It was Didier. Zach could see him in the wheelhouse, walkie-talkie in one hand, gun in the other. Zach lowered the glasses and turned to Cassel.

'I'm here, boss,' said the skipper. 'We heard shooting. You okay?'

'Just Dhuc and Léo trying to go solo and take over the party. Gone gold mad. Tried to pull their guns on me, would you believe?'

Zach looked like he'd been punched in the guts. His eyes went wide and his mouth opened in disbelief. Léo? Pulling a gun on the boss? It couldn't be.

'Get Zach and Milagro over here fast,' Didier continued, moving on to more important business. 'We need to shift the gold.'

'*T'as pigé*,' Cassel replied. 'You got it. They're on their way.'

Zach frowned. 'He wants us to go back for him? In the Zephyr?

447

Why doesn't he come to us . . . use the boat he's got? Much easier.'

Cassel put down the walkie-talkie. 'You heard the man. He wants you there. Just do it.'

And then, over Zach's shoulder, Cassel saw movement. A kilometre off, appearing round an outcrop of rock. Another boat. Coming in from the east, the lowering sun glancing off its curved windshield, the sculpted bow slicing through the water.

He snatched the binoculars from Zach and trained them on the approaching vessel, recognised the sheer lines of an Adagio 60 and remembered the one they'd passed just that morning in Calanque d'En Vau. And Cassel knew that there weren't enough of the latest Adagios around to see two in one day. It had to be the same one.

The question was, who did it belong to?

And what were they going to do about the unexpected arrival?

He handed the glasses back to Zach and reached for the walkie-talkie.

'Boss? We got company.'

121

HAMID, *DÉSIRÉ*'S SKIPPER, HAD RUN a wide arc from the mainland out to Pénitents but had kept the island close on his starboard side. If anyone aboard *Corsaire* had spotted them, they would have assumed that *Désiré* was just another pleasure cruiser heading east towards Cassis, Bandol or Toulon. But the moment *Corsaire* was out of sight, Hamid eased the wheel to starboard and turned into the sun, coming in fast and low for the island. A hundred metres out he'd levelled off and hugged the rocky shoreline until finally, up ahead, he spotted *Corsaire*'s radio mast and navigation lights the other side of a low, intervening headland.

'Come in slow, like we're looking for a good mooring, and get in close as you can,' said Duclos, sitting in the middle of a cream leather banquette built into a corner of the bridge. The leather was warm and smooth and creaked when he moved, and not two metres away, standing at the wheel, was Hamid – the long white socks and plimsolls, the smooth brown legs and shorts creased tight to the buttocks. 'Are the boys ready below?' Duclos asked, savouring the view.

'They're all set,' confirmed Hamid, taking *Désiré* wide to pass the headland and coming now into full view of *Corsaire*, neatly pegged at anchor and lying abeam to them, her decks deserted. He eased off the throttles and coasted into the cove, no more than two hundred metres from *Corsaire*, spotting on his port side, drawn up near the beach, the other boat, *Constance*.

He couldn't see anyone on board the small cutter, but something else caught his eye, something in the water, between the launch and the shore. He reached for his glasses and holding the wheel with one hand, he trained the binoculars on *Constance*.

'What is it?' asked Duclos, seeing Hamid's attention focused on the beach and not *Corsaire*.

'It's the launch, boss. And two bodies by the look of it, in the water. Maybe a third, it's difficult to tell.'

Duclos smiled. 'They've got the gold then,' he said, almost to himself. 'Loaded it aboard, and got rid of the skipper and his lady friends. Looks like we made it just in time.'

Hamid pulled the glasses away from the beach and set them on *Corsaire*.

'There's movement in the stern. Looks like they're going to lower a Zephyr.'

'Let them do it. An open target just makes it easier for us.'

Closing now on *Corsaire*, with just a hundred metres between them, Hamid swung *Désiré* in a lazy, elegant turn that put them beam side on to *Corsaire*. Leaning forward, he punched a button on the console and from the bows came the rattle and clank-clanking of an anchor chain.

122

IT WAS DIDIER WHO SPOTTED the new arrival first, over Jacquot's shoulder, a sleek thirty-metre motor cruiser coming round the headland, its blue-black shining hull settling into the bow wave, a line of deck level cabins set beneath the swept-back tinted glass windows of an enclosed bridge.

'Get down,' he snapped at Jacquot, 'and get in here quick.'

Jacquot did as he was told and, crouching low, scrambled over the stacked gold and into the wheelhouse. Didier had slid down from the skipper's chair and was peeping over the sill of the wheelhouse side windows, gun in one hand, still trained on Jacquot, walkie-talkie in the other. At the mouth of the cove the new arrival drew to a halt about eighty metres from *Corsaire*'s port side, and dropped anchor, both boats bow on to the beach.

When the anchor went down with a rattle and splash, Didier cursed.

'You know who they are?' asked Jacquot, still stunned by what had happened to Dhuc and Léo.

'Course I don't,' Didier spat angrily, 'but right now is not a good time for someone to start messing up my arrangements. Whether they mean to or not.'

'This time of day, with some weather coming in, they'll probably be mooring for the night,' said Jacquot. 'And you've got a couple of bodies floating out there. If they decide to come ashore . . .'

'*Alors*,' whispered Didier, 'if they decide to come ashore, they'll regret it, *n'est-ce pas*? And if you don't keep your mouth shut, sailor-boy, so will you.'

But their conversation was brought to an end by the sound of a single gunshot.

Both men ducked below the window.

'*Merde*,' said Didier. 'What the fuck . . . ?'

123

THE FIRST BULLET SMASHED THROUGH a port-side window on *Corsaire*'s bridge and struck Milagro in the left shoulder as he reached forward to slide it open. No one on *Corsaire* had known who the new arrival was but Cassel, the skipper, wasn't taking any chances. After letting Didier know that another boat was approaching, he'd sent Zach down to the salon to tool up the crew and told Milagro to break out his bolt-action M40 sniper's rifle. Which was exactly what he was doing when the 9mm slug, flattened from its passage through the glass, hammered into him. It wasn't a fatal shot but the force of the blow lifted him up from the banquette where he was kneeling and spun him across the bridge, his M40 tumbling after him.

Whoever the newcomers were, Cassel now realised, they weren't friendly.

It was Beni on *Désiré* who'd pulled the trigger. Raking his binoculars across *Corsaire*'s bridge he'd spotted the Mexican taking up position, keeping low. And seen the rifle.

'They've got a sniper on us,' he'd called out and, tossing aside the glasses, he reached for his gun.

'You certain?' shouted Hamid, ducking down below any possible line of fire, while Duclos scrambled for cover below the overhang of the instrument panel. None of them had expected things to start so quickly.

'*Oui. Certain.*'

'Those dirty Polineaux bastards,' spat Duclos. 'It's a trap. They've set us up.'

'So what do we do?' Beni looked at Hamid and Duclos.

'Take the fucker out,' replied Duclos. 'Just put him down. All of them.'

And that's what Beni had done. Leaning back in his seat, he'd held his Browning Hi-Power in both hands, supporting the gun on his bent knees, squinted down the barrel at the bottom left corner of the middle window on *Corsaire*'s bridge where he'd seen the gunman, and let off a single round.

There were maybe twelve seconds between that first shot from Beni and the fusillade that followed, not enough time for the two crew members working on *Corsaire*'s Zephyr to reach cover. They were the first to go down, taking three or four bullets apiece, blood blossoming across their whites as they crumpled to the deck. With Milagro down as well, *Corsaire*'s compliment of gunmen might have been reduced to Zach, Cassel and the three remaining members of crew, but they returned fire with a blazing enthusiasm – Zach and Cassel firing from the bridge, the three crew members taking up position on the lower deck.

On *Désiré*'s bridge, windows shattered and tinted glass splinters showered Hamid, Beni and Duclos as the gunmen on *Corsaire* returned fire. Aris and Jo-Jo, down in the salon, had the worst of it, along with the crew members they'd staked out on the rear deck. Pinned down by a raking sweep of machine gun fire, they were unable to get off more than a few shots, with Aris taking a ricochet hit to his leg and Jo-Jo a flesh wound to his upper arm. Two of the three remaining crew were not so fortunate. A lucky head shot and chest shot only seconds apart sent them sprawling back on the deck, their lives leaking out of them.

Up on the bridge, ducking up and down from the shattered windows like targets in a fairground shooting gallery, Beni and Hamid returned fire, Hamid hitting one of *Corsaire*'s crew as he stepped out from behind a companionway to take aim, Beni winging another crew member.

'My boat,' seethed Duclos, hunkering down beneath the instrument panel as another volley thudded into *Désiré*. 'My fucking boat! I'll fucking kill the *salauds*.'

On *Constance* Didier and Jacquot watched the exchange of fire in stunned silence, the sound of gunshots ripping around the cove and battering back from the slopes of Pénitents.

'Who the hell are they?' asked Didier.

'Someone else who knew about the gold,' replied Jacquot, praying that they didn't become a target, and wondering how he could turn the firefight to his advantage. Before he could work out how to do it, Didier kicked out with his foot and caught Jacquot on the shoulder.

'How much fuel you got?'

'Half a tank, maybe more.'

'So let's get moving.'

'Get moving? Where?'

Didier smiled, nodded towards the two cruisers. 'Where do you think? Out of here.'

On *Corsaire*'s bridge Cassel was bleeding from the cheek, a warm flow of blood that spilled down into his collar. Either it was a near miss, or a splinter of glass had done the damage. Beside him, Zach was reaching his pistol through one of the smashed windows and firing blindly at *Désiré*, finishing a full clip and pulling a fresh one from his pocket.

'Last clip,' he shouted at Cassel, as bullets whined through the bridge just centimetres above their heads. 'What about you?'

'Another clip and I'm out,' Cassel shouted back. 'Time to leave the party,' he said, peering through a shattered window.

'What about the boss?'

'You want to go get him?'

'I sure as hell don't want to leave him. Alive, that is.'

Cassel chanced another peek through the windshield.

'Doesn't look like you'll have to. *Constance* is on the move.'

With Didier's gun trained on him, Jacquot had squirmed forward using the wheelhouse for cover and crawled over the main cabin roof to bring up the anchor. As he passed the skylight over the for'ard cabin, he glanced down and saw Claudine and Delphie trying desperately to undo their bindings.

'Stay down,' he called to them. 'And stay in the cabin.'

'What's going on up there?' cried Delphie, eyes wide and frightened.

'Just do as I say and stay where you are. When we start moving, get on the floor and pull the mattress over you.'

Back in the wheelhouse, he turned on the engine and, keeping low, backed *Constance* away from the beach.

'Take her to the left,' said Didier, peering over the instrument panel. 'Between *Corsaire* and the rocks. There's easily enough room.'

Jacquot did as he was told, keeping to the edge of the cove and aiming for *Corsaire*. It was, he realised, the only sensible route, the bulk of the cruiser providing cover as they closed on the gunfight. With just fifty metres to go, the first bullets from *Désiré* smacked into *Constance* and whined past the wheelhouse, one of its windscreen panels shattering as a lucky shot tore through the glass and bit into the aft deck.

As they closed on *Corsaire*, Didier backed up behind Jacquot's legs and started firing as *Désiré* loomed up ahead, emptying a fourteen-round clip into the Adagio 60's superstructure before *Corsaire* blocked out the target.

With just ten metres between *Corsaire*'s rising hull and the rocky edge of the cove, Jacquot held a steady course, eyes flicking to either side to guage his clearance as Didier loaded another clip and

456

prepared for a fresh line of fire. But as he scooted forward to the starboard side and raised the gun, *Jacquot* came out of *Corsaire*'s lee and into open water. As they did so, a heavy swell smashed against them, the water much rougher than when they'd arrived that morning, driven now by the strong easterly that *Jacquot* had been warned about.

'*Merde*,' cried Didier, as a gout of water slapped up from *Constance*'s hull and splattered over him. But before he could scrabble back into the shelter of the wheelhouse, another cresting wave caught them square on. *Constance* lurched to port and Didier and the gold bars were sent slithering across her tilting aft deck, crashing into a seat locker.

'The bastard's making a run for it,' shouted Cassel, as *Constance* raced past his stern. He could see Didier squaring up to take a shot from the aft deck, a scatter of gold bars, and another figure at the wheel. He'd expected the launch to kill its speed and come in on the blindside, using *Corsaire* for cover to unload the gold. But whoever stood crouching at the wheel wasn't doing that, heading straight past them instead, and making a getaway. And Didier, judging by the angle of the gun in his hand, aiming to take out anyone he could see who planned to get in his way. Either on *Corsaire* or *Désiré*.

Gritting his teeth, Cassel raised his own gun and took a bead on the lurching craft, making heavy weather of the incoming swell. He knew there was no chance of hitting Didier, almost out of sight in the tipping craft, but the man at the wheel was a different proposition.

Standing firm, a good wide target.

Following the swing and lurch of the boat, steadying his target in line with the barrel of his gun, Cassel's finger was tightening on the trigger when a sledgehammer blow caught him between the shoulder blades and sent him staggering forward, toppling him over the edge of the bridge.

The last thing he registered before he hit the deck below was a shape, spray sluicing off its bow, racing in fast round the western edge of the cove.

Coming out of the sun. But not so fiercely backlit that he couldn't make out the red, white and blue chevrons slanting across its grey hull.

Unmistakable.

It was the last thing that *Corsaire*'s skipper would ever see.

124

JACQUOT, WHO HAD SEEN THE rougher water up ahead, was prepared for it, feet braced, knees bent, hands gripping the wheel as he came out of *Corsaire*'s lee. He knew what would happen, and when Didier lurched backwards as they hit the first swells he didn't waste an instant. Didn't think about it. Just turned the wheel to starboard, pushed forward the throttles and flung himself at his adversary.

Didier was younger and fitter, but Jacquot had the advantage, dropping his full weight on to the crumpled man. Bringing his right fist down in a series of hard, sharp jabs into Didier's face, he reached for the flailing gun with his left hand, snatching at the man's wrist and banging it down hard against the lip of the locker.

As *Constance* tore forward into the swell, bucking up and down with every incoming wave, Didier managed to get off another couple of rounds, close enough to part Jacquot's hair before smacking into the wheelhouse. But Jacquot paid no heed. Gripping Didier around the throat, he kept on smashing the man's gun hand against the edge of the locker until the gun slipped from his bloodied fingers and slithered away across the seat, coming up short where locker lid met transom.

If the gun was out of reach, it didn't stay that way for long. As *Constance* rose over a swell and crashed down into a following trough, the gun came sliding back down along the seat. Both men saw it at the same time, and snatched wildly for it as they, too, were sent spilling forwards, Jacquot's head crashing into the base of the binnacle as the gun slid off the seat and into Didier's lap.

Dazed, trying to blink away the stars in his eyes, Jacquot used the next incoming swell to help lift him to a sitting position, pulling up his legs to get his feet under him. But that was as far as he got. Out on the aft deck, Didier was scrabbling away from him, bringing the gun up from his lap, trying to keep himself steady and get his finger through the trigger guard as *Constance* battered her way through the swells.

And then, as *Constance* rose up on the next wall of water, Jacquot saw what Cassel had seen, coming in fast.

'*Attention*!' he screamed, pointing behind Didier.

And Didier turned, as Jacquot had prayed he would.

Which gave Jacquot precious seconds to launch himself sideways and drop through the open wheelhouse hatch, the knuckles of his backbone rattling over the edge of the five companionway steps leading down to the main cabin, his head hitting the deck with another dizzying crunch.

But there was no time to brace himself, no time to reach for something to hold on to. Seconds after his head hit the deck, the police launch he had seen coming straight at them crashed into *Constance* with a sickening thud and scraped along her port side with a splintering, grinding screech, first tipping the smaller craft over to starboard, before its higher, rising hull pulled her hard down to port, all in a matter of seconds, great gouts of water bursting up between the two clashing hulls.

Jacquot's body followed both impacts, first rolled like a loose piece of timber to his left, then picked up off the deck and flung against the side of the chart table like a bag of washing as *Constance* tilted back again.

A sluicing torrent of water cascaded through the hatchway and splattered over him. Wiping the water from his eyes he saw Didier slide into view, his broad shoulders jamming into the hatch, his drenched polo-shirt clinging to his body. There was a volley of gunfire, easily heard over the sound of the engines and crashing hulls and the swells battering against their bows, and as Jacquot ducked out of any incoming fire, he saw three red roses bloom one by one across Didier's back and a bloody mist spray down on to the chart table.

125

ISABELLE CASSIER, APPROACHING FAST ON the police launch she'd requisitioned just an hour earlier from the Gendarmerie Maritime, hadn't been expecting to see *Constance* race towards them, streaking out of the narrow gap between *Corsaire* and the shelf of rock at the edge of the cove.

And nor had her skipper.

There was no time to avoid a collision.

If *Constance* hadn't veered away to starboard after passing *Corsaire*'s stern, the two launches would have hit head on. But that readjustment served only to delay the impact, the two boats brushing up against each other, beam to beam, with a jarring, screeching intent, the larger, heavier police launch getting the better of the contact, tipping *Constance* sideways, then rising up over her port side and pulling her down under the weight of her hull.

Up on the bridge the police skipper was the only one who wasn't sent sprawling by the collision, Isabelle crashing first into Laganne and then staggering into Salette whom she'd tracked down after Laganne told her about *Corsaire* and *Désiré*, praying the old boy would know where Jacquot had gone. And he had, parlaying the co-ordinates that Jacquot had given him that morning into a place on the launch.

'You,' shouted Isabelle, recovering her balance and pointing at

462

Salette. 'You stay here, *compris*?' Then, turning to the skipper, 'Keep her alongside as long as you can, got it?'

Reaching for handholds Isabelle hauled herself across the tilting bridge and, with Laganne close behind her, she clambered down on to the aft deck where, suddenly drenched with spray, she made her way to the starboard side, the two boats rising and falling through the swells, clashing together with never more than a metre between them.

Berettas drawn, bracing themselves against the battering swells, she and Laganne peered over the side, through sheets of seawater, at the sliding, sprawling figure of a man on *Constance*'s aft deck, also with a gun in his hand, even now bringing it round to take a bead on them.

The three of them blasted off almost simultaneously, seven or eight shots whining through the salty spray thrown up between their two craft, three of those bullets finding their target.

126

'GET US OUT OF HERE,' shrieked Duclos. 'Get us the fuck out of here. Now!'

Like Cassel, he, too, had spotted the police launch, and knew the game was up. They might have dealt with *Corsaire*, but the cops were quite another matter. Even now he could see the long grey shape of a Coastguard cutter bearing down on them from the open channel. What they had to do now was get the hell out of there, as fast as they could.

Hamid threw down his gun and stepped up to the wheel, preparing *Désiré* for departure while Beni kept up a solid rate of covering fire, confident now that they had the advantage, ever since he'd taken out *Corsaire*'s skipper. But the cover he provided wasn't quite as effective as it should have been.

Zach, peering out from *Corsaire*'s bridge, watched as *Désiré*'s anchor broke surface, the cruiser turning gently, its speed increasing as the manouevre was completed. As *Désiré* moved away, straightened, increased speed, Zach could clearly make out her skipper crouching at the wheel, and another man, on his belly, firing off a fusillade of random shots in their direction. But the shots were wild and it was clear that the gunman hadn't spotted Zach. Reaching for Milagro's M40, he tucked the rifle stock into his shoulder and lined up the crosshairs of the sniperscope onto the skipper's back. By now the *Désiré* had picked up some speed and was heading out of the cove. His finger found the trigger, the crosshairs stayed steady on the skipper's back, and Zach squeezed gently.

Hamid was punched forwards, his arm catching in the spokes of the wheel and tugging it to the right, his body falling on to the throttle levers. With a roar of power, the Adagio 60 spun round to starboard and with an astonishing burst of acceleration that lifted her bow high out of the water, she surged towards the rocky shelves of the cove's headland.

127

TIMING HER JUMP, ISABELLE LEAPED from the police launch and landed on *Constance*'s aft deck, rolling away from the body in the wheelhouse, a gun still held in its hand, bringing up her own and levelling it just in case.

But there was no movement from the body, just a swaying and tipping in time with the motion of the boat, the head slumped forward on the chest as though examining a polo-shirt soaked in blood.

A moment later Laganne also made his jump from the launch, landing more clumsily than Isabelle, his feet shooting out from under him, sending him crashing into a seat locker.

Getting to her feet, Isabelle made it over to the wheelhouse, grabbed the wheel and brought *Constance* clear of the police launch, pulling back on the throttles as she steered away from the swells and back into the relative shelter of the cove.

To her right, *Corsaire* lay still in the water, no movement on deck. But to her left, *Désiré* had started her engines and was preparing to make a dash for it.

They wouldn't get far, she thought, watching the Coastguard cutter that the Gendarmerie Maritime had called in for support, squaring up to block any attempt at escape, or prepared to follow and apprehend should *Désiré* somehow manage to make it through.

But there would be no escape.

Behind her, from *Corsaire*'s bridge, Isabelle heard the mighty crack of a rifle shot and ducked instinctively. But the round wasn't meant for her. While Laganne and two of the crew on the police launch returned fire, she looked ahead and saw *Désiré*'s skipper go down, slumping over the controls. With a whine from her engines, the boat turned, her bow rising up as she accelerated towards the rocks.

Fifty metres away.

Twenty metres . . .

But Isabelle never saw her hit.

128

LAGANNE FOUND JACQUOT IN THE for'ard cabin with the two women. The three of them were standing in a tight hug, arms round each other, murmuring words of reassurance, whispers of comfort, the cabin a tumbled chaos of glass, books and bedding.

'You okay, Danny?'

Jacquot turned, smiled. 'We're okay. Is it over?'

'It's done,' replied Laganne, but the smile was not returned.

'What's happened?' asked Jacquot, stepping away from the sisters, knowing immediately that something was wrong.

'You need to come with me,' Laganne replied. 'Up top,' he added, nodding over his shoulder.

Isabelle Cassier was lying on the aft deck, legs splayed, arms at her sides, her head resting on Salette's lap. The old harbour master looked up as Jacquot came on deck, stepping over Didier's body, a single small hole in his forehead added to the three bullets that had brought him down, but not killed him.

When he saw Isabelle lying there, Jacquot hurried over, dropping to his knees, searching for a wound, some blood, something to explain why she was down.

He caught Salette's grim look.

The old sailor shook his head, a tiny, almost imperceptible movement, as Jacquot took his place.

Her eyes were closed, but as he pushed back a slick of wet black hair from her cheek they fluttered open, widened on the sky above her, then moved and settled on Jacquot's face. She frowned, as though trying to remember who he was. Then she smiled. She knew.

'You owe me,' she whispered, so low he had to bend down to hear the words. As he did he saw the blood welling out of the armpit in her Kevlar vest, pooling behind her neck until a swirl of seawater pinked it, washed it away across the deck.

'Lunch. Wherever you want,' said Jacquot with a smile that was hard to find. He knew there would never be any lunch. Judging by the flow of blood, the bullet she'd taken had hit her on the left side where the velcro side straps kept her Kevlar vest in place, a few centimetres below the armpit. He knew the terrible damage that bullet would have done. A lucky shot, from a dying man, but a deadly one.

'Make it dinner?' she whispered.

'For you, dinner.'

Isabelle winced, licked her lips.

'I'm dying, aren't I?' she managed. 'This is it. I always wondered . . . My last . . . my dying minutes.' She hunched painfully, gave a cough, more a guttural clearing of the throat that brought a bubbling dribble of blood to her lips. 'That's all I've got. Just minutes. And, ohhh . . . so much I wanted to do.'

'You're not dying,' said Jacquot softly, stroking back her hair, reaching for her hand, ice cold to the touch, no strength in the fingers. 'If you were dying, you'd be . . .'

Isabelle tried to shake her head. '*Non, non, non* . . . Tell me about dinner instead. That's what I want to hear about. What we would have done. You and me. Like . . . Mirador, that first time. Remember?'

She closed her eyes, squirmed a little, tried to get comfortable.

Jacquot knew she wasn't interested in dinner. He was right.

Her eyes opened, widened, settled on him, as they had before. 'Tell me you love me. Really.'

Out of the corner of his eye, he saw Claudine and Delphi standing in the wheelhouse. Claudine had her arms wrapped around herself. Delphie clung to her. They were both watching him.

He turned his attention back to Isabelle and smiled. 'You wer right,' he said. 'You're the one.'

Isabelle's lips curled into the tightest little smile, her finger tightening around his hand.

Then she sighed, clear and deep for a moment, but when mor blood bubbled up she began to choke, tried to swallow, rolled he eyes and died in his arms.

129

IT WAS ON A SUNDAY morning, three days after Isabelle Cassier's funeral in Marseilles' Saint-Pierre cemetery and two days after Delphie caught the train home to Paris, that Jacquot stepped aboard a Gendarmerie Maritime launch in the port of L'Estaque.

He sat up on the bridge with the skipper, a slim, crisply uniformed young man who knew better than to notice his passenger's shorts, T-shirt and espadrilles, happy to exchange the usual professional pleasantries until they passed the breakwater. Then, with a nod to Jacquot, the young sailor took off his cap, slipped on a pair of mirrored Oakleys and pushed forward the throttles, the sound of the engines and a buffeting whip of sea-breeze bringing all conversation to a halt. Which suited Jacquot just fine, leaning back in his seat and watching the sprawl of the docks and the city speed past, the sea low and calm, a high blue sky softened by a sheet of milky gauze. A perfect day to be out on a boat, he decided, and had she not been confined to the Malmousque yards for repairs, that boat would have been *Constance*.

'*Plage* des Solitaires? Is that where you want?' asked the skipper thirty minutes later, cutting back on the throttles and closing on the northern slopes of Île des Pénitents.

That would do just fine, Jacquot told him as the rocky shoreline drew closer, a low soundless chop splashing up against it. Five

471

minutes later, the skipper steered them past the burned-out hulk o
Désiré and into the Solitaires cove, bringing the launch to withir
a couple of metres of the shingle.

'It's as close as I can get us,' the skipper called down, but Jacquo
waved aside the apology. Dropping off the side of the launch intc
chest-high water he waded ashore, the shingle slipping beneath hi:
feet, a rucksack slung over his shoulder.

Ten minutes later he stepped across the first of the prison's wal
footings and followed the path he'd taken with Delphie and Dhuc
and Léo through its ruins.

When he reached the open courtyard, Jacquot went straight tc
the low section of wall where Philo and Eddie had buried thei
gold, and where Dhuc and Léo had made him re-bury those fou
last bars. He'd forgotten all about them until driving back to the
millhouse after Isabelle's funeral, and it had taken a few phone
calls before he'd been able to hitch a lift with the Gendarmerie
Maritime. Had he said anything about gold bars, they'd have go
him out there in a finger-flick. But he'd given no reason for the
trip, just put in a request through official channels.

Now he was there, looking at the section of low wall where he'c
packed away those four gold bars.

But he didn't bother squatting down to dig them up.

Instead he put his hands on his hips and smiled.

Someone had beaten him to it.

130

ON THAT SAME DAY, ON the western slopes of Cap Ferrat, Patric Polineaux, the last of the great *parrains*, died in his sleep.

Not at night, in his bed, but in the afternoon, in his wheelchair, on the terrace of Hauts des Pins.

When he drew his last breath, he was dreaming of a fine old English sports car, red as blood, that smelled of leather and petrol and made a sound like growling thunder, of a girl with wavy blonde hair, and bars of gleaming gold.

He was reaching for the gold when that last breath came.

A long, rattling gasp that made him reach out a hand, knocking his brandy glass from the terrace table.

It was the sound of the glass shattering on the tiles that brought the butler, Jarrive, out on to the terrace to check that everything was all right. He could see that his employer was dead before he reached him, the old man's body slumped – almost deflated – in his wheelchair, head tipped back, mouth open, bony arms hanging down at his side.

Delon, the nurse, had taken the day off, but Jarrive knew what to do. He placed two fingers against Polineaux's neck to check for a pulse. When he found none, he left the body where it was and went inside to call emergency services.

It took the ambulance just twenty-five minutes to reach Hauts des Pins, during which time Jarrive had opened Polineaux's safe removed the two twelve-kilo bars the old man had put there, and transferred them to his small apartment over the garage.

He'd be out of a job, now that Polineaux was gone.

But given the rising price of gold, it might be a while before he needed to look for another position.